THE MYSTERY

AT

SEYMOUR LAKE LODGE

Susan Winters Smith

THE MYSTERY AT SEYMOUR LAKE LODGE

Website for book: http://wintersmithbooks.com

Published by Wintersmith Books

ISBN-10 Number: 1453806601
ISBN-13/EAN 13 Number: 9781453806609
Front Cover Art: by Brandy Sue Bushey
Edited by: Victoria Wright, BookmarkServices.net

BISAC Subject Headings:
FIC022040 FICTION / Mystery & Detective / Women Sleuths
NAT011000 NATURE / Environmental Conservation & Protection
FIC026000 FICTION / Religious

For more information, please contact the author at
Wintersmithbooks@yahoo.com

Dedication

This book is dedicated to Brian and Joan DuMoulin who have made the Seymour Lake Lodge a comfortable and welcoming home-away-from-home.

Disciaimer

Although this story is fiction, most of the setting for the story is based on extensive research into the lodge and the area. However, no details or information herein is intended to be taken as absolute fact. The Seymour Lake Lodge is a real and wonderful place, although some of the fine points of architecture and décor, as well as the geography of the surrounding area have been changed to accommodate the story. Please visit www.seymourlakelodge.com to learn more. Some of the characters in the book are based on real people, but are not completely accurate descriptions of them or their lives. The Abenaki shaman is a fictional character and his words are not meant to represent the philosophies of all of the Abenaki people.

For more information on the Abenaki and the Hawk Clan of the Northeast Kingdom, see www.clanofthehawkinc.org.

Acknowledgements

My most sincere thanks begin with my amazing husband, Steve, who is my rock. Next, I thank my fantastic and talented children, Steve, Andy and Sandi, my shining star daughter-in-law Amy, and my wonderfully creative grandchildren Nathan and Kira for being my inspiration. To my dearly loved sisters Sheryl, who was my playmate, and Jane and Kathy, who listened to my stories when they were little, I give much gratitude, as well as my sisters-in-law Rosemary and Annemarie, who are always there with support and a hug, and my niece Brandy Sue Bushey, the talented artist who created the cover picture. My gratitude also to: Darlene Smith-Ash, talented writer and advisor; Victoria Wright, who diplomatically edited this novel and taught me many tricks in the process; my creative writing teachers Thomas Byron Saunders, T. Alan Broughton, and Betty Bandel, whose writing and teaching skills put me on this path long ago; Natalie-Kinsey Warnock for her expert advice; my good friends Andy and Donna Chambers who loaned me their cabin when I needed a retreat; Ralph Dolan, gifted writer, musician, and wise confidant; Allan Ballinger, master cellist and poet, who inspires me to reach higher; Andy Snyder, positive and sensitive supporter; Pastor Bob Livingston and Pastor Kathy Faber, for their spiritual guidance; Pat Banning, Cindy Chapin-Howell, Sara Moriarty, Dot Wilbur, Fran Sellers, Liza Maynard, Carol Faille, Carolyn Wessel, and Jan Birnie, and all of the warm congregation of the Enfield Congregational Church. Of course, my deep gratitude is sent to Joan and Brian, who made the Seymour Lake Lodge such a wonderfully comforting place; to Maggie who gives me courage and Bonny who mends hearts; to Richard Tessier, owner of the Great Northern Moose Lodge, who educated me about moose facts; to my brother-in-law Phil Badger, my expert on auto mechanics; and to Chief Lone Cloud of the Hawk Clan of the Abenaki, who so graciously sat and talked with me on sacred land and gave me his acceptance. Above all, my thanks and praise to God and the Great Mystery.

Table of Contents

Chapter 1: Into the North Woods........................ 1

Chapter 2: Presence....................................... 11

Chapter 3: Dawning....................................... 18

Chapter 4: Balance Rock.................................. 35

Chapter 5: Shades of Blood.............................. 48

Chapter 6: Campfire 59

Chapter 7: The Bog.. 71

Chapter 8: Demons and Dilemmas..................... 85

Chapter 9: Hurricane Road 103

Chapter 10: Evansville 116

Chapter 11: Sizzle.. 135

Chapter 12: Daydreams and Danger 149

Chapter 13: Songs of the Muse 167

Chapter 14: Evacuation 181

Chapter 15: The Newport News 192

Chapter 16: Relaxations and Revelations 205

Chapter 17: Élan 218

Chapter 18: Cloud Patterns and Candle Flames 230

Chapter 19: Smoke and Rain 245

Chapter 20: Stalemate 269

Chapter 21: Lightning Strikes 286

Chapter 22: Confrontation and Compassion....... 301

Chapter 23: Encore.. 310

About the Author 318

Chapter 1: Into the North Woods

Jan's little red Mazda glided around the bend, heading east toward Seymour Lake in northern Vermont. As if on autopilot, the car followed the familiar road along the river as its exhausted driver struggled to stay awake. Only another fifteen or twenty minutes and she would be at the lodge, her safe haven from the world, where she could crawl into bed and sleep away the problems of the past two months. Whatever trouble her friends, Ida and Philippe, were going through at their lodge, she was sure it would not interfere with her long-awaited vacation, and her chance to regain her balance from her husband Sidney's devastating declaration of divorce. Jan's anxieties were lessened by taking in the scenery of late June in the Northeast Kingdom of Vermont, when the green mountains are the color of emeralds and the blue sky dances with ever-changing clouds. The warm air and beautiful scenery always made Jan feel that this is what heaven would be like. This year her stress level was at a new high, and just the thought of the tranquility of previous visits allowed her to relax.

Jan perked up a bit when she arrived at the T of Route 5A and was looking straight ahead at the Cow Palace restaurant with the elk farm behind it. Turning right, she laughed out loud at entering the last leg of her long six-hour journey from southern Connecticut. Driving through the small town of Derby, she soon saw the crosswalk sign marking the left turn onto Route 111 East and next the white rail fence with the sign that read, "Morgan 9 miles. Population 675."

The little village of Morgan, just seven miles from the Canadian border, had become an adopted hometown to Jan over the past three years, and she was grateful now to have this place of shelter and comfort. After some rolling fields and then a big yellow house, the road bent to the left and then a couple of miles ahead on the right she saw the sign for Lake Salem, another of Vermont's pristine mountain lakes. She was almost there. Now it was up and down hills for eight miles. The back and forth movement of the car as it turned right and then left along the curving Vermont road was almost hypnotic. Dusk was falling and wisps of wood smoke were beginning to settle down into the valleys. Jan felt her tired brain trying to shut down.

She jumped into full wakefulness as her foot jammed down onto the brake at the top of a small hill. Her heart pounding loudly in her ears, she stared straight ahead into the glowing eyes of the biggest moose she had ever seen. "Wow, is he beautiful!" she thought. "Just look at the size of that velvet rack, and it's only June. This is one huge bull. I bet he weighs in at a thousand pounds or more!" She admired his long legs and his still slightly ragged shedding coat as he stood there in the beams of her headlights. His piercing eyes gave Jan the once over and he sauntered off into the brush.

Jan got control of her breath and began to drive forward when a blaring horn and flashing lights came barreling at her from behind. She gripped the wheel and hung on tightly as the gigantic log truck screamed past her on the left, without so much as a cautious change in speed. The Mazda rocked from side to side with the force of the truck, and Jan shrieked.

"Well, I guess I've arrived in the north woods. So much for peace and tranquility. Oh Great Spirit, what am I in for?" She looked in the mirror and gave her dark-red wavy hair a quick combing with her fingers. Her blue-green eyes were now fully open.

After a few additional miles of more cautious and wakeful driving, the investigative reporter shed tears of relief as she crested the last hill and saw the moonlight shining on the still waters of the lake. Driving down around the curve of the beach, she spotted a lantern shining from the porch of the Seymour Lake Lodge. The white columns and railings reached out to welcome her, and the lights in the windows glowed with the warm feeling of home.

She drove up the small hill on the grassy driveway to the left of the lodge, passing the row of cedars and the poplar trees with their leaves shimmering in the moonlight. She parked in the gravel parking lot behind the lodge, hopped out of her car, and Ida's old black lab ran out to greet her. "Hi, Seymour!" Jan called, reaching down to rough up the dog's graying coat. Together they followed the handicap ramp around from the back of the lodge to the front porch, where Ida greeted Jan with a big hug.

"Home at last! Ida, it's so great to be here! I almost hit a moose and didn't make it."

"Well, you ought to know more about those moose than anyone, You've studied them enough. There have already been nineteen deaths in Vermont this year from moose accidents. Thank God you're okay."

The porch of the lodge was softly illuminated by the lanterns, and shadows of antique wooden geese, swans, and ducks greeted Jan's arrival. A rocking-horse nodded its head from the top of an old trunk in the corner near the door, and the wind chimes gently tinkled, "Hello, hello." Passing the deer-hoof coat rack, Jan and Ida went in the front door to the dining room, where Ida had a fresh pot of chamomile tea ready to serve with a plate of just-baked shortbread cookies. Jan indulged her hunger, happy to look at her friend's sweet face framed with soft brown hair. Ida's warm presence wrapped around her like a fuzzy blanket.

The Seymour Lake Lodge was a welcoming place, a renovated turn-of-the-century farmhouse with ten guest rooms, a huge eat-in kitchen, large dining room, and the great room. In one end of the long shed out back was a small suite, called 'the green room' because of the green rug and lamp shades used when it was set up and furnished. Decorated in antiques, most of which were for sale, the lodge was a year-round vacation place where guests could entertain themselves with fishing and moose watching in the spring, swimming and boating in the summer, hunting and leaf-peeping in the fall, and snowmobiling, cross-country skiing, and ice-fishing in the winter. Jan discovered the lodge a few years before, and loved it as a place to relax, write, and photograph nature.

"I'm so glad you could get away from the paper for a while, Jan," Ida said, "but tell me, what is bothering you? On the phone you sounded stressed and said that there was a problem."

"Oh, Ida. I was really hoping that somehow it wouldn't get this far, but Sidney now wants a divorce. He is adamant about it, and won't even consider counseling."

"Are you serious? Oh, Jan, I'm so sorry." Ida gave her friend a big hug. "That man must be out of his mind, to want to lose a terrific woman like you! I am really shocked."

"Well, it's funny, but although I'm the one who gave the ultimatum, it seems to have amazed me as much as anyone else," Jan sighed. "I'm not sure what went wrong, or how I screwed up in this marriage, but I guess deep down I sort of knew a long time ago that we were going to come to this end. I kept hoping things would change, but in truth, it now seems that we were never really right for each other. I ignored the obvious signs when I met him at Lake Winnipesaukee six years ago. He was just too high-class for me. He is Wedgewood and I'm Fiestaware."

"Excuse me?" Ida leaped to her friend's defense. "The truth is that you have too much class for him. You have real class. You are a caring, aware 'people person', and, I'm sorry, this may be judgmental, but Sidney could be—okay I'm going to say it—a narcissist."

"Hmmm. You could determine that from meeting him all of two times?"

"Yes, and of course from the many stories you have told me. You know I'm a good judge of character. There's just something about him that calls out, 'Me, me, me'. But I don't mean to be harsh. I know you are hurting. There is no simple answer to that situation and I'm here if you need to talk about it."

"I know you are, Ida. That's why I was happy for an excuse to come up here. You said that things were getting rather creepy. So, what's happening here that has you scared?"

"Jan, you're not going to believe it. You'll think I'm making it up. But it's gotten so nerve-wracking that we just don't know what to do next. For two weeks now, there seems to be some evil presence in the lodge. We have been praying a lot, and had a special prayer service here, with chanting and the burning of incense. It was fascinating, but it didn't work. Weird things are still happening. Guests are missing food that they stored in the refrigerator and pantry, lights are going on and off when no one is near them, furniture and antiques have been moved around at random, and the phone rings at odd times. When we answer it, often no one is there, or they hang up. Ms. DiPersio in room nine has had clothes missing from her drawers and closet. She has also felt an eerie presence at night and heard shuffling noises."

"Wow, I didn't realize that it was this serious. I'm sure there must be a simple answer though—some disgruntled customer perhaps? Have you talked to the local police?"

"Our constable? Oh, yes, Fred says he's on the case, but I'm not sure he's taking us seriously."

"Well, what makes you think I can figure this out? I'm no detective."

"Of course you are! Your investigative reporting is amazing. Your story on the beach vandal in Connecticut was remarkable—helping the police nab that guy, and making the beaches safe again. Didn't you get an award for that story? Besides, you have great insights. Remember when we had our pontoon boat stolen, and you located it over in Barton? You're sharp."

"Yeah? If I'm so clever, why doesn't Sidney give me any credit? My husband—or my soon-to-be-ex-husband, just assigned the biggest story of the year to a new reporter." Jan hung her head.

"Sweetie, I can't answer for Sidney, but I think he likes to keep you insecure. You are just not your strong self around him. When you get away from him for a few days, you become a different person—more assertive. Somehow he weakens you. Anyway, I know you are one smart investigator, and I need your help. I'd like to get this figured out without a big public to-do that would scare off potential guests."

"I'll see what I can do, Ida, but really I'm afraid I'll let you down with the state of mind I'm in." Just then Lola, the lodge's Siamese cat, jumped up onto Jan's lap.

"Well, hello, old friend. What's up?" Jan stroked the cat's sleek fur, and Lola nudged her chin.

"She's very nervous, Jan," Ida said. "She's been acting peculiar, and so has Seymour. They know something is different around here. But I think Lola knows you are here to help."

"Maybe I'm just here to pet her and to take pictures of moose and loons. Seriously, I'm not so sure how strong I am even away from Sid. Sometimes I think I'm just naturally too intimidated, and I hate myself when I'm weak."

"What was it that brought things to this point with Sidney? I thought that six months ago things were improving." Ida poured more tea for her friend.

"I thought they were too. But I was just kidding myself. I can't believe I actually thought that after five years of marriage, we were both ready to have a child, and since I'm 33, I feel like time's running out. But, when I pressed him on it, he said that he now knows that he definitely never wants one, and that I should be happy with the life we have with just the two of us. It just isn't enough for me. Being the editor's wife— entertaining Sid's newspaper colleagues—is so unfulfilling. I know that some women find accomplishment in being the hostess, planning parties, working with caterers, shopping for the latest fashions and jewelry, decorating and redecorating their houses, but I was never good at any of that. Sid wanted me to be better at it. He expected me to make him look good, and I think my lack of style embarrassed him. He actually sent his secretary over to help me when we were expecting guests. That was embarrassing, but I went along with it. I guess I was hoping that my reward would be that he'd agree to have a baby. He kept telling me that it wasn't time, and eventually I insisted. I told him that I wanted a family, or I wanted out of the marriage. He said, 'So long, have a nice life.'"

"Just like that?"

"Basically. That was a month ago. We've been tiptoeing around each other since then. I was hoping he'd think about the prospect of actually losing me and change his mind. I thought we loved each other. I am not even sure what love is any more. Last week he started talking about divorce lawyers and whether I wanted to keep my job at the paper." Jan's eyes began to fill. "He just seems not to care at all. I just can't believe that something that seemed so wonderful could turn out to be such a mistake."

"Well, he's an idiot if he loses you, and he'll regret it."

A loon from across the lake sounded its long, mournful call that seems to say *Where are you? Where are you?*

"I'm glad that I'm here right now, Ida," Jan said wistfully.

"Me, too," Ida patted Jan's arm. "We have a houseful of interesting guests for you to meet—a family from Kansas, a painter and her father, a couple from New York, a wildlife photographer, a hunter and a poet. Oh, and three teenagers in the green room. Business is good, but with the bizarre happenings, I'm nervous about the rest of the summer season. I'm worried that word will get out that we have ghosts here, or some such thing, and people will leave."

"I'll do what I can, Ida. I'll start looking into this tomorrow and I'm sure we'll find the answer. Don't worry. Now, I'm exhausted. What room do you have me in?"

"I saved you room three, of course," Ida said, picking up the empty cups and plates and taking them to the kitchen sink. "You probably don't need me to show you the way."

Jan started toward the stairway with her duffel bag. "No, I think I could find my room with my eyes closed, and they almost are."

"Call me if you need me," Ida said, pointing to the intercom. She left to go next door to the log cabin where she lived with her husband, Philippe.

Jan climbed the curved wooden staircase to the second floor and settled in to room three, the one with the deck overlooking the lake. Although this room was the largest in the lodge, other than the room nine suite or the green room, Jan stayed in this room whenever she came here. It had come to feel like her private space. Only twice had she shared it with Sid, when he reluctantly agreed to accompany her to her retreat here in northern Vermont.

The same pink, purple, and mauve quilts were on the two beds, one double and one single. The same pictures were still on the walls, one of a meadow of grass pinks under a blue and white sky, one of white-tailed deer leaping over rail fences in autumn, and one of a beautiful sunset on Seymour Lake. Jan dropped her duffel bag on the larger bed, and turned down the sheets on the smaller one, nearer the deck doorway.

She opened the sliding glass doors and went out to look at the stars. Jan loved how bright and beautiful they were here in the North Country, with no light pollution, and tonight they were indeed spectacular. The Milky Way sparkled like a sequined scarf as it stretched across the sky. Jan inhaled several deep breaths and savored the beauty and the freshness before she went inside. Closing the screen, she left the outer glass door open so that she could feel the breeze, smell the sweet Vermont air, and hear the loons. Indeed, as soon as she was snuggled under the quilt and ready to doze off, she heard the bird's maniacal laughing call—a call much different than the long eerie sound heard earlier.

What's so funny? Jan wondered. She drifted into a foggy pre-sleep state and saw a vision of the loons on the water as the cares of the day faded and the long low sounds from across the lake now lulled her into a deep soothing slumber.

Chapter 2: Presence

"Ayeee! Help. Help. Ayeeee!" Jan was jolted from her dreams by a high-pitched scream which seemed to come from the hallway outside of her room. Fully awake, she heard it again, this time clearly coming from downstairs. She jumped out of bed, but hesitated before going to open the door. Looking around her room for a weapon, Jan grabbed a lamp from the dresser and inched her door open, cautiously peeking out into the hallway. The guests from room two—a man and a woman—were running down the stairway, and Jan could hear a commotion in the dining room below. Setting the lamp back on the dresser, she followed the couple downstairs.

The low lighting in the room made the antique furnishings seem peculiar and a little ghostly. An old cast iron wood stove on one end of the room sat like a squat Buddha, adorned with antique kitchen utensils. A wooden swan flew from the ceiling attached by a wire. The carved ducks and geese around the room all seemed to be watching as if they had an uncanny knowledge of the events.

A tall, thin, blonde woman was pacing back and forth. "There was a man in my room! There was a man in my room!" she shouted. Someone buzzed Ida while other guests tried to calm her.

The agitated woman was Annette DiPersio, the poet in room nine, the small suite off of the dining room. She was an extremely tense woman, very thin, possibly anorexic.

"I was so scared!" she gasped. "First I woke up because I thought I heard someone shuffling around the room. But then I realized that I had the window open, and maybe someone had walked by on the porch, so I calmed down and started to doze off again. Later I woke up with a terrible feeling of dread, and then I saw a shadow of a man run across the foot of the bed, and my bedroom door opened and closed. I screamed. It was awful."

"Are you sure it wasn't a dream?" Ida asked.

"Well, I suppose it could have been," Annette said crabbily. "I was groggy from my sleeping pills, but it felt so real. I'm sure I heard something, saw something. If it was a dream, I'm sorry, but I think it was real."

A man, who Jan figured from Ida's description was Mr. Loomis from Kansas, spoke up. "Too many strange things are happening around here."

"What strange things?" Jan asked him.

"And you are?" Loomis asked Jan, abruptly. He was a bit chubby, but harmless-looking despite his curtness.

"I'm sorry, Nate," said Ida. "This is Jan Whitlock. She is the investigative reporter I told you about. She's come to help us figure out what is going on here."

"Well, it's about time," said Loomis. "We have had our sandwiches stolen from the refrigerator twice now, and my son has had his boogie board taken right off the front porch."

"I had a six-pack stolen from the fridge myself," another man offered. Ida introduced him to Jan as Ralph Ledger, a hunter from North Carolina. A bit scraggly-looking with his long, thick black hair, beard and moustache, wearing a worn red plaid flannel shirt and gray sweatpants, he spoke with a slight southern accent, "I went to get a cold one after my hike yesterday, and there were none left."

"So there's someone around who's extra hungry and thirsty," a third man joined in. "There are three teenagers in the shed who seem like the natural suspects."

"Who are you?" Jan asked.

"Matt Abbott, photographer for *American Wildlife* magazine." He reached out to shake Jan's hand. "We've all been waiting for you. And here you are to solve the mystery," he grinned.

"I think that's a bit optimistic," Jan responded, not failing to notice the captivating smile or the tone of his voice. "So far, it's a shadow and some missing food. Not a real crisis."

"And ringing phones!" Annette DiPersio added. "All hours of the day and night, startling people and there's no one on the other end when we answer. It's spooky. And the lights go on at odd times. I'll have made sure all of the dining room lights are off when I turn in and then I'll go out an hour later and they're on again. One night I even woke up to find the light in my room on, right over my bed. I admit that the writer in me finds it intriguing, but it's getting just a bit unnerving."

Jan grabbed a pencil and a sheet of paper from the motel desk near the kitchen and began to take some notes.

"The phone rings over at the log cabin also," said Ida, "I shiver when no one is on the other end."

Mr. and Mrs. Shapiro, who had run down from room two, also had a story to tell. "We've loved coming here so much, because it has always been so peaceful, a place of spiritual renewal. Now it's nerve-wracking. One of the signs over the kitchen stove says *Nearer my God to thee*. That used to make me feel like this was the Garden of Eden, and now it means 'Watch out!' We were really scared the other night, when we were sitting in the great room playing Parcheesi, and someone kept rapping on the window that looks out onto the porch. We went out the door and looked a few times, but no one was there. It's kind of creepy. And then, we are careful to turn the lights off in our room whenever we leave it, but twice we have come back to find them on again."

Now there were more guests coming down to the dining room in their bathrobes and slippers. Diana Peabody, a watercolor painter, and her elderly father, Amos, came in, both looking annoyed. "Who's screaming?" Diana asked. "My Dad isn't getting any sleep around here, what with phones ringing and people banging on windows all night. Good gravy, Mother Murphy. We may need to go find a motel somewhere if this keeps up." The stocky woman, with her gray hair in a ponytail, led her frail father by the hand, and both of them sat down at one of the tables.

Jan now realized how threatened people were feeling, but still thought that it might be as simple as pranks, someone stealing food, ringing phones, knocking on windows, and a neurotic poet with a bad dream. "Sounds like Mr. Abbott could be right about it being teenagers," she said.

"That's not really fair, Jan," Ida spoke up. "They are really good kids. They're part of the Youth Conservation Corps, working summer grants at the wildlife refuge."

"Of course you're right. We really shouldn't jump to conclusions too quickly. I'm sure there's a simple answer and we need to allow for all possibilities. People should relax and not let their imaginations get out of control. We'll figure it all out. Now, did anyone see a man running away from room nine? Or did anyone hear the front door open and close?" The blank faces told Jan that the answer was no.

"So what woke everyone up was Annette's screaming, right?" The guests began to murmur to each other while casting sideways glances at the lady poet.

"I suggest we all try to get some more sleep, and I'll talk privately with each of you tomorrow." Jan tried to sound authoritative, knowing that someone had to be confident and in charge.

The guests began to drift back to their rooms, and only Annette, Ida, Matt, and Jan were left in the dining room.

"You must be the one who got room three? I don't suppose you'd switch with me?" Annette asked of Jan. "I wanted room three and Ida said that it was already reserved. I offered to pay extra but she wouldn't give it to me. I love the deck and room nine is so disturbing. That's where the former owner was murdered, you know."

Jan caught her breath and glared at Ida, who winced with an expression of one who has been caught in a lie.

"I can't believe that in three years you never told me this!" Jan said, jumping up and stomping around the room.

"I try not to tell people," Ida said apologetically to Jan. "It just makes them nervous. Annette knows because she was here around the time that it happened. It's been six years now. I'm sure that it's irrelevant to the current situation."

"Ah, but it's way too soon to declare any fact irrelevant." Jan was now intrigued with the mystery, and wanted to know everything. "You have to tell me that whole story, and anything else that you may have filed away under 'irrelevant'."

"Oh, all right," said Ida. "But not tonight. I'm so tired. I promise to tell you all about it tomorrow."

"Fine, but I want the whole truth."

"Yes, I know. But perhaps privately," Ida said quietly, glancing toward Matt.

"This is going to be fun," said Matt. "And I thought it was only going to be a dull photography trip." Winking at Jan, he turned and headed for the stairs.

Annette continued to whine and rock back forth in the chair and Ida tried to comfort her. "Annette, I'm sure that you are perfectly safe. I'll leave Seymour here in the lodge tonight for your comfort, but really, you must try to relax and get some sleep."

"I'll try. I really am exhausted." Annette turned to Jan, "I am glad you're here. But maybe Ida should lock the doors for once?" She then turned and went timidly back into room nine. "Maybe I'll take another pill."

"Ida," Jan said, "I hope you and Philippe aren't depending on me too much."

"Oh, but we are counting on you," said Ida. "There is no one else who can do this—be here at the lodge and find out who is causing trouble. We need you."

The phone on the kitchen desk rang twice and stopped. Ida grimaced and turned to Jan. "Please?"

"Well, I'm here. I guess I'm supposed to be. So, let's get a couple more hours of sleep and get to work." Jan tried to sound positive, but all of the muscles around her belly tightened.

The friends hugged again and Ida left to go back to the log cabin, leaving Seymour at the lodge as guardian. Jan made sure that all the downstairs lights were off and then started up the stairway on the west side of the lodge. As she turned to go into her room on the left at the top of the stairs, Matt came out of the bathroom and went in the other direction down the hallway to room one. "Good night, Ms. Whitlock," he said with a smile.

Jan nodded but did not respond. She went into her room, and sat on the bed. Looking down at her left hand, she thought, "These rings are strangling me right now." She removed the rings and put them in the top dresser drawer, then set her alarm for six A.M. so that she could be up before everyone else.

Chapter 3: Dawning

Rrrinnnnng. The old Baby Ben alarm had a disturbing clang, and for a moment Jan couldn't remember where she was. As her eyes opened and she realized that it was becoming light outside, she hurried to the sliding doors and looked out, hoping to see the sunrise. But the sky over the deck was already a beautiful blue, painted with a few white clouds, just enough to be picturesque. Wanting to be the first one downstairs, Jan grabbed some clothes and headed for the bathroom in the hall, which she now knew she shared with the Shapiros, next door in room two, and Matt Abbott in room one at the end of the hall.

The old lodge was a fascinating place, with antiques in every room, and the bathrooms were no exception. The tub in this particular bathroom was cast-iron, with a pedestal base. The faucets in the tub and sink were metal with white porcelain. The chrome shower frame attached to the end of the tub held a blue-and-white-flowered curtain, and the small electric vanity lamps over the sink looked like Easter lilies in bloom. The walls were papered with light blue fleur-de-lis and held wonderful miniature prints of Maxfield Parrish paintings. The old wide floor boards were thickly covered in a gray-blue paint, and accented with an oval braided rug. The window looked out on the back yard of the lodge, and the woods and fields leading up Holland Pond Road.

Jan washed quickly and headed down the curved staircase, covered with the same gray-blue paint. The shelves around the stairway opening held more antiques; a white wooden pig, a pair of old snowshoes, and wooden geese of various styles. An old window frame over a mirror graced the wall and made the stairway appear more spacious. Jan heard the front door slam before she got to the bottom of the stairs, and as she entered the dining room, she saw through the window the dark shadow of a man leaving the right side of the porch.

Running over to the window, Jan tried to get a good look at the man, but he disappeared behind the cedar trees. "Maybe it was Philippe," she thought. "Seymour's not here barking, so that's probably the answer." She made a mental note to check with Philippe later.

Jan went to the kitchen off of the large front dining room and started a pot of coffee, taking note that the kitchen light was on. The continental breakfast was set up for the guests to serve themselves—a system that Jan loved—as she enjoyed being alone for a while in the early morning and having that first great cup of java. She looked at the array set out by the innkeepers: four kinds of cereals—bran flakes, instant oatmeal, cranberry-almond granola and fruity puffs; bananas and oranges; breads and muffins; jars of locally-made jams and jellies; toaster waffles and real Vermont maple syrup. The refrigerator held milk, juice, eggs, and butter. Pouring herself a bowl of the granola and grabbing a banana to slice onto it, she chose to sit at the small cozy table here rather than to go out to the dining room. The vinyl placemats had pictures of birds: a ring-necked pheasant, a killdeer, a loon, and a godwit. The bright ringed eye of the killdeer stared up at her as she sat at the table. Then, looking over at the godwit, she thought, "Does God have a wit? Is this all a big joke?"

Jan still found it difficult to think that the crisis here was anything more than some trivial incidents getting blown out of proportion. However, since she now knew that Ida had kept the murder that had happened here a secret from her for three years, she wondered what other revelations would appear. She really didn't want to play detective right now. She wanted just to relax and think about what was happening with Sidney. Instead, she was being called upon to use her analytical brain, which she felt was not operating at full capacity. The coffee finished perking and she poured a cup, spilling some of the coffee onto the counter. After cleaning it up and adding some more to her cup, she put in extra milk and one sugar, and then strolled around the kitchen, the back part of which doubled as a small antique shop. Over the big old wood stove were two framed embroidered sayings, her favorite being *Home is Where the Heart Is.*

"Ida and Philippe are very spiritual," Jan thought. "I wish I had their faith in God and life." She sat for a minute at the kitchen desk in the corner, amused by the old black rotary telephone still in use for guests, and at the collection of antiques on the shelves around the room. Bearing tiny price tags in pastel colors were Depression glass, old cooking utensils, milk cans, piggy banks, chalk ware, old dolls, children's books, dishes of Wedgewood and Blue Willow, and paintings of various types on the walls, including some intriguing portraits of somebody's great grandparents, Vermont pastoral scenes and the occasional religious image. The painting that Jan loved the most was a large picture of Jesus the good shepherd, placed high on the wall next to the big old oak desk. He could be seen from the dining room, and from the front door as one walked into the lodge. Somehow it was comforting knowing that He was there, with His shepherd's crook in hand. This one bore no price tag because it was a permanent fixture in the lodge.

Sitting back down to finish her soggy cereal, Jan spoke out loud to no one. "Where was my good shepherd when I was marrying the wrong man?" and then "Here I am talking to myself. I guess I'll be doing a lot of that from now on." Jan wondered what Sid was doing back in Branford, the wealthy town in Connecticut where they had lived in an elegant shorefront home since their marriage five years ago. It was about time for him to get up and go to work at the *New Haven Courier*, where he was editor. She loved her job as a reporter when she started working there along with Sidney. She thought then that the world was rolling out a red carpet at her feet, and now it had been ripped out from under her. With all of her hard work and training in investigative reporting over the last few years, Sid had recently been giving the big stories to others, and now had given the very important story on Hartford's Mayor Perez to her rival, Serena. That stung. She was very suspicious, though, that it was not entirely about the woman's reporting skills. She had suspected him of fooling around on her in the past, and although she couldn't be completely sure of that, she now knew that Sid was not the man she thought he was.

"Some detective I am," she thought. She had let her feelings override her common sense. Sid was handsome and charming, but really always shallow. She had seen that but ignored it. "And children—how could he not want children?" That's what brought all of their problems to the surface. He wanted so much attention—all of her attention—and everything his way. He had no interest in sharing their life with children.

Tears began to form in the corners of her eyes, but Jan heard footsteps on the staircase, and shook them away. After pouring herself a second cup of coffee, she went into the dining room. The Shapiros appeared, greeted Jan briefly and went into the kitchen to fix themselves some breakfast. Ward came back first and settled down at one of the other tables near her. Small oil lamps set on hand-crocheted doilies served as centerpieces on the four maple tables, and the placemats were laminated needlepoint pictures of New England seasonal nature scenes.

Jan greeted the couple. "I hope you got some sleep after the two A.M. surprise."

"Yeah, I slept okay, and I think Avis did also," said Mr. Shapiro. "My name is Ward by the way. And you are Jan, correct? Or shall we call you Ms. Whitlock?"

"Oh, it's Jan, thanks. And where are you two from?" Jan asked, reluctantly thinking that she might as well begin interviewing the guests.

"We're from Long Island. I'm a stockbroker. We love coming here, for the outdoor sports and fresh air. The only thing I'm not crazy about is that it's hard to keep connected with my New York office. There is one outlet in the dining room for internet, but the cell phone doesn't work here unless you walk down to the far end of the beach. Of course, Avis thinks that it's a plus to have more of my attention. We love this place, but this past week it hasn't been as enjoyable as we remember, what with the strange happenings. It's a bit disconcerting."

"Yes, I am aware that it's harder to communicate with the outside world from here." Jan also suspected that by now Sidney would have left several messages on her cell phone, but she had not checked. She had told him that she was going out of town, but had not informed him of her specific plans and she was not ready to talk to him again yet.

"You're not kidding!" Avis chimed in, carrying her hot coffee and granola in from the kitchen. "One phone in the whole lodge, and every time I try to dial long distance, the circuit is busy. I mean, I know we come to Vermont to get away from the rat race, but a little contact with home would be nice. I mean just to check on the dogs."

"I guess that depends on how you look at it," Jan responded. "So, Avis, tell me about your family in New York. Do you work in your husband's business?"

"Stock brokering? Heavens, no. That's Ward's life, and I guess he enjoys it, or at least the financial rewards of it. I'm a buyer for Macy's. Much more fun. And, no, we have no children. Our parents are gone. We each have one sibling, neither of whom we ever see. We are pretty much our own family. Which is too bad really, because we have a lot more money than we need and no one to spend it on. In fact, Ward just inherited more from his father. We do have two sweet fox terriers at home, but we don't like to travel with them, even though Ida allows pets at the Inn. We need a break from them sometimes and we have a good kennel. I worry about them, though."

"So, why are you way up here near the Canadian border for your vacation?"

Ward answered for them. "Well, it's a good deal, and a clean lake, and it's easily accessible from the interstate. We like to swim and kayak. I've caught some beautiful lake trout, and we've made ourselves some fantastic dinners. It's a whole different world from New York. It's slower paced—almost like going back in time. And the wildlife! The other night we were driving back from Island Pond and we saw a moose in the road. It was fascinating. Once, on a ride over to Lake Willoughby, we saw a black bear."

"The nature here is really wonderful," Jan said.

"Oh, yes. And the scenery is so spectacular, wherever you go," Avis agreed.

Just then Matt, the wildlife photographer, came in from the great room. "So where do I go to find all this wildlife?" he asked. "Where can I get a good bull moose picture?"

"Many places nearby," Jan answered. "especially at dusk and dawn. Moose are pretty much nocturnal. Although they are unpredictable, and I've seen them at noon, and in all types of weather."

Matt poured a cup of coffee, spread some homemade raspberry jam on a blueberry muffin, and leaned against the registration desk while he ate it. An old cash register made by the George A. McLean National Company still sat on the old desk where it had been for many years, and jars of homemade jam were lined up for sale, along with postcards, locally made greeting cards, and Vermont maple syrup and candies. Matt flipped through some of the pictures of local scenery and wildlife that were available for sale.

Jan had learned from Ida that Matt was thirty-seven years old, a widower from Pennsylvania with a young son. He seemed to be taking in all that was going on, and enjoying every moment of it. He had a sparkle in his eye and a smile on his face. "Well, I'd like to find some of these moose. I've taken a lot of animal pictures in Pennsylvania and Ohio, but of course, we don't have moose down there."

"Well, maybe you'll get your chance while you're here," Jan said, as she turned to greet Diana just coming in from some watercolor painting out at the lake. The large woman was wearing a tent-like purple jersey shirt, and blue jeans that stopped just above her white ankle socks and sneakers. Her ponytail needed re-doing.

"You were out early," Jan said to the woman. "You must have been up at the crack of dawn."

"Yep, the early artist catches the sunrise," Diana answered. "It was a bit breezy, but warm, and the sunrise was just the right shade of blue-green with drifts of orange and yellow." She held up the canvas she had been working on.

"That's lovely," Jan told her, admiring her painting of morning clouds and color on the lake. "It really captures the feel of the dawn here at Seymour. But tell me, did you happen to see anyone or anything strange that early, as you were heading out? Like a man you didn't recognize?"

"Nope, there wasn't a soul around."

"How about the dog? Did you see or hear him?"

"Come to think of it, I didn't see Seymour. Wasn't he here last night, guarding us? I guess there must have been someone up before me who let him out, because I never ran into him."

"Perhaps Philippe or Ida was over here at daybreak or before. They sometimes come early to set up the breakfast," Jan offered in explanation.

"Well, I don't think I want to answer any more questions right now, if you don't mind. I'm going up to get my dad and we'll be down to eat. If he gets up and doesn't see me there, he may panic. It's the Alzheimer's. I have to keep careful track of him," Diana said as she left through the great room.

"I don't think she felt like being questioned," Matt said. "Or else she wanted more praise for her painting."

"Well, I expect to annoy more people before the day is out."

"Is that hard for you?"

"I don't know. I guess so. I know that a lot of reporters like to get in people's faces and drag out their feelings. I have a hard time with that."

"Like when someone has just had their family burned up in a fire and the reporter asks them what is going through their mind?"

"Yes. Like that."

"So you find it hard to be ruthless?" Matt asked.

"There ought to be some line of propriety, where media people can get a story without total lack of concern for the human beings involved."

"And where would you put that line, Ms. Whitlock?"

"I guess I'm trying to figure that out."

Jan noticed that Avis was writing in the guest book, and walked over to her.

"I'm writing the story about the early wake up call," said Avis. "I think it's a good one to add to the lodge stories, don't you?"

"Oh yes. I've always enjoyed reading through the pile of journals, full of guests' adventures around the area. Ida encourages people to write whatever they want in there, and they surely do. I've seen pictures drawn by famous artists and wonderful poems and storytelling. They make you want to go out and see what they saw. Sometimes there's a complaint in there, but not often. Mostly people rave about the glories in the Northeast Kingdom."

Ward arrived and the Shapiros then went out for a morning drive to the St. Johnsbury Museum, and Jan and Matt were left to chat.

"Can I pour you some more coffee?" Matt offered.

"Sure, why not," Jan answered. "I can't believe you have never photographed a moose. Have you ever seen one?"

"No, regretfully, I've never even seen one," Matt said, pouring the coffee. "I hope you'll help me remedy that."

"We'll see. Are you any good as a detective? I could use some help on this case and you seem interested."

"Well, I think I used to be pretty good. I did do some investigative reporting for a while. I'm a photographer mostly, and sometimes a writer. I've only been working for *American Wildlife* for a few months, so I've been concentrating on writing from the naturalist's viewpoint. But, I could try—help you brainstorm. Sometimes my articles do require research and investigation. It's kind of intriguing, isn't it—this spooky old lodge and people getting scared out of their wits? It makes me wonder if it isn't a publicity stunt."

"Oh no, I'm sure it's not. In fact, Ida is afraid of bad publicity. If it gets around that there is a thief around scaring people to death, the lodge could lose business. It takes a certain kind of person to come to this lodge as it is, and it has taken a while for Philippe and Ida to build up a clientele."

"Aha, then maybe she's not trying to attract guests, maybe she's tired of innkeeping and wants to get rid of them."

"No, that's not the Ida I know. She does think about retiring sometimes, but I'm sure she likes what she's doing. It's just that she knows that this lodge is not like most of the others. It's for people who like a place that is homey and unusual, but not too "unusual"."

"You mean that most guests who come here wouldn't want excitement beyond stuffed wild animals on the shelves and meat cleavers over the doorway?" Matt teased, pointing around the room.

"Is that what that thing is?" Jan asked, looking up over the doorway into the kitchen. "I thought it was some kind of old fashioned tool for cutting hay."

"Nope, it's a tool that the butcher uses to cut up a cow. I've seen them in Pennsylvania. And I'm sure you must love this room, too. I have been finding it fascinating."

Matt gestured and Jan followed him into the great room off of the dining room. It was furnished with two old overstuffed sofas, a few odd chairs, a huge handcrafted wooden box, several old tables with games and puzzles piled on them, and a TV in the corner atop a large scale from the St. Johnsbury Scale Company. Two large handmade braided rugs warmed the floors, and a ping-pong table stood in the back corner. Other decorations were a set of moose antlers on the wall over a small wood stove, various wooden items, including a stork, a penguin, and a large model of a World War II airplane hanging on wires from the ceiling. At the far end of the room was the back staircase which was the access to the "pet-friendly" rooms on the right-hand side of the second floor. At the base of the stairs, on the back wall, was a huge oval mirror in a thick wooden frame, with leaves and pinecones carved into it. Room eight was tucked in back of the great room under the stairway.

"Have you ever seen such an odd arrangement of décor?" Matt asked.

"That's why they call it a great room! Did you check out the lavatory?"

"That one in the corner? Not yet." Matt peeked into the small bathroom in the corner of the room where there was a sign that read, "First flush toilet in the town of Morgan. It originally sat on the porch of the inn and people came from all around to see it."

"Well, that's unique," Matt laughed. "This place just gets more fascinating every minute."

It was now about eight A.M. and the Loomis family came down the back stairway from their two rooms—

four and five. Their entourage consisted of Nate and Frances, and their children, Nate Jr., Albert, Dora, and the baby, Celeste, along with a blonde cocker spaniel named Rosebud. After greeting Jan and Matt, Nate got the children seated in the dining room, and Frances went into the kitchen to make French toast for them all. Guests were allowed to use the small electric stove to cook for themselves, as long as they cleaned up their own dishes, pots, and pans. It looked like quite an ordeal for Frances Loomis, who soaked two loaves of bread in egg, milk, and cinnamon, fried them up on the griddle, and served them to the family, along with five glasses of orange juice and two cups of coffee, with refills. She placed the butter dish and jug of maple syrup on the table, next to her husband, who helped the children sweeten their French toast. Nate did a pretty good job at keeping the kids contained in the dining room, although the same could not be said for the cocker spaniel, who stole syrupy toast from Dora's plate and ran with it into the great room.

"Have you found out who the culprit is yet?" Nate asked Jan. "We are tired of having our things stolen."

"I'm working on it, Mr. Loomis. What else are you missing besides sandwiches and a boogie board?"

"Well, Dora's bathing suit is missing this morning. We hung it in the pink bathroom last night, and it is not there now. We checked the other bathroom in our wing also—the blue one—just to be sure. Who would want a little girl's bathing suit? She'll have to swim in shorts and T-shirt today."

Just then four-year-old Albert knocked over the jug of maple syrup, which went running over the edge of the table and was licked up by the greedy cocker spaniel.

"No, Rosebud!" yelled Frances. "Nate Jr., help clean up this mess. Who left the syrup in front of Albert anyway? You know he always spills."

"Have you kept all of your children in your sight these past few days?" Jan asked with hesitation, not wanting to insult the guests. "I mean, are you sure that Nate Jr. didn't put his boogie board somewhere else besides the porch, and hide his sister's bathing suit?"

"Oh, we can understand your thinking that," said Frances with a laugh. "Little Nate is pretty forgetful sometimes, even for an eight-year-old, and he does tease his sister. But, we know how much he loves his board, and he keeps really good track of it. He knows that if he picks on his sister too much while we are on vacation he might not get to go in swimming. We just know it isn't him."

"Well, I'm glad to hear that." Jan said. "I really didn't think so, but I have to check out every possibility. So, tell me. What do you two do in Kansas?"

"I teach biology at the middle school," answered Nate, "and Frances runs a craft and quilt shop called 'Fran's Fantasies'. We're pretty busy most of the time but do love to get up here to Vermont in the summer."

"It is beautiful, I love it here myself," Jan said. "Is it all right if I ask you some more questions later?"

"Sure. I hope you ask everyone all the questions you need to. Someone needs to figure this out," said Nate. "But I hope you will keep your questions connected to the lodge and our visits here, and not get into our private lives in Kansas."

Jan nodded. She got the message.

The Loomises went upstairs to change before they all headed for an early swim at the beach, leaving a rather sticky trail behind them in the dining and kitchen area. Ida came over to clean it up, and at the same time, the three teenagers from the green room came in. Stan, Jeff, and Cliff wanted to catch a quick breakfast before heading over to the wildlife refuge. Jan greeted them and introduced herself before she began asking them questions.

"So, you are all on government grants this summer?" Jan asked the boys. "What exactly do you do at the refuge?"

"I don't see why what we do there should have anything to do with the stuff going on here," Stan snapped. "but since you must know, we mostly follow the ranger around and learn from his superior wisdom,"

"We don't just do that," the one named Jeff spoke up. "We take notes on all of the plants and wildlife. We learn about what is poisonous or dangerous. We learn the habits of the animals, like how to tell bear scat from that of a fisher cat, and how deer prints are different from moose—things like that. It's cool. We are all here for different reasons. I have to write a paper to get some college credit and to be invited back next year."

"Sounds fascinating," Matt jumped in. "Have you seen moose in the refuge?"

"One, so far. A lone female. She surprised us one morning," Jeff again spoke for the trio. With his smooth dark hair and glasses, Jan thought that he looked more like a computer whiz kid than an outdoor guy training to be a ranger. She soon learned from Ida that he was a high school honor student from Bedford-Stuyvesant in Brooklyn, New York, who had earned a grant to study the boreal forest for the summer for college credit; Stan was court-ordered to be there, and Cliff was part of a special-needs program for Vermont teenagers with mild Asperger's syndrome.

"We saw three baby foxes yesterday," offered Cliff, a short husky young man with a cheerful disposition. "They were playing in the roadway, and didn't even run away when we drove by them. They weren't at all afraid of us."

"Wow, foxes! That would be a great picture," Matt exclaimed. "I'd be happy to get that one, or a bobcat, or a fisher cat, or anything else unusual." He stayed and talked more with the teenagers, while Jan went upstairs to help Ida change the sheets.

With the lodge at almost full capacity, there were a lot of beds to make. They began on the west side in room two, since Jan insisted that her sheets did not need changing.

"Okay, my friend, time for you to talk," Jan confronted Ida. "I can't believe that you never told me about a murder here. I thought I knew everything about this lodge."

"I never wanted to ruin your vacations," Ida responded. "And Philippe and I had made a pact never to speak of the murder to anyone who didn't know. It just didn't seem necessary. We wanted people to be able to relax here, and not be afraid."

"And Annette knew?"

"Yes, because she has been coming here for many years, and knew Mr. Baggett."

"And you put her in the room he was murdered in?" Jan said in disbelief.

"Oh, she's so funny about that. She wanted that suite when she couldn't have room three, because it's bigger. She could have had room eight, but she refused it. She likes the extra space, and she has stayed there many times. Sometimes I think she really loves the drama, too. We've had other writers who have asked to stay in the 'murder room' and a psychic who was hoping to see a ghost. Too bad they're not here now, they'd probably see one."

"So lots of guests knew about it?" Jan crossed her arms, nodded her head and glared at Ida.

"I'm afraid so. The word has gotten out some, mostly to earlier guests who knew Mr. Baggett and inquired about him, or because they read about it somewhere or someone told them. We didn't. Jan, I really am sorry to have kept it from you. I guess it is part of the lore of the lodge, whether we like it or not. But no one has ever seen or heard anything that could have been a ghost—until now."

"That reminds me, did either you or Philippe come into the lodge early in the morning to let Seymour out?"

"No, we set up the breakfast the night before, as usual. Why?" Jan told her about the man leaving at six, and that Seymour had not been there to bark at him.

"Seymour did come home rather early. He was sitting on the step when I looked out at six. We thought you had let him out. So what are you thinking, Jan? It sounds like you have an idea."

"It's all very strange," Jan said. "I really don't have a clue yet as to what's going on."

"Well, we need to find out soon, or guests will start leaving. I have an elderly lady coming in this afternoon. Miranda Picket, a cousin of Philippe's friend, Ed, is coming here to stay for several days, while she has her floors stripped and varnished. We are getting paid extra to keep a close eye on her, and Annette has volunteered to keep an ear out for her at night. She is quite lively and agile for eighty-nine, but has a touch of dementia and can occasionally wander off. We don't need her getting scared. I will be putting her and her cat in room eight; the one behind the great room, so I must remember to make sure the bed is made up. I appreciate your help. Sometimes I do get tired of the constant upkeep of this place."

"No problem. Frances Loomis said to skip their rooms. They don't need clean sheets every day, except in the crib, of course. I notice you managed to change the subject away from the murder, Ida. So talk."

"Jan," Ida pleaded, "Could we save that story for later? I promise I'll tell you everything when we have some time to sit and relax."

"Putting me off again? Okay, fine, just until later, but I want it all—every detail, with nothing held back," Jan insisted. Ida nodded.

When the beds were all made and the kitchen and dining room cleaned up from breakfast, Jan and Ida were about to sit down for tea when the local constable came to the door.

"Hi, Fred, what's up?" Ida asked. "Have you gotten any information or ideas that might help us to understand what is happening here? I hope that you haven't told anyone about this though. I don't need nasty rumors flying."

"No, Ida, I'm sorry. I haven't really had time to investigate the petty thievery at the lodge, or who's leaving your lights on. I'm just letting people know that they still haven't captured that guy who escaped from the prison in Drummondville, Quebec a couple of weeks ago, and now they think the guy may have headed down this way—may even have a contact in Island Pond. I'm warning people to keep their doors locked and their eyes open. He may be dangerous."

"Oh, great," Ida said, looking over at Jan. "That's all we'd need."

Chapter 4: Balance Rock

"Why didn't you tell the constable about the man I saw leaving the lodge?" Jan asked Ida early that afternoon, as they were sitting on the porch swing, people-watching.

"Because we don't know who or what that was," Ida answered defensively. "I'm sure it wasn't that escapee. I mean, why would he come here and bother with our lights and all? That was probably just one of our guests going out early."

Ida got up and went down into the flower garden in front of the porch. The lupine was in full bloom, and so were the weeds. She began pulling them up with a vengeance. It hadn't been a great spring for the perennials. The squirrels had dug up the tulip bulbs, and the deer had nibbled the phlox down so low that it would take a lot of rain to bring them to bud. The forget-me-nots and pink and blue columbine were beautiful, though, and the lupine spikes were spectacular.

Guests were beginning to come outside to enjoy the fresh air on the porch. Ralph Ledger came out, lighting up a cigarette, and Ida asked him to please not smoke on the porch, so he made a face and wandered off towards the beach. Jan watched him walk away and wondered about this scruffy man—why he would hang out here at the lodge to try to find out about good places to hunt next October? The idea of guns in the lodge, even those meant for hunting, was a little unsettling under the circumstances.

Diana brought Amos out to sit on the porch while she painted. The old gentleman had recently celebrated his eightieth birthday. Although he was not as sharp as he used to be, he was still a character. He loved a good joke and a glass of fine wine. He delighted in traveling with his daughter, watching her paint, and chatting with people about the weather, the government, and the Red Sox. He sat in a rocker near the front edge of the porch, while Diana set up her easel down on the lawn where she could paint a view of the lodge looking up from the road.

"Hey, don't forget to paint your handsome father into that picture!" Amos shouted to her. Sitting there in the porch rocker, looking out at the lake and the beach, Amos looked like there was no place on earth he'd rather be.

The weather was exceptionally warm for June in this area, and the beach today was crowded with swimmers trying to get cool. Some kids were running and jumping from the dock while others were playing "Marco Polo" in the clear, cold lake water. A couple from a nearby cottage paddled out into the lake on a canoe, and a group cruised by on a pontoon boat. Jan looked out over the sparkling pristine Seymour Lake, which the local Native Americans originally called "Namagonic", meaning "salmon spearing place". She felt a strange chill go up her spine as she thought about the ancient land and the importance of the Nulhegan Basin and the boreal forest.

"We wouldn't even be able to breathe without this forest," Jan thought reverently. She hoped that the article she was writing could capture the spirit of the area and stir up some support for the state to preserve more of the land around the Nulhegan basin. As she looked up at the blue sky and the few white clouds hanging there, she noticed that one was shaped like a wolf, and the evil look of it made her shiver. Jan went over to Ida in the flower bed.

"Well, I understand your not wanting to stir up negative publicity, Ida, but that could have been significant. Someone snuck out of the lodge at dawn, and probably let Seymour out earlier. In fact, it must have been someone that Seymour knew, or who was very good with dogs. I don't understand why you don't get the constable more involved."

"Well, I don't know, Jan. Maybe it's because he has a big mouth and also a reputation for not being much of a help. Anyway, Seymour came back, but Lola is missing. Philippe called over earlier to tell me that he's worried because he hasn't seen her since yesterday afternoon. She's a homebody Siamese and never wanders off very far."

"Oh, no! Well, if she doesn't turn up by lunch time, we can get a search party going. I'm sure we'll find her. Maybe she just needed a break from the craziness around here. Speaking of which, you seem to keep walking away from me when we start to talk. It's time for you to tell me about the murder!"

"I will, I will. I just want to get this weeding done first. Okay?"

"No, but I'm not sure I have a choice." Jan started back inside and then turned back toward Ida.

"It feels like it's going to be a very warm day, and I'd really like to take a hike in the woods where it will be cooler. Do you have any suggestions?"

"Hmmm. There's a criminal running around and you want to go for a hike?"

"Why not? The constable mentioned that he could be headed to Island Pond, so I'm sure the guy is not hanging out in the woods. Besides, I need to think." Ida ignored Jan's frustrated tone.

"Well then, have you ever been up to Balance Rock? That's a fascinating spot. It used to be a very popular hiking destination, but for some reason the forest has been left to grow up around it, and it's not easy to find the trail anymore. Only those of us who know about it can find it."

Matt, who had been standing behind the screen door came out and asked if he could join her on the hike. "Maybe we'll see a moose up there in the woods?" he asked. He took the liberty of sitting next to her on the double swing which hung from chains in a little alcove near the railing on the east side of the deck.

"I suppose if you want to come along, it's always safer than to go alone," Jan answered, a bit coolly. "Let's get going, then, before it gets any hotter around here."

"I'll have a big jug of iced tea for you when you get back," Ida offered. "And then we can sit and try to figure things out. Matt can join in if you really want him to. Miranda is coming in with her cat, Princess, sometime soon, or I'd go with you to show you the way. You'd better get directions from Philippe, though, as I'd probably mislead you."

Taking her advice, Jan and Matt went around the lodge to the long tin-roofed shed in the back, its old gray sides decorated with big antique signs for Coca-Cola, 20 Mule-team Borax, Thelma's Real Estate, J.J. Lillicrap Trucking and Texaco gas. The back half was a big garage and barn for maintenance equipment. The middle part of the shed had been made into an antique shop, filled with hundreds of antiques purchased by Ida and Philippe all over the country, and the front third of the shed was the new three-person suite they called the green room.

They found Philippe in the garage working on the engine of the lawn tractor. He looked up when he heard them approaching. "Hey, there's our city girl." He gave Jan a hug and apologized for his greasy hands.

"Hi, Philippe. It's great to be here, but not so great that you are having this problem."

"Oh, what's one more problem? When you run a lodge, that's all there is—problems." The handsome dark-haired French-Canadian said with a grin. Philippe was a strong, common-sense guy, with a lot of faith in God. He never worried too much, as he also believed in the ultimate good of humankind. "In fact, I have a problem right here with this tractor. It was running fine yesterday, and today it won't even turn over. I wonder if it's the humidity. This heat wave is a bit much for this time of year. It makes me think that it might be time to air condition the lodge, even though it's usually only a few days of the year that we even think that way."

"Well, it may be global warming steaming things up," said Matt.

"Oh," Jan said, remembering why they were there. "Matt and I want to take a hike up to Balance Rock while it is still fairly cool. Ida said you could give us good directions to it."

"Sure. You just go along the road toward the west along the lake, start up the hill, and look for an old post up on the bank, across from a big butternut tree. Go up in there, and you'll find blue paint markers on some trees. Follow those in until you come to a dry gully. There are no more markers after that. Follow the gully until you come to a big fallen log across it. Then go up the side of the gully on the left, and the log will be pointing over in the woods toward the big rocks. Go toward the biggest rock, and around it, and then look north and you'll see the balance rock. It's easy to find if you know the way," Philippe grinned. "Just yell loud if you get lost and maybe someone will find you." He laughed. "Or maybe not. You can take Seymour along if you want, and follow him home. Oh, and watch out for poison ivy. It's virulent this year."

Assuring Philippe that they would heed his warnings, Jan and Matt headed out. The walk down the road along the beach was easy going, and they strolled along, with Seymour leading the way. Matt wanted to chat about moose sightings, while Jan wanted to ruminate about the events in the lodge.

"So, are you going to tell me where you think the best place around here is to find a moose?" Matt asked.

"Well, maybe. But first I think you should help me brainstorm this mystery at the lodge, as you promised."

"Fine. Shoot. You storm and I'll brain."

"Hmm. Not sure I like the sound of that, but here goes. We have food missing, a boogie board and bathing suit missing, phone calls at odd hours, lights apparently going on and off on their own, shadowy figures around the lodge, and what else? That's it. It's not all that terrifying."

"Right. The food is the teenagers. The boogie board and his sister's bathing suit have to do with Nate, Jr."

"What about the phone and lights?"

"Crank phone calls, and old wiring."

"And the shadowy figure seen by Annette, and the man I saw leaving early this morning?"

"Now, that was a ghost," Matt said with a smile.

"Oh, you're helpful. Could you be serious?"

"I'm kidding. Can you lighten up a little? You look like you've lost your best friend. It's not so terrible. In fact, this mystery is a challenge. It's fun. Let's have fun." He raised his eyebrows flirtatiously at her and brushed his brown hair off of his sweating brow. They reached the hill and, with the noon heat growing humid, the walking was more difficult, but they kept on. Soon they were at the post that marked the entrance into the woods. Matt stopped and aimed his camera at the top of the post and began taking pictures. Jan was curious and went over next to him.

"What are you doing, taking pictures of a post?"

"Look closely," Matt said, pointing to the top of the post. Jan saw that the surface was covered with strange lichen, with tiny spikes shooting up out of it. The tops of the spikes wore little red caps. "Those are called 'British soldiers'," Matt told her. "This is *Cladonia cristatella*, a lichen found in the north woods. I've heard of it but never seen it. It's amazing that it's growing here on the post."

"You have an eye for detail," Jan said.

"Well, you're the investigative reporter," Matt said. "You probably look closely at things too—notice patterns."

Jan stood close to him and felt him breathe in deeply a couple of times.

"Your hair smells nice," he said.

She looked up at him, frowned and then turned away towards the bank that led up into the forest.

They hiked up the hillside into the woods, keeping a careful eye out for the poison ivy. Seymour began to move faster ahead of them.

"I'm sorry, I'm not great company," Jan said apologetically. "It's not the problem at the lodge that is getting to me. It's my impending divorce."

"Oh. Now I'm sorry," said Matt. "I didn't know. I had heard that you were married, but you weren't wearing rings, so it wasn't clear."

"Well, that's what's happening and I don't want to talk about it."

Seymour led them up the gully and over the fallen log. Looking ahead they saw large boulders, many of which were moss covered. The forest was beautiful, with fascinating plants all around, and so lush that it felt almost jungle-like. The ferns were huge, like short palm trees, and there were vines that wound around trees and hung down as if inviting travelers to swing on them. Jan pointed out a scattering of pink lady slippers, and Matt took pictures. A little farther up the path they saw wild columbine, commonly called rock bells, dangling in the breeze with their little red-orange caps and yellow feathers.

"That must be it!" exclaimed Matt, charging up the hill, with Jan right behind him. In the clearing in front of them a huge rock balanced—precariously, it appeared—on top of a smaller rock. The big rock was at least seventeen feet across. Matt pushed on it, as if he thought it might move. It didn't. The rock was solid. Then he climbed up on the top of it and bounced on the overhang.

"Typical guy," Jan called up to him, finally offering a smile. "You just had to do that, didn't you?"

"Of course," Matt said. "Here, take my picture." He handed down his camera, and posed on top of the rock, while Jan photographed him. Looking through the camera lens, she realized that Matt was quite an attractive guy, even reminding her of an old boyfriend with his playful mannerisms.

"Come on up! The view is spectacular," Matt urged.

The back of the rock was a bit slippery and Jan nearly fell back down, but eventually she was up beside Matt. "What view? We're in the thick of the woods."

"Well, a few minutes ago, it was quite lovely." He winked.

"You know, you are annoying," Jan said, sitting down on the top of the mossy rock. Matt sat beside her.

"Sorry. I can't help myself."

"Not as annoying as Ida is today, though."

"Oh?"

"I can't believe I let her get away with putting me off again. I'm such a mouse. Damn, I hate it when I realize an hour later that I should have said something."

"Wuss."

"Yes, I am, thank you. They asked me to do a job, and I need to do it, even if they are part of the problem."

"Well, now you're showing some fire."

"So what is life like in Pennsylvania?" she asked him, thinking that she might as well start investigating whether the lodge's troublemaker could be Matt.

"Aha, you know where I'm from, and I didn't tell you. What else do you already have in your notebook about me?" Matt asked, swatting at his arms which seemed to be under attack."

"Why don't you tell me what I should have there?" Jan shot back. "All that I already know comes from Ida's guest register."

"Okay," Matt paused. "I see how it is. Well, I'm afraid my life isn't very exciting. I have no aliases, no prison record, no weird fetishes, and no missing relatives. I never was investigated for anything. I'm a boring guy who grew up on a farm in Pennsylvania. Ouch, what kind of bugs are biting out here?"

"These are called 'no-see-ums'," Jan said, smacking at her own neck and arms. "because..."

"We can't see um. I get it."

"And do you still live there—in Pennsylvania?" Jan asked.

"My son and I live there with my mom. My dad passed away two years ago, a year after my wife, Julia, died of cancer."

"I'm sorry about your dad, and losing your wife. That must have been a really difficult time for you."

"Yes, my son, Ethan, was seven when his mom got leukemia. We moved in with my folks and my mom took care of Julia and Ethan while I drove an hour and a half commute every day to work. It was rough, yes."

"When did you become a photographer?" Jan changed the subject.

"I started taking pictures when I was a kid. It relieved the boredom of the farm. I got my bachelor's in journalism at Penn State, married Julia, and went to work in Philadelphia, writing local news and later taking pictures for the *Philadelphia Inquirer*. That's it— nothing spectacular."

"I have a feeling there are a few interesting stories in there, and now you work for a prestigious magazine."

"Yeah, that was a fluke." I had taken some shots of a black bear that had wandered into the suburbs of Philly and when the Associated Press picked it up, it got noticed by an editor at *American Wildlife* who emailed and invited me for an interview. One great shot and I was in. That was just a few months ago. I'm still getting used to hunting down wildlife, and spending more time outdoors. I love it, though."

"That must have been some picture."

"Well, the bear was a huge male, and he had been accosted by some neighborhood dogs and was holding them off. Yes, one of my best all-time photos. I had it enlarged and framed, of course." Matt smiled at Jan and then began fiddling with his shoelaces. "Now I'm looking for the greatest of all-time moose picture and I've never even seen a moose. I mean in person. Or is it in moose?" He laughed.

Jan smiled. "Tell me about your son."

"Oh, Ethan's a great kid. I miss him. Wish I could bring him with me when I travel. I sometimes do, but he wanted to try Boy Scout camp this year, and we thought it would be good for him. I know from experience that just hanging around a Pennsylvania farmyard in summer can bore a kid to death. Our closest neighbor is five miles away, and there's not much in between but cornfields. Ethan's nine and in the Cub Scouts. He wants to earn an Eagle Scout Badge some day."

Matt grew quiet, and Jan let him off the hook. "So, do you have any instinctive feelings about the guests at the lodge? Does anyone seem suspicious in any way? Or do you think we are looking for someone who is coming in from the outside?"

"Or just a series of strange coincidences maybe?" Matt added. "I'm not really ready to believe that the spooky events are all from one source. Guests at the lodge? Well, I do think the teenagers, or one of them, could have something to do with this. I did have a long chat with them this morning. Stan was in juvenile detention in Burlington for a few months. His job at the Conte is really his opportunity to fulfill the community service part of his sentence. He is a child of a single mom, with an edge about him, and I think he bears watching, but I don't really think he's malicious. Jeff seems conscientious—he's trying to get a college scholarship. Cliff has Asperger's and social problems. He could be a prankster, but would likely have trouble keeping it a secret. I think we have to look at Annette, and also at Ledger. But, truthfully, I think it's all mischief or small infractions of propriety—stealing someone's sandwiches and all. Basically, I think these people are all harmless, except in the sense that some of them could have overactive imaginations and play off of each other, increasing the anxiety. People seem to look for a crisis just to add excitement to their mundane lives."

"But then, we know that sometimes people who appear to be completely above suspicion are hiding some serious aberrations."

"Ha!" Matt laughed. "You are getting sucked right into this group delusion, aren't you? You love it."

"I guess I am getting into the mystery. I don't love it, though. I wanted to come to the lodge to relax, think through Sid's announcement, and maybe work on a freelance article on the Silvio Conte Wildlife Refuge. Ida called and begged me to come sooner than I'd planned. She's very worried about losing their summer income if travelers are scared off. So, a part of me is intrigued, yes, but I'd be thrilled if I found out today that it was all a joke."

"Well, Ida's lucky to have you for a friend," said Matt. "But now I want to ask you a question. You said you didn't want to talk about your impending divorce, but I am very curious, and I told you a lot about myself. So, how could any man want to divorce you?"

The corner's of Jan's mouth turned downward and trembled. "I suppose we weren't right for each other from the beginning, and I just didn't see it. There I was, a small town Vermont girl over at the beach for the day, and there he was, on vacation from his family's estate in Old Lyme, Connecticut, stopping at the Weirs harbor with his yacht on a shopping trip from their summer condo in Wolfeboro. I think I just was never in his class, and now he realizes it."

"Well, he must be an idiot." Matt looked thoughtfully into Jan's green eyes, his own dark brown ones sparkling. She looked back and he held her gaze for an extended moment, just until they heard a long, low howl coming from the ledges above them.

"What was that? A loon up here?" Matt asked.

"That was no loon," Jan asserted. "It sounded like a wolf, and I'm not going to hang around here and find out. Besides, I'm getting all bitten up."

They heard the primordial wail again and goose bumps prickled up on Jan's skin.

"Let's go," she said, standing up and brushing the moss off of her blue jeans. Without an argument, Matt followed her down from the rock and with the help of Seymour they made their way back to the lodge.

Chapter 5: Shades of Blood

Ida's mint iced tea was ecstasy to the hikers after the long hot walk back from the rock. Jan and Matt each drank a couple of tall glasses of it while resting in the great room with Ida. Although the lodge was not air conditioned, the two big fans in the shade-darkened room made it quite comfortable. All of the other guests were out at the beach or otherwise occupied, so the three of them were alone.

"Has Lola come back yet? Jan asked.

"No, and I'm worried. Philippe and I have walked all around the area and called and called, but no sign of her. We're going out again later. Now, I did promise to tell you about the murder."

"Yes. It's about time. We're ready."

Ida began to talk. "And are you sure, Jan, that you want Matt to hear this also?"

"Yes, he's now part of the team," Jan said, half-skeptically. She still wasn't sure that this was a serious investigation, or that the six-year-old murder had any relevance.

"Well, Philippe and I only heard the story secondhand, of course, when we were looking into buying the lodge. Mr. Baggett's lawyer and executor, Jake Hawkins, was trying to settle the estate quickly, so we were able to get a fantastic deal. We were the first to make an offer, and it was accepted right away, although we had to wait to take possession until the initial investigation was over. That about six months. Then, for several months after that, there were still police detectives popping in occasionally to examine room nine. That's where the body was found, just inside the door. He had been stabbed."

"Stabbed? How many times? Did they find out who did it? Was it a robbery? Were there guests around?" Jan was taking notes in her old leather binder.

"Well, we were told that it was a pretty bloody stabbing, and in fact, there are still some bloodstains under the rug there. No murder weapon was ever found. It was in the late summer, in the slow season after summer vacations and before fall foliage and hunting. The few guests who were there hadn't heard a thing. They were all interrogated before they could leave town, and none was implicated. I really hate even thinking about it. Poor John Baggett, dying like that, alone on the floor. He must have been terrified. When we started getting odd happenings here, I thought maybe it was his ghost coming back to haunt us. That's when we had the prayer service and asked Jesus to protect us. But, really, I don't think what's happening now has anything to do with that murder. That was just a sad and strange event in the history of this lodge."

"And who investigated? Was there anything stolen?"

"It is our understanding that the Vermont State Police came in and determined that there was no robbery. Perhaps someone was going to steal something, but was surprised by Mr. Baggett. We may never know. The case is still open, of course."

"Well, what about John Baggett? Why would someone want to kill him? Did he have any enemies?"

"Not around here. Everyone liked him. He had come up from Baltimore five years previous, and had completely renovated this old lodge. It was a thriving business year round, with the usual spring and summer visitors—a large clientele of hunters in the fall; and snowmobilers, skiers, and ice fishermen in the winter. Fall and winter are still very busy for us."

"Did he have any family?" Matt asked. "A wife? You haven't mentioned a Mrs. Baggett."

"He was alone here—a widower. He had a son, James, back in Baltimore, who actually called us soon after we bought the lodge, wanting to know if we would sell it to him. We declined, of course, and we never heard from him again. Rumors are that before the murder he was in trouble a lot and he and his father were estranged. I'm not sure why he wanted to buy the lodge."

"Rumors?"

"Well, after we took over, the locals used to occasionally tell us what they knew about John Baggett, which wasn't much. I think he was well-liked, but a private person, like many who come to the north woods. He minded his own business. He left his Baltimore past behind and didn't talk about it. No family came to the funeral here. His lawyer handled everything and had him buried right over there in the Morgan cemetery."

"Well, you're right," Jan said, "there doesn't seem to really be any connection between the murder and what is happening now, especially since it was six years ago. I'd say Mr. Baggett should be resting in peace, but Ida, if you remember anything else about it, please let me know, even if you think it is unrelated, all right?"

"Sure."

"And you said his lawyer's name was Jake Hawkins? Where is his office?"

"Over in Island Pond. More iced tea?"

"No, thanks," Jan answered, jotting down some notes. "I'd like to look through the lodge's history books though, as well as the guest books and desk registers for the past six years."

"Well, they're right here in this cabinet. You two can look at anything in here. I have to go out for supplies and to pick up a guest. I do hate remembering about the murder." Ida got up to leave.

"May I ask you one more question?" Jan asked. "You said that Annette was 'around' at the time. Was she in the lodge at the time of the murder?"

"I only meant that she had been a frequent guest, even before that, and that she knew Mr. Baggett. I don't think she was actually a guest at the time of the murder, but I can't honestly say for sure. She returned that first summer that Philippe and I were here, and I know she had read the story in the papers also. I do think that the writer in her loves the sensationalism of it all, because she often asks for room nine. May I go now?" Ida rubbed Jan's arm several times, her eyes drooping and showing dark shadows.

"For now. Remember, you wanted me here to do this."

"I know, Jan. I just wish it wasn't happening. God must be putting us through a trial." Ida walked away with a sad smile, and Jan and Matt began looking through the old books and photo albums.

"Wow, I didn't realize that this lodge has hosted a lot of hunters and fishermen over the years," Matt exclaimed. "Although with stuffed partridge running around on the tops of tables, and moose and deer antlers and mounted fish adorning the walls, I should have known. Look, here's a picture of some guys posing right out here behind the lodge with their dead deer, and another one with six guys holding up huge fish. I wonder why we don't have anyone catching fish like that right now. It must not be as popular as it used to be."

"Probably a silly question, but do you hunt?" Jan asked him.

"No, I could never kill an animal. My uncle once took me hunting out in western Pennsylvania. He shot a deer and hung it up and gutted it with his hunting knife. I can still see the blood running onto the ground, and the sad eyes of the deer. I know I shouldn't judge the hunters, because we all contribute to the slaughter of animals in many ways, and I don't judge them. I just don't want to see it. I have done a little fishing, but I don't like watching the fish squirm on the hook, breaking their spines to kill them, and all of that. Here's a picture of John Baggett with a huge fish. He looks kind of familiar. Paul Bunyan look, maybe. What kind of fish is that, do you know?"

Jan studied the picture. "Looks like a northern pike. People sometimes catch them over on Lake Memphremagog."

"I hear that the lakes around here are spectacular—deep glacial water. I'd like to go explore them sometime soon, but I need a tour guide," Matt said, looking wistfully at Jan.

"I have work to do," she answered. "But it could be important to know more about the area. It's an unusual world here in the kingdom." Jan examined the photo of Baggett, a tall man in overalls, with a thick dark beard and moustache. "Mr. Baggett looks like a pretty rugged individual. I'm surprised that he couldn't fend off his attacker. He must have been surprised by him."

"Or her," said Matt. "Maybe it was a woman. Say, look at this article about a snowmobile accident. The picture indicates that it was pretty nasty. Two people killed in a collision on the Toad Pond trail. It's a rough life here in the north woods, isn't it, Jan?"

"It can be. Snowmobiling is big in the winter, but there are always a lot of accidents and a dozen fatalities."

"Why do they call it the Northeast Kingdom?" Matt asked, changing the subject again.

"I believe it came from an old speech by Governor Aiken back in 1949. Look, here are some pictures of the Silvio Conte Wildlife Refuge, and some brochures about its history. This could help with my article. And here are pictures of the bog, which is a unique place."

"What exactly is a bog?"

"Well, sort of a swamp, but this bog, the Mollie Beattie Bog, has plant life that is found nowhere else in the world. Look, here's a picture of red pitcher plants in the bog."

"Beautiful! Looks like a place we should go to. Any moose in this bog?"

"I've seen their footprints."

"Who's Mollie Beattie?"

"Matt, I'm surprised that you don't know, since you work for a wildlife magazine," Jan teased him. "She was the first woman director of the United States Fish and Wildlife Service. She died in 1996 of a brain tumor. For years, she defended the Endangered Species Act, fighting proposed budget cuts, and insisted on protecting whole ecosystems, rather than just individual at-risk species."

"Well, then, I honor her," Matt said seriously, raising his iced tea glass. "and, I'd like to see her bog."

"Look at this strange picture," Jan said, showing it to him. "It looks like there are candles in the bog—unless it is a badly developed picture, or a double exposure or something."

"Aha, another mystery."

"Here are some articles written about the lodge over the years—one in *Vermont Life*, one in *Old Inns of New England*. Ida always says that a lot of writers find this an inspiring place. The lodge guestbook is full of the autographs of writers, artists and musicians drawn here by the creative energy of this rare southern tip of the boreal forest. It's a mystical place."

"Boreal forest? Down here?" Matt asked.

"Yes, the Nulhegan basin is a unique geological phenomenon that draws the forest down into it. I belong to the Friends of the Nulhegan Basin, a group working to preserve it. Vermont's Governor Douglas helps by keeping a focus on environmentalism in Vermont."

Just then, Ida came in with an elderly woman who carried a cat in her arms. Jan and Matt stood up to be introduced. "I'd like you to meet Miranda Picket," said Ida. "She's going to be staying with us in room eight for a while. And this is her cat, Princess."

Jan petted the small black and white cat, and welcomed Miranda, a short, frail little woman with her white hair wound up in an old-fashioned bun held in place with an antique tortoise shell hairpin. Her flower-print cotton dress covered her knees, but not the tops of her rolled down support-hose. Matt said a brief hello and excused himself to go down to the beach to take photos, and Ida escorted Miranda and her cat into room eight.

After quickly shuffling through the rest of the lodge scrap books, Jan slipped a couple of pictures into her notebook and returned the albums to the cabinet. Catching up to Matt on the beach, she invited him to join her in a walk to the nearby cemetery.

"I want to see where John Baggett is buried," Jan said. "Ida said that it was right here in Morgan."

Matt was happy to accompany her as they walked the eighth of a mile up the hill to the old Morgan cemetery, just beyond the Renaults' log cabin. Wandering around among the mossy, weathered old stones, they made note of many interesting names from the area. "Here's a Holland," Jan said. "I wonder if he's related to the Holland Pond Hollands. And here's a Morgan." She read the stone, "'Theodore Morgan, 1870-1932, beloved husband. Gone but not forgotten'."

"Here's a pitiful one," Matt observed. "Three children of John and Sarah Pease. They all died in the same year, within months of each other. Philippe's friend Ed is a Pease. I wonder if they're related."

"Look around. There are quite a few little family groups like that in this cemetery," Jan said. "That year was one of the influenza epidemics."

"How do you know that?"

"I've done some genealogy. Look at this one. 'Here lies Dolores, third wife of George. Eleven children and never bored.' That's funny!" Jan laughed aloud and turned to Matt. He was standing a few yards away.

"Well, I found Mr. Baggett, but it looks like someone else found him first." The stone was knocked over backwards, and it had been smashed around the edges.

"Matt, this is significant," Jan exclaimed. "This is the only stone damaged in the whole cemetery. Why only Mr. Baggett's stone? And why now? It definitely looks like a recent incident. There's no moss on the broken edges. Perhaps there is some connection between the events at the lodge and the Baggett murder. I mean to find out more. I need to talk to the state police and to the local newspaper people. Are you with me?"

"I'm in. This is more exciting than looking for moose. But I'm not sure how I'll explain it to my editor if I don't get that moose picture soon."

"You'll get it, I promise you. Let's get back. Help me with this, and I'll make sure that we run into that moose."

"Oh good, more blood on the highway," Matt smiled, following Jan as she slid down the grassy hillside back to the lodge where they found the guests in a commotion.

"Someone's been smashing antiques!" Annette announced to Jan as she came up the steps. "We've found two broken ducks here on the porch, several smashed dishes in the kitchen, and a $200 soup tureen from the antique shop was shattered right on the back step."

"And this, too," Ida held up an antique wooden airplane with its wings dangling."

"This is definitely looking like an inside job," Jan said. "How else could someone break dishes without being heard unless they knew that there was no one else around?"

"Well, I don't know," said Ida. "We still leave the lodge unlocked all the time. Maybe we'll have to reconsider that policy. Annette found the broken dishes and got cut when she tried to pick up the pieces." Annette, slightly paler than ever, waved her bandaged hand at Jan. Blood was still seeping through. "I'm taking her over to Doc Williams' office to get stitches."

"Oh, I do hate to cause a problem for anyone," Annette whined.

"Nonsense, Annette. It's no problem, and you know you love the attention." Ida looked at Jan and rolled her eyes.

"And you are going to inform the constable of this," Jan urged.

"I'm not sure," Ida responded. "Let's wait and see. Maybe it was one of the kids." Annette followed her out to the parking lot and they were off to Island Pond for treatment.

Jan collapsed onto the porch swing, her thoughts racing. Matt sat down beside her. With a report like a gunshot, his side of the swing let go and he fell to the floor. Jan tumbled down on top of him, and the heavy swing swung like a pendulum towards their heads.

"Ouch, now that hurt!" Jan cried, struggling to get off Matt's warm body. He was holding her head tightly against his chest, trying to guard her from the still swinging wood and chain. "Let go of me," she hollered, and as he did, she managed to roll away from the swing and get upright.

"I'm sorry. I was only trying to protect you," Matt tried to reassure her. "Here, look at this chain, it has been cut. It looks like it was sawed almost through, and our weight finished the job." Jan looked at the chain, and then went over to sit on the porch steps.

"Are you all right?" Matt asked of the now silent Jan.

"Yes, at least physically. I guess my pride is a bit injured."

"You've nothing to be embarrassed about," Matt said.

"Well, things are getting worse around here, and what have I done? I haven't begun to figure this out. Ida should talk to the state police and get a real investigator in here."

"You are a real investigator, remember? It's your job, isn't it? Why are you putting yourself down?"

"Oh, I don't know. Maybe I'm feeling a bit like a failure these days."

"Because of your marriage? It takes two to make it work. You know what you should really be investigating—yourself! You need to find out who you are, and how valuable you are. Do you really want to save your marriage? If so, why are you here in Morgan? Do you really belong in investigative reporting? Why are you writing an article about the preservation of nature? And, why do you not believe that your work is of high quality, when you have the awards to prove that it is?"

"I suppose Ida told you about that. Were you talking about me?"

"Maybe a little."

Jan frowned. "I hear what you are saying, and I don't have the answers to those questions. I guess I need to work on finding them. First, I have to help Ida."

Frances Loomis appeared. "Look at this!" she said, handing the guest book to Jan, opened to the last autographed page.

Jan read aloud the inscription, "LEAVE THE LODGE" signed, R.E. Payer.

Chapter 6: Campfire

River Jordan is chilly and cold, alleluia
Chills the body, but not the soul, alleluia

The gentle melodic tune being sung around the evening campfire seemed most appropriate to Jan, given the circumstances. Philippe and Ida Renault were religious people and although discreet, were not particularly hesitant to express their own beliefs. And, this did seem to them a suitable time to sing a Christian song. The threatening message in the guest book had made the guests and proprietors of the lodge jumpy and everyone needed to relax, if possible.

Campfires were a regular event on summer evenings at the lodge as long as the weather was dry, and the Renaults were joined this evening by several of their guests and their good friend Ed Pease, elderly owner and operator of the old farm up at Holland Pond. No one knew exactly how old Ed was, but there was no one in Morgan who could remember when Ed wasn't around. This man, who resembled Father Time with his long, white beard, was tall and thin, elbows sharp like a hatchet, legs like bean poles and a neck twice as long as necessary and too slender to hold up his head.

Ed was considered by the locals to be the expert on just about everything in the Northeast Kingdom, and people loved to listen to his stories of the early times— the days before the roads were paved, before telephones and electricity, and before people had to get permission from one government or the other before crossing the Canadian border in either direction. He could tell you about when the local wildlife, particularly the moose, bobcat, lynx, and wolf became endangered, when they disappeared, and when they returned to the area. He could tell you when the natives of the area moved in and out of the territory, and where they now resided, as well as who was who among the Abenaki people who lived in the area in and around Morgan. He was definitely the one to consult on the best fishing holes, winter or summer, the most likely bear, deer, and moose-spotting places, and which rock ledges still occasionally were home to timber rattlers.

Ed's best friend was Joseph Rainwater, the local Abenaki shaman, and if there was anything that Ed couldn't tell you, then probably Joseph could. Ed suggested to the group that they call Joe in to seek his wisdom during this stressful time. "Joe has a knack for hitting the nail on the head without too much trouble," he said. "He'd figure things out darn fast. And, he'd love to tell you a few good yarns about his adventures, sure as sugar."

The lodge guests who had gathered around the campfire—Jan, Matt, Annette, Miranda, Diana and Amos, the Shapiros, and the Loomis family, had all been anticipating hearing a story or two from Ed, and he was not about to disappoint them. After a few verses of "Down by the Bay" and "On Top of Spaghetti" accompanied by the soft mournful wail of Ed's harmonica, there followed a recitation of one of Annette's poems, which in general had religious themes, or were sentimental rhymes about trees and flowers. This time she read one called Daily Bread, which went like this:

Give me this day some daily bread,
And please, a place to lay my head,

Some shelter from rain and snow and sleet,
A place to escape the summer's heat,
A simple dress to cover my bones,
And maybe a few less whines and groans,
Someone to care would sure be nice,
A job—a simple one would suffice,
A little challenge, a bit of fun,
But still, oh Lord, thy will be done.

Someone said, "Amen."

Matt asked Ed if there were any wolves still around the Morgan area. He mentioned that he and Jan thought they heard one up by balance rock.

Philippe jumped in, "Oh, it was probably a coyote. There are a lot of them around. I don't think there have been wolves for a long time. Not since the Wolf Ledge incident a hundred and fifty odd years ago."

That was all the opening that Ed needed to begin telling the history of the lake, doing so in his thick Vermont accent that occasionally needed translation. "Lake Seymour is the second largest lake that is entirely in the state of Vermont—second only to Lake Willoughby. Memphremagog is bigger, but it is mostly in Canada. Seymour is the cleanest in the state and the second cleanest in the country. It's fed by a few streams and by several springs that bubble up around the edges of the lake. Folks can hear these springs bubbling from a distance and they used to say that it was the lake spirits rumblin'. This here lake is 300 feet deep in some areas, especially east of Weeks Point. It's a great lake for fishin', with bass, lake trout, brown trout and salmon. If you want pike, you need to go to Norton Pond, and for muskies, over to Memphremagog. There are some damn big fish around this neck of the woods. Joseph caught a land-locked salmon in Willoughby once that fed his whole tribe. I tell you, though; you don't want to get caught in a storm on Willoughby. A storm on a deep glacial lake like that will stir up from the bottom and rock your boat like crazy, and if you happen to be caught between the two facing cliffs of Mt. Pisgah and Mt. Hor, the choppy water could capsize your boat like it was a child's toy. I've seen it happen."

"Are there a lot of storms in this area?" Matt asked. "It seems like the weather has been wonderful since we arrived."

"Oh you've been lucky. The weather up here is unpredictable. In fact, there's a sayin' in Vermont, 'If you don't like the weather, wait a minute.' Those summer storms can surprise you all the time. They can come up sudden and flash through in minutes, leaving the air crisp as a fall frost. And then there are the lingering storms. Oh those are the worst." Ed looked up at Philippe, who moaned.

"Those are the ones that are so bad for the tourist business," Philippe said. "They crawl in slow, build up steam with rumbling and flashing, then settle in deep and get stuck between the hills, just hanging in there with a nasty drizzle for days and days. I've seen 'em last for two weeks here in the north country, while the rest of New England is clear and blue."

There was a moment of silence, and a whippoorwill called in the distance. Nate Loomis brought out a bag of marshmallows and several people joined the kids in toasting the sweet treats over the fire pit.

"Aaaagh," Albert hollered. The four-year-old had burned his tongue on a hot marshmallow and jumped around, flailing his arms. Frances took him inside to put an ice cube on it.

"Now as for your question about the wolves," Ed began again. "Back in the 1800s, there were many bears and wolves in this area. In those days, people didn't think much about the rights of wild animals, especially when their flocks and even their children were endangered. Sometime around 1820, there was an incident where a big black bear was seen swimmin' in the lake, not too far from where some children were playin', and someone came out and shot and killed it without a second thought. Today the animal rights groups would be up in arms."

"Wow, a bear," exclaimed Nate Jr. "Would we see one now?"

"Not likely," Ed answered. "Bears are a lot more scared of us than we are of them. They pretty much hide out way back in the woods. You might see one once in a while in a field, or crossing the road, but they won't hurt ya."

"Now in 1838," Ed continued, "that's when there was a fairly large pack of wolves roamin' the hills around the lake and ravaging the sheep. One night, farmers heard a considerable amount of howling up on Elm Hill, and the next day, a message was sent around the countryside for a hunt. A hundred farmers and about the same amount of hunters gathered the next evening and formed a thick line driving the wolves out to the point, and then they closed in and killed a great many.

"A hundred farmers? That seems like a lot," Matt said.

"There were a lot more farms up here back then," Ed explained. "The population has actually gone down. Anyway, in those days there was a government bounty of a half a dollar on a wolf, so they not only saved the sheep but made some good money on the deal. The point was named Wolf Ledge after that. But, yes, there are some wolves around today. There are more coyotes, but all of the wildlife is comin' back. Wolves have been spotted several times, along with bobcat and a few lynx, and there is talk, though I suspect mostly wishful thinking, of the catamount returning to Northern Vermont. Banjo Dan even wrote a song about it that was on his last album. Now you take the moose. They are everywhere these days, but back in the '40s, '50s and '60s it was rare to spot one moose up here. You'da had to go into Quebec or far northern Maine. Now they are so thick that, even though a lot are killed in the fall hunts, and others by vehicles or moose ticks, their numbers are still growin'."

"And yet I haven't seen one," Matt complained.

Ed then took out his harmonica and began to play. His tune was soft and spiritual like a country church hymn. No one really knew the tune, but they tried to hum along with it. It was a sweet song that made you go deep inside and dream about a day gone by, with bears and wolves around the lake.

Next Annette read another poem, this one a bit disturbing.

It seems to come from way up high
Or is it somewhere deep inside?
I worry but do not know why.
At night I dream I hear a cry.
I sit at evening near the pine tree,
Wondering just what could the matter be.
A restless stirring seems to haunt me.
What can I do to set my mind free?

"Interesting," said Ida. "It kind of describes the feeling of anxiety that is increasing around here, doesn't it?"

Jan nodded, wondering if there was more to Annette's anxiety than they knew.

The Loomis children were escorted off to bed, and now the campfire talk turned to the recent strange events, which Philippe recapped for Ed—the ringing phones, the missing items, Lola's absence, people seeing shadowy figures, and now broken dishes, smashed wood ducks, the chain of the porch swing being cut, and worst of all, the threatening entry in the guest book. Even the story of the unsolved murder came out, with Annette and other guests whispering pieces to each other, and then wanting to know the whole truth.

Ida decided to let the others in on the murder story, with Annette adding what she knew about it. Their reactions were more intrigued than shocked or scared.

And now Jan added another piece. "When Matt and I were at the cemetery, we found that John Baggett's gravestone had recently been turned over and smashed. His was the only stone damaged over there. It does indicate a possibility of a connection. Why only his stone? Why does someone want to do harm to the lodge, and to the former owner's grave?"

"People could get hurt in this," Ward Shapiro chimed in, "and I may have to think about bringing Avis home if this is not resolved very soon."

Avis glared at him. "Me? Bring yourself home. I'm doing fine."

"I'm sorry," Ida said sadly. "I'm sorry that guests are feeling nervous. I'm sure that it's not as scary as it seems. I'm sure no one really is meaning to do real harm."

"Well, if Jan hadn't fallen on top of me," Matt grinned facetiously "she might have gotten really hurt when the swing broke. It is possible that there is an evil mind behind this, and I'm starting to think that there might be a connection to the murder. I'm sorry Ida, but I think we have to be very cautious and keep our guard up."

"Well, the murder was never solved," Ed stated. "Has someone from the past come back to stir things up? Maybe someone needs to go talk to the state police over in Derby."

"That's near the top of my list," Jan responded. "But first I want to find out everything that I can around here. What do you think the townsfolk know about the incident?"

"Well, now there's where you really should talk to Joseph," said Ed. "One way or another he hears everything that is going on, and he is pretty good about putting things together. I remember that Baggett didn't have any enemies around here. Whether or not he had back in Baltimore I don't know. He had a son, but we never saw him. We had heard that the son was in trouble back in Baltimore. He never came up here to the lodge that I know of. Do you think that the missing items have any significance?" Ed asked. "What were they—clothes, food, and some beer? Those seem pretty harmless, and could be explained. What else?"

"Well," Philippe admitted, "I didn't want to say, but there have been some knives missing from the kitchen."

"Knives!" Avis squealed. "This is getting creepy."

"Doing fine now, sweetheart?" Ward asked. Avis scowled.

"And that is a connection to the murder," Ed added. "A stabbing wasn't it? Certainly all of the guests need to be frequently updated, in case they want to leave."

"If anyone wants to leave," Philippe said to the guests, "You can have your money back, no problem."

"I'm staying," Annette asserted. "It's interesting, and I'm not afraid. I really think it's mostly imagination."

"This from the one who woke us all up at two A.M. with her screaming," snorted Avis. "But I agree. I'm not ready to chicken out yet, even if Ward is."

Most of the guests declared their intentions to hang around for a while to see what happened. Even the aged Mrs. Picket, who sat with Princess on her lap, did not appear to want to run away from whatever was happening.

"How can you say that this is all imagination?" Jan asked of Annette. "Was Mr. Baggett's bloody body in room nine imagination? By the way, were you a guest here at the lodge when that happened?"

Agitated, Ida got up from her place near the fire pit and strode into the darkness. Her shriek a moment later scared Princess right off of Mrs. Picket's lap and into the flower bed, and brought Philippe, Ed, and Matt running. Ida, in great distress, stood over the carcass of a spruce grouse, its neck slashed. Blood ran down the steps onto the walkway.

"This is too much!" sobbed Ida, turning to Philippe and hiding her head in his chest. "I can't take much more of this. Someone is going to get hurt. I think we'd better talk to the state police."

"I'll put in a call right away," said Philippe, heading into the lodge. "Don't anyone touch the bird."

Jan helped Miranda catch Princess and then walked them back to room eight. Matt sat on the porch steps away from the bloody bird and talked more with Ed, Annette, and the Shapiros. Then Ralph Ledger's SUV pulled in, with the three teenagers inside. Stan, Cliff and Jeff saw the group gathered by the steps, and then saw the grouse.

"Holy smokes," Jeff said. "That's a spruce grouse, falcipennis-canadensis. They're protected. Who did that?"

"Are you sure that it's the protected grouse?" Matt asked.

Ida answered him. "You can't miss his dark coloring, the white bars on his black chest, and the bright red eyebrows. I look for those feathers whenever we are out in the woods. The Abenaki use them in their crafts, especially to make the dream-catchers. They pay good money for those feathers."

"Do the Abenaki hunt them?"

"No, never," Ida said. "They respect the laws of man and nature, and understand endangerment. They wait for the feathers to be shed, or gather them when a predator kills the bird."

"I don't think whoever did this was thinking much about endangered species," Matt answered. "This is meant to scare us off." He and Ida sat quietly with the dead bird, in reverence for the beautiful creature that had apparently been killed solely to threaten them.

State Police Officer Parker arrived in a half hour and questioned everyone. Ralph and the teenagers had to explain where they were when the bird was killed, and the boys related how they had missed getting their usual ride home with Ranger Matthewson because they had stayed too long in the refuge. They had started to walk back the nine miles to the lodge when Mr. Ledger had come along and picked them up on his way to Island Pond, deciding it was more important to give the boys a ride than to do his errand. Everyone was questioned about the other events, the missing items, and especially the broken swing.

"It could be that the swing chain was just worn," the officer said. "And, really the broken and missing items could indeed be some of the kids—let's not rule out the teenagers or the Loomis kids just yet."

The boys objected to being suspects and indignantly asked to be excused. They headed over to the green room in the shed.

"What about this grouse?" Matt asked with a tone of agitation, "and that chain has an obvious clean cut. It seems like you are minimizing everything. I know I thought at the beginning of all this that maybe it was all silly pranks, but killing an animal just for laughs is not funny."

"Well, your cat was missing," said the officer, looking at Philippe. "Doesn't she ever kill a bird? Maybe she got hungry after being out for a couple of days, and she dragged home the grouse. Cats do that."

"Well, not Lola," Ida objected. "She doesn't have the strength to catch a bird this big and drag it onto the porch. Besides, she is not back. She's still missing." Ida's eyes were teary.

The officer took another look at the grouse. "You're right," he said. "It has a pretty good-sized slash that could possibly be a knife, very fresh. If so, then this grouse was knifed right here while you all were at the campfire." A frown came over his face, he confiscated the bird, told everyone to stay in town until he gave them the okay to leave, and said that he'd be back tomorrow afternoon. After he left, most of the guests went inside and tried to settle down for the night. Philippe hosed the blood from the front steps, and scrubbed it with bleach until there was no sign of it.

Jan announced that she was going to go over to Silvio Conte tomorrow and talk to the ranger there. She had some questions that only he could answer. Matt asked if he could go along, but Jan stung him by saying she just wanted to go alone.

"I thought that I was helping you brainstorm on this," Matt protested.

"I know, and I'm sorry. I just need to be by myself for a while in the morning."

"Okay, look, I'll go moose hunting on my own, and I'll also ask around town about Mr. Baggett, and see what I can find out. We can compare notes afterwards."

Jan smiled at him. "Thanks for being understanding."

Later, unable to sleep and hearing the loons out on the lake, Jan recognized that a part of her was just a little afraid of what she was feeling about this man, who actually seemed to be accepting of her agenda and not trying to take control. She thought of Sid, and wondered if he was at all concerned about her, and if he was at all reconsidering her wish to have a child. Was he thinking about her? Did he even care? Was he even the person she thought he was? Was this marriage really over? Jan turned the light back on and opened the night stand drawer. She took out the Gideon Bible and read herself to sleep.

Chapter 7: The Bog

Jan knew that the visitor center at the Conte didn't open until nine, but that the ranger was often out early, checking on the eagle nesting sites, and watching for deer poachers and unlicensed fishermen. It was only seven, but she decided to see if she could find him. Her Mazda sputtered slightly as she turned into the dirt road beyond the visitor center, and headed into the forest.

"Must be the morning dampness," she thought, dismissing the engine noises.

Her slow ride through the refuge was delightful, with treats for the eyes and ears found only in this area of New England, where the boreal forest reaches a thin finger down into the Northern Appalachians. The clearings and roadside ditches this June were vibrant with early summer wildflowers—columbine, lupine and blue flag iris adorned with delightfully delicate butterflies including swallowtails, whites, sulphurs, meadow fritillaries, and the iridescent blue and purple Bog Copper.

The woods were a mix of spruce, fir, and conifer, especially black spruce or jack pine, with some hardwoods including quaking aspen, white birch, and maple. Many bird species ornament the trees; cardinals, blue jays, gray jays, thrushes, small osprey, hawks, cedar waxwings, and an occasional eagle. This refuge, Jan knew, was home to the endangered spruce grouse and the rare three-toed woodpecker.

Jan had been there before with Philippe, so she was confident that she knew her way around the wildlife preserve. The roads were not paved, but they were wide enough for two cars to pass, and smooth enough that she could dodge the occasional rock that might take out her gas tank—she hoped. She decided to look for the ranger at the tourist spots along the route—the Lewis Pond Lookout and Mollie Beattie Bog, especially. She figured she had to run into him somewhere around the main loop. About eight miles into the refuge, after a brief stop at Lewis Pond, she saw signs that read, "Spruce Grouse Protected Area" and, after making educated guesses at several crossroads, she saw the sign for the bog and parked her car in the designated clearing. The rare bog sedge, drooping bluegrass, red pitcher plants, and mossy logs among the black spruce greeted her as she stepped onto the boardwalk and walked into the bog.

A man with a multi-colored tunic over his blue jeans sat on the wooden bench along the boardwalk's main viewing area. Startled, Jan turned to go back to her car, but instead, felt intrigued enough to approach him. As she did, he peered up at her, and she looked straight into his deep black eyes and felt a sense of peace. Observing a few feathers in the long gray braid down his back, and colorful beadwork on the upper part of his shirt, she realized that he was probably one of the local Abenaki, and greeted him warmly.

"Hello. I'm Jan Whitlock, and I'm looking for Ranger Matthewson. You wouldn't have happened to see him, would you?"

The man held a small burlap sack in his left hand, and with his right, he was holding a variety of plants, which he placed into the bag. He replied, "I do believe that he is somewhere here about. Perhaps if you sit here and wait a while, he'll show up."

A thousand thoughts of caution rushed through her head, as if some inner child was wondering whether she should talk to this stranger. Yet those were rational thoughts and her emotional mind allowed her to feel quite comfortable here on the boardwalk with the dark-eyed man.

"You are safe," he said to her.

"Oh, I wasn't thinking—" Jan started.

"You were, but it is better to feel than to think."

"Oh, really?" Jan wondered how this person knew her thoughts.

"You are troubled."

"Good guess," Jan responded sarcastically. "Isn't everyone?"

"No. Many find peace in what others see as trouble. But you are in pain."

Jan glared at him, not sure she wanted this intrusion into her feelings, but somehow at the same time, she was captivated.

"It looks like love pain," he continued. "It may be a need to receive, or a need to give."

"Well, really, I'm distressed about things that are happening to my friends," Jan began, but caught herself, realizing that she didn't even know this person, and wondering why she would consider telling him anything. He could be the sneaky perpetrator wreaking havoc at the lodge for all she knew. As soon as she thought that, another thought popped into her head, that perhaps this character could help. "I told you my name, but I don't believe you told me yours."

"I am Joseph Rainwater of the Hawk Clan."

"I should have known!" Jan exclaimed. "You are the Abenaki shaman—friend of Ed Pease."

"Yes, and you are the investigator from New Haven who has come to help the innkeepers."

Jan looked at him quizzically.

"You told me your name," the man said, answering her unasked question. "And Ed told me about some of the events over there. Not everything is a mystery. In fact, nothing is a mystery once we understand. And, yet there is what we call the 'Great Mystery.'"

"I thought that was the 'Great Spirit'," Jan said.

"The term 'Great Spirit' belongs to the natives of the plains. But the Abenaki recognize different spirits, and a balance of nature, as well as the 'Great Mystery'. I can not give you details since you are not a member of the tribe."

"Well, it's a mystery to me why just when I need a vacation and plan to go to the one place in the world where I can relax and catch up to myself, I am given a big problem to solve, and my place of peace has become a pit of stress."

"It was given to you only because you drew it to yourself," the shaman informed her with a tone of authority.

"What? Are you saying that I wanted this?" Jan protested.

"In some way, you wanted it, or needed it. It's all an orchestration for you. Your spirit reached out to the north woods when you were in need, and you felt it drawing you here. The spirit of the lake and forest calls you. The spirit of the sky watches over you."

"That's outrageous!" Now Jan was becoming angry. "Don't tell me that I brought this evil to the lodge—that I wished this on my friends."

"It is likely that something in them also called upon the spirit of growth and change."

Jan's red face portrayed her distress, and she got up to leave. Joseph touched her arm with only one finger. "The bog spirit has something to say to you. Listen." She rolled her eyes upward, but Joseph pointed to the bench, his eyes directing her to sit. Jan sat on the bench and listened for what this bog spirit might be saying.

"I don't hear anything," she said.

"Shhh. Listen."

She took a deep breath and listened. There was not a sound. The black spruce trees stood tall and wispy all around. The bog grasses were still. It was humid, but not oppressive. Soft warmth surrounded her. A few bushes grew here and there in the spongy bottom of the bog, and some orange mushrooms pushed out from rotting logs among the fading yellow lady slippers and the bright red pitchers. Pockets of clear water reflected the conifers and the few cottony clouds in the blue sky overhead. The only visible movement was in the calm drift of the clouds. No bird sang. No frog croaked. No bug stirred. No mosquito landed on her arm, and no bee buzzed. The silence was so overpowering that Jan wondered for a moment if she had suddenly gone deaf. She flicked her earlobe and heard a scratching sound. There was silence again. No sound at all.

"I guess I can still hear," she thought. "This must be what it means when one says 'the silence is deafening'."

"This is amazing," she whispered to the shaman, not really wanting to change the mood. "It's like the bog is dead. My ears feel stuffed. I hear nothing at all. It is emptiness—dead silence."

"And what else?"

Jan listened again, sitting absolutely still for several minutes. Then she felt it. "But it doesn't really feel dead. It feels incredibly alive. It's like you can feel the plants growing, moving, and it... I feel something inside, like a longing... pulling on me. What?" she looked at Joseph.

"A vacuum?" he asked.

"Yes. It seems to be drawing me into it." Jan heard her own voice and looked at the shaman. A tear formed in her eye. "Oh," she said. "Oh."

"You must listen to the spirits of nature," he told her. "You must hear the song of the wind and the birds, as you did when you were a child." Jan nodded at him in recollection.

"You must watch the clouds in the day, and the moon, the fireflies and the will-o'-the-wisp at night. But you must sense with your heart and not your mind."

"I'm not sure how to do that," Jan said sadly. "I'm not sure at all that I have any awareness or any capacity to interpret anything. I've made so many mistakes."

"You will learn. You must open your heart to this call for growth. The lake and the woods have beckoned to you and brought you here."

"But you are an Indian, a native. You have a special connection to all of this."

"You do, too. We all do. It is in your genes, in the very structure of your cells. Just as the monarch butterflies know to fly to Mexico, you know inside of your own spirit where you must go. And you have guides to help you."

"I do?" Jan really wanted to know who these guides were.

"One is the moose. The moose is your totem and your primary guide. It will appear as a warning or a premonition," Joseph told her. "And this is your flower." He handed her a small plant with yellow flowers which looked to her like a weed.

Jan suddenly felt overwhelmed by all that she was feeling. She cradled her head in her hands and closed her damp eyes. When she looked up, Joseph was gone. She looked down the length of the boardwalk, and there was no sign of him.

"People sure do disappear around here," she said to herself. She'd wanted to ask him what he knew about the Baggett murder. She sat for another moment listening to the bog, sensing that it was indeed telling her something. She felt a growing tension, and decided that in spite of not finding the ranger, it must be time to go back to the lodge. People would be getting up for breakfast, and a cup of hot coffee and a bowl of granola would feel very good right now.

As soon as Jan left the end of the boardwalk and crossed the dirt road to the grassy parking lot, she heard sounds. A blue jay called, a breeze rustled the leaves of the hardwoods, and a cricket sang. "That's weird," Jan thought. "It's as if noise was banned from the bog and all of the creatures know it."

She turned the key in her Mazda and heard another silence. The car was dead. "Oh, damn," Jan said out loud, pounding her fist on the steering wheel, and realizing that she should have paid more attention to the sputtering engine on her ride out here. "That will teach me." She tried the key a couple more times before she realized that the situation was not immediately fixable. She reached for her cell phone, but quickly realized that there was no service in the refuge. Chiding herself that she had not brought a bottle of water along, and that her hat was back on the porch of the lodge, she got out of the car and began to walk in the direction that she was sure led back to the entrance, perhaps seven or eight miles away. The morning mist was lifting and the sun was breaking through with the promise of more heat and humidity.

Hoping to run into the ranger, Jan walked for about two miles down the dusty dirt road. She came to an intersection where there was an old post with a small board across it, which probably used to bear the names of the roads, but now only showed faded scratching. Jan was sure that she had turned right in coming towards the bog, so she turned left. Walking along the next mile, she muttered to herself about the shaman. "What a strange event that was. 'Spirit guides' my foot." She reached into her pocket and took out the little yellow flower. "Just what are you supposed to do for me?" she asked it. It didn't answer, so she tossed it to the side. Then, after a few steps forward, she turned and went back to pick it up. "I might as well identify you for my article," she said, shoving the weed back in her pocket. Plodding along, Jan had no choice but to chat with her inner thoughts.

She remembered how wonderful her first visits to the refuge here had been, how she had gone out in a canoe into the streams of the Nulhegan Basin and encountered her first bull moose in the shallows. She had startled him, and he swam for the shore as fast as he could and disappeared into the thick woods. Seeing him was wonderment, and since then she had always thought of the moose as her special animal. There was something about the huge primordial beast that inspired awe in her, and called back those times of wonder that her childhood in Shady Rill, Vermont had given her—the first time she found a spotted turtle, her first dog-toothed violets in the spring, and the first time she saw the trout flashing red as they spawned in the brook. Recalling these, she also remembered how only a few years ago she had come to feel that there were no more magic discovery moments to be had— that once you were an adult, life became boring. She had learned that there was no Santa Claus and that there were no fairies in the woods by the stream. She had given up writing her little poems about the powers of fairy dust, and now only wrote realism: science, history, and political investigation. She had given up creative writing for journalism, and married Sidney, who was practical and logical. Although she had fallen madly in love with a musician once, she had been so deeply hurt and disillusioned that she vowed never to be so deceived by emotion again.

She had her house in order, and her mind connected to reality. "I really have no time for bog spirits or totems," she thought. "But then again, I probably could use one right now. What am I saying? The last thing I need now is for a big moose to come charging at me."

The sun grew hotter, and Jan walked on. She decided to follow the advice of the shaman and listen. "What do I have to lose?" she asked herself. "I've nothing else to do." She heard the wood thrush trilling his morning cascade, and the cardinal singing "Pretty, pretty, pretty." But then she heard the crows that seemed to be laughing at her with their "Haw, haw, haw."

"Great," Jan said to herself. "My totem is probably really the crow." Then she heard the unnatural sound of some kind of machine, and upon listening more closely, concluded that it was a grader working on the roads. She was now at another crossroads, and decided to try to walk towards the sound, hoping that the person operating the machine could help her. She walked in the direction she thought the sound was coming from, but did not find the grader. A weasel darted across the road and startled her, and soon afterwards she came upon a partridge—the ordinary ruffed grouse, common cousin of the endangered and more beautiful spruce grouse killed on the lodge steps. The bird stood still on the edge of the dirt road, apparently believing that she would not notice him, but as she continued towards him, he puffed up his feathers in challenge. Then he flew off. Jan smiled, feeling the fondness she had always had for wild creatures.

As she walked, she remembered another encounter with a partridge in the cedar woods near her home in Shady Rill. She has been only eight years old the first time that she walked into a thicket and scared up one of these fascinating birds. It so startled her that she ran all the way home. "Why can't you just play with dolls like other girls?" her mother had scolded. After that, she learned more from her dad about the woods and was not afraid. She slogged through swamps, once stepping barefoot on the back of a large snapping turtle. She hopped from rock to rock over brooks and bathed in frigid waterfalls. When she was ten, she rowed out into the middle of ponds and fished for hours, watching a little red bobber bounce around until she finally landed a twenty inch pickerel! Nature thrilled her. She was in love with the mountains and the waterways of New England.

When she met Sid, she was so sure that they had this love in common. They both loved the cottage on Lake Winnipesaukee, and driving along the ocean shores in southern Connecticut, especially the rocky ledges between Groton and Stonington. She thought he loved the beach as she did, walking along the sand, observing the ebb and flow of life, collecting the scallop and slipper shells tossed up on the sand, watching the tiny green crabs scurry away into the rocks, and the sea gulls cracking clams on the breakwaters. She wondered now if she had only thought that they had shared the same interests or values. Looking back, she remembered how he loved to flex his muscles on the beach and to ride around the harbors in his boats. "Were we really the same?" she asked herself, "Or was I deluded?"

They had seemed so compatible and happy for the first two years, and then they seemed to just drift apart. Jan joined a church and made new friends. Sid refused, but she felt that that should not come between them. Jan wanted a child, but Sid wanted to wait. Soon they were taking separate vacations, Sid going to Las Vegas or Thailand, and Jan discovering the lodge in Morgan and becoming friends with the innkeepers.

Jan's mind kept drifting away to her favorite New England hideaways as she trudged along the dusty road through the refuge. She had often enjoyed spending time with her only sibling, Eleanor. Eleanor's family of husband and five children lived near a small pond in Frankfort, Maine. Jan loved to spend time with the children, making up stories to tell them, and taking them hunting for treasures in the woods. Sid went once and then apparently had no desire to go back with her; he always had something more important to do.

Jan and Eleanor were close as children. Their father, now deceased, had been a financial planner for a big company, but had always made time for walks in the woods. Their mother was an amateur artist, a creator of wonderfully fanciful pictures in oil, who worked as an apprentice in stained glass to make some extra money. Recently, Jan was working on getting to know her mother better, and appreciating some of her mother's unfulfilled dreams. She was also trying to understand why she felt that she was never able to please her mother, the way that Eleanor had. Eleanor was the perfect daughter, while Jan was the tomboy who loved playing with snakes and frogs. Eleanor was successful now, a mother of five, while Jan was still waiting. Often she wondered why the artist in her mother did not appreciate the writer in her. Yet, she knew that her mother felt that a newspaper job was only secondary to her being a wife and mother.

Jan remembered the day she told her mother that she was engaged to Sid, and her mother's response was, "Okay, now you've got a man. See if you can keep him." It seemed like her mother's primary goal in life was to get her daughters married off. No wonder she hadn't told her about the divorce yet. She was not looking forward to that conversation.

A strange brown blob inched along the road. It was a large colony of ants whose home had somehow been disturbed—probably by the vibration of the grader. They were moving as one entity, many of them carrying white eggs that were as big as they were. They worked together and maintained a steady pace. Jan wondered if humans were any more intelligent than these ants, or if we were all just more complicated insects, going through life trying to keep ourselves secure, and perhaps somehow connected by that collective unconscious that Jung wrote about. She watched the ants until the whole troop turned off into the undergrowth.

After what felt like another hour with the sun beginning to seriously burn her fair-skinned face, Jan noticed a post that she had passed before. "Oh great," she thought. "I'm just going around in circles." Now there was no more engine sound.

Incredibly thirsty, Jan tried to figure out where she was, and realized that if she could head east, she would probably get back to the visitor center. Walking along toward the sun with her head down, she noticed the beautiful flowers in the ditches—buttercups, daisies, purple vetch and orange paintbrushes—and remembered the magnificent closed blue gentian that lined the ditches last August—the last time she had visited the lodge. She had taken a break away from Sidney then also, and recalled that there had been signs then that the relationship was going under, but she hadn't wanted to believe it. Now she wondered if she should just cut her losses, agree to the divorce, and quit her job on the *Courier*.

Would she be able to stay there and work with him as her boss? What would that be like? Would she be able to watch him interact with Serena, and other women if indeed he had had an affair, as she now believed? Or should she go back and fight for the marriage—insist on counseling and try harder to make it work? What if Sidney would just give it a try? Would it be possible? Should she even give up the idea of having a child? Dozens of questions entered her mind and she found herself mentally going around in circles, just as her feet were doing. As she approached another crossroads, Jan called out loud. "Help! I need help! Where are those guides of mine?" Jan looked around at the trees and down again at the ditches. Then she looked up at the sky. Although she did not really want to believe it, and told herself it was pure foolishness, she saw a cloud above the pine trees that was shaped like an arrow. "Oh, what the heck," she thought, and decided to go in the direction of the cloud arrow.

Within minutes, Jan came upon the grader by the side of the road, with its driver sitting in the shade of the machine, drinking coffee and munching on a doughnut. Jan was hot, tired, thirsty, and miserable.

"You look like you need a ride," the road worker said.

"I sure do. Are you going my way?"

"There's only one way you'd be goin' and I'll take you there." Jan hopped up into the grader, holding back tears.

"Aren't you going to ask me why I'm out here?"

"Nope. Ain't my business."

"Aha. A fellow Vermonter."

"Yup. Born and bred." The grader bounced up and down.

"Whoa. Kind of bumpy, huh?" Jan laughed, beginning to feel better as they headed to the visitor center.

It was now after ten o'clock and the place was buzzing with visitors. Jan approached the desk, realizing that she was dust-covered, sunburned, and sweaty. She borrowed the phone and called AAA. Next she asked for Ranger Matthewson, but found that the ranger on duty today was Jeff, the boy from Brooklyn. A bit embarrassed, she told him what had happened and complained that the refuge needed to have road signs on its many forks so that people would not get lost. Jeff gave her a brief lesson on how to mark her trail, and then showed her to the employee lounge where she could wash up and rest.

Visitors to the center turned to look when the big green truck from Boom Chain Towing showed up in the parking lot, and Jan hopped aboard to ride with them back to the bog. Fortunately, they knew the way.

It was late morning when a sunburned, exhausted Jan finally returned to the lodge in the tow truck that was pulling her little Mazda behind it. Philippe agreed to look it over, and had them leave the car out back by the shed.

The cold coffee that had been left out for a couple of hours tasted like ambrosia to Jan, and the rhubarb bread she had with it was food for the gods. She took the treats up to her room, and hoped for a short nap before lunch. Within minutes, she was sleeping to the melodious songs of Enya on the old Art Deco radio.

Chapter 8: Demons and Dilemmas

Jan's afternoon nap left her groggy and reaching back deeply to remember the fine points of a dream. She was wandering through a maze of roads in the forest, with dangers at every turn. She had a vague memory of a wolf at one bend of the road, and at another, a madman. Lying still and allowing her mind to slip back towards the dream state, she remembered that the wolf was mostly black with a little gray and kept charging at her with bared fangs. The madman chased her and blocked her path as she tried to run from the wolf. The two were both menacing, until, at the end, it seemed as though the wolf turned on the madman, who turned out to be Sid.

Not wanting to review more, she rolled over and slid out of bed. Her legs ached from miles of walking, and the skin on her face, arms and legs stung with fire. After washing up with cold water and slathering the sunburned parts of her body with aloe lotion, she went out to look for Philippe. She found him near the back garage leaning over the engine of the Mazda.

"This has definitely been tampered with, Jan," Philippe said with an anxious tone. "Look here, there's a hole in the fuel line. What that does is cause the line to suck air, which causes the sputtering. You can go for a few miles before you're done. Someone didn't want you to have a good day."

"Great. Now this is getting personal."

"And that's not all. My tractor was sabotaged too. Look at this, the ignition wire was cut." Moving over to the tractor, he held up the end of a wire for Jan to see.

"Looks like it's another call to the state police. Maybe this time they'll get serious about investigating."

"I hope so, Philippe. I think this is more than I can handle on my own. We need all the help we can get. I have a meeting with Ranger Matthewson this evening, to ask him a pertinent question. This time I made an appointment though."

Philippe laughed. "That's good. I don't think your car could take another trip through the refuge."

"Nor could my legs," Jan winced. "Can you fix the fuel line for me?"

"Sure. No problem. Be done by evening."

Jan thanked him, grateful that Philippe was so accomplished in so many areas. For six years, he had maintained the lodge, able to fix just about anything in the areas of plumbing, heating, electricity, or carpentry. He took care of the lawns and shrubbery, could fell a tree, shingle a roof, field dress and butcher a deer or a moose, scale a pike, and fix a motor on a boat, a bike, a snowmobile, a car, or a truck like a kid playing with tinker toys.

Trusting her Mazda to Philippe's capable hands, Jan went back to the lodge, looking for guests to interview. Ralph Ledger was on the front porch, leaning over the old pine trestle table with a cup of coffee.

"Do you mind if I ask you some questions, Mr. Ledger?" Jan began tentatively, still feeling like she was intruding on people's vacations.

"Not at all, ma'am," he responded, dipping a homemade doughnut into his cup. "Glad to help if I can. Have you found my missing beer yet? Whoever took that is going to have to deal with me when we catch him."

Jan wondered just how she had become a "ma'am" and admitted that she had not found the beer. "I heard that you were looking for the best places to hunt moose up here. So does that mean you will be back in October?"

"Oh, yes, ma'am. I plan to bring my pals with me, and then show them how to do it."

"And your pals are from where?" Jan asked, reading the lettering on Ledger's black T-shirt which spelled out "One Shot One Kill". It reminded her of the reasons she wasn't especially fond of hunters. It wasn't that she was moralistic about killing animals, nor a vegetarian. It was just that it seemed so violent.

"Hagerstown." A catch in his voice made her feel as if he hadn't wanted to answer that. "Hagerstown, Pennsylvania." He reached over into the pocket of his brown leather jacket and pulled out a cigarette package. "Don't worry; I'm not going to smoke here. Just checking to see if I need to get some more at the store right away." He added, "Oh, I also noticed two packs of cigarettes missing from my room this morning."

"Really? From your room? Room seven?" Jan found it hard to believe that the thief had now been entering bedrooms. Of course, in this old lodge, the only locks were the hook locks on the inside of the doors, and most people never even used those. For all of the three years that she'd been coming there, she had never heard of anyone ever invading another guest's privacy. However, that was before. Now, given the fact that several people have found things missing from their rooms, as well as lights turned on when they had turned them off, it wouldn't surprise her if guests' rooms had been violated.

"Why is there a 'B' monogrammed on your jacket?" Jan asked, wondering why anyone would be wearing a leather jacket when it was 85 degrees outside.

Ledger looked down at his front pocket, laughed and said, "Oh, that stands for 'Bear Hunters'. It's a hunting club I used to belong to."

"Have you ever shot a bear?" she asked.

"Sure," he said. "Well, once. See this gun?" He showed her a small shotgun he had beside him on the porch. "This may not look like much to a non-hunter like yourself, but it's damn powerful." Jan knew nothing about guns, but took note of the gun he showed her.

"And have you ever hunted moose up here before?" she asked him.

"No, that's why I want you to show me your favorite moose hideouts."

"Oh, I should show you where my totem animals are so you can shoot them?"

"Aha, you don't approve of hunting, do you? You're one of those folks who like to eat animals, but not kill them."

"Oh, it's not that I think hunting is a terrible thing," Jan said, realizing that she had stepped into the murky water of the disagreements between the North Woods hunters and the naturalists and that Ida would not appreciate it if she insulted a hunter-guest. "I understand that the moose herds have gotten very large and that thinning them down can be a good thing, what with the number of road accidents and that parasitic brain disease that affects deer, elk, and moose. I do eat meat. I guess I just don't like to think about the animals getting killed, especially the moose, because I think they are beautiful—and majestic. They mean a lot to me."

"Well, you wouldn't think they were so beautiful if one came crashing through your windshield at ten o'clock at night and kicked you to death in the front seat of your own car."

"I suppose not," Jan agreed, sickened by the scene that had formed in her mind.

"Well, it happened to a friend of mine. He was slashed to pieces, blood and guts all over the place."

"I get the picture," Jan said, hoping he would end the lecture. No such luck.

"Life isn't always the pretty picture you want it to be, Missy. Sometimes it's outright down and dirty, and dog eat dog—or man eat moose. Take it from old Ralph, lady, if you're afraid of the blood and guts, you won't survive long in life."

"Okay, well, I don't believe I have any more questions today, Mr. Ledger," Jan hoped to slip away to calm her insides. She wished more than ever that she hadn't missed church this morning.

"Have you ever seen a wolf take down a deer?" Ledger continued. "Now that's a sight to make you think about things. What you environmentalists don't realize is that it's all nature. People and machines are part of nature, too. We all gotta live. If you shoot your food or write stories to get money so you can buy food others have shot, or you cut down trees and sell logs to get money to buy food, it's all the same. People do what they've gotta do. Plain and simple."

"I see what you mean," Jan stood up and attempted to walk away.

"Nature survives, remember that, too." Ledger seemed determined to educate her. "Anyway, the natural predators are coming back. The wolves and coyotes, eagles, fisher cats, bobcats...they're all coming back. The moose herds will go back down and then we won't be able to hunt them any more and then you moose-lovers will be happy. It all balances out."

"I appreciate your input, Mr. Ledger. Let's talk some more later," Jan said, now walking away, hoping she was finished with this character.

Questioning Ralph Ledger left Jan with her muscles twitching and screaming for exercise. She turned her thoughts toward unfinished business with Sid. Jan knew that ignoring his calls was probably not a good idea. It was late afternoon, and time to check for messages. Remembering to put on a sun hat to protect her damaged skin, Jan reluctantly walked the half mile to the far end of the beach, to the spot where cell phones were somehow able to receive signals. Along the way, memories flooded back of the early days with Sid, the thrill of the elegant parties, beautiful gowns and fine dining that were all a part of the world he grew up in which she had admired. "Was I an idiot?" she thought. "Was I wrong to want to have nice things as well as love? Or is it possible to have both? I thought that I had both."

When she arrived at the clear spot, she sat down on the grassy shore and dialed her voice mail. As she had expected, there were several calls from Sid and the tone in his voice was exactly as she had known in her soul that it would be—cold and callous, forcing her to face the reality of their relationship. She listened to all of his messages, and a few others—one from her friend Margaret at the paper, one from her mother and one from her sister, Eleanor; but she had no psychic energy to return any of them.

Sid sounded so angry. He apparently wanted things over and done with. He was demanding answers from her regarding how they were going to proceed, and he was insisting that they should both use his long-time lawyer and friend, Dave Maloney, and save some huge fees. He was sure that they could agree on everything, and he wanted to get started right away. He was firing questions at her in every message. "Do you plan to stay in the house? Do you want to keep your Mazda? Do you want to stay on the paper, or are you job-hunting somewhere else? I need to know." Sid wanted answers. He was mad that she left before discussing and settling these things.

Jan could not process all of his demands. She felt overwhelmed with betrayal and dismay at her own ignorance for having kept faith in the marriage, when it obviously had been over for years. "How could this have been love?" Jan asked herself as she stood up and began to drag her aching body back to the lodge. "I thought we were happy. I thought I made him happy. He did criticize how I did things, but I assumed he wanted to help me learn how to fit into his world. Did he really ever love me? I feel so stupid."

Why was she here now, when perhaps she should have stayed in Branford and tried to save her marriage? How had events synchronized to create this upheaval in her personal life, just when Ida and Philippe were in the midst of their own crisis and needing her? Was there really some supreme being who orchestrated all of this? Was the shaman right that she had been drawn here for a reason?

Jan meandered past the long row of cottages on the opposite side of the road from the lakefront, noting the signs of happy families on the porches and in the yards. Towels were hung over railings, bikes and balls were strewn on the grass, and kids were running to and from the beach. A dog chased a ball thrown by a toddler whose brothers were wrestling in the grass. Moms were carrying crying little ones in for their naps and dads were washing cars and untangling fishing lines. Wonderful smells of hot dogs and burgers on the grill filled the air. Jan drew a deep breath. Right in this panorama was all she'd ever wanted: kids and an occasional trip to the beach.

"Is this really too much for me to ask of life?" Jan was filled with doubt and afraid of what might lie ahead.

Arriving back at the lodge, hot and tired, her legs still throbbing from yesterday's hike through the refuge, Jan put on her bathing suit and went to cool off in the lake. She waded out slowly, walking along the side of the dock on top of the smooth pebbles and gradually letting her body sink down into the chilly water. Floating on her back, she looked up at the sky, but no cloud patterns stirred her mind. Knowing that she had a commitment to Ida, Jan tried to focus on the problem at the lodge, but all attempts failed, so she pulled herself up onto the dock.

Cooler now, she lay on her towel on the sun-warmed boards listening to the gentle waves slap against the pillars underneath and the hum of an outboard motor coming across the lake. The air smelled like musty-sweet pond water and distant barbecues. The beach buzzed rhythmically with the voices of children playing. Jan opened one sleepy eye. Matt sprawled in a lawn chair just on shore close to the dock. He was taking a video of some loons diving in and out of the gentle wake from the motorboat.

Jan sat up on the dock, dangling her feet over the edge. As she considered heading back to the lodge, a loon swam towards the dock and directly toward her feet. She kept her feet still and the loon stopped about eight feel away and then dove. It came up farther away and again swam toward her. Jan kept motionless. The loon came closer, to about five feet away, and then dove again. Jan watched the water. The loon came up eight feet away and swam toward her again. Jan turned her head slightly and noticed Matt videotaping this game. She swished her feet at the loon and it dove. Again it came up, this time about ten feet away, and came closer. Jan stayed still. It came to within a yard from the dock, paused, and stared at Jan. It dove, and popped up much later and much farther away. She looked over at Matt, who had put the camera down. The loon kept coming toward her, until finally some kids ran out on the dock, jumped off and scared it away.

Jan was slightly unnerved, and more than a little curious about this loon behavior. Joseph Rainwater had said to watch nature. What did the loon mean? Was it some kind of a message? Jan asked herself. "If cloud shapes can be messages, could this be also?" She looked over at Matt, who had folded up his chair and was coming her way.

"How about going for a ride to find some dinner?" he asked.

"Sure. I'd like to sit and brainstorm some of the recent events, but first I have to stop at the Visitor Center to see Ranger Matthewson. He's meeting me there at seven."

"It's a deal. Wow, Jan, are you okay? Your skin is so red."

"Don't remind me."

They walked together to the lodge to shower and change.

"I'd be glad to rub some lotion on those burns," Matt grinned.

"I just bet you would. No thanks, cowboy. I can handle it."

Jan found herself searching through her duffel bag for something pretty to wear. "Why does it matter?" she pondered. "This isn't really a date, after all. I'm still married, and we're just working together on this investigation. Why didn't I put in my mint-green pullover?"

They took Matt's Bronco, since her car was still being repaired.

"Do you have 'night-shot' on your camera?"

"Yes. Why?"

"Because we may see some moose."

"Really? Fantastic."

"No promises, but as dusk falls, it's very possible along this road."

Jan asked Matt to wait while she went into the center to meet with Matthewson. At first he just sat in the car, thinking it would be only a couple of minutes, but when it appeared that it would be longer, he got out and roamed around the outside of the building. He took a few pictures of the local wildflowers and caught a shot of a chipmunk on a rock. Twenty minutes later, he wandered inside and chatted with the woman in uniform at the desk. She directed him to the fifteen minute movie on the Nulhegan Basin that was about to start, so he sat and watched it, keeping one eye out for Jan to emerge from the Ranger's office across the hall. After the movie, trying to keep from getting more irritated than he already was, Matt roamed around the center, looking at the exhibits and posters, impressed with the care and planning that had gone into the place. Back at the desk again he asked the young dark-haired woman, "Have there been any recent moose or black bear sightings in the refuge?" She laughed. "Every day. There was a young moose sighted just an hour ago right out there on the road." She said, pointing out to the paved route 105. They don't seem to know that the refuge is a safer place to be."

"Darn, I can't believe that I just missed it again," Matt said, disgruntled, and then said out loud to this total stranger. "I seem to be missing the boat all over the place. I can't quite figure out this woman I'm attracted to. I suppose that I should realize that since she's going through a divorce, she probably hates men right now, so it's no time to give up. Wouldn't you agree?"

The woman at the desk smiled and shrugged.

When Jan finally emerged from Matthewson's office, they were both laughing like old friends. "Thanks, Donald," Jan said to the ranger, "I really appreciate your input."

Matt noted how she gently shook his hand and he gave her a big smile as he went back into his office.

"Well, that was a long discussion!"

"Hmm? Oh, I'm sorry, Matt. I guess I forgot you were here. Yes, I did get quite a bit of information, and I have one more little piece to gather."

Matt just rolled his eyes upward at the "forgot you were here." and stared as she went to the desk, took a packet of waxed paper out of her pocket and unwrapped a wilted yellow flower to show to the attendant. He tried to convince himself that his ego could handle the little stings that this hard-to-get woman was sending his way.

"Can you tell me the name of this flower?" Jan asked the woman at the desk.

"Swamp candles," the woman answered. "It's a member of the loosestrife family. It grows in and near the bogs, and sometimes out in fields." Jan smiled, and rewrapped the plant, and put it back in her pocket.

"I'm ready, Matt, and I'm hungry. I really am sorry I kept you waiting so long. Accept my apology?"

"Oh, sure."

Matt led the way back to his Bronco and they were off to Island Pond.

"Did I tell you that you must never go over the speed limit in Island Pond—not even a tiny bit?" Jan warned.

"No." Matt touched the brake, slowing the jeep down to the required speed. "Are you serious?"

"Oh, yes. Many people have learned the hard way up here that the Island Pond Constable just loves to ticket people for speeding—especially flatlanders."

"Swell," said Matt, "so we'll have a leisurely ride."

In just about twenty minutes they arrived in Island Pond and spotted the Buck and Doe, a highly rated north country restaurant, famed for its bison burgers and venison stew. All of the public parking spots in town were parallel with the sidewalks, and most of them were full. The only one not taken was about two blocks away, which presented the opportunity for a brief tour of most of the center of town, consisting of a couple of gas stations, a police station and town hall, a small church, a smaller fire station, two restaurants, one realty office, a hotel, and a half-dozen retail stores, two of them being gift shops for tourists.

"There's a feeling up here that I can't quite figure out," Matt said as they stood on the corner at the one big intersection in the town. "It's very different from the small towns in the South and Midwest. It's like people aren't aware that others are here. In Pennsylvania people would be staring at us and checking us out."

"Oh, you can bet that they are peeping out windows and keeping an eye out for strangers," Jan responded. "But Vermonters tend to mind their own business, or at least pretend to, for the most part, and this town has more reason to than most."

"How's that?"

"Well, about thirty years ago, a fringe religious group moved into town, and when the townspeople panicked about their ways, and worried that the children of the group were being abused, it created a very difficult time for the Island Ponders. They are still recovering. I think that atmosphere actually made it possible for the over-zealous constable to entrench himself in office."

"So, what happened?" Matt asked, as they arrived at the door of the Buck and Doe and went inside. The place was snug and unpretentious, with a mock fireplace glowing on one side wall, and knotty pine paneling all around, with North Country pictures and rustic chandeliers over each knotty pine table. They were seated at a small table near the front window, the only vacant spot, as if it had been saved for strangers who came to town, in order that they could be observed more closely. Jan and Matt noticed a discernable lowering of voices when they entered, and although it was subtle, being the keen observers that they were, they were aware of being checked out by the locals. Someone even gradually turned down the volume of the country music station coming through the wall speakers.

"We'll have to talk very quietly," Jan answered. "Ears will be tuned this way, even if they are all chatting."

"Fine, we'll whisper sweet nothings to each other." Matt smiled and looked across at his dining companion. She gave him back a slight smile, but he wanted more.

"Now there's some real country music." Matt changed the subject. "And that's the same wherever you go in the country, whether it's the Great Smokies, the Rockies or the Appalachians."

"That's because it's music from the big stations. It's national music, not local. Local Vermont music is different."

"How so?"

"You'll see. We'll run into it."

"Okay, so tell me about this fringe group thing."

"Well, there is a religious community here, which is in some ways similar to the Mennonites, and in other ways more like the Moonies. When they arrived in 1978, some of the town's adolescents left home to join them, and people panicked. Stories came out about the abuse of women and children, and the state got involved. Children were removed from the sect and placed in foster homes, where more stories surfaced, or were invented. In the end, the state had to return all of the children, and the people had to accept the group into the community. They have shops in town, but attend their own schools and churches, so it's hard to know what really goes on inside. Anyway, it's a great case for religious freedom... allowing people to do what they do as long as they don't hurt others. I believe there is still some question about whether the corporal punishment of children constitutes abuse, but here in the north, many people still believe in not sparing the rod, as well as a live-and-let-live philosophy."

"Wow. Well, I know that back home, Pennsylvania's Amish have suffered discrimination in the past. I'm all for letting people live their own lives. It's always a dilemma though, when it comes to the children, who have no choice in the matter."

"Right. So many children are living in less than happy circumstances. I keep thinking that if I never have any of my own, or maybe even if I do, that I possibly could adopt a few. I want to be a mother. In fact, I guess it's the issue that has caused the end of my marriage."

"And is that marriage over?" Matt asked, with an earnest desire to know the answer.

"I guess I have to accept the fact that it is. Yes, according to Sid, it is, and I could never live with him now. My eyes have been opened, although emotionally, it's hard to accept. I guess I have held on to a fantasy that things could change. His recent phone messages have been really cold and cruel, and yet, somehow, I realize that they are not really out of character for him. I just refused to see it before."

"So, have you been talking to him?"

"No. I haven't called him. I told him I was leaving, but not where I was going. I will have to do it soon. He's ready to have his own lawyer draw up an agreement for us."

"Really? Are you going along with that?"

"I thought for a brief time that I would. It would save costs and be simpler, and I know the lawyer. He seems like a straight-shooter."

"But now?"

The answer to Matt's question was interrupted by the waitress, a pony-tailed teenager in blue jeans, who took their order for Kingdom ribs for two. Matt had said that it sounded enticing, and the waitress said that it was popular with the tourists.

"But now I know that would be foolish. Sid was always very persuasive, and I have always let him take charge, even when he really never considered my viewpoint on things. I don't know why I was so submissive. I'm ashamed of myself really. And, I guess I'm still a little afraid of him. I hate myself for that."

"If you want my opinion," Matt said, "I think women are submissive out of love. They want to show love, and hope for love and respect in return. They don't always receive that, and it's the shame of men that they don't. I believe that someday we will evolve to a higher level, where a real harmony between men and women can create happier marriages."

"I can't believe you just said that," Jan said in amazement. "I was just reading an article about that very theme. Some psychologists believe that that is exactly what is happening—that because women are getting stronger, and asserting themselves, that men have to respond with growth, and that since, at least in the Western cultures, they are no longer able to hold onto their women with brute force or financial power, then they have to become men who women want to live with. It makes sense. And it goes both ways of course. Marriages will last only because of love, not power or wealth."

"It makes sense to me. Before Julia got sick, we had begun to see how our differences could inspire creative harmony rather than critical bickering and power struggle, which often happens to people." Matt smiled gently at Jan. but then his face dimmed as though a cloud had been drawn across it.

"And you've had to grow up out of necessity I guess, to raise your son without his mother," Jan reached out and patted Matt's hand and he pressed his thumb onto hers for a moment.

"Yeah. But I have had my mother there, thank God. She's the calm one. Ethan has attention deficit disorder, with the hyperactivity component, and hasn't been an easy child. He's bright and creative, but not focused."

"I can see where that would be difficult."

"Yes, but also rewarding. I love him so much, and he keeps a piece of Julia with me." Matt's eyes took on that misty look once more and Jan looked away.

Changing the subject again, Matt asked, "So what information did you need from Ranger Mathewson, if I may ask?"

"Well, at first I just wanted to learn more about the basin and the dispute with the bordering landowners for my article. Then today, after talking to Ledger, I wanted to know more about types of guns and what they are used for."

"And did you learn anything interesting?"

"Oh, yes. I learned that the landowners have been convinced to will their land to the Friends of the Nulhegan Basin. That was most encouraging." The bouncy waitress arrived with their meals. Matt's other question would have to wait.

After they had devoured the maple-barbecued ribs, and reviewed the creepy events at the lodge one more time, Jan and Matt walked back to the Bronco, in the darkening town.

"There are only two street lights in this whole town!" Matt exclaimed, looking around.

"We're lucky there are any. We'd better hurry, it's just dusk and the moose will be out."

They drove slowly back along Routes 114 and 111, partly to avoid getting a ticket, but also because of the very real danger of a moose collision, which Jan had already been made sharply aware of on her arrival in Morgan. Just when it seemed that they would get back to the lodge uneventfully, one medium-sized female moose abruptly slid down the bank at the side of the road. Matt stopped, his eyes widening, reaching for his camera, but she turned quickly and vanished into the trees.

"Holy smokes!" Matt cried, his hands shaking and nearly dropping his camera. "I saw a moose—a real moose! It was huge."

"You haven't seen anything yet. That's just a tease. We'll go out in the morning when it's easier to see them. Of course, you'll have to get up at five."

"I don't care. I'll get up at four. I can't wait. I want to see more of these creatures. Jan, did you get a close look? It looked to me like she was wearing a collar. Am I nuts?"

"No, you're not nuts. I saw it, too. It was probably a tracking collar. Some of them have them. I forget what group is doing that, probably the Vermont Fish and Game."

Matt continued driving, and they were soon back at the lodge. After some lively conversation with the Shapiros about moose sightings, moose lore, and moose pictures, the lodge guests began settling in for the night. Matt was restless and knew that he wouldn't get to sleep right away, so he took a book on wildlife up to his room with him.

Jan crawled under the cool sheets and let her mind's own organic computer go to work on processing the day's events and thoughts. She was so full of new ideas and perspectives that she, too, was having difficulty dozing off. Her brain rambled for an hour, but she couldn't integrate the angry tone of Sid's phone messages into her own dream of having his child. "Did I want his child?" she asked herself, "or did I just want a child? And did I want a child because I was not getting what I needed from the relationship and I thought a child would make things better?" Jan agonized.

Hearing a muffled cry outside of the window, Jan sat up in bed and listened. The sad, pleading cry wailed louder, and she went out on the deck to check it out. There on the grass in the front yard, she saw the bloody, bedraggled Lola, eerie in the moonlight. Jan grabbed a towel from the bathroom, ran down the stairs and out onto the lawn.

"Oh, poor baby," she cried. "What happened to you? Lola kitty. Oh, kitty. You're hurt. Okay, baby. I've got you." Wrapping Lola carefully in the towel, Jan gently picked up the injured cat and ran with her to the log cabin.

Chapter 9: Hurricane Road

In her dream, Jan was lost in the thick, tangled heart of the forest, hearing a woodpecker drumming a loud message on an old dead tree somewhere. She tried to follow the drumming, and searched through the spruce and the hardwoods, falling over stumps and scratching her limbs on briars and branches, but she could not find the bird. As the drumming grew louder and more insistent, she awoke in realization that someone was knocking on her bedroom door. Rolling out of bed and opening it carefully, she saw Matt with a pleading look on his face. "Hey, lady, it's almost 5:30 and you said to be up at 5 o'clock."

"Oh gosh, I forgot to set my alarm!" Jan said drowsily. "I didn't get very much sleep. Give me a minute and I'll be down, okay?" She shut the door and Matt went downstairs to wait, mumbling something about women and always having to wait around for them. Once they were on the road, this time with Jan driving her repaired Mazda, she told him about Lola.

"We were up for hours with the poor kitty. Ida was too distressed to go, so Philippe and I took her to Dr. Jacobson, the vet over on the Evansville Road. She was bruised from head to toe and needed a dozen stitches. It could have possibly been an attack by a large animal, like a coyote, but Dr. Jacobson suspects foul play of the human kind. He is sending a report to the state police."

"Oh, as if Parker would be concerned about it," Matt said. "Well, who knows, maybe this will get through to him."

"I don't know. I have to wonder why we aren't getting more response from Parker."

"Who would do such a thing to a helpless animal?" Matt asked with a look of disbelief and disgust. "Let's hope it was another animal. At least that would make it easier to take. Ida and Philippe must be pretty mad."

"They're angry, yes, and heartsick for poor Lola," Jan added, "and scared, too. Ida is wondering if it is really safe to keep the lodge open at this point, or if guests are in danger. We can't let this go on, Matt. We have to figure things out to end this misery at the lodge. This is not a joke. Someone really wants all of us to leave the lodge, and they are getting very determined about it."

"You're right. Do you want to cancel our moose-hunt this morning?" Matt asked, feeling a bit guilty for pursuing his own photography career when pets and maybe people were in danger.

"No. I promised you a moose, and we will find one. We can analyze while we ride, but later I need you to go with me to Evansville to the Abenaki trading post. I want to find Joseph Rainwater and get his advice. Philippe will be calling Officer Parker today about Lola, but sometime very soon I hope to question Parker in detail about how the Baggett murder investigation was handled six years ago. Also, I want to talk to Jake Hawkins, Baggett's lawyer, and go over to the *Newport News* to dig up any articles that were written about the murder and whatever details they may have discovered and filed at the time. I may be on the wrong track, but I really think that there is some connection to that murder."

"Somehow I'm not sure that a north woods newspaper is going to do an in-depth investigation, even into a murder," Matt said cynically.

"Well, we'll see," Jan said, as they headed up Route 114. "Keep a close eye out on this road, Matt. It's still pretty dark, and moose can jump out unexpectedly."

"I'm watching. I'm ready for those moose. This camera does well with available light, so bring 'em on."

"I'm going to pull in here on Hurricane Road," Jan said in a short while. "It leads out to the Bill Sladyk Wildlife Management Area, a very rough and rugged terrain that I wouldn't want to go too far into with the Mazda, but we can go as far as the pond." They drove in slowly, to be as quiet as possible, and within a mile or so, rounded a curve by a swampy area and came upon Hurricane Pond, a rather small, shallow pond, that was actually a small cove of Norton Pond. Jan pulled the Mazda off to a turnout on the side of the road opposite the water.

"We'll sit here and wait for a while," Jan whispered to convey to Matt that quiet was of the essence. As first light grew brighter, Matt's restlessness took over.

"This is beautiful!" exclaimed Matt, in a muted burst of joy. "I have to get out and take pictures."

"Well, fine, but if you want to see a moose, you need to stay by the car, and stay as still as you can. No sudden movements."

"You got it, boss. Don't worry. This camera has a silent shutter," he said, turning to Jan with a grin and a wink as he slid out of the car, being careful not to slam the door. Jan got out also and tiptoed beside Matt along the edge of the road by the long, shallow pond. The water was high, almost running into the road. On the far edge of the pond, dark fir trees reached into the morning fog, which painted wispy garlands across their pointed tops. The water's surface was smooth as polished granite, but broken in dozens of places with the tall gray spikes of dead Jack-Pine, leaning this way and that in an eerie arboreal graveyard. Near one end of the pond, a beaver lodge claimed squatting rights, and all through the dead pines, large spider webs sparkling with dew were draped like doilies on a clothesline.

Matt took dozens of pictures as the heavy layer of fog lifted and a thin mist began to rise from the pond, causing the myriad webs to twinkle in the breaking sunlight. He turned to Jan with a huge smile, and she put her finger to her lips to remind him of the need for silence. A ripple broke the surface of the water several yards away, and they watched as a beaver paddled through the steamy surface with a leafy twig in its mouth. Matt smiled at her again, raising his eyebrows, and then edged along the pond rapidly snapping photo after photo.

Smack! The beaver slapped the surface of the pond in a loud warning, and disappeared under the water. All was still, and Matt's face conveyed a bit of disappointment. Jan touched him on the arm and beckoned him to follow her. They walked further along the pond's edge and came to a large boulder where they could sit still and watch. It wasn't long before a few mallards appeared, drifting along the grassy banks within a few feet of them, and nibbling on young arrowroot plants. Following the mallards, a couple of red-headed mergansers came by, but declined to venture too close to the strange creatures on the rock.

Jan turned toward Matt in time to see him looking through his lens at her, and raised her hand to her face. He lowered the camera. "What, you don't want to be in *American Wildlife*?" he whispered.

"No, thanks. Not the way I look this morning," she whispered back.

Matt studied her silently with a softness that made her tear up, blush, and turn away. He was about to comment, when a loon appeared out in the center of the pond and caught their attention. It cruised smoothly along, occasionally dipping its long-billed head down under water. Matt snapped a few shots with the telephoto.

Other birds came back closer, including a couple of the mallards and a merganser. All of a sudden, the loon rose up on its legs, spread its wings out and then charged toward the merganser, thrashing at it with its spear-like bill. The merganser took off and the mallards followed.

"Darn, I should have had the video cam ready for that one."

"I've never seen that before," said Jan, "A loon attacking another bird."

"Well, apparently they do," Matt said. "They can even kill another bird, and it is not uncommon for them to do so, especially if they feel that another species is encroaching on their nesting territory."

"How do you know this?" Jan looked at Matt in surprise.

"Well, I took one of Ida's wildlife books to bed with me last night, and I read up on loon behavior. I thought I might find an explanation for the nuttiness of the loons on the lake yesterday."

"You did that?" Jan was impressed. "And what did you find out?"

"Well, loons are not the sweet, placid, mate-for-life creatures that many people think they are."

"Really?"

"Right. There's no proof that they keep the same mate, and some studies show that although they often go back to the same nesting area, they have no problem getting a mate from whoever is around."

"Sounds like some people I know," Jan said.

"Ha. Yeah, for sure. Also, they can be aggressive. As I said, they will kill over territory. That long sharp bill can pierce the head of a merganser, and they think nothing of murdering other bird's chicks when they find them near their own nest."

"Wow. I never suspected."

"They are quite complex and intelligent also. I read that they have four unique calls, and then some variations. They have that long, low wail that can sound like a wolf, that I guess is meant to locate a mate. Then they have a short hoot, which means 'hello', and a yodel, which is three notes slowly rising, followed by undulating phrases. That is a territorial declaration. It means 'This is my spot, keep out.'."

"So, the fourth must be that loony laughter that gives them their name?"

"Correct. This is called the tremolo. It is sounded when they are excited or agitated. It is also used in flight to check out ponds and lakes below to see if they are occupied. They cry a variation of this call when flying, and if they receive back the responding 'hoot' they move on to find a vacancy somewhere else."

"Fascinating. You read all that last night? Did you find out anything about them acting aggressively towards humans?"

"Not much, really. Just that they will sometimes behave that way to protect their nests. Other times they just abandon their nests and give up if humans are around. Those loons yesterday weren't nesting though, so that's not an answer. I did read about one study that seems to indicate that loons can learn new behaviors, and where their territories overlap with humans, such as in tourist areas, they adapt and develop strategies for dealing with humans. Those loons yesterday may just have been curious."

"All right. I'll take that for now. Thanks for checking that out." Jan gave Matt the smile that he had been waiting for, and he grinned back. They sat quietly, watching the mist rise from the pond as daylight advanced.

"I'd like to see a curious moose right about now," Matt said. "Well, at least I got some great bird pictures, and some spider webs."

"Well, your trip isn't over yet. How long are you staying, anyway?"

"I certainly hope that I can stay long enough to see your investigation through to the end, but no more than another few days or a week, max. To please my editor, I need to get some more animal shots; even those baby foxes would be great. I'd like to spend more time in the refuge."

"You may also see animals on the main roads, almost everywhere, and we're going out to Evansville later."

A few sunbeams began to break through the mist, streaming down on the pond's smooth black surface. The sound of splashing water, at the left edge of the pond just beyond the beaver lodge, made Matt turn his head.

"Oh, my god!" Matt exclaimed in a muted cry. "Jan, it's a moose." He raised his camera, adjusted the telephoto and clicked several shots, as the long-legged female waded out into the pond.

"My first moose picture! She's beautiful! This is incredible!" Matt whispered excitedly as he snapped picture after picture with his soundless digital camera.

Jan stared at Matt, wondering if she was going to see his eyes fill up again; his face was so alive with excitement and joy. She watched the moose, too, wishing she had brought her own camera.

"What could be better..." she asked Matt in a whisper, "than a moose in the pond in the mist?...except perhaps for the baby moose following behind the mother." She pointed toward the rim of the pond, just as the ragged, lanky little calf stepped carefully out into view, dipping its young toes into the water's edge where the tender cattail shoots and arrowroot grow. Matt's mouth flew open, and his fingers clicked away.

The calf followed its mother along the bank, reaching down to pull up water plants and chew them. The mother moose sometimes put her head way down under the water, seeming to hold her breath for a very long time, before she came up with greenery hanging out of her jaws. Matt got some wonderful pictures of both of them with water dripping from their mouths in front of spectacular backgrounds of pine forest and misty sky.

Jan and Matt watched the mother and baby for over half an hour, until the mother suddenly picked up her head, looked in their direction, flicked her ears and then sauntered off into the woods, with the calf following right behind.

Matt's eyes followed them into the woods, and he put down his camera and sighed. "Wow. They are beautiful. I can understand why you have a special love for these amazing animals. Thanks Jan, for making that happen."

"Hey, I've been to this pond dozens of times, and it never happened before."

"Really, I thought it was a favorite moose spot."

"It is. Ida says lots of people have seen them in here, and I always hoped I would." Jan smiled at him. "Sorry it wasn't a big bull though."

"Well, that's okay. They were wonderful. I'd still like to see a bull sometime though. Do you think that's possible? Can you take me to a likely spot sometime soon?"

"I will, really. I sometimes think it's all arranged though, by some higher power—God, or the Great Spirit of the woods."

"I don't know what I believe about all of that," said Matt. "I just know that the world is full of many wonders. You seem to have a spiritual connection with the woods, and that shaman saw that in you, didn't he?"

"I guess so. He also said that the moose would bring me messages. I wonder why it was a female and calf, and not a bull."

"That's obvious. Because you want a child," Matt said. "Maybe the Great Spirit is telling you not to lose hope, that one day you will."

"I think the Great Spirit is God," Jan said. "There is no difference. It doesn't matter if some people see several gods in nature, or we see only one. It's all the same, no matter what we see. God is what He is, I suppose. Or She. Some churches I've been to now refer to God as 'He' and 'She'. Perhaps it is all the 'Great Mystery', and unknowable, as the Abenaki say. I feel bad that I missed church yesterday, while I was lost in the Conte."

"Do you suppose She is mad at you?" Matt asked.

"I don't know how He could be mad at me, if, as I believe, He arranged for me to get stranded there. Besides, if the moose is a message to me, what about the moose wearing a collar?"

"That's easy," Matt ventured. "That's about Sid having a hold on you."

"Hmmm. This is getting heavy," Jan sighed.

"Then how about some breakfast? I'll buy," Matt offered.

Jan nodded and got up from the boulder. She and Matt walked silently to the Mazda and headed over to Island Pond, this time to check out the cuisine at

Jennifer's Diner. The day was growing warm and bright, a glorious summer day in the Northeast Kingdom. They parked a couple of blocks away, and strolled into the small restaurant. Although it was quite full, they managed to find a table for two against the center of the far wall, with a red-checkered vinyl tablecloth, chrome-capped salt and pepper shakers, a ketchup bottle and a pourable sugar container. On the wall next to them was a huge northern pike with a small perch in its mouth.

"Wow," Matt exclaimed. "I wonder where I could catch a fish like that one."

"You could probably catch that same one wherever they released it," Jan responded. "That's a fiberglass release mount."

"A what?"

"Most fishermen now get a fiberglass replica of their fish and then release the real one, so someone else can catch it later."

"I should have known that," Matt said. "That sounds like a good article for the magazine." He looked around the diner and chuckled. "I feel like I'm back in Pennsylvania. It's amazing how small-town diners are all the same." The waitress, wearing blue jeans and a T-shirt that read "L.L. Bean", took their order for the blueberry pancake special. The customers wore a variety of up-country attire, very casual, denim slacks or green work pants, plaid flannel shirts and button-down blues over T-shirts of every variety. Many of the men sported baseball or hunting caps. A cup rack on the wall was a sure sign that most people here were regulars who were served with their own favorite cups—a tradition not uncommon in the Green Mountains.

"Well, it kind of makes me feel at home wherever I go in the country," said Jan.

"Have you traveled much, Jan?" Matt asked reaching for the Cabot butter, the only brand served at Jennifer's, and the real Vermont maple syrup.

"Well, Sid and I went across the country and back a few times, and to Hawaii, and on a European tour once."

"And where is home? Wow, this is good coffee."

"It's the best. Vermont Coffee Roasters. Home is here. The North Woods. New Hampshire, Vermont, and Maine. It's where I belong."

"Not Connecticut?"

"Well, I guess not. I tried to make it mine, but I suppose I failed, at least so far. Who knows? Maybe I'll stay down there though, since the job opportunities are greater."

"So you wouldn't stay on the *Courier?*"

"Well, assuming Sid even wanted me to, I'm not sure that would be a good thing. But I don't know if I might just to prove that I'm not a quitter. I have mixed feelings about it."

"Would you stay in investigative reporting?"

"Ultimately, I guess, although sometimes I think I'd rather be freelancing, and writing nature stories like the one I'm working on now about the Conte refuge. There's no money in that, however."

"Yeah, what about that? Where will you sell it?"

"Who knows? It's not even done. It might never be done. I am trying to help Ida and Philippe solve the problem at the lodge first."

"Okay, I understand that. I believe you will. Maybe with some help from the state police. Maybe. But after that, if you finish the article, I'd like you to send it to my editor."

"At *American Wildlife?* Do you really think it's good enough?"

"Now that's really believing in yourself. Why do you do that?"

Jan looked at him, and bit her lip. "I don't honestly know. I don't think I used to be so down on myself. Maybe I feel like a failure because I'm being divorced, and, rationally I know that that is not the case. It's not necessarily my fault or failure, but..."

"But nothing. You know it's not your fault."

"Could we change the subject? I'm trying to enjoy these pancakes, and you're giving me stress."

"Sure. Let's talk about this music. I bet this is a local radio station, because it does sound different than the music at the Buck and Doe."

"WCOW."

"No way."

"Way. It's the local station, all right. The song is 'I'll take the Hills' by Banjo Dan and the Midnite Plowboys."

"I kinda like it," said Matt.

"Me, too. It's about as local as you can get. Northeast Kingdom music. Now let's do some brainstorming. Things are pretty serious at the lodge, and I'm out here doing moose hunts and discussing music."

"Okay, let's examine the lodge investigation again, though we've gone over it so much, I don't know what we could have missed. You now have some more serious happenings—scary notes in the guest book, antiques and equipment being broken, an endangered grouse killed, a cat injured, a gravestone overturned."

"My car was definitely tampered with, and so was Philippe's lawn tractor."

"No kidding? You didn't tell me that. What else are you holding out on?"

"Nothing. I just forgot to mention it. Philippe only told me that yesterday after he examined my car."

"Okay, well, what do we have, and what can we rule out? It's way beyond people's imaginations getting carried away, or forgetting that they ate their leftover pizza. So, who is doing this? Who do you suspect?" Matt looked worried.

"I have suspicions about Ralph, Annette, and even Stan."

"And what is your reasoning?" Matt asked, playing devil's advocate.

"Annette was here at the time, and writes some strange poetry. Stan has a record in juvenile court, and I just don't like Ralph Ledger."

"Ah, the scientific approach?"

"Now, don't discount a woman's intuition, pal," Jan retorted.

"Oh no, I wouldn't do that," Matt chuckled. "But I do put a bit more stock in science. So what's next?"

"We'll go back to the lodge and check in with the state police and the *Newport News*. Then we'll ride out to Evansville to find Joseph Rainwater."

"Okay, I'm game. Let's go." Matt left the money for the check and a good tip on the table, and they left the diner followed by several pairs of curious eyes.

Chapter 10: Evansville

"Jan, you won't believe this," said Philippe, agitated about his talk with the state police officer. "Sergeant Parker acts like there is nothing serious going on here. He says he doesn't believe that your car was tampered with, because, he says, I'm not a professional mechanic to make that judgment. He believes that Lola was probably hurt by a fox, even discounting the phone call he got from the veterinarian, and he now thinks that she was the one who killed the grouse because a cat could have made a big gash that looks like a knife gash. He thinks the broken swing was just because it was old, and the message in the guest book, along with the missing food and broken antiques, was just the teenagers. He just told me to come up with something serious and he'd take a look at it. I can't believe this. My state taxes are paying this guy's salary, and he's dismissing me. I'm about ready to call our state representative."

"Wow. I can understand your anger," Jan said. "Doesn't he see how this adds up? What about the gravestone?"

"Just graveyard vandalism, he says."

"But it was only Baggett's grave, no one else's."

"I know. I explained that to him. 'Pure coincidence', he says." Philippe was pacing the floor.

"Well, I'm going to call him myself."

"Good luck, Jan. I hope you have more success than I did." Philippe left the lodge and returned to the log cabin while Jan dialed the Derby Station of the Vermont State Police. She got through to the main number, but when Parker was not available, she left her name and the lodge number, requesting a call back.

Next she called the *Newport News* and asked to talk to the reporter who had handled the story on the Baggett murder six years ago. Unfortunately, that reporter had passed away, but she was put through to Kyle Dorsey, who had been a reporter there for four years, and now handled all of the biggest stories.

"Sure, I'd be glad to talk with you about that case," Dorsey said. "I remember reading about it when I was an intern on the *Burlington Free Press*, and I have often wondered when that murder would rear its ugly head again. I'd love to find out what has stirred up interest in it."

However, he explained that due to the big story about the escapee from Drummondville prison having crossed the border and probably being in the Island Pond area, breaking news of a deer poacher in Barton, and the story of the possible arson over at a hotel on Lake Willoughby, the earliest that he could meet with Jan was Friday afternoon, which was three days away. However, he promised to have the information for her by then. She was not happy about having to wait, and had some serious questions about north country reporting, but decided to continue seeking other ways to get information. One of them was to go find Joseph Rainwater.

Matt and Jan took the Bronco to Derby Center and down route 5A through Charleston, one of those little Vermont towns about which it is said, "If you blink, you miss it." Matt was surprised at just how small it was, but was finding these little towns to be picturesque. He wanted to take photos of everything. At one point, they rounded a bend, and came upon the Clyde River Bridge, where the river slowed, curved and widened through rich farmland. There they saw a herd of cows lolling around on the riverbank. It struck Matt as reminiscent of a Robert Duncan painting, and he had to have a picture, so they pulled over. The cows were a collection of several varieties: Jersey, Guernsey, Holstein, Black Angus, and even a couple of red and white Ayrshires. The river and the weeping willow trees created a marvelous backdrop for the pastoral scene.

"This is a sweet mental break from the stress at the lodge, isn't it?" Matt said to Jan. "It kind of brings you back to a more balanced reality."

"Yes," Jan agreed. "But I can't shake the feeling that my friends are in some serious danger. There is someone out there who has evil intentions, and I want to find him before it's too late. I can't believe that Dorsey won't have the information for me until Friday. I must not have given him a feeling that it was important."

"I don't think it's you, I think it's the laid back attitude one often sees in the country."

"I hope you're right, Matt."

Driving along, they passed more wonderful Vermont farms, fields, and forests. Brooks and ponds popped up here and there, and a country home or two, an old antique shop—Hudson's Harvest, a white-spired Congregational church and a one-engine fire station. Soon they came to the Trading Post, a long building resembling an old barn, with a couple of gas tanks in front. From the outside, it didn't look much to Matt or Jan like an Indian outpost. Inside they found a typical country store with groceries, a deli, movies, books, magazines and postcards, a few hardware items, and hunting and fishing gear. However, in a room in the back were several shelves of Indian souvenirs. There were Native-American dolls, necklaces, earrings, animal carvings, knick-knacks, rabbit-skin vests and gloves, peace pipes, Indian music, and several kinds of dream-catchers.

Jan picked up a few of the dream-catchers and examined them, becoming especially drawn to a medium-sized one with bits of pinecone, wildflowers and feathers attached. There was something about this particular one which made her feel comforted and hopeful. As she looked closer at it, she could see that the feathers were loon feathers, and that there were tiny red beads sewn around, to represent the red eyes of the loon. Jan decided to buy it, along with a couple of ham and cheese sandwiches and sports drinks for the road.

At the checkout, she asked the clerk about the Abenaki shaman. The clerk laughed, and said to her, "Joseph Rainwater? If I could direct anyone to his whereabouts, I could probably make a few bucks on the side." A couple of men standing nearby broke into vigorous laughter and she realized from their ruddy complexions and their leather jackets that these were tribesmen.

"Are you real Abenaki?" Jan asked, feeling a little bit more like an outsider than usual. The men laughed again, causing Jan to blush bright red, but she was determined to stick to her plan. "I'd really like to find Joseph. Do you have any suggestions? I need his advice on something."

"Really, he's hard to find," the tall dark-haired man at the checkout said to her. "And, yes, we are Abenaki. Sorry for laughing. We don't mean to laugh at you, but more with you, since we all have had a hard time finding Joseph when we want him. He does seem to show up when we *need* him, however. You just kind of have to think about him, send him a mental message, and he may find you. You might go and talk to the chief, if it is really serious."

"It is. Where can I find the chief?" Jan asked, studying the face of the Native American, and feeling more like she was in a foreign country than in the hills of Vermont.

"You can find Lone Cloud, Chief of the Hawk Clan, out on route 5A. Just look for a bright yellow mailbox with a hawk painted on it, on the right hand side of the road. Go down a slight hill and you will find him. He loves to have company. This looks like one of his dream-catchers. A good choice, especially if you like the loon."

"I do. Thank you so much for the directions," Jan said, and then, in a strange moment of inspiration, she asked, "By the way, do you know of any homes on the water for sale around here? I'm interested in buying a place."

Matt came out from the back room in time to hear this request and was a bit surprised.

"Homes for sale? Well, there's a funny thing about that," offered one of the other tribesmen who had been standing nearby listening the entire time. "As soon as any waterfront house goes on the market around here, it's bought up quickly, even sometimes before it's on the market."

"Really?" Jan was interested.

"Right. In fact, some people around the lakes have had realtors stop in and offer them great prices for their homes. Most people don't want to sell though."

"Have there been any offers they couldn't refuse?" Jan wondered. The men laughed.

"Not that we know of. We have heard though, that several camp owners over on Lake Willoughby have sold out. That's just a few miles south of here."

"Yes, I know Willoughby. I heard there was a fire at a hotel there yesterday, and that the state police suspect arson," Jan ventured. "Have you heard anything about that?"

"Yup. It was the Sheldrake Inn, the largest building on the lake. It's going to need a lot of repair. The owners are sick over it."

"I'm sure they are. Well, I appreciate your help, guys," Jan said. "I'm sure I'll be back, and I will try to find the chief."

Jan and Matt drove towards Willoughby, and did find the home of the chief, who unfortunately was not in. Jan left a note explaining that she hoped to talk to the shaman, and she and Matt continued on toward Willoughby to check out the site of the fire, and to perhaps find a peaceful spot for a picnic lunch.

The ride around Lake Willoughby was spectacular, with the view of Mt. Hor and Mt. Pisgah, across from a long stretch of beach with vacationers swimming and sunbathing. They passed several lovely cottages and arrived at the Sheldrake Inn. Jan hopped out and went up to the door and knocked, but no one was around. The smell of charred wood was very pronounced, and on the door was a large pink sign that read, "Closed temporarily due to smoke damage."

"Well, we won't learn anything here today," Jan said to Matt. "I'd like to find out about the sales of the cottages here, though. Let's take a ride down to Barton. I know of a real estate agent there." Continuing around the lake, the road curved in and out and the couple was treated to unique scenes around every corner. One side of the road was next to the huge rock cliffs, while the other side ran along the edge of the enormous glacial lake. At a scenic turnout, Matt and Jan stopped to admire the view. They walked across the road to a hillside spring where clear, cold water tumbled from a pipe in the rock and into an old concrete basin. Matt returned to the Bronco to collect a few water bottles that were piled on the floor in the back. He handed a couple to Jan, and they filled them, watching a fisherman on the lake pull in a very large fish. They found a small beach area down the road and stopped to eat their sandwiches at a picnic table.

"Something fishy is going on here, in more ways than one," Matt said.

"You bet there is," Jan agreed. "I'm starting to be convinced that the problems at the lodge were no inside job by a guest at all. No pranks either. It's serious business." They ate quietly; relaxing and watching some small children play in the sand with pails and shovels.

"They're so cute," Jan said wistfully.

"They sure are. The boy reminds me of my son when he was little like that. He loved the beach. He still does."

"You miss him a lot, don't you?"

"Yes. He and my mom are the only reasons I do want to go back to Pennsylvania. I've been traveling a lot lately on this job, and I'm missing out on a lot of his growing up. As much as I am growing to love wildlife photography, I often have thoughts about finding a job with less traveling."

"It must be great to have a son, though. I wonder if I'll ever have a child."

"Sure, you will. You just have to find the right guy to be the dad."

"I wonder how one does that, in reality," Jan said. "How do you really know what anyone is like, until you are years into a relationship. Then if you find out it's no good, you're stuck, or you start over."

"It's always a risk. No doubt about that," Matt said.

"Well, I think I have a long road ahead of me before I get to have one of those little munchkins running around."

"You have plenty of time, Jan," Matt said sympathetically. He reached for her hand, but she pulled away, grabbing their picnic trash. On the way to Barton, a smooth and pleasant cruise, they both refrained from conversation. As soon as they arrived in the little village, they spotted a sign for Crystal Lake Realty, and went in. Jan told the woman who rose from the desk to greet them that she wanted to buy some waterfront property in the area.

"Well, there isn't much available at the moment," the friendly brown-haired young woman explained. "They sell as soon as they go on the market, although they're very expensive. I'm Margo Sanders, by the way," the woman said, reaching out her hand to Jan.

"Jan Whitlock. This is my friend, Matt Abbott."

"Do you have a price range?" Margo asked.

"Well, not really. I do have some money coming to me soon, though," she fibbed, "and I'd really love a year-round place on a lake."

"Any particular lake? Crystal? Willoughby? Seymour? Salem?" Margo seemed eager to help.

"Oh, any of them. They're all beautiful. I favor Seymour or Echo Lake. Perhaps Crystal Lake is a bit more populated than I would like, though. But I would consider one there. Have you nothing for sale right now?"

"No. But we're expecting to sign one soon on Lake Salem. I could call you as soon as we get the listing. Frankly I'd much rather sell a property to you than to Rambling River."

Jan looked at Matt, who gave her a raised-eyebrow look that acknowledged her brilliance.

"Rambling River? And what is that?" Jan asked Margo.

"Rambling River Development," she answered. "They are buying up land around the lakes. They pay whatever price is asked, and have even knocked on doors and made extravagant offers on property that isn't for sale. Sometimes people take them up on it. Others are wondering if there's gold in the lakes, and they hold on for even better prices."

"Just what is Rambling River Development developing?" Jan asked.

"I couldn't tell you, really. I have heard rumors about them being a bit shady. So far, they are just buying property. Vermonters don't let go of their land easily, but for the right price..."

"Okay." Jan sighed. "I would appreciate it if you'd let me know of anything that comes up for sale." She gave the woman her cell phone number, as well as the lodge number, and she and Matt were on their way. They took the long way around the lakes back to Morgan.

"A dime for your thoughts," said Matt.

"Wow, the price has gone up a bit," Jan laughed.

"Well, I want you to know that I value what you think about things. I wanted to ask you something, but you seemed a bit annoyed with me when I reached for your hand back there."

"Forget it. It wasn't personal. What did you want to chat about?"

"The Abenaki. I just wanted to know more about them. Ed told us a little bit at the campfire, but I'd like to know more."

"They are an interesting people. They moved their tribes around a lot to escape the wars of other people, and now they haven't been able to get recognized as an American Native tribe, because they traveled back and forth across the border so much throughout their history."

"I see. I guess they didn't accept the lines drawn on the maps by the white people who moved into their territories."

"Right. And, really, they were here in New England as long as any other tribe. It's all a political thing, and I don't know all the details. If we could find Joseph, maybe we could learn more. Here we are. Home again, home again..."

"Jiggety-jig."

Jan laughed. "I can't believe you know that old nursery rhyme."

"Country is country," he laughed, "whether Vermont or Pennsylvania."

They could smell the garlic, sausage, oregano, and basil as they pulled into the driveway. Frances Loomis had started a big pot of sauce for a spaghetti supper, and the guests were excited about having a group dinner. Ward and Nate were heading over to the Fat Belly Deli across the road, to find some bread, while Avis and Annette were beginning to chop vegetables for a huge salad. The air in the lodge was saturated with the great smells that make one hungry, and Jan and Matt were starved from their day's adventure.

"Can I help?" Jan offered.

"I think it's under control," Frances said. "You two are doing enough, working on the investigation. Let us make you dinner."

"Right!" added Avis and Annette together.

"It's the least we can do," Annette said, while she fiercely sliced a cucumber with a large oriental chef's knife. Have you found our culprit yet?" Pieces of celery and onion were flying around the counter as she continued to chop.. Matt ducked as a piece of red pepper went flying towards his face.

"No, but when we do, we'll let you at him," Matt chuckled.

Nate and Ward came back from the deli with four big loaves of Italian bread. They were laughing like men who had been friends for years. Slicing the big loaves down the middle, they slathered them with butter, sprinkled them with minced garlic, wrapped them in foil and popped them into the hot oven. The old country kitchen was full of busy people joking with each other and working around each other to create a feast for all. Philippe located a couple of big pots and began boiling water for the pasta, while Ida pulled down plates to set the tables.

Diana and Amos came downstairs, oohing and aahing at the smells and sounds. "Is there enough for us?" Diana asked.

"We've cooked enough for an army," Nate declared. "Seat yourselves and dinner will be served." Miranda came softly into the dining room and chose a seat next to Diana. Ralph Ledger was nowhere to be seen, but Ed Pease came in saying, as he winked at Ida, that he could smell the sauce from up on Toad Pond Hill. He kissed his cousin Miranda on the cheek and sat down near her.

"Will someone go and knock on the door of room seven to see if Ralph is around, and then go out to the green room and see if the boys are hungry?" Ida requested.

"Now, sweetheart, when would teenage boys not be hungry?" Philippe teased.

"I'll go," offered Matt, feeling rather in the way. He soon returned with three eager boys right behind him. Ledger was nowhere to be found. Avis had put out silverware, napkins and glasses, along with pitchers of lemonade, and the spaghetti was ready to serve.

"Man, a real home-cooked meal!" Cliff exclaimed, as plates were handed out piled high with the steaming pasta and sauce.

"I hope you washed your hands, dorko," Stan razzed him.

"Knock it off, Stan," Jeff said, defending his friend. He was obviously annoyed with Stan.

"Oh, and you're my boss, now?" Stan retorted.

"I don't think you need any more bad reports, do you?" Jeff challenged. "I just want you to leave Cliff alone. You have harassed him all day." He motioned to Cliff to move to another table, and Stan was left sitting alone. Soon Matt joined him.

"What's up, Stan?" Matt asked. "You guys not getting along?" He reached for the basket of garlic bread, and offered some to Stan.

"Those two are such wusses," Stan said. "Brown-nosing the ranger and racking up points."

"So? Why do you care if they make a good showing on their summer projects? It has nothing to do with you, really, does it?" Matt pressed.

"Not directly. But if they keep pointing out what a fuck-up I am, then I could get canned, and I need a good report for my probation officer."

"I'm sure you'll be okay, as long as you haven't broken any laws." Matt gave him a questioning look. "Are you fucking up?"

Stan grinned and looked over at Jeff and Cliff, whose face darkened as he stared at him.

"Nah. No more than anyone else."

"What does that mean?" asked Matt.

"Don't worry about it, man. Get off my case." Stan got up and went out to the porch. Matt thought of going after him, but just then, Philippe sat down beside him and asked about their ride to Evansville.

"Did you find out anything interesting?" Philippe asked.

"Maybe. We'll see where it goes." Matt didn't really want to give away too much information before he and

Jan had discussed it. He changed the subject. "Look at those kids enjoying their spaghetti!" Nate Jr. and Dora were sucking up spaghetti noodles and getting sauce all over their faces and shirts. Albert was feeding pasta to Rosebud under the table, and Amos Peabody was sitting across from them laughing as if he were a child again.

"This is just like the old days here at the lodge, Matt," Philippe said with a slightly sad smile. "Families having fun together. Kids playing. Great meals and great friends. This is how it should be. We've lost that feeling here lately, and I hope it comes back."

"Will there be a campfire tonight?" Cliff asked loudly.

"You bet there will, and we're making s'mores!" Philippe promised, as he got up and began to clear the tables. "Men do the dishes tonight. Ladies night off."

"What?" protested Ward Shapiro. "We made the garlic bread, and it was great. We did our part."

"I have spoken!" said Philippe with a hearty laugh, and Nate, Ed, Matt, and Amos followed him into the kitchen, with Ward reluctantly dragging behind.

"It's not that bad, Ward," Amos said. "I've done many a dish in my day, and I rather like it. It gets the grime off my hands." The guys laughed. In a short time, the kitchen and dining room were clean and all that lingered was the smell of the garlic.

Now the makings of the s'mores—chocolate bars, graham crackers, and marshmallows, were gathered up and brought out to the fire pit. "Time for dessert, everyone!" Ida announced, and the group gathered around. A few people sang as the marshmallows were toasted, and then, in a moment of quiet, the lodge phone began ringing. It rang twice and stopped, rang twice again and stopped. Again and again it rang twice. Ida went in to try to answer it, just in case, and grabbed it on the first ring, but, of course no one was there. The mood around the campfire now changed.

"Well, it was nice to forget about our fears for a while," Diana said. "But obviously, our problems are not over. I am wondering if I should take Dad home to Delaware."

"I thought I heard a scream last night," Miranda said, out of the blue. "I didn't say anything about it, because I thought every one else must have heard it, too. I was too scared to get out of bed, and I did fall back to sleep."

Ida's eyes met Jan's briefly, and by unspoken agreement, neither woman mentioned the cat.

"Come on kids," Nate Loomis called to his children. "It's bedtime." Nate Jr. protested, but they followed their dad, and left the campfire. Frances held up baby Celeste to say goodnight to the others.

"Good night, sweet baby," Amos cooed and kissed her on the cheek, while others gave her hugs.

"Does anyone want to hear some Zydeco?" Ed offered, buzzing a little on his old harmonica.

"What the heck is Zydeco?" Cliff asked, chomping on his third s'more, with chocolate and marshmallow stuck to his lips.

Ed grinned. "It's music from Cajun country in the Louisiana bayous, a little bit of European folk music, and a bit of bluegrass with a French accent."

"Oh great," Stan moaned. "There's not one radio station up here that doesn't play country music, unless of course it's all French-speaking, and now we get Cajun?"

Philippe went back into the shed where antiques are stored, grabbed an old washboard and a smooth wooden spoon to rub it with. Then he accompanied Ed in the upbeat tempo. They started off with the "Bosco Stomp" and "They Stole My Chicken".

The music was lively, and soon people were tapping their fingers on the benches, clapping their hands and stomping their feet. A few got up to dance around the fire to the cheerful sounds of the "Old Plank Road". Amos was having a ball, clicking his feet around like an Irish step-dancer. Between songs, guests talked about the ongoing disturbances.

"I'm missing two more six-packs!" Ledger declared, as he arrived at the campfire. "I just got back from the woods and I went to the fridge, and all my damn beer is gone. I'm fed up."

"I'm sorry. I'll go get you some from my place," Philippe said, as he got up and headed for the log cabin.

"I finished another painting," Diana offered. "Does anyone want to see it?"

"Sure," Jan said. "I would. You are quite talented. I like your style with the watercolors." Diana left to get her painting.

"We should all just try to be positive," Avis Shapiro proclaimed. "No more negative talk."

"And who put you in charge?" her husband snapped back at her. "Don't be so bossy."

"I'm just saying," Avis flushed, "I think we keep getting all worked up."

"Well, you can't tell everyone else what to say or do," Ward said. "Just take care of yourself."

"Why are you crabbing at me?" asked Avis. It began to sound like an argument.

"I'm not crabbing. I'm telling you to stop telling other people what to do and what to feel. You're not in charge here."

"I didn't say I was in charge, but I have a right to an opinion, don't I?" Avis hissed. "You have no problem offering your opinions."

"Okay, you two," Ida jumped in with a forced smile. "Let's not fight with each other. Everyone's nerves are shot."

"How about a poem while we're waiting for Diana?" Annette offered, and when Ida nodded, she began:

She saw the hairy creature through the trees
Lumbering toward her, casting foul odor on the breeze.
As it came closer she could see quite clear
The sharp yellow fangs that filled her heart with fear.
She raised her gun and aimed straight for the eyes
And so the furry beast met his just demise.

Stan laughed hysterically, and Jeff chastised him for being rude.

"Oh shut up, Jeff," Stan said. "You're no saint. And, it's funny."

"I don't think it's funny," said Miranda, now holding Princess in her lap. "It's scary."

"It is scary," Amos defended Miranda, as he moved over closer to her on the campfire bench. "I'll stay right here and protect you." Miranda smiled at the attention.

"Are you scared, Dad?" Diana asked her father as she returned with the painting.

"Hell, no," Amos answered. "This is the most excitement I've had in years! But if the lady is scared, I'll look after her." He winked at Miranda and she giggled.

"Well, you're scaring me," Ralph laughed, "Oooo, I'm so terrified and not much scares old Ralph Leggett."

Jan made a mental note that he had mispronounced his name. Perhaps he had had too many beers already.

"Let's see the painting," Ida said. Diana held it up in the light of the campfire. The view was of the lodge from down near the beach. There were dark storm clouds above the roof, and eerie shadows on the porch and lawn. The trees around the lodge looked like skeletal arms and hands and the rain dripping down from the clouds contained blood-red droplets. A light behind the windows glowed like cat's eyes, and the porch railing gave an appearance of a sinister smile. The lodge itself seemed to be an evil personality.

"Oh my," Miranda whimpered. "I think I want to go to bed now." She picked up her cat and Amos walked with her into the lodge.

Philippe came back with some beer for Ledger and then he and Ed played a couple more songs, "Sweet Tater Pie" and "Bayou Blue Boy", and then sat down to take a break.

"I had some bad news today from my friend Pete Delaney," Ed began. "He's had a hard time making his mortgage, and his place was put up for auction. Some guy named Roger Orton outbid everyone else and snagged the place. Pete said it was the same guy who bought up the Morrison place a couple of months ago, and the guy was a cold-hearted businessman. He never even pretended to care about the owners who were losing their property."

"That's sad for your friend," Jan said. "Are you sure it wasn't some development company who bought those places?"

"Pete didn't mention any company name. Only this guy, Orton. Do you think there's something weird going on, Jan? Like some damn land-grabbing?"

"Maybe. We're looking into that. Ever heard of Rambling River Development?"

Ralph choked on his beer. "Damn cigarette cough."

Ed paused. "Can't say as I have. You might ask Joseph, if you see him."

"Yes, I'd like to see him," Jan said. "How can I arrange that?"

Ed laughed. "Funny thing is, you won't find him by looking for him."

"I've been hearing that," Jan said. "I met some Abenaki today who told me the same thing."

"Well, you're learning about the Abenaki tribe then," Ed continued. "They're an elusive group, especially their shaman." The Abenaki survived the great wars by splitting up and disappearing into the forests. It's in their blood. However, I do know some of Joseph's hangouts. One is the bog, as you know, where he goes to find medicinal plants. Another is an old logging camp which is now part of the Bill Sladyck Refuge. He keeps a little cabin out there and grows a few vegetables."

"Thanks for the tip," Jan said, smiling, her brain immediately planning her next shaman hunt. "I think it's time to step up this investigation."

"I'm really worried about our safety," Diana said, kneading her hands. "I feel so on edge, like we just don't know what will happen next. What dead animal will end up on the porch, and what antique will fall down on our heads?"

"You've had enough of those s'mores," Ward snapped at Avis, who glared at him and threw the rest of her dessert at him. "You eat it then."

Stan then began throwing pinecones at Jeff. Annette yelled at them to please stop, putting her hands over her eyes, and Philippe stood up and spoke. "Calm down everyone. We're all getting too frustrated around here. I know it's a rough time. We're working hard to find the answer here, and keep everyone safe. I assure you that it's not as bad as we're making it out to be."

"I hope you're right," Ida added. "And, I hope that Officer Parker is right, and we're overreacting. But I don't know how long we can let this go on without closing down the lodge."

Jan looked at Matt. They were now sure that it was not so simple, and that perhaps they had actually been under-reacting.

"Relax," Philippe pleaded. "There are some great warm summer days ahead. Let's just enjoy them. Don't let a few strange events here ruin your vacations."

"Yes," Ida said, working hard to sound cheerier. "We have to have faith in God, and be positive. We'll work on planning something extra fun, like a pontoon boat ride or a picnic up at Shady Brook."

Diana smiled, and Avis nodded. Ward said, "Fine. At least we'll be away from the lodge." Then Stan piped up, "What about inviting the whole town for an all night party? That would be more fun."

Chapter 11: Sizzle

The muggy Tuesday morning grew slowly brighter with no dramatic flare. It just quietly appeared with the promise of sun, sweat, and sizzle. Jan treated herself to a cool shower before heading down for breakfast. She found Matt, Philippe, and Ward sitting out on the porch, bemoaning the unusual Vermont heat wave.

"How about some iced coffee?" Philippe asked, handing her a tall frosty mug of the muddy brew.

"Yes, thanks. Now, how about some air-conditioning in this old lodge?" Jan teased, gratefully accepting the perker-upper.

"I know, it was an oppressively humid night, and I guess there are several more days of it to come. Did you get any sleep?"

"Some," Jan answered. "But besides the heat, I had a brain worm."

"A what?" Matt asked, with a look of wonder.

"Oh, I just kept hearing "Down on the Old Plank Road" over and over in my head. Part of me wanted to get up and dance."

"Oh," Matt laughed. "Brain worm. Where I come from, we call it an earwig. I got stuck once on "Red Rubber Ball" and it lasted for weeks."

"Maybe the restlessness has something to do with the heat," Philippe said. "Anyway, that sun sure was a red ball early this morning. How does that saying go? 'Red sky at night, sailor's delight...'"

"'Red sky in the morning, sailors take warning,'" Jan finished. "That would imply that a storm is coming."

"Right," Philippe agreed. "But the heat should make it a good day for swimming. In fact, Matt has already jumped in the lake."

Jan looked at Matt and gave him a coy smile. "Well, that ought to keep you cool for a while! I hope there are some blueberry muffins left." She started to get up, when Philippe said, "Sit down, Jan, I'm making breakfast for everyone this morning—French crepes with strawberries."

"Oh my God, Philippe, you just made my day, no matter what else happens." Looking at Matt again, she said, "Philippe makes absolutely the most perfect French crepes ever. Wait till you taste them—thin and sweet, with a crisp lacey edge."

"Same way I like my women," Philippe laughed, heading for the kitchen. Matt chuckled and nodded in agreement.

Ward's face was drawn and he was biting a cuticle.

"How are you this morning, Ward?" Jan asked. Did the heat keep you and Avis awake?"

"Well, it kept Avis awake, and so of course she kept me awake," he said, disgruntled. "We are really thinking of leaving. Avis is getting anxious. But in some strange way, I like the mystery going on here."

"You do? I thought you were the nervous one and Avis was more adventurous." Jan said daringly. "What do you like about it?" Matt watched her question the Long Island stockbroker.

"Oh, you know, the excitement, I guess. Wondering what will happen next."

"Who will be scared out of their wits today?" Matt nodded. "Yeah, that is just never-ending fun."

"Well, I suppose my life isn't that exciting."

"What? You live in New York! Don't they have a killing a minute down there?" Matt asked.

"Well, that stuff gets boring after a while—drug wars, neighborhood drive-by shootings, arson fires. But I don't know anyone in my neighborhood who has found a dead grouse on their steps."

"You have a point there, Ward," Matt agreed.

In a short while, the aroma of the crepes and the maple-smoked sausage filled the lodge, and guests were straggling out to the front porch. Ida began bringing plates out on trays. A big bowl of fresh chopped strawberries and another of real whipped cream were set out along with jugs of maple syrup, for all to help themselves. More pitchers of iced coffee and orange juice circulated among the guests, and everyone seemed delighted.

Annette and Miranda set up a small table in the porch corner and borrowed some antique tea cups to enjoy an elegant breakfast reading poetry to each other. Miranda's little cat, Princess, roamed around the porch getting acquainted with Lola and Seymour. Soon the Loomis family came bounding down the stairs with Rosebud, and the children's chirpy voices filled the air.

The teenagers arrived from the green room, ready for a day of work in the refuge. "This is terrific," said Jeff, appreciation glowing on his face, "and we even have time to sit a minute, and not just grab and run." Stan helped himself to a huge pile of crepes and Cliff followed suit. Philippe was making them as fast as he could in the kitchen, but could barely keep up with the demand.

"Wow, this is sooooo good," Matt said to Jan.

"The iced coffee?"

"Everything! Crispy crepes, real whipped cream, and especially the company," he said with a wink.

Jan ignored him and moved to a bench near the front of the porch, letting her mind wander out over the flower beds where the late-blooming tulips were just opening beside the lupine. Thinking for a moment about the incongruity of tulips in a heat wave, she observed that the lake was smooth and quiet with the majestic Elan Hill rising pyramid-like on the far side. A small pontoon boat was crossing about a quarter mile out, a large white bird flew over—probably an egret—and a quartet of mallards floated along the edge.

"So peaceful," she thought. "Who would think that anything evil could happen around here?"

Diana was at her easel on the far end of the porch, painting an image of the lake and the mountain. Amos was rocking away in a colonial slat rocker. Jan had noticed in interviewing Amos that, just as Diana said, he did have a bit of dementia, as he told her the same story several times, of how he had succeeded in the business world of greater D.C. and how he had met several presidents. She only questioned him to be thorough, but didn't expect any real information from him.

When all had eaten their fill and the boys had left for the refuge, Philippe, Ida, and Jan cleared away the breakfast dishes. Jan remarked that a dishwasher might be a great addition to the lodge, and Philippe scolded her playfully. "Now listen, city girl, you have to stop trying to modernize this place. Some of us don't mind a little old-fashioned work. You just go write your story, and keep thinking about our perpetrator here. I'll take care of this mess."

"Okay," Jan said with a laugh. "Philippe, I don't know how you manage to stay so cheery and positive through all of this. I don't think Ida is as sure as you that things will be all right. I feel like she's ready to close down and sell out."

"Well, there are days when she has had it with all the work of running a lodge, but she doesn't really want us to quit. At least I don't think so." Philippe got quiet and turned toward the sink.

Back out on the porch, Jan took out her note pad, rested her feet up on a milk can and began to write. Sometimes she felt that the brain-hand connection worked better with pen and paper than it did with the laptop. The big antique Coca-Cola thermometer on the porch column registered 91 degrees and it was only ten o'clock. The air was so still that the leaves of the big tooth poplar trees by the driveway showed no signs of twinkling, and the nearby quaking aspen were not about to quake. The rocking horse balanced precariously on top of the old steamer trunk, where it usually rocked in the slightest breeze, but now moved not a smidgeon, and the tire swing on the old maple tree appeared to be strung on a rigid pole.

Jan tried to work on her article but was distracted by the movements of a big, brown and yellow striped orb spider in the corner where one of the nine porch columns met the roof. "There's an enterprising character," she thought. "She seems not at all slowed down by the summer heat. Maybe she's even energized." Jan started to draw on her note pad, sketching a web growing bigger and bigger along with the one being created by the spider. What would the shaman say was the message in this little piece of nature? A tangled web we weave? A maze like the roads in the refuge?

Jan saw the spider as a potential hero in a children's story, and began to write:

On a hot June day in Vermont, nine-year-old, Clarissa Canterbury, in her new yellow dotted Swiss dress that matched her long blonde braids, sat at the antique wrought iron table on her front lawn with her two new friends, the strange Magruder twins who had moved next door. The twins wore their hair in top knots that stuck straight up from their heads, and when they talked, they spoke exactly the same words at the same time. Clarissa drank the sour lemonade that they had poured for her, and felt a little tingly as her body shrank to the size and shape of a butterfly, and light blue gossamer wings grew out of her back. She tried to fly away towards her bedroom window, but soon became tangled in a huge black spider web at the edge of the roof. She twisted and turned, but the more she struggled, the more the web clung to her body and wrapped her tight. Now her wish to be a butterfly had gotten her into a big mess...

Jan scratched out what she had written and went back to her refuge article, writing in the shade of the porch until Ida arrived in her gardening gear and began to tear away at the weeds in the flower bed in front of the lodge. Jan put down her pad and pen, grateful for a break, and bounced down the steps to help. When the late morning sun hit her full force, she began to wish she had taken Philippe's suggestion about jumping in the lake.

"Not those!" Ida gasped, as Jan grasped a large clump of rose mallow about to bloom.

"Yikes, I'm sorry. They looked like weeds. Aren't these weeds? Our gardener in Branford always pulls these out."

"Well, they may be weeds in Branford, Connecticut," Ida said. "But here in Morgan they are wildflowers."

Matt appeared with a large pitcher and several glasses.

"Ice water, anyone?"

"Not while we're working," Ida answered. "It can turn your stomach when it's too hot."

Slightly rebuffed, Matt relaxed in the Adirondack chair and worked on the notes for his recent wildlife photos. A story was growing in his head about the moose in the Hurricane Pond. Hiding behind his notebook, he took a closer look at this woman who had caught his interest.

Jan was eagerly helping Ida trim up the small flower garden, bending and then standing, kneeling and shifting as she did so. Matt observed and admired every move. He liked the way her denim shorts fit snugly around her hips without being too tight, and how they were just long enough to be conservative but still revealing of some spectacular legs. Her dark red hair glowed with highlights in the morning sun, the length of it just brushing her shoulders. Oh, those smooth shoulders, exposed around the thin yellow straps of her tank top and glistening with perspiration as she pulled weed after weed with an apparent vengeance. Matt studied her, entranced. Suddenly realizing that she was being watched, Jan turned to face towards him, the yellow top damp from her labors barely concealing the rounded perfection of her upper body. Grabbing up a handful of limp dandelions, she tossed them onto Matt's lap. "And just what are you looking at?"

"I just like watching other people slave away while I relax," Matt laughed, catching the dandelions. The ladies continued weeding and Matt went in to look at maps and make a plan for an evening ride in his Bronco later, hoping to spot some kind of wildlife along the way. Miranda and Annette sat in the dining room writing poetry, Amos went up for a nap and Diana continued to paint her lake scene.

By lunchtime, the heat and humidity were oppressive, sending Ward and Avis out to find an air-conditioned restaurant over in Newport. The strawberry crepes still sat heavily in Jan's belly and food was of little interest, but she nibbled on some fruit salad that Philippe had prepared for the gardeners.

"That's enough gardening for today," Ida declared. "We probably disturbed the roots too much in the heat anyway. I'll have to soak the bed good tonight."

As hot as it was, Jan suddenly felt that she needed to check her phone messages again, so she took off toward the far end of the beach, for once regretting that this remote Vermont town had such poor cellular reception. The pavement seemed to burn through the bottoms of her flip flops as she walked along the road and the air was hard to breathe. She wished she had brought along a bottle of water, although the spot that she was headed for where there was cell phone reception was only a half mile away from the lodge.

Jan sat on the grassy bank by the lake and dialed up her messages. Sid's cold voice was the only one she heard. He was demanding that she call him and discuss divorce plans, as he now wanted to get it over with as soon as possible. His words and his tone caused her to feel like she had been hit by a truck, wondering whatever happened to the love they had known. What happened to the man who had kept her dancing all night at the Renaissance Hotel? Where was the man who said she was his queen and that he would build her a castle? Jan lay back on the grass, and as she heard a distant rumble in the sky, she noticed a few dark clouds in the west. She felt like she couldn't move. Was it the heat or was it the power of Sid's awful condemnatory attitude? She closed her eyes, for just a few minutes, but soon a loud series of thunder claps startled her, and she sat up. The dark thunderheads were now moving quickly in over the lake, and a few sprinkles of rain hit her face. Just above Elan Hill a large bolt of lightning shot down from a black cloud and seemed to hit the peak.

"Cool rain would feel good," she said to herself. "But lightning would not." Quickly Jan got up and began walking swiftly, and then running, toward the lodge. More raindrops hit her skin and the trees along the lake began swishing back and forth, gently at first and then more fiercely.

A strange hissing sound rose up from the pavement, like steam escaping from a pressure cooker. Loud claps of thunder frightened her, and wind and rain now drove in on the attack. Jan was caught in the storm. The lightning seemed to come closer as she ran as fast as she could. She contemplated knocking on the door of one of the cottages and asking for shelter, but could not bring herself to do it. Feeling very alone and afraid, Jan ran, as well as one could run in worn out flip flops. She then remembered someone saying that the lightning would get you if you ran so she slowed a little, and waited for her hair to stand on end, the sign that lightning was about to strike. She knew that if that happened she would have to hunch down in a ball and hope it missed her. Jan trotted toward the lodge. Never had the beach seemed so long.

Then, as suddenly as it had come up, the storm subsided. The black clouds moved off to the east and the moisture lifted off of the still warm ground in misty swirls. Jan slowed her pace as she approached the lodge, and there on the grass at the lower edge of the long rolling lawn, stood a huge bull moose. Jan's first thought was, "Oh, my God, I have to go find Matt!" but then the moose took off up Holland Pond Road, and Jan heard a scream from inside the lodge.

Crashing through the screen door, dripping wet, Jan glanced around the dining room for Matt. Most of the guests were there talking and Miranda was crying, with Amos trying to comfort her. Jan realized that it was the old lady who had screamed.

"What the heck happened to you?" Philippe said to Jan. Ida grabbed a towel from a pile of linens on a chair and brought it over to help Jan wipe off the rainwater. "Did you get caught in that cloudburst?" Ida asked.

"Cloudburst? That was a hurricane!" Jan said. "I was scared to death. But what happened here?"

"Miranda saw a ghost," Frances Loomis said. "She was screaming out of her wits."

"It was real. It was real," wailed Miranda.

Ida hugged the woman. "Calm down, now. What actually did you see?"

"I was heading over to the restroom near the back stairs, right there, with Princess," she pointed to the back of the great room where the stairway went up to the east wing.

"I was by the mirror there, and I saw him—a man with black shaggy hair. Imagine looking in the mirror expecting to see your own face, and there is a hairy man. I heard a crash and then turned around to see if he was behind me, and he wasn't there. It had to be a ghost." Miranda was shaking. Frances brought her some chamomile tea and had her sit down at a table.

"Calm down everyone," Philippe urged. "I'm sure there's an explanation for this. There's no hairy man here now. Let's all just relax. That storm was pretty wild and it could have stirred up some people's imaginations, if you know what I mean."

Jan was not so sure that the hairy man in the mirror was a figment of Miranda's imagination. Standing in the spot where Miranda had stood, and looking into the mirror, Jan noticed that the big round mirror held the image of the mirror on the far wall of the dining room. She held the mirror by the edge and tilted it level with the wall and the image disappeared and she saw her own reflection. "That's odd," she thought, letting the mirror fall back in place, again. Just then, Matt crossed in front of the dining room mirror and his image appeared on the round mirror at the bottom of the stairs.

The phone rang in the kitchen and Ida picked it up.

"No one there?" Jan asked Ida, who slipped into the great room, her face pale.

"Right, and, look at this." Ida opened the guest book and showed Jan the latest entry.

"U WIL ALL BE SORY FOR WHAT U DUN. R. E. PAYER."

"Oh, no, not again!" Frances wailed.

"This guy needs a good kick in the butt!" growled Diana. "I'm getting tired of this."

"It's infuriating!" scowled Nate.

"Repayer. Hmmm," said Jan. "What is this character repaying?"

"I don't know," responded Ida, "But you're still soaking wet, Jan."

"Yes, and its keeping me cool, but I am going to go change. Let's think about how this guy is getting into the lodge, or if he's already here. This is important. Are you locking up?"

"At night, yes," Ida said. "I really hate to. We've never had to lock the lodge before. But, it's open all day because people are coming and going."

The guests began to drift away from the turmoil. Jan left for her room, Diana went back to her painting, and Amos sat with Miranda, patting her shoulder.

"I'm getting mad, too," Miranda grumbled.

"Well, just let me get my hands on this guy," Amos promised her, "I'll show him what it is to be scared. I've fought in two wars, you know."

Later in the evening, Jan and Matt were alone on the porch, sitting and relaxing on the repaired swing when she finally had a chance to tell him about the big moose.

"What? I can't believe it. I missed him, and I was out on the porch until just before Miranda screamed!"

"I'm sorry," Jan apologized. "I immediately thought of you and tried to go get you, but he ran off and then I heard her screaming. I feel bad that you haven't seen a bull moose yet."

"Oh, hey, it's all right Jan, really. There are better things in life than getting the great moose picture. In fact, it's the hunt that's the best part. You know—the anticipation." He smiled, and Jan looked away.

"Jan, look at me," Matt pleaded. "Is this really all business?"

"Yes. Matt. Listen, I admit I find you attractive, and that you give me a lift. But, I'm still technically married, and emotionally I'm still confused. I don't think I'm going to be feeling free for a while. I need to ask you to back off. It's too difficult right now, to try to concentrate on this case, and to cope with all of my feelings."

"Okay. I get it. Enough said."

"I'm sorry."

"No. Don't be sorry. I'm an idiot. We'll stick with being platonic friends, all right?" Matt said. "However difficult that might be."

"Yes. Thank you," Jan said with relief, and then began to go over the events and possible perpetrators.

"I've been leaning towards this being an inside job, and I still am, but now there appears to be an outside influence," she said.

"Rambling River?" Matt asked.

"You can see the possibility, right?"

"Sure, at least it deserves looking into."

"I want to go over everything with you today, Matt, if we could," Jan said. "I don't want to miss something. Philippe noticed this morning that there were more knives missing from the kitchen. That concerns me. If it's not an inside job, then someone is getting in here."

"Okay, so, which insiders do you include as suspects at this point? Is anyone from the lodge really a possible perpetrator, or are we now looking at something bigger?" Matt asked.

"Well, we have to assume everyone is guilty until we rule them out. I have ruled out Ida and Philippe, and the Loomis family, and, of course Miranda and Amos. Everyone else is suspect."

"Are you sure you can rule out Ida?" Matt asked, earning a scowl from Jan.

"Of course. Don't be an idiot. Ida wouldn't do anything like this."

"Annette?"

"A suspect. Absolutely. She knew about the murder. She is a drama queen. Maybe her poetry reflects her guilt. Maybe she broke the dish that cut her hand. She likes being in the *murder* room, and remember how violently she chopped the veggies? I have nothing concrete on her. I just haven't ruled her out."

"Diana?"

"Don't know enough to rule her out. I suppose she's improbable."

"Ward and Avis?"

"Avis is unlikely. Although Ward keeps saying she doesn't want to be here, she says she does. But maybe she is creating an excuse to go home—farfetched, but possible. Ward is another story. He is the anxious one, but also appears to like the excitement, and maybe is creating it."

"I think he's more of a businessman than a mystery writer though," Matt said cynically. "Personally, I'd go with the teenagers. Not all of them, but very possibly Stan."

"Really?"

"Right. I learned that he has a long record with juvenile court and this is about his last chance to reform. He is on probation doing public service on the refuge, mad at the whole system, and may have the desire to get back at someone. He is an angry young man who could use some therapy, or a father. I really hope, though, that he can get it together and do something worthwhile with his life. He has potential."

"Well, he bears watching then, and so does Ralph. I don't like him at all for some reason."

"You said that before. Is it the animal killer thing?" Matt asked, questioning Jan's perspective.

"Well, I think he's a phony. I don't think his name is Ledger. The other day he called himself 'Legget'."

"Really? Messed up his own name? Interesting."

"By the way, Matt, you are from Pennsylvania. Ever hear of Hagerstown?"

"Hagerstown? You mean Havertown?"

"No, Hagerstown, with a 'g'."

"There is a Havertown, Pennsylvania. No Hagerstown. There is a Hagerstown, Maryland, though."

"Well, he either has a bad memory for names, is one of those people who just pronounces things wrong, or he is lying about who he is and where he's from," Jan declared, "and I intend to find out what's up."

Chapter 12: Daydreams and Danger

Early on Wednesday morning, Jan sipped her iced coffee on the porch and munched on one of Ida's fresh strawberry muffins while she watched Lola stalk the chipmunk who lived under the steps. The old Siamese was recovering well from her injuries and apparently feeling the return of her kittenhood. She lay on the second step down and watched and waited for the chipmunk to come out to get the cracked corn that Ida had placed on the stump of the old maple tree. Only her tail moved, swishing back and forth. Once the chipmunk ventured out from under the porch latticework, Lola pounced, pretending to want to catch the little creature, who quickly scrammed back to his lair. This scene was repeated over and over throughout the morning; with Lola never actually catching the chipmunk. However, the chippy apparently understood the rules of this game, as he would wait a short time while Lola perched herself back on the step and then the game began all over again.

Rosebud ran around the yard in circles, chasing the kids or the birds, or nothing at all. Lola ignored him entirely. The cocker spaniel tried a few times to interest Seymour in a little fun, but the old lab lay on the porch in a shady corner, and was definitely not himself. He seemed very anxious, barking at anything that moved, and occasionally getting up to pace around among the guests.

Ida joined Jan, who began firing questions at her. "Tell me what you said earlier about Ralph Ledger being from North Carolina. He told me he was from Pennsylvania. And you said that Mr. Baggett's son once tried to buy the lodge. Did he make an offer, and do you know where he was calling from? Did you get any other offers?"

"Could you slow down a little? One question at a time," Ida said. "Yes, Ralph signed in as being from North Carolina. It's in the guest registry."

"Oh, really? I don't know how I missed that. So, he actually wrote that down. Interesting."

"James Baggett did call early on, wanting to buy the lodge. That was soon after we bought it. He didn't offer much beyond our buying price, and of course we were not interested in selling. He seemed annoyed, but we didn't think much of it at the time. I don't think he said where he was calling from and I didn't ask. Is this important?"

"Every detail is important. It seems odd that he didn't inherit the lodge from his father, but then I guess they had been estranged for some time. Did anyone else make an offer on this lodge?" Jan asked while writing in her notebook.

"A realtor did come by about a month ago and ask if we were interested in selling. I don't remember his name at all, but he did give us a card. I could look for it."

"Would you, please?" Jan requested. "It could be significant."

"I probably tossed it in the desk drawer. I'll go look."

While Ida went to look for the card, Jan found herself staring out over the lake and fighting off intrusive thoughts of Matt. "I just can't let myself get involved. It's really bad timing."

As if on cue, Matt slammed out the screen door. "What's up for today, partner?" he asked. "You said we might go out to that Bill Sladyck Area to look for wildlife. How about it?"

"Maybe later, Matt. I have a couple of things to do first." Damn, he was attractive.

Ida came out from the lodge with the card in her hand. "Here it is," she said. "Roger Orton Realty. He's the one who came by."

"Roger Orton?" Matt asked. "Isn't that the name of the realtor that Ed Pease said was buying up foreclosures? It sounds like he's kind of a scumbag."

"Well, at least it's not Rambling River," Jan said. "Thanks, Ida. Hold onto that card, though, okay? I'm going to Lady Pearl's to see if they can fit me in for a haircut."

"What?" asked Matt. "The lodge is in danger, and you're going for a haircut?"

"It's necessary, Matt. How about talking with Annette and Ward while I'm gone? See if you can pick up anything suspicious."

"Sure. No problem. Just don't cut off too much of that beautiful red hair," Matt said, clearly disappointed that he was not invited. But at least she had said they might go back to the woods later. He watched her drive off, with her hair blowing in the breeze.

Lady Pearl's boutique, Jan knew from experience, was a great place to pick up information on the locals, and hear about anything exciting that was going on in the area. Historically, women spill their guts to their hairdressers and the beauticians are thrilled to have something to talk about. Lady Pearl remembered her right away.

"Hey, you're Ida's friend. You back at the lodge for another visit?"

"Yes, I am. And a great place it is to relax. It's nice to see you, Pearl."

"Thanks. It's Jan, right?"

"You have a good memory. That's a good thing to have."

"Usually, although I'm starting to get old, and sometimes I do forget a name. What can I do for you, girl?"

"I'd just like a little trim, you know, get rid of some split ends."

"Sure thing. Have a seat. I love to work on hair like yours," Pearl ran her hands through Jan's hair. "It's such a gorgeous color, like my mahogany dresser, and so thick and wavy."

"Thanks, Pearl. Say, since you have such a good memory, do you remember anything about the murder at the lodge six years ago?"

"Oh, yeah, it was the talk of the town at the time. We don't get many murders up here in Morgan, right, Bea?" The wide blonde woman at the desk nodded.

"All I know," said Pearl, "is that it was very bloody and never solved. That poor man, Mr. Baggett. He seemed like a good guy, too. Some of the townies turned out for his funeral, but not one relative of his showed up. We heard he had a son, too, down in Baltimore. How come you're so interested?"

"Oh, I'm just writing a story about this area," Jan fibbed. "Are there any other interesting events you might tell me about?"

"Well, I just heard there was a big fire at the Sheldrake Inn over on Willoughby. That's the latest gossip," said Pearl, "and, of course, that two big landowners are selling out."

"Really? Where is their land?" asked Jan, trying not to show the intensity of her interest.

"Well, one big parcel of land over on Willoughby was sold, and another on Lake Seymour, the Addison land, over 200 acres of farmland abutting the lake with 300 feet of lakefront on the back side. I heard that Addison got big bucks and is going to retire to Florida."

"Wow, that's a big deal," Jan said, one eyebrow rising. "Who bought these places? City people?"

"No," said Pearl. "Both were bought up by a company called Rambling River Development, from down in Concord, New Hampshire. "No one knows much about them, which is kind of strange, since usually everybody knows everything about everybody's business up here. People sure are wondering, though, and Constable Fred says he's going to look into it—for what that's worth. Several landowners around the lakes have been approached and offered pretty good money. Not many want to sell, though."

"I heard they bought land around Crystal Lake, also," Jan said casually.

"Really?" Pearl asked. "Well, that's another one for the list. I wonder what they plan to develop. I hope it's not a bunch of hotels. People say we can't stop progress, and that hotels and resorts are good for the economy, but Vermonters really would rather be poor than have too many people around. We like our rural areas. If we wanted to live in Vegas or L.A., we would move there. I tell you though, I heard that some of the places they bought—they just right away turned around and sold for a profit."

Pearl finished up the haircut and Jan headed back to the lodge. The beautiful sunny day had the guests out enjoying the beach and sunbathing on the sweeping front lawn. Ida greeted Jan as she arrived at the front doorway.

"Mr. Ledger has had more beer stolen," Ida said. "At least that's what he's saying. I really wonder if he had that much beer around. I'm not sure I believe him."

"I'll talk to him," Jan responded. "I'll just make a sandwich and sit on the porch."

"I made you some lunch," Diana said. "It's a curried chicken salad plate with dilled cucumbers and cantaloupe. It's delicious. How about it?"

"Why, that was very sweet of you, Diana," said Jan, since she was rather hungry and didn't really know how she could refuse. The two women sat and chatted in the shade of the big porch.

"Early on, I chose colors like turquoise, spring green, and marigold with just a splash of magenta. Now it seems I'm going for something deeper, like sienna, burnt umber and olive."

"Why do you think your mood has become so much darker, Diana?"

"I don't know. Probably the creepy things going on around here. Sometimes I think I look for something weird to happen to get me in a strange mood, just to see what will come up on the canvas."

"Really? And just how far would you go to create a mood like this one?" Jan asked, looking at Diana's latest painting. It showed a view from the porch, this time looking down at the lake. The water was choppy and muddy-looking. The sky was streaked gray, and the mountain was a very creepy olive green, with just a suggestion of an evil face within the ledges.

"Well, I didn't have to go very far. The mood was already here, right?" Diana said defensively, though not really understanding what Jan was getting at.

"Of course, you're right, Diana," said Jan as she put down the painting and went back to her salad plate. "This is an excellent lunch, thank you again."

"Don't mention it. You are doing a lot for us here, trying to figure things out."

"I just remembered," Jan exclaimed, jumping up from the table. "Rambling River Development? No wonder that name has been pounding on my skull. Excuse me, Diana. I have to make a phone call." Jan ran inside and used the house phone on the desk to call her friend Margaret, back on the *Courier* in New Haven.

"Jan, where are you?" her friend asked. "Sid has been driving us all nuts wondering where you are. Are you okay?"

"I'm fine. I just had to get away and think things through. I suppose I should have let someone know that I'm all right."

"Duh. Yes, I think so. Even your mother has called here. We were wondering if we should send the missing persons squad after you."

"I'm sorry. Listen, Margaret, I don't have time to explain right now, but I need some information. What was the name of that development company that caused the huge problem up in Maine a couple of years back? I believe it was your story? Something about pollution and extensive damage to a pristine lake in the North Woods."

"The Moosebegone Lake fiasco? What brings that up? Are you in Maine?"

"No. I'm in Vermont, and I'll call Sid tomorrow, but I need to know this now. Do you remember the name of the developer? It's important."

"Let's see. Raging River, no Restless River. That's it, Jan, Restless River Development. They did so much damage that the EPA had to go in and shut them down."

"Restless River?" Jan asked. "Are you sure it wasn't Rambling River, Margaret?"

"Pretty sure. I'll double check, but I do remember that it all gave me a restless feeling, and that word stuck with me. A lot of people were raging about it, too, which is probably why I said raging."

"Thanks, Margaret. Thanks much. Could you pull up your article and read me what you found out about them? I need to find out everything I can."

"I will, but can I email you soon? I'm actually on the line with Senator Dodd's aide at the moment, and I put him on hold to talk to you."

"Okay, I'll check for your message in a while."

"But Jan, are you really all right? Do you know when you're coming back? Sid is a jerk, and even more of a jerk without you. We're all sick of his attitude."

"There's nothing I can do there, right now. He's not going to be my jerk much longer. I'm very appreciative of you looking up that information, Margaret. I'll be in touch again, soon. Take care and thanks again." Jan hung up the phone and went to find Matt, who was out in the green room with Jeff, helping him with some editing. Jeff and Cliff both had the day off and Cliff was swimming at the beach, while Jeff was trying to work on the written part of his summer project. Jan knocked loudly on the door.

"Matt, I'm sorry to interrupt, but are you ready for the ride out to the Sladyck?" Jan's voice betrayed her excitement. "We can talk on the way. I have some things to brainstorm with you, and I need to find Joseph. He may have a hangout in an old logging camp out there."

"Ah, yes," Matt answered. "I'm there." He excused himself from Jeff, promising to help him more with the project later on.

Matt grabbed his cameras, easily convinced Jan to ride in the Bronco, and they were off to the Bill Sladyk Wildlife Preserve, a part of the Nulhegan Basin. They drove in past Hurricane Pond and deep into the woods. The road became grassy in the middle, and wet and muddy in places where the beavers had dammed the streams and re-routed the flow over the roadbed.

"I see why you agreed to go in the Bronco," Matt said to Jan, who returned a sly smile.

"You don't think I want my Mazda covered with mud and blowing out a gas tank, do you?" she asked.

"A wise woman you are, Ms. Whitlock," Matt said. "Have no fear. This baby can handle anything we put in front of it."

"We'll see," Jan said, as they came to an old wooden bridge over a stream. It looked rotted and Matt stopped the SUV, hesitating.

"Is this really safe?" he asked, eyeing the disintegrating edges of the bridge.

"Well, people do go in here fishing a lot, so probably," Jan assured him.

"Probably? Uh, okay, no worries, then," Matt said as he eased his vehicle over the boards. He sat high in his seat as if he didn't want to add his weight to the load.

Jan was smiling.

"What's so funny?" Matt asked.

"Oh, just seeing you look so afraid. Actually, huge logging trucks went over these old bridges for years, so they are built really rugged and probably would hold six of your Broncos."

"Okay, go ahead and laugh. You'll see what this truck can do, lady." Matt continued down the narrowing road, deeper into the Sladyck area to the remains of a huge old logging camp. Logs were left here and there, and occasionally they came upon rusted machines and fallen down shacks. As they drove along, the road began to get very wet and soggy.

"Yikes, it looks like we're going into a swamp!" Matt said.

"You're right, but we're safe," Jan reassured him. "See those logs going crosswise? They're a little grassed over, but they're solid."

"That stuff that kind of looks like a boardwalk?" Matt asked, skeptically.

"Right. That's an old corduroy road, made by laying the logs down horizontally to get the trucks over the soft spots."

"Okay. I'll take your word for it," Matt said, easing the Bronco onto the log road and continuing through the swampy area. They bumped along over the logs until they reached the other end and came out to a row of small shacks and then a longer building.

"That's the bunk house," Jan said. "Let's stop here and look around."

Matt turned off the engine and sighed "I don't suppose there's another route back?"

"Nope," Jan answered, laughing out loud and heading for the bunkhouse. She walked through the decayed old building, but saw nothing that spoke of the presence of an Abenaki shaman. While Matt wandered around taking pictures, Jan poked her head into every old building she could find, but no Joseph.

"Maybe if I call him," she thought, and began loudly yelling his name. When she received no answer, she looked for Matt, and found him climbing up on an old logging machine.

"Hey, be careful," she called up to him in warning.

"Yes ma'am, you got it. What is this thing, anyway?" Matt asked.

"It's called an alligator—kind of an amphibious vehicle. It's a boat that could move big floating logs around in the water, but it could also crawl over the land from one body of water to another."

"This is really neat," Matt said. "Let's see what else is here. I saw a path or an overgrown road back there by the bunkhouse. Jan followed him down the recently worn walkway to a shack with a small flower and vegetable garden growing beside it. The front door was slightly open, so they went inside.

"I feel kind of guilty going in, but I think we've found Joseph's hangout," Jan said. The little shack was old and rustic, but the floor was swept and the shelves lining the walls were dusted underneath the artifacts of various kinds that rested on them—animal skulls and furs, wooden ornamental objects and flutes. Drying plants hung from the ceiling in one area and, and dream-catchers hung in the four windows and over the doorway. In the back corner was a cot with a quilted comforter.

"Look," said Jan, "here is a burlap sack like the one he carried in the bog. Maybe he'll be back here soon to check his garden, and if I leave him a note, maybe he'll come talk to me at the lodge."

Matt found paper and pen for Jan in the Bronco and she wrote the shaman an extensive note, mentioning Rambling River Development and the company's dealings in Maine. She hoped that he would know something about this and help her decide what to do next.

"Let's go," Jan said, and Matt willingly followed, ready for any adventure that might pop up, and wondering what this woman was planning. A beautiful butterfly, which Jan recognized as a pink-edged sulphur, landed on Jan's shoulder as they walked back up the path to the bronco. She stopped and held out her hand as it flew upward.

"Hey, don't touch that butterfly, lady!" Matt said, teasingly. "Remember the butterfly effect! You might start a monsoon somewhere."

Jan smiled and smacked Matt playfully on the arm. Matt chuckled and then got serious again.

"So, you're focusing on Rambling River as the culprit here?" Matt asked, starting up the bronco and heading back over the corduroy road. "I don't quite get it. What about your theory about Ledger?"

"Well, I'm not so sure about Ledger now. He is a strange character, but I have to admit, I've been prejudiced against him. He irritates me, but he's just a crotchety old bachelor. I think that perhaps this developer wants the lodge, or the land that it's on, or at least for them to go out of business," Jan said.

"Wow. Do you think that is what's happening? Rambling River is really trying to scare everyone out of the lodge?" Matt noticed a beaver pond that they had not paid much attention to on the way in. "Let's check this out," he said. "Maybe I can get another good beaver picture."

Jan and Matt got out and walked to the pond, stepping carefully around the edge, watching out for poison ivy. No beavers showed themselves. The pond was quiet. Matt took a picture of the big beaver lodge near the far edge of the pond, and then shrugged. "We might as well go, huh?"

Jan was about to turn back to the Bronco, when she thought she saw an animal on the other side of the beaver house. She told Matt to look and she pointed to the big black bear as it came into view.

"Holy cripe," Matt whispered, powering up his movie camera. They stood there silently, Matt recording, while the bear climbed up on the beaver lodge and began tearing into it with his huge paws. Sticks were flying in all directions.

"This is very odd," Jan whispered. "I've never heard of a bear attacking a beaver lodge. The lodge under the sticks is made of hardened clay that he shouldn't be able to break through. It's very strange. Maybe we'd better get out of here."

"And miss these pictures? No way," said Matt. "Besides, it's not all that strange. I read a story once about the black bears in Ontario breaking apart lodges to eat the baby beavers. Just then, the bear lifted his head and sniffed the air. He then appeared to stare right at them, and turned and slipped away into the forest.

"Amazing," Matt breathed. "Fitzgibbons will be thrilled when I cut some stills and send him pictures of that big bear."

"It's weird, though," said Jan. "Joseph would say there is some message here, in a big shaggy black bear wrecking the beaver lodge. What could it be? Maybe it's a clue about the person attacking our lodge?"

"Ah, maybe it's Bigfoot!"

"Oh, stop."

"Well, that gives you something to think about—you and your wood spirits, and here's something else for you to ponder. I saw a poster at the deli about a concert tonight on the green in Island Pond. It's that singer you told me about, Banjo Dan. So, how about going with me?"

"You mean, a date? I thought we agreed to keep things platonic."

"Absolutely. Platonic is my middle name."

"Oh yeah, I bet," Jan was hesitant, but said, "I suppose it could be fun, since I haven't heard Banjo Dan in concert for years, but I'm going to need to do some thinking and writing first. You ready to go back now?"

"If we must."

Back at the lodge Jan pulled out her laptop, hooked it up to the net service in the dining room, and spent some time reading her email and taking some notes on the computer. Her mailbox was loaded with unanswered questions from Sid, Margaret, Eleanor, and her mom. Margaret's newest email was most interesting. She told Jan that the owner of Restless

River Development had been banned from Maine for fraudulent real estate deals and destruction of wetlands. Jan wondered if it could be the same people, changing the name and starting over in another state.

At seven, Matt interrupted her concentration stating that he was starving and wanted to head to the Island Pond green for some sausage grinders and to get a good spot on the lawn before the concert started.

"Let me take a quick shower and I'll be ready," Jan said.

"Fine, I'll be waiting," Matt said. "So what else is new?"

"Huh?"

"Nothing. I'll be wandering around downstairs, looking at the postcards and handmade photo cards for sale at the front desk. I bet I could make some money making cards out of my own photos."

Jan took her laptop upstairs and searched through her clothes for something decent to wear. An unusual sound from outside near the deck caught her attention and she went out on the deck to see what it was. A pileated woodpecker was pounding on the dead branch of a nearby maple tree. Jan watched and listened for a while, thinking about how wonderful it was to be at the lodge and how much she really loved nature and the Great North Woods. Finally she went back inside, grabbed her clean clothes and her shower caddy with her toiletries and headed for the bathroom.

Jan undressed and stepped into the shower.

"Ahhhhhhh! Oh, my God!" she screamed, and Matt bounded up the stairs. Jan stood in the hall with only a towel wrapped around her, shouting, "Catch it! Catch it! It's in the bathtub!"

Matt moved past her and looked into the tub. A striped garter snake about fifteen inches long was slithering around trying to climb up the tub walls.

"How the heck did this get in here?" Matt asked as he reached in and picked up the snake. He carefully carried it out of the bathroom, with Jan standing there in the towel, her hand up to her whitened face.

"Relax, it's just a harmless garter snake. A small one at that."

"Just get it out!" Jan exclaimed. "Someone put it there, of course. What will they do next?" Aggravated, Jan went back into the bathroom to take her shower. As the hot water ran over her shaking body, Jan felt her frustration rising.

"I really want to get this guy," she said aloud, "This was done on purpose by someone who expected people to be afraid of snakes. Whoever it is, he is keeping up a steady stream of misery around the lodge. It is time for him to be stopped.

"And here I am going out with Matt again. Talk about frustration. I should be spending the night in my room figuring this out. Come on Jan, stop talking to yourself and get moving. Okay, one last date, maybe a little relaxation listening to my favorite country singer will get the image of bears eating baby beavers out of my mind. After this, it's all down to business. Right. Who are you kidding?"

Jan dressed to go out, ignoring her own inner voice of warning, as it was overridden by her need to feel like a desired woman again.

"This tee-shirt is so plain. Oh, well, it's just an outside concert." Jan thought.

The evening air was very warm in Island Pond, but the slight breeze was refreshing. Matt spread the army blanket out on the grass midway between the stage and the snack bar. "This ought to be handy," he said. Colorful blankets and quilts decorated the lawn along with people of all ages carrying coolers and bags of potato chips. Children ran laughing and chasing each other around.

"Sure, I know you just can't wait for one of those sausage things," Jan said.

"Well, they also have plain old hot dogs. Does that suit you better? I thought you were adventurous."

"I am. Bring on the sausage. It actually smells good." Jan tried hard to relax as Matt went to get the eats and the band began setting up on the stage.

"Oh, baby, this will kill you or cure you of anything that ails you!" Matt announced when he returned with two piping hot grinders loaded with sausage, peppers and onions, and two large lemonades to cool down their throats afterwards. He had just settled down on the blanket next to Jan when Banjo Dan began to sing. Matt was impressed with the opening song, "The Catamount is Back".

"Wow, is it true that the mountain lions are back?" he asked Jan.

"I'm not sure. It may be speculation or Dan's wishful thinking," she answered.

"That would be an incredible coup, a picture of a Vermont catamount."

"I wouldn't count on it, hot shot," Jan said, grinning.

He smiled back, and she thought, "What am I doing?"

Jan concentrated on the light and lively music and began to relax as they enjoyed their meals and the summer breeze. Dan sang of the return of the peregrine falcon to Lake Willoughby, snowfalls and hills, ghosts of covered bridges, old cellar holes and other Vermont nostalgia. Jan was in heaven. "This is really where I want to be. I wonder if I can find a way to live up here in northern New England."

"This is great," Matt said softly in Jan's ear, leaning close and moving near her on the blanket.

"I told you it would be," she said, edging away from him just a little. The warm evening zephyrs and the lights around the gazebo shining on the water just beyond the green created a romantic ambiance that few could miss.

Jan and Matt sat quietly near each other on the old blanket enjoying the music, the party atmosphere, and the sweet Vermont air. They laughed at the funny songs and looked wistfully at each other during the songs that stirred the soul with longing. Finally, Matt leaned in and kissed Jan very gently on her lips. She kissed back, but then pulled quickly away.

"That was a mistake," she said.

"You can't deny the attraction here," Matt responded.

"Oh, yes, I can," Jan said, "I am just vulnerable, and so are you! We need to stop being foolish."

"Why is this foolish?" he asked.

"Because you are not over your grief and neither am I. I want to leave now. It's almost over anyway." Jan got up and gathered up her sweater and their trash and headed for the Bronco. Matt grabbed the blanket and followed her, his face betraying the unmistakable ache in his chest.

The ride back to the lodge was very quiet until Matt spoke up. "Say, that was a great concert, wasn't it? Keep your eyes open, Jan, because a wild catamount might just jump out in front of us."

Acknowledging Matt's attempt to lighten the mood, Jan agreed, "That would be something, Matt." The rest of the ride home was more peaceful than fun.

When Jan lay in bed that night, the light from the window lit up her new dream-catcher that she had placed on the wall over her bed. "Another spider web to untangle," she thought.

Chapter 13: Songs of the Muse

On Thursday morning, Jan awoke early and went downstairs to get coffee and a cranberry-orange scone to bring back to her room. She wanted to spend time alone thinking about the possible perpetrators of the disturbing events at the lodge, but somehow her mind kept wandering back to her attraction to Matt and last night's kiss on the green. She decided to concentrate on her other project, her article on the Nulhegan Basin.

What was the big picture? Of course, the refuge was somehow connected. This problem was about preserving the beautiful natural areas that are left. If developers could come in and buy up lakes and destroy wilderness areas, and there was no way to stop them, then what hope was there for humankind? This was not just about the beautiful northern lakes becoming tourist resort areas, the destruction of trees, and fragile rare plants and animals, it was also about where our hearts and souls are in the universe. What kind of creatures are humans if we can't think ahead and plan ahead for a better world, if all we can do is greedily grab up whatever makes us rich, or just gives us some momentary pleasure?

Jan sat down at the dressing table, opened her laptop and began to write. "Where Is Our Refuge?" she titled the piece. Questions ran through her mind about the meaning of the boreal forest and the lodge that feels like home, and the Great Mystery of the woods.

"Who will save us? Will we save ourselves? Do bog ferns matter? Do conifers, warblers and lichen matter? Are we worthy stewards of the earth? Is it our right to cut down trees and kill animals, or is it our responsibility to protect the balance of life?" Jan wrote for hours. She wrote until her fingers hurt. She wrote out her heart. When she was finished, she went to find Matt. He was at the little kitchen table enjoying a bowl of Ida's famous broccoli-cheddar soup.

"My article is finished. Would you look at it, please?" She put the laptop in front of him. Matt put down his soup spoon, looked at Jan with wide eyes and began to read. Jan walked outside.

Miranda was on the porch with Princess, who was playing with Lola, mimicking and annoying the old Siamese. The younger cat bounced around the elder, batting her paws at the other's tail, and jumping back when Lola struck out playfully with her paw. Amos sat near Miranda and whispered sweet things to her; Philippe and Ward stood near the bottom of the steps, debating the advantages of country life over life in the city; and Ralph Ledger sat at the end of the porch, sipping a beer and listening to others' conversations. When he thought no one was looking, he threw peach pits at the cats.

"Hey, stop that!" Amos yelled at Ledger.

"Oh, I'm just giving them something to play with," Ledger grumbled, lighting up a cigarette.

"Ralph, I'm sorry, but there's no smoking here on the porch," Jan said to Ledger. He glared at her and got up and walked away onto the wide front lawn, mumbling, "She's the damn porch police, now."

Soon Matt came out and went over to Jan with her laptop. He knelt beside her and looked in her eyes. "This article is wonderful. It's really powerful, Jan. I'd like to send it to my editor, if you don't mind."

"Do you really think so? You're not just saying that?"

It appeared to Matt that she did not know the strength of her own voice. "Yes, Jan," he said. "I really like it, and I'd like to see what my boss, Andrew Fitzgibbons thinks, if that's okay with you." Jan nodded and they went inside to email the article to *American Wildlife*. Matt plugged Jan's laptop into the only outlet in the lodge that had the internet connection. "You'd think Philippe would upgrade this place to be wireless," Matt said.

"Sure. After they get air conditioning and a dishwasher."

"There," Matt said when the article had been sent.

"Thanks for doing that," Jan said to him. "Thanks for believing in me."

"It's about time you believed in yourself, lady."

"I'm trying to, really. I guess I've gotten knocked down a bit lately, but I'm working on it. I do believe that being here at the lodge inspires me to write. It's so wonderful to be surrounded by all of the beautiful trees and sky and animals—everything is wonderful, even the rocks and dirt and moss...."

"It sounds like this is a very healing place for you, Jan," Matt said. "I think perhaps for me, too." He winked and bent down to tie his shoes. "I'm going for a walk. Be back in a while." Jan followed him with her eyes until he disappeared over a small hill, and she thought it was a good thing that he was doing some alone time.

Lunchtime came and Jan was feeling pretty good about her morning's project, when she joined Annette on the front porch. "This might be a good time to find out more about our resident poet," she thought.

"Annette, do you mind if I bring my sandwich out here to join you?"

"Not at all. That sandwich looks better than mine. What is it?'

"This? It's chicken salad with walnuts and raisins, from the deli. Do you want half?"

"Oh, yes. Here, I'll give you half of my ham and cheese, and some lemonade."

"You've got a deal. Say, tell me something about your poetry, would you? Have you been published? How do you get your inspirations?"

"Well, I have had a few published in our local newspapers, but I want to do a small poetry book."

"You mean self-publish?"

"Yes. Lots of poets are doing it these days. There's not a lot of money in poetry, but it's very satisfying to collect your works."

"And what would be the general theme of your book?" Jan asked.

"Well, there are a few themes, really. One that I write about a lot is people's darkest fears. Another is the sorrows of women. I have thought of combining these into a two-part book. I know it sounds morbid, but it isn't, really."

"Oh, no, I understand that poetry is a lot about feelings. It sounds like most of your work is very emotional. Have you done a lot of work with women's issues in any capacity?"

"You mean like a counselor? No. I have sure known a lot of victims, though." Annette's face hung down and her eyes became misty.

"And have you been one yourself?" Jan pressed, but softly.

"Yes," Annette sighed. "Most of the men in my life have let me down. Most of them have been abusive."

"And the furry beast poem—was that about a man?"

"Not a particular man, but men, yes. Is it that obvious?"

Jan nodded, "Probably not to everyone, but I saw that in there, just from my newspaper work. I have had an interest in man-woman relationships for some time. Wish I knew more about it myself, and maybe I wouldn't be getting divorced. Sometimes it does seem like men and women are two entirely different species."

Jan's mind was putting images together. "The furry beast. The dangerous male. The black bear. I wonder if Joseph would say that the bear was an omen of some kind," she thought. There was something disturbing about this image, but Jan wasn't sure what it was at the moment.

"Do you ever write poetry, Jan?" Annette asked.

"Oh, I used to try once in a while, but I just couldn't make the sentences rhyme."

"Oh, but poetry doesn't have to rhyme. It's just putting your feelings on paper, and letting it flow. I bet you'd be good at it."

"Well, I seem to be better at facts than feelings, lately. But, who knows? Maybe I'll try again sometime."

Philippe stuck his head out the door, and told them that Constable Fred was on his way over to talk to them. "We'll want you to come in, too, Jan," he said.

"Sure thing," she answered, as he ducked back inside.

"Annette," Jan began, "Do you mind if I ask you some more questions about Mr. Baggett?"

"Of course not, but why me?"

"Well, you were here a few times when he was alive, correct?"

"Yes."

"You never answered my question about whether you were here at the lodge the night he was murdered. Were you?"

"No, Jan. I had been here a few days before, but you could have found that out from the old guest registry."

"I suppose so, but I haven't gone through all of those yet. What was he like—in your opinion?"

"He was a really nice man. He was quiet, but could be philosophical. I enjoyed talking to him in the evenings. He wasn't like most men. He actually cared what women thought. He would listen to me. He was always calm, never harsh. He seemed distant and sad a lot, though."

"It sounds like you got to know him quite well. Would you say you were good friends?"

"We were getting to be, yes. He mostly kept an emotional distance, though. It was strictly platonic, if that's what you're getting at. I liked him, and I admit that if I thought he'd been interested, I might have pursued something more."

"Really?"

"Well, yes. He was a great guy. But he didn't seem to show any serious interest, other than enjoying my company, so that was that. In fact, sometimes he was a bit mean." Annette's tone became slightly annoyed.

"You seem a little defensive. I wasn't meaning to accuse you of anything," Jan said, "I'm just digging for information on him. There seems so little to go on."

"Well then, it sounds like you think that this current situation is related to his murder," Annette said.

"I didn't say that. I don't know. We're just not ruling anything out."

"Well, I don't have much to add. We talked a lot about philosophy, but he didn't talk much about his past or his family. He was a very private person. If I sound defensive, I guess it's just hard to talk about. I did like him. Actually, I found out later that he did like me, too, but it was too late then." Annette looked down at the floor and wiped her eye with her hand.

"What do you mean?" Jan asked.

"Oh, nothing."

"What was it like at the lodge then? Did he have campfires?" Jan asked.

"Oh, no. He didn't have campfires. Some guests made them on their own. He allowed that, but he didn't get involved with the guests much, except for sometimes talking like he did with me. It was harder for guests to get to know each other, also, probably because there weren't organized campfires and activities. It's much more fun now. I do miss John, though. He had his grumpy side, but he was a good person." Annette's gaze fell again to the floor.

"Then you don't think he had any enemies?"

"No," Annette answered. "The state police asked us all of that back then. You might be able to get their reports."

"Well, I'm hoping to."

Just then Constable Fred drove up the driveway in his shiny dark blue Crown Victoria.

"Even here the cops drive Crown Vics?" Jan said, surprised.

Annette smiled. "He does. But he also has a beat up old 4 x 4. Sometimes he likes to play the big shot."

"Good afternoon, ladies," Fred greeted them, tipping his brown buffalo Stetson. "Are the innkeepers around?"

"Yes, they're inside waiting for you, and I'm joining you," Jan answered, stacking the lunch dishes to bring inside. Philippe opened the door and shook Fred's hand.

"Come on in, Constable. We have information and a lot of questions for you," Philippe said.

"Well, I may have some news for you, too," the constable stated, sitting in one of the maple chairs nearest the kitchen, and setting the Stetson on the table.

"Darn nice hat there, Fred," Philippe remarked.

"Yup," Fred responded in his thick Vermont accent. "I got this on eBay, of all things. I said I'd never get into that online shopping, and now I'm doing it. It sure beats running over to Burlington just to get a hat or a pair of boots."

"I should say so," Ida added. "It's very stylish too, Fred. Can I get you some coffee? Light and sweet, I think is how you like it?"

"Oh, you're talking my language, ma'am," the constable chuckled. "Coffee is just what I need. Now, you mentioned on the phone that some more incidents have happened. So far you've had some strange noises and thievery, which could be pranks, right?"

"Well, it's much more than that," Ida answered, pouring coffee for all four of them. "We've had a dead spruce grouse on our porch, a snake in the bathtub, a car and a tractor tampered with, the porch swing chain cut so it would break, the cat injured, and a threatening note in the guestbook."

"Well, so far," Fred started, "It sounds like a lot of mischief and coincidences. These things happen all the time. The other day, a guy up at Toad Pond had an injured raccoon crawl up on his porch and die."

"Fred," Philippe responded, "Officer Parker of the state police didn't think most of this was anything serious, but he was willing to allow that the grouse may have been killed and left there on purpose. And I know that the vehicles were disabled on purpose. This is not a joke."

"Maybe some Abenaki is putting a hex on you," Fred said.

"Oh, Fred, you know they don't do that," Ida scolded. "We need your help and you are making a joke of it all."

"Okay, I'm sorry. Here's another idea. Maybe you're harboring the escapee from Drummondville."

"No, we aren't concerned about him," Ida said. "He'd be long gone by now, hiding out far away."

"Besides, since Parker is investigating, you don't need me, now do you?" Fred pointed out, hoping to be off the hook.

"Never mind what Parker is doing or not doing. What I need is for you to talk to me about something else," Jan said. "I have a concern that may or may not be connected to the lodge, but something strange is going on around here, and it bears looking at."

"Okay, I'll bite. What's buggin' you?"

"I know that you have heard of the Rambling River Development Company and been asked to look into them. Right?"

"Yes, ma'am, I have."

"Well, what do you know about them?"

"Well, I know that they have been buying up land in the area, especially foreclosures. What they are doing may be heartless, but it's legal. Then some others are selling out for a profit though, and then Rambling River is making more profit. There haven't been any official complaints. Why?"

"Well, I believe that they are the same company that had some illegal dealings up in Maine and caused a lot of damage to a pristine lake. I'm trying to find more information on them."

"Really? You think they're not legitimate? Do you think there is a connection between their deals and what's happening here?"

"I'm not sure. I just have a bad feeling about them. Will you look into it?" Jan asked.

"Sure thing. I'll get right on it this afternoon. Matter of fact, a few other people in town have had concerns about them, and I've been meaning to investigate. Meanwhile, you find out what you can, and Philippe, you need to lock the lodge at night, and keep a close eye on everyone. Call me if you need to. I'll check in with Parker and we'll see if we can put our heads together."

"Parker is a skeptic, and I think he may look for the easy way out," Philippe said.

"Maybe so. But if we have information that he needs to look at, then we'll call him on it," said Fred. "Sometimes we have to light a fire under those state guys."

Philippe stifled a smirk, as he thought about the difficulty he and others had in getting Constable Fred to act on anything.

Ida brought out some sandwiches for the constable and they changed the subject. Fred told his story about catching the twenty-seven pound lake trout out in Seymour Lake.

"I hear that someone just broke that record, Fred, with a 34-pounder. Looks like you'll have to go back out to defend your honor."

"Oh, no, you're kidding me, Ida!" Fred whined. "Some punk kid, I bet. They get the beginner's luck."

The constable stayed an hour or so, and then excused himself to head back to his office in Morgan Center. Jan decided to take a walk along the beach. She waded in up to her knees and enjoyed the cool lake water. Looking up at Elan Hill, Jan thought, "I have to do something to help preserve this wonderful natural area. If developers come in like they did in Maine, they could really make a mess of things." She decided to go back to her room and to write some more about the whole Silvio Conte Wildlife Refuge that ran the entire length of the 7.2 million acre Connecticut River watershed, from its source at the Connecticut Lakes to where it empties into Long Island Sound between Old Lyme and Old Saybrook. This time she would write more about the ecosystem and less philosophy. After a couple of hours of writing, she dozed off for a short nap.

Jan woke up sweaty and decided a swim was in order. Matt soon joined her at the beach and they talked while swimming around the end of the dock. "I heard from Andy this morning," Matt told her.

"Andy? Oh, your editor. What did he have to say?" Jan was very curious about his reaction to her article.

"He said that your article was 'different' and that he wanted to read it more thoroughly before he got back to us on it. I think that's a very good sign. Also, he wants me to write more on the wildlife up here. He was excited about what I've sent him on the bear on the beaver lodge, and the mother moose."

"I'm happy for you," Jan said. "You're a really good writer and photographer."

"Thanks. I think I've improved because I love what I'm doing now. I really love this Great North Woods, Jan. I think it is even more beautiful than the lower Appalachians, including the Great Smoky Mountains."

"Well, now you're making sense," Jan teased. "This is the only place to be. I've about made up my mind that after my divorce I'm settling up here."

"I just might want to do that some day myself," Matt said.

"I really am not that interested in where you live," Jan snapped, heading for shore. "I'm hungry. I'm going over to the deli to get something to eat."

After drying off, Jan wrapped her towel around her like a skirt and went to the little deli next to the beach.

"Hey, those calzones smell great!" Matt said.

Jan turned and rolled her eyes as she realized that he had followed her. "Yes, they are tempting."

The Fat Belly Deli was really like an old country store, with essential groceries, homemade baked goods, salads and sandwich fixings, pizza, a few postcards and games, and those wonderful homemade doughnuts found only in Vermont.

They bought a couple of calzones to take back over to the lodge for their supper.

The campfire that evening began with a discussion about evil spirits, and the question of the lodge being possessed by some agitated ghost.

"Oh, stop," Philippe pleaded, not wanting to support any more fears of the events at the lodge being supernatural. "We already had a prayer service to get rid of any ghosts, and I'm quite sure that there is a logical, rational explanation for all of this."

"Oh, you don't believe in the supernatural?" Annette asked. "What's the difference between religious visions and hallucinations?"

"I know a lot of people get some silly ideas about visions," Philippe said. "One needs to be careful about that. It might come from God or the devil."

"Ha. Or schizophrenia!" Annette added.

"I had a wild dream once that came true," Diana offered. "I dreamed that my dad fell down the stairs, and the next day he did. Cracked a rib, too." Amos nodded in confirmation, frowning and rubbing his side.

"I used to be into some Jungian dream analysis," Avis added, "and I attended a workshop on hallucinations, dreams, and visions. I do believe that people can have visions, and see signs."

"Signs? You mean like Jan following a cloud arrow out of the refuge?" asked Matt.

"Isn't that omenism?" Ida asked. "I think that can be dangerous territory."

"Well, I don't know what I believe anymore," said Matt. "But I do believe that there are many things that happen that we can't explain."

"Besides, Ida, all through the Bible people followed signs," Avis defended Jan. "Like when the Israelites were led by God and followed a cloud by day and a fire by night. And what about the burning bush?"

"Right," added Ward, "I believe that God interacts with man today, also."

"And what about women?" Annette asked.

"Humans, I mean," Ward corrected himself.

"Aha," said Matt teasingly. "But Jan was led by the spirit of the north woods, according to Joseph Rainwater. Is that the same as God?"

"One could argue that theologically," said Ward. "He can have many names—God, Allah, Abba, Yahweh."

"Or She," Annette interjected.

"I've had some unusual experiences," said Diana. "I often see a sign that leads me. Once I was trying to find a friend in Concord, and had no idea what street she was on, and I kept seeing roses everywhere, until I remembered Rose Street. I drove down Rose Street and there she was, outside watering her yard."

"That's what Jung called 'synchronicity'," said Avis. "Amazing coincidences. I do believe we can get psychic messages that way."

"I'd expect this from a poet and a painter," Philippe said. "You gals are very creative."

"Doesn't all creativity come from God?" Jan asked. "And aren't we all a part of creation?"

"I believe in divine orchestration of things," Diana said. "And I think that Jan is here at just the right time for all of us."

"Well, thanks, I guess," Jan said. "I happen to believe it was the Good Shepherd who brought me."

"Speaking of poems and art," Annette spoke up. "Would you all like to hear another poem?"

At first no one answered, but then Ida said, "Sure, go right ahead."

Annette read her latest.

Every shadow in every corner hides a startling mystery.

Every thought is working towards unraveling of a history

A horrible fate creeps up on us, and time moves much too slow.

To stop the beast we must be fast and brilliant too, you know.

Jan listened carefully to the poem and felt a chill go down her spine. "I almost think that she knows something, intuitively...perhaps."

Chapter 14: Evacuation

Jan jumped out of bed on Friday morning with an odd feeling like someone shaking her shoulder. Seymour was barking somewhere downstairs. Then she smelled it. Gas. It was still dark outside, with a little light of breaking dawn and a quick glance at the clock told her it was just five. She knew that most of the guests were still asleep, so carefully she went to wake up Matt, gently knocking on his door.

"Matt. I need help. Don't turn on a light. The lodge is full of gas." She asked him to run through her room to the back hallway and evacuate the east wing. "Don't turn on any lights or light any matches!" she warned him.

"I know, I know. I'll get them out. You'll call the fire department?"

"Yes. Good, your window is open."

Matt ran down the hall with his pants in his hand. Jan roused the Shapiros, telling them to run to the log cabin and get Philippe and Ida, as she was afraid that using the intercom could cause a spark that would ignite the gas. She then checked their windows, ran downstairs, got Annette out safely, then ran to the kitchen to turn off the gas burners which were all on without being lit. She then opened all of the downstairs windows and quickly dialed 911 on the desk telephone. After making sure the firemen knew where to go, she went outside, with Seymour following her. Matt had gotten the Loomis family, Diana and Amos, Ralph Ledger, and Miranda Picket out and then run to get the teenagers out of the green room. All of the guests were accounted for on the lawn of the log cabin when the fire trucks arrived.

"It's a good thing everyone had their windows open!" Jan remarked to Philippe. "We can thank the heat wave for that. Only the downstairs ones were closed."

"And a good thing you woke up and smelled it," he answered.

The firemen set up huge fans to blow the gas out of the building. "There does not appear to be a defect with the stove," the fire chief said to Philippe. "The knobs were all in good shape. Ms. Whitlock had turned them all off and there was no more leakage. I don't think that this was an accident. Not if all of the knobs were on, as she said."

Soon Constable Fred arrived, and chatted with Philippe about the sequence of events. He decided again to leave the investigation to the state police.

"It must have been that intuition of yours that woke you," Matt said.

"I suppose," said Jan. "It felt kind of like someone shook my shoulder. But no one was there in the room."

"You have to have a woods spirit guardian watching over you," Matt said. "You're getting to be spooky."

"What do you mean by that?" Jan asked.

"Oh, you know, cloud arrows, loons attacking. There's something about you that is very tuned in to the pulse of things."

"Hmm. I think if that were true, I'd have solved this case by now." Jan sighed and went over to the log cabin to find Ida.

In a short while, the gas was cleared out, the firemen left, and the guests straggled back inside. Then, within an hour, Sergeant Parker arrived and began an investigation by rather rudely demanding that the innkeepers and all of the guests stay near the lodge until he was finished, and then insisted on getting all of their stories regarding where they were when Jan smelled the gas. Jan informed him that all of the other guests had to be wakened.

"Well, I still have to question them," Parker said, "and I'm going to have to search the whole place, including the sheds. Everyone will have to stay out of their rooms until I do so."

"Wait a minute," Philippe said. "So far you have minimized our problems here, and now you want to search the whole place? Do you have a warrant?"

"As a matter of fact, I do. I'm not as dense as you think. I picked it up yesterday." Parker handed him the official paper and began searching Annette's suite.

"Well, what do you know," Philippe said to Jan. "We're getting some attention from the state police now."

"I'm not sure that's such a good thing," said Ida, her voice shaky.

Jeff called the ranger station at the Conte Refuge to let him know what was happening and that they might not get in today. The ranger said that they could work Saturday instead.

Kyle Dorsey, the reporter from the *Newport News* arrived. After speaking briefly with Philippe, he asked for Jan. Philippe introduced them, and soon Dorsey was sitting on the porch swing with Jan, chatting as if they were old friends.

"Do you have any idea who did this?" Dorsey asked, leaning so close to her that his long black bangs brushed her cheek, and whispering, ostensibly to keep their conversation private.

"No," Jan answered, moving away from Dorsey on the swing. "I do have some feelings about who could be the perpetrator of all of the scary events around here, but nothing conclusive, and I don't want to accuse anyone without more evidence."

"You'll have to tell the state police your theories. They know that you have a head start on them."

"Are you kidding me? I've been trying to get a good conversation going with Parker for days. Anyway, I'm sure I'm missing something," Jan said, frustrated. She looked over at Matt, who nodded in agreement. The three teenagers were standing around on the porch whispering to each other, when Jeff called Philippe over to them.

"We have a confession to make," he said. "We have beer in the green room."

"We?" Cliff yelled, then put his hand over his mouth.

"Shhhh," Jeff cautioned him.

"We're going to be in big trouble if Parker finds it," Jeff continued. "Can you help us?"

"We don't know how it got there, anyway," Stan said. "Someone must have planted it there. Probably the same person who did all the other weird stuff."

"Yeah, I'll bet," Philippe said "Okay, guys. I'm going to go out on a limb here. I'll sneak the beer back into the fridge, but we are going to have one serious talk later. How much is there?"

"Two six-packs left," said Cliff.

"Oh, ho," laughed Philippe. "So you drank some? How much was there to start?"

"Three six-packs," Stan said. "But that doesn't mean we took them."

"Well, *we* didn't," Cliff glowered at Stan.

"Cliff, just be cool," Jeff said. "I'll get the beer, Mr. Renault. Thanks."

While Parker was occupied upstairs, Jeff brought out the six-packs in a grocery bag and handed them to Philippe, who met him at the door of the green room.

"Now you guys just hang out and lay low until Parker wants to talk to you. I'll take care of this."

The teens headed for the front lawn with an old boom box they'd found in the green room, ironically blasting "Paint it Black" by the Rolling Stones, and Philippe disappeared into the back door of the kitchen. He came back out onto the porch later to find Jan and Ida talking with Kyle Dorsey at the big table. Matt was sitting on the swing.

"Philippe, I asked Mr. Dorsey not to make a big deal about this, because we don't want the bad publicity," Ida said.

"Ida, the man is doing his job. Don't tell him anything you don't want to be in the papers, or at least tell him that it's off the record."

"I'll get the whole story from the state police if I don't get it from you," Dorsey said. "I'm not going to sensationalize it, but I am interested in this lodge and its history. Jan and I have talked some about that. I think our readers would be interested in all of the recent events and if there is a connection to the past tragedy."

"Actually," Jan responded, "I was hoping you and I could work together on investigating this, before we get people all keyed up. We don't really know if there is any connection, or just our imaginations going wild. I'd like to go over the details of what we've already found."

"Okay, well, we still have an appointment for four o'clock today, right, so let's talk about this then, but I do have to report the basics here, and in tomorrow's paper."

"Can't we talk now for a while?" Jan asked.

"For a few minutes, but I have to be somewhere else soon and I came here in a hurry and didn't bring you the articles I found. Besides, when you come over to Newport, I'll buy you dinner," Kyle smiled and gave her the once over. Jan didn't notice, but Matt did. He winced, glanced her way, frowned, stood up and walked around the corner of the lodge. Jan saw his face and wanted to call after him, but she didn't.

Officer Parker did a quick search of the whole lodge and then began calling guests into the kitchen for questioning. His brusque attitude caused many of them to be anxious, and Ida tried to calm them down.

"Everyone relax and I'll make some lunch," she said. "Jan, would you help me get everyone to relax?"

"Sure," she said. Dorsey followed her to the middle of the front porch, where the guests sat around the tables.

"Parker says he'll give me a press release in a while," Dorsey said. "I can't wait long though."

"I wish I knew what the story is here," Jan said. "Everyone was asleep when it happened. It must have been someone who snuck in and then left."

Miranda was questioned first. "I just don't know what to think," Miranda said to Parker. "I saw a weird man in the mirror, and there was a dead grouse getting the steps all bloody, and Jan's car was disabled. It's awful."

"Don't worry, Ma'am," Parker said to the older woman. "We'll get this figured out. Don't you worry yourself about it." He quickly realized that Miranda wasn't going to have anything significant to tell.

Philippe called over to the deli and ordered up two dozen sandwiches, since it looked like Parker would be around a while, and the guests were asked not to leave. Lunch was served on the porch, because Parker wanted everyone out of the lodge except for the one he was currently questioning. Philippe had some fans blowing on the porch, but the air grew hotter and heavier by the minute. Iced tea helped cool everyone off.

Parker questioned Annette for a half an hour, leaving her very stressed out. He then called Ledger into the kitchen.

"This is ridiculous," Ledger complained to the group, "and the last time I'm coming to this lodge for a vacation. It's been nothing but trouble." Parker asked him for details about where he had been on the days of the grouse killing and other events.

Jan sat on the porch with Dorsey, as Matt came back to sit near them. He grabbed a sandwich and sat without speaking.

Annette had returned to the porch and sat near Jan. "I feel like I'm being treated like a criminal," she sobbed. Jan tried to comfort her.

"Parker's got the wrong idea," Jan said. "It can't be any of the guests here. Everyone was sleeping and we had to wake them all up."

Dorsey looked at his watch and got up to leave. "Well, much as I hate to leave, Jan, I have a lunch meeting down in Montpelier, so I'm going to check in with Parker later. See you in a few hours." He winked at her and left, peeling out of the driveway in his pale green Porsche. Matt frowned. The teenagers watched him take off, and Stan whistled.

"Now, that's a car," he said. "I didn't know reporters made that much money."

"They don't," said Jan. "He must be independently wealthy."

"You know, Jan," Matt said to her "we don't really know if everyone was sleeping. They could have been pretending."

"But why would anyone stay in the lodge if they had turned the gas on?" she asked.

"Maybe they were going to be the hero, but you beat them to it," Matt answered. "Or maybe you are the perpetrator," he added with a slight grin.

"That's not funny!" Jan said, "That's annoying."

"Well, if I were in charge of the investigation, I'd look at you," Matt continued. "You have motivation. You wanted a chance to show what you could do. And you had opportunity. You know the lodge pretty well. And, you were the one who smelled the gas."

"Now you're really making me mad," Jan glared at him. "I supposed I wanted to fall off of the porch swing, also? And how did I start the whole thing even before I got here? You're a more likely suspect, since you were here when the lights started going on and off and the phones were ringing all hours of the night. You own a cell phone and maybe you wanted a big story from this yourself." Jan slammed her glass down on the maple table.

"Relax. I'm putting you on. You're letting all of this get to you. It's just a mystery, and you're going to solve it." Jan put her head down, and Matt reached over and took her hand. "It's okay. You're doing a good job."

"Am I? It sure doesn't feel like it. It's a good thing the state police are here."

"Oh, yeah. They did such a good job solving the murder six years ago," Matt said sarcastically.

One by one, the guests talked to Parker and returned to the group visibly shaken.

"I've never been treated like a crook before," Diana protested. "And he's even questioning my old dad who has Alzheimer's." Amos soon came out, insulted because Parker said he had no more questions for him.

"I bet I could have told him a thing or two that might have helped, and he isn't even interested. No one wants the opinion of an old man. We old folks do know a thing or two, you know. Didn't live eighty years for nothing."

Once Parker left and guests were allowed to go back into the lodge, Philippe and Ida called for a pow-wow in the great room with Matt and Jan and the three teenagers to discuss what had happened with the beer.

"Okay, okay, I admit we took the beer from the fridge and it was probably Mr. Ledger's beer," said Stan.

"Not *we*," protested Cliff, innocently. "Stan did it all by himself."

"Okay, Cliff," Jeff spoke up. "He took it, but we drank some of it, so we're just as guilty."

"Only part guilty," Cliff said sternly.

"We agreed not to tell on him and he shared it, so, yes, we are just as guilty. I'm really sorry, Mr. Renault," said Jeff.

"So now you squealed, so you are a couple of loser wusses," Stan griped at the other two. "I guess I can't trust you two at all."

"Things changed when the state police showed up," Jeff asserted. "We would have all been in very deep hot water if Mr. Renault had turned us in."

"Which I may still do," Philippe raised his voice. "Give me one good reason why I shouldn't."

Now Cliff turned white, and Jeff hung his head, while Stan crossed his arms in an "I don't care" attitude. "Go ahead. It's only a matter of time, anyway. They'll get me for something."

"What do you mean, Stan?" Ida asked.

"I'm labeled. Once you're labeled, they just wait for you to commit some crime, anything, no matter how trivial, and off you go, to the big house."

"Stan, that's a bit exaggerated, but is that what you want for your life?" Philippe asked him.

"Nope. Nothing I can do to stop it is all."

"That's bullshit," Matt said, angrily. "Look, you guys. You have a good thing going here. You got these jobs at the refuge that lots of kids your age would just about kill for. What the hell do you think you're doing, Stan, risking blowing your big chance for a couple of beers? And you, Jeff, do you want to lose your chances at a good college?"

"No, I don't," Jeff answered. "I feel like an idiot. I shouldn't have gone along with Stan."

"Yeah," Cliff joined in. "I feel like an idiot, too. Now we are going to be in big trouble, huh?"

"You should be. If my son pulls a stunt like you guys did, he'll be in big trouble with me," said Matt. "What would your parents think, if they heard about this?"

"Calm down, Matt," Philippe said, patting Matt on the shoulder. "We can work this through."

"My parents wouldn't give a crap," Stan said. "I haven't seen my dad in years and my mother's busy with her own life. She cut me loose when I went to juvenile hall."

"I don't have parents," Jeff said. "My grandma has worked hard to see me go to college. It would break her heart."

"My mother will be crying," Cliff said tearfully. "Please don't tell on us, Mr. Renault. We won't do it again, I know we won't."

"Look, guys. I'm going to think about this," Philippe said to them. "I'd like you all to go hang out in your room or down at the beach for a while, separately, and give some deep thought to what you've been doing this summer, and where you want to go from here. I want to talk to you some more later."

The teenagers left, and Philippe, Ida, Matt, and Jan went out to the porch to discuss their next move.

Soon, Ralph Ledger came out to join them. "Hey, my beer is back! Some of it, anyway. What do ya know? Maybe your perp is reformed." With that, he headed out to his truck, with a beer in hand.

Soon Diana and her dad came out to the porch. Amos sat on the swing while Diana came over to the others, carrying the guest book. "Look at this," she said. "I was going to write a note about the evacuation this morning, and look what I found."

Scrawled in the guest book, in big black letters, was, "I TOLD YOU TO LEAVE!"

Chapter 15: The Newport News

Jan decided to let Matt go along with her to Newport for her appointment with Kyle Dorsey. After all, she had told Matt that he was her partner in this investigation. She was fully aware that both of these men were attracted to her, but that was really their problem, and not hers, she figured. She wasn't really interested in anything other than a platonic relationship with either of them. At least, that's what she tried to tell herself.

The ride to Newport took a leisurely twenty-five minutes from Morgan, with spectacular views of meandering rivers and rolling hills enchanting the travelers along the way.

"What gorgeous scenery in Vermont! I can't get over how beautiful it is," said Matt.

"I really like it when we can ride with the windows open, and just feel that wonderful breeze," Jan commented. "I like it even more than air conditioning."

"This heat wave is unusual for up here, isn't it?" Matt asked. "Philippe said that it's the longest and muggiest stretch he can recall."

"Right. Well, I guess it has something to do with some hurricanes brewing down in the islands, and pushing up some tropical air.

"Or someone messed with a butterfly," Matt teased.

"Very funny," Jan laughed. "However, it is supposed to rain in a day or two, so maybe it will cool things off."

"So what do you think you'll find out from Dorsey?" asked Matt.

"I'm hoping he can look up the old stories about the six-year-old murder," Jan answered. "Basically, I just want to gather in all of the facts that I can about Mr. Baggett's murder, on the slim chance that there is some connection to what is happening now. There may not be any, though. The gravestone thing may just be a fluke."

"So what is Newport like? Is it a city?"

"I guess it's called a city because of its form of government. It's not like cities you might know, however. It has only about 5,000 people. You'll see. It's busy, but not overpowering. Here we are."

They entered Newport from Route 5, with their first view of the lake coming into their vision on the bridge to South Bay on Lake Memphremagog.

"Wow, what a spectacular lake!" Matt exclaimed. "How big is it, anyway?"

"Well," Jan answered, "I know that it's 32 miles from top to bottom, mostly in Canada, but about a fourth of it in Vermont. Some call it the gateway to the US from Canada. Newport is on the southernmost shore of the lake. Up on the north shore, the Canadian side, is the city of Magog."

"'Memphremagog' sounds like another Indian name. What does it mean, do you know."

"Yes, it means 'beautiful waters' in Abenaki. 'Magog' means 'waters' or 'lake'."

"Well, it sure is beautiful. I really love New England and its northern forests and lakes," said Matt. "It's so fresh and clean."

"You might not feel that way in the winter. The long frigid winters keep most flatlanders away."

"I think I could deal with that, as long as I could still find some wildlife."

"You'd probably like to see the South Bay Wildlife Management Area then. It's pretty impressive."

"Do we have time to do that?"

"I don't know. I guess it depends. We could always come over another day in our hiking gear. I'll give you a quick tour through town before we meet Kyle. His office is back across the bay, but we can look around here for a minute. I love this kind of village. I think it's typical of small towns in the USA that have a downtown area. So many places now are like sprawling shopping malls that sometimes it's hard to find out where the center of town is."

"Oh, I agree," said Matt, noting glumly that she was referring to the reporter as 'Kyle' instead of 'Mr. Dorsey'. "People now hang out more in the center of the mall than on the town green."

"Some people are actually considering building a big Wal-Mart up here. I think it would be terrible," Jan said, driving down the main street. "Look at these quaint shops: Pick and Shovel Hardware, Needleman's, Simon the Tanner, Montgomery's Kitchen and Café, First Base Collectibles, Alexandra's Kitchenware, Bumwraps, Landing Bridal, Mountain Country Soaps, Urban Access. Wow. There are so many great stores here. I should have allowed more time for shopping."

"Look at that!" Matt pointed at a sign. "Sign up for a cruise on Lake Memphremagog on the Newport Bell. That might be fun. How about it?"

"Maybe next time," Jan answered, heading back over the bay and up Hill Street to the *Newport News*.

Kyle greeted them at the door of the newspaper office, giving Matt a brief glance before he complimented Jan on her upswept hairdo. "Wow, that style is great on you. It brings out those adorable freckles on the back of your neck."

"Thanks, I guess," Jan responded.

"Come on in. I've found most of what you wanted," Kyle led them through the large outer room, where a half dozen people worked in their cubicles, and to an office in the back, next to that of the editor, Pete Lamson. "This is going to be my new office, since I'm now the assistant editor."

"Really? When did that happen?"

"At my lunch in Montpelier today. John Rancourt retired and I'm his replacement."

"No kidding? Congratulations," Matt offered, trying to be more than a third thumb in this encounter.

"Yes, congratulations," Jan added. "I'm impressed, but why Montpelier for the announcement?"

"Oh, it was a meeting of newspaper people from all over the state. Pete wanted to honor me with a surprise public announcement. Here, sit down, and let's have a look at this information." Jan sat down on the very expensive-looking leather sofa, as Kyle pulled out a rather large file folder. Matt quickly sat next to her, which brought a frown to Kyle's face, and an elbow jab from Jan into Matt's rib.

"I've made you printouts of all of the articles I could find about the John Baggett murder," he said. "I'm not sure you'll find anything here that adds to what you know, but at least you'll know what the reporters and police know about it. "This first article just tells about the bloody murder. Basically, it was a stabbing or cutting with some kind of a long, wide knife. This other article describes the services. The man was buried here in Vermont, which you already know. This second one also explains that the investigation was ended with no closure."

"Okay, what else?" Jan asked, her computer brain pulling up connections.

"There apparently was a will, leaving almost everything to a niece, the daughter of his sister, who also predeceased him. He apparently also left some money to a woman who was not related to him."

"Really? A woman, huh?" Jan asked. "And nothing to his son?"

"Not a dime, apparently. This article says that the niece told the investigators that Baggett and his son had not seen each other for a long time."

"Well, I wonder where the son is today?" Jan ventured.

"I have no clue, and I tried to find out," Kyle said. "I've done several people searches and FBI file searches. Nothing yet."

"Well, I do appreciate your work," Jan said, smiling at Dorsey.

"No problem, Red," he said, grinning flirtatiously. "Does anyone ever call you Red?"

"Only if they don't know about my quick temper," Jan joked. "But, I wonder if I could trouble you to look up something else?"

"And what might that be?"

"Any stories that might have been done on Rambling River Development."

"Oh, those guys. Sure. We have had stories on them. That's a resort builder specializing in remote areas of New England. I believe they have been implicated in scamming elderly farmers and grabbing up foreclosures. However, no one can really prove that they've done anything illegal, so far. Let me look them up." Kyle turned to his computer on his desk and began searching for articles, while Jan and Matt read through the file on Baggett.

Kyle's search turned up two articles. One was about Rambling River buying the Addison property with waterfront on Seymour, and the other was about the sale of the Morrison land by Holland Pond to Rambling River.

"Look at this, Matt," said Jan. "Rambling River bought the Morrison land. Didn't Ed tell us that the Morrison land was bought by Roger Orton?"

"I think you're right," Matt answered. "Do you suppose they are one and the same?"

"Oh, I'm really beginning to think so. Unless Ed made a mistake, but why would he?" Jan and Matt huddled together over the articles, and Kyle frowned and went back to his computer.

By six o'clock, Kyle announced that he probably had no more information for them at this time, and that he was hungry.

"Do you still want to go to dinner, Jan? Or do you have a date with someone else?" Jan then had to admit to herself that she had ignored Kyle's intent to be alone with her. She felt a twinge of guilt, but quickly dismissed it. "I don't owe him anything," she thought "and besides, it's all in the interest of the investigation."

I don't have a date, really," Jan answered, looking towards Matt. "But why don't the three of us go to dinner, Dutch treat?"

"Hey, why not?" Kyle agreed, thinking that he was at least going to spend more time with this gorgeous redhead, and maybe he could still catch her interest. "We'll go to the Eastside on Landing Street. It overlooks the lake and has great steaks and seafood."

"How about lobster?" Jan asked.

"Sure thing, kid," Kyle joked. "Vermont lobster right out of Memphremagog."

Jan looked at him and laughed out loud. "Okay, Kyle. I'm not really as naïve as I may look."

"Yeah, but you are a flatlander aren't you, from Connecticut?"

"Not really. I was raised in central Vermont, just a couple of hours south of here. We may not have an ocean in our state, but I do know the difference between salt and freshwater."

"Touché," Kyle said, with a grin, fully intending to win this girl over with his great sense of humor and his good sportsmanship. He gestured for Jan and Matt to precede him out the door to his car, hoping to show off his Porsche.

His hopes were short-lived however, when Jan said, "It will be simpler if Matt and I go in my Mazda and meet you at the restaurant, and then we can just head back to Morgan from there after dinner." She turned away, heading for her car and giving him no opportunity to object. Matt went along, prancing a bit like he had just won an inning.

The menu at the East Side Restaurant was tantalizing. Matt ordered a barbecued bison burger with sweet potato fries and Kyle ordered lake trout with curried rice pilaf.

"Wow, both of those sound good," Jan said, "But since they don't have lobster, I guess I'll go with the baked stuffed shrimp and rice primavera."

"How about some peppered crayfish appetizer?" Kyle suggested. "I guess that's the closest Memphremagog comes to lobster."

"Oh, I don't think so. Thanks anyway," Jan answered, and to the waitress, "I'll have a glass of white Zinfandel with that, please."

"Is Beringer okay?" the petite platinum blonde girl asked. Jan nodded approval.

"And drinks for the gentlemen?"

"What do you have on tap?" Kyle asked.

"We have Bud, Bud Light, Sam Adams, Long Trail, and Amstel."

"Okay, make it a Long Trail. This is Vermont after all."

"I'll go with that too, then," Matt added. He sat at the table next to Jan, but then wished he had chosen to sit across from her where he could look into her eyes and flirt, as he noted that Kyle was now doing.

"So, Ms. Whitlock, how is the investigation going anyway?" Kyle asked her. "Have you gotten it figured out yet, and did I add anything helpful today?"

"Oh yes, some of what you gave us is very helpful. We have quite a bit to follow up on."

"Well, good then. You'll solve your case, and I'll get a big story, and we'll all be happy. I trust you will clue me in when you get the breakthrough, won't you, Jan?" Kyle leaned towards her and said her name with softness in his voice that betrayed his interest.

Matt didn't miss it, and jumped in to answer the question and break the mood he feared was growing. "It seems only fair," he said.

"Yes, of course," Jan agreed. "You gave us good information, and I don't even know any of your competition. Is the *Newport News* the only paper up here in the Kingdom?"

"Well, we have the widest circulation. There is a small paper in St. J., but most people look to us for the really big stuff," Kyle asserted, throwing a glance at Matt.

"I guess it's a really big deal if any crime happens up here, isn't it?" Matt needled Kyle. "I mean, it can't all be cow auctions and moose-tagging."

"Oh we get plenty of international excitement. By the way, my article on the lodge's evacuation due to gas will be out in tomorrow's paper."

"I don't suppose we could get an early peek at that?" Jan asked.

"Sorry, lady, you'll have to wait."

Matt rolled his eyes. "I just don't know if I can stand it till morning."

The food was delicious, but the competitive banter between the two men became tiresome to Jan. She chose not to drag out the evening any longer than necessary.

"Well, Kyle, we really have to get back, but will you email me if you find anything else, or anything more on that escapee from Drummondville?"

"Sure, you got it, kid," Kyle got up and helped Jan with her chair.

"My goodness. Chivalry isn't completely dead, is it?" she remarked, rewarding him with a smile.

"Just hang around, and you'll see how alive it is," Kyle promised. Matt felt the jab, but quickly reminded himself that he was the one riding back to Morgan with this intriguing woman.

Kyle walked with Jan to her side of the car and reached to open the door for her, but hesitated, then spoke quietly as she came near.

"So, Jan, is there anything going on between you and Matt?" he asked.

"No, Kyle. Not that it's any of your business, but we just met at the lodge recently and he's been good enough to help me with the investigation for Ida and Philippe. I barely know him. Besides, I'm married."

"Married? I assumed you were single or divorced."

"Well, I will be divorced in the near future, but for the moment, I'm still married." Jan felt strange in voicing the words. She was feeling less and less married with every passing hour. In fact, she was beginning to enjoy the idea of dating again, and getting some male attention. "Thanks for your help, Kyle," she said to him, as she got into her car, and playfully adding, "I'm sure we'll be talking soon, and getting you your really big story."

The ride back to Morgan was uneventful, and Matt had decided it wise to play his cards close to his chest.

Determined not to sound any more like a jealous teenager than he was afraid he already had, he kept his eyes open for moose and made only small talk.

"That was a great dinner, Jan. Thanks for letting me tag along. I appreciate it."

"You're welcome. But, after all, you are helping me brainstorm this thing. I think we have some interesting new information to dig into, don't you?"

"The Orton-Rambling River thing? Oh, yeah, definitely. I'm not sure what it has to do with the shenanigans at the lodge, but it certainly hints of something strange going on up here."

"And don't forget about the will, and his leaving money to some woman," Jan said.

As they approached their end of the lake, Jan and Matt were surprised to see the lodge lit up like a huge jack-o-lantern, with every light on, including the spotlights in the outside corners. People were milling all over the lawn and the driveway.

"Something's wrong," Jan turned the car hard into the driveway, kicking up dirt. "I knew it—I knew we haven't seen the last of this crap. Oh, no!"

Ida ran over to them. "Princess is missing and Miranda is so upset. We have everyone looking."

"We'll help, Ida," Jan said, slamming the car door. She and Matt joined the searchers.

Diana and Amos were looking around the lodge porch, Ward and Avis examined the bushes between the lodge and the log cabin. Philippe searched the flower beds and the lawn. Miranda stood on the front step crying and calling, "Here, Princess kitty, here, kitty."

Annette was visiting friends in Troy and Ledger and the teenagers had not been seen since morning.

From somewhere nearby, Seymour howled, an eerie wail that made them all pause in the search. Again he howled and before they could find him, he ran to the front of the lodge and grabbed Philippe by his pants cuff, pulling him towards the wooded area on the other side of Holland Pond Road, with Ida and the others right behind him. Miranda stayed behind, a look of fear on her face.

"Oh, Lord," Philippe said with a grimace, as he looked down to where Seymour was pointing in the underbrush. "Someone give me a towel or a shirt." Matt took off his plaid button-down and gave the tee shirt underneath to Philippe. Soon Philippe came up from the underbrush with a wrapped bundle in his arms and walked wearily over to Miranda.

"I'm so sorry, Miranda. Princess has met with a very sad fate."

"Oh, my kitty. My Princess." Miranda took the shirt from Philippe and pulled back the edge to see the face of her little friend, stiff and bloodied. "Oh, my Princess. Oh, my Princess," she said, beginning to tremble. Ida wrapped her arm around her and led her back to the lodge. Silently, the rest followed. Jan's stomach turned and she knew it wasn't the shrimp dinner.

After yet another call to Sergeant Parker, Ida called Miranda's cousin, Ed Pease, who came down to get her.

"You'll come stay with me for a while, honey," Ed told her, giving her a hug.

"By the way, Jan," Ed said. "Joe was by today and said to tell you that he got your note and that you must think with compassion, whatever that means. He didn't explain." Then, leaving the cat to be examined by the police, Ed took the weeping Miranda up to his farm.

Philippe turned off the outdoor spotlights just as the three teenagers arrived back at the lodge in Ledger's truck.

"We missed our ride again," Cliff explained. "And along came Mr. Ledger to save us like he did before."

"Well, you're lucky, I guess. Remember, you can call here for a ride if you need one."

"Thanks, Mr. Renault," Stan said.

"Philippe!" Ida called from the kitchen. "Sergeant Parker is on the phone. He says he's not coming over for a dead cat." Philippe went in to talk to Parker.

"Dead cat!" gasped Cliff. "Not Lola?"

Ida explained the evening's sad events and Cliff and Jeff expressed their sympathies. Stan shrugged.

"Just a damn cat," said Ledger, disappearing up to his room. The teens went off to the shed and Jan sat down on the porch swing. Matt joined her.

"Jan, do you think cats go to Heaven?" he asked her.

"Well, if Jesus can have sheep, why not cats?" she answered. "Poor Miranda. That cat was her baby. I know one thing for sure. We have some work to do tomorrow." Jan looked at Matt. "And you can put your shirt back on now."

"I feel much cooler this way," he said. "How shall we start tomorrow?"

"I want to question Mr. Ledger, and then I want to make some calls and find out more about Orton."

"Why Ledger?"

"As I said. I just don't like him."

"Is that your intuition, or is it being judgmental?" Matt asked. Jan was a bit stung by the question.

"Are you saying I'm not being fair—that I'm being influenced by my own prejudices?"

"No. Just trying to figure you out."

"Well, then, I just have a deep feeling about him. I think it needs exploring. But it's probably just that I don't like him. He's probably just a mean old guy."

"Okay, whatever you say, boss." Matt reached out to take her hand. "I think you've had a rough day. How about we just relax and watch the stars over the lake and listen for the loons?"

"Only for a few minutes," she said, withdrawing her hand. They sat together in the stillness for a short while, looking out over the lake, disturbed only by Annette returning from Troy. They decided to let someone else tell her about the evening's events.

After another brief moment, Jan spoke. "I think I'll turn in early. Matt, Joseph said that I need to think with compassion. Do you think he means that I'm not compassionate?"

"Not at all, Jan," he said, gently touching her arm. "I think he meant to use that quality which is within you."

"I think you're being kind."

"Not at all. That's what I think."

Jan headed upstairs, turned back briefly and said, "Good night, Matt."

"Sweet dreams, kid," he answered.

Chapter 16: Relaxations and Revelations

When Jan went downstairs at dawn on Saturday, Philippe and Ida were in the kitchen drinking coffee and talking about closing the lodge.

"You can't mean that!" Jan interrupted after hearing a piece of their conversation. "You can't close the lodge. You love it, and so many people love coming here."

"We don't want to, Jan," said Philippe, handing her the morning newspaper. "but Ida is really afraid that someone could get hurt. So far it has only been animals, but a person could be next. Here, check out Dorsey's article."

Ida looked down at her hands. "This is not going to be good for business."

Jan skimmed the article and shook her head. "This is a bit sensationalistic. Listen, just hang in there a little longer, you two," Jan pleaded. "I think we are closing in on the culprit. Between Officer Parker, Constable Fred, Matt, and me, we will get this thing figured out."

"We'll have to take it day by day, Jan," Philippe said. "Parker is not much help. He's hot and cold. And Fred is leaving it mostly up to Parker and us. We have to protect people. We will now be locking the outer doors at night, and I'm thinking of sleeping here in the lodge in the great room. I think Parker is taking us a little more seriously, so perhaps we will get his help. We do appreciate you and Matt doing all that you are."

"Hey, I love you guys," Jan said. "You've been life-saving to me, and I love this lodge and the lake. It all has to work out somehow. Just please, give it a little more time before you make a big decision like that. After all," she said, pointing to the painting over the desk, "The Good Shepherd is watching over you."

Philippe and Ida smiled at Jan and nodded. Jan took her coffee into the great room and noticed that Ralph Ledger was sitting in a dark corner. The television was on, giving the morning weather.

"Good morning, Mr. Ledger," Jan said to him. What's the forecast?" She decided to seize the opportunity to engage him in some serious conversation for a change.

"Well, chili today, hot tamale," he said with a half-grin, but a scowling voice.

"Ha. That's funny," Jan laughed. "But really. I don't think today will be chilly."

"Nope. Hot and humid. Some rain may come in by Monday, though. That tropical storm brewing east of the Keys may come charging up here. Then again, it might just go out to sea, as usual. People up here get all worked up about hurricanes. You'd almost think they wanted one. Not enough excitement, I guess."

"Well, I'd say we've had our share here at the lodge, wouldn't you?"

"Yeah. And did I hear the owners say they were thinking of closing down?"

"You may have overheard that. I'm sure they won't though. They're just nervous. We still don't know what's going on exactly, and how many of these scary events are actually tied together."

"Well, if I was them, I'd consider selling out. This old place is just too much trouble. You own a place like this and you're workin' it twenty-four/seven with never a break, and it can't make that much money with the cheap rates they charge," Ledger grumbled.

"You may be right about that, Mr. Ledger," said Jan. "But of course, they are not in it just for the money. Philippe and Ida love this old lodge, and the lake, and most of all, the guests that they meet from all over the country."

"Oh yeah, and it's international too," Ledger joked. "In fact, isn't the west wing actually in Canada?"

"Oh, you are funny today, Mr. Ledger," Jan continued, trying to build a rapport with this man. "You're not from Canada, are you? Didn't you say you were from Pennsylvania?"

"Did I?" Ledger asked. "I'm from all over. I'm cosmopolitan—a man of the world. And, you can call me Ralph if you like, Missy. After all, we're all getting to be good pals around here, aren't we, now?" Jan looked in his eyes and her stomach quivered.

"Well, sure, Ralph," she said. "I bet you have a lot of stories to tell, and I'd like to hear them. I'm going in for more coffee. Would you like some?"

"Okay. Lots of cream and three sugars," Ledger handed his cup to Jan for the refill, and Jan went in to the kitchen, thinking perhaps she really now had a chance to find out more about this character.

In the kitchen, Philippe excitedly told Jan his plan for the day. "We're trying to drum up business for a hike up Shady Brook. Anyone who wants to can go along. The green room guys are working in the refuge this morning, so they won't be able to come along, but the Loomises and Shapiros are interested. Diana said she'd have to stay here with her Dad. He's not much of a hiker these days. I'll let you invite Mr. Ledger, since you seem to be getting chummy with him," Philippe teased.

"Oh yeah, we're good buds. I will certainly ask him," Jan said as she refilled the coffee cups. "I don't understand though, Philippe. Why a hike at this crazy time?"

"Well, just to get people away from here for a little while, and see if that helps in some way. I really want to try to keep the faith that everything will be all right."

"Okay. Maybe Parker will have things all figured out before we return, ha ha." Jan went back into the great room.

"Here you go, Ralph, extra sweet."

"Thanks. Don't expect a tip, though," he said.

"Oh, don't worry. I have no such expectation. I just thought I'd like to get to know you better."

"Really? Or would you be trying to psych me out, Missy?"

"My name is Jan."

"Ha. Okay, Jan. I'll play. What do you want to know?"

"Oh, anything you want to tell me. I'm interested in people and their stories. What have you done for a living? What got you interested in hunting? That sort of thing. Married? Children? You know. All that."

"Nope. No marriage. No kids. I'd never have a kid. I'd be afraid I'd be a lousy father. I'm not made for raising kids. How about you? Kids?"

"Well, I guess that's fair. No. I'd love to have kids, though. I think I'd be a good mother. Why do you think you'd be a bad father?"

"I'm a grumpy guy. No patience with kids or cats." He studied Jan's face as he said that, but she revealed nothing. "I'm okay with dogs, but I'm just like my dad, really—lousy father material. Smacked me around whenever he felt like it."

"I'm sorry to hear that, Ralph, that you had a mean father. What about your mother?"

"Died young. Left me with a drunken, rotten s.o.b. of a father."

"Well, that doesn't mean that you have to be like him."

"Can't take the chance. I'm a mean cuss. That's why I like hunting, I suppose. Take it out on a creature that's legal to shoot."

Jan could really not believe what she was hearing from Ledger's mouth, but she decided to keep him talking for a while. "I guess it wasn't much fun growing up in Pennsylvania, was it? You seem to have a slight southern accent, which is what made me think it might not be Pennsylvania as you said before."

"Well, it was North Carolina mostly," Ledger said. "My folks moved around a lot. I guess my dad just couldn't hang onto a place, what with his drinking. Finally broke my mother's heart and killed her off. I went to live with an uncle for a while after that. What the heck do you care anyway, Missy Jan? No one gives a damn about my sorry life."

"No? Why not, Ralph?" Jan told herself that she was beginning to feel just a bit of compassion for this guy, and suddenly the message from Joseph came back to mind. "Think with compassion."

"Ralph, a group of us are going on a hike up Shady Brook for a picnic, would you like to come?"

"No thanks, and you don't have to pretend to care about me. No one ever did, and I don't need that," Ralph Ledger asserted. "And I don't care about anyone else, either. I take care of myself, and leave the rest to mind their own business." At that, he made a face at Jan and went up the back stairway to his room.

A bit taken aback, Jan went out to the kitchen to sit with her friends, have a bowl of granola, and regain her footing. "He certainly is a strange one," Jan thought, "I don't think he is really evil, though."

Ida was now pressing Philippe to follow up on the plan to do something to change the mood around the lodge, if they were going to keep it open. The Loomises had come down and were having a little breakfast, but were definitely showing signs of stress. Albert and Dora were picking on each other more than usual. Nate Jr. was whining about wanting grape Fruitios for breakfast, and the baby was fussing for something that no one could figure out.

The Shapiros soon joined the party and were snapping at each other about who was going to do the laundry later. Annette was sitting by herself out by the campfire pit smoking cigarette after cigarette. Jan watched as Ledger went out to join her. Both were chain smokers. Soon Annette got up and came back into the lodge.

"That man is so rude," she said. "I keep trying to get friendly with him, but he's nasty."

"I think we need a hike and a picnic!" Philippe announced. "Who wants to go? I'll head over to the Morgan Country Store and pick up some makings for sandwiches, some drinks and snacks and stuff. I have to go to the post office anyway. We can hike up Shady Brook to the waterfall. It's so nice and cool in there on a hot day. We can wade in the water and eat in the shade. It'll be just what we need."

"We'd love to go, but we don't hike with the baby," Nate Loomis said.

"Leave the baby with me!" Diana offered, coming in from the great room with Amos. "I have to stay here with Dad, anyway. His hips can't take a hike like that, and the baby will get his mind off Miranda and her cat."

"Well, I suppose we could, if you really don't mind," Frances Loomis said, quite cheerfully, probably thrilled at the idea of a break from the little one.

Philippe made a quick trip to the Post Office, in the back of the Morgan store, which also served as an eat-in diner, bookstore, and local gathering place. He whipped up some of his specialty grinders with pastrami and tomatoes on whole wheat baguettes, along with some peanut butter and jelly sandwiches for the kids, and loaded them into a back pack. He added some spicy tostada chips, brownies, and several cans of cold soda and iced tea, and they were ready to go.

"Who's coming with me?" Philippe asked, heading out the front door. Ida, Jan, Matt, Annette, Ward and Avis, Frances and Nate with Nate Jr., Dora, and Albert all followed after him. "Now you're all at my mercy."

"Are you sure the little ones can make it?" Frances asked.

"Oh, they'll do better than most of us. Kids are great at brook-hopping," Philippe answered.

"What about Stan, Jeff, and Cliff?" Matt asked.

"At the refuge," Jan answered. "They had to work this morning, but they'll be back later."

One mile up Holland Pond Road brought the troop to a stone wall lined with maple trees and a pathway along the other side of the wall that led into the woods and down to Shady Brook. The boulders in the deep shade of the brook were large and rough, so they were easy to hop on and off as the hikers made their way up the shaded rocky way. The brook led up to the top of Holland Pond Hill and to Toad Pond, where Ed's farm was, but along the way were small cascades and wading pools, and one special spot with a larger waterfall that Philippe had in mind for their picnic.

Matt tried hiking along the edges of the brook, but the rocks there were moss-covered and he slipped, banging his ankle on a boulder, and almost dropping his camera bag.

"I can tell you're no experienced brook climber," Jan teased, just as her arm was tangled in some raspberry bushes and she nearly fell in.

"What's that you were saying, Smarty-pants?" Matt chided as he leaped from rock to rock and took the lead up the brook. Jan stopped to wash the bloody raspberry scratches on her arm in the cool brook water and then leaped up after him, soon passing him as he tried to maneuver a tricky jump.

"You are a flatlander after all," she said, "We New Englanders grew up boulder-hopping up brooks."

Jan took the lead, followed by Philippe and then Matt, Ida, Annette, and the Shapiros, with Nate and Frances slowed down a bit by the smaller children. Nate Jr. was holding his own, however, and loving every minute of it.

The brook led them through a forest of pines and spruce, with almost budding pipsissewa growing along the ground in the pine needles, and red squirrels zipping around looking for treats. A cowbell in the distance signaled that the troop was not far from the south pasture of Ed Pease's farm and the trees beside the brook opened up onto a cow path that led up into the pasture.

In the wide pool beneath the big waterfall, the brook trout were spawning, flashing around in swirling circles of red, mimicking flames in the sunlight on the water. The group stood watching in awe, until Albert kicked off his shoes and made a sudden dash into the water and the trout vanished upstream, leaping up the waterfalls with a splash of red light.

"Oh, they're gone," Annette lamented. "I was hoping we could watch them a while."

"Sorry," Frances smiled sheepishly. "He was too fast for me."

"That's quite a sight to see," said Matt. "I even got a short video."

With the spawning trout now departed, the hikers began following the little boy's lead, shedding their shoes to wade into the cold water of the brook.

Jan sat next to Annette on a boulder, both of them with their bare feet dangling into the water. The children went swimming in their clothes, and all of the adults were wading around looking for shiny stones speckled with mica.

Nate Loomis was turning over rocks near the edges of the pool, and coming up with small salamanders to show the children.

"Here's a northern two-lined salamander," he called. "We don't have these in Kansas and I've only seen them in my science books." Nate Jr. held the tiny creature up to his face.

Jan slid off the boulder and waded over to see it. "Oh, I used to hunt for these when I was a kid. Their little faces are so cute."

"It's smiling at me!" the boy squealed.

"What a great idea you had, Philippe," Ward exclaimed. "It's so cool and pleasant here. I could just stay here the rest of the day."

"Well, there's no reason to hurry back right away," Philippe answered, skipping a flat stone across one end of the wide pool.

"Wish I'd brought my fish pole," Nate Loomis said. "Now that I know there are trout here. Maybe we can come back fishing one day."

"Or just head on up to Holland Pond and meet the trout up there!" said Philippe. "Aha. Six skips—a new record."

"So, Annette," Jan gently probed, as she sat on a cool rock next to the poet. "Tell me more about your friendship with Mr. Baggett. You said he talked to you more than to most of his other guests, and that he was sometimes mean. Was there anything unusual about him, anything that might make someone want to kill him?"

"No. No, not at all. He was a sweet man, mostly," Annette declared. "He seemed lonely a lot. Talked about his wife, and how he missed her. He said he had a lot of regrets, and that he wished he could do some things over, but I don't think he had any dark secrets. I mean, he wasn't a hit man or an ex-con or anything."

"Just a normal guy then?"

"Well, he did admit that he drank too much when he was younger, and wasn't a good father to his kid. But, hey, we all have our sins, don't we? I gathered that he had reformed, joined A.A., and made amends, or at least tried to."

Jan recorded these bits of information in her memory, since she had neglected to bring paper and pen. Something about Annette's story was nagging at her like a briar stuck in her skin.

"Time for eats!" Philippe announced, pulling the sandwiches out of the back pack and passing them around along with the chips and drinks. A hush fell over the group as they ate and relaxed in the cool shade of Shady Brook. Nothing was heard for a while but the tumbling of water down the waterfall and the occasional trill of a pine warbler. Everyone enjoyed the sandwiches, even an uninvited guest.

Young Albert screamed as a gray, black, and white bird snatched his lunch right out of his hand. "Ma!" he yelled. "That bird!"

"That's a Whiskey Jack for you," laughed Philippe. "The Gray Jay will smell people-food from miles away and sneak up on your campfire, steal your hot dogs right off the grille, and fly off without even a thank you. I never saw one steal a sandwich in the middle of the day, though."

Frances gave Albert another PB&J and then asked with a sigh, "I suppose now we have to hike back down that steep brook? I'm not sure the little ones can do it. Albert already wants to be picked up. I wonder if we could go through Ed's farm and out to the road to walk down the hill."

"You could, but it's pretty hot out there on the road, and we actually have a better plan. Ed's going to give us all a ride down the hill in his hay truck."

"A hay ride! A hay ride!" Nate Jr. and Dora jumped up and down cheering.

"Let's head on over to the farm, then. It sounds like we're ready to go back to the lodge," Ida said. She had been very quiet for most of the hike, and now seemed glad to have it over.

The gang from the Seymour Lake Lodge trudged up through the pasture, avoiding a herd of curious cud-chewing cows, and arrived at the Pease Farm, where Ed was waiting with the hay truck.

"Pile on!" he called out. "I'll drop you all off on my way down to Evansville!" The weary hikers complied and crowded together on top of a layer of hay.

"Oh, I'm going to itch like crazy," Annette whined.

"Feel free to walk if you'd ruther!" Ed told her.

"Oh, that's okay. It won't last," Annette admitted.

Back at the lodge, some guests decided to take naps inside with fans blowing, while others headed out to the beach. After a cool swim, Jan lay on the warm dock, chatting with Matt who was half in the water, with his arms hanging on to the edge of the old gray boards, going under every so often for a cool dip as they talked. She couldn't help admiring the sharp lines of his body, probably nicely carved from working out. She tried to focus on the situation.

"I don't know, Matt. It's all kind of discouraging. I thought we would have figured this all out by now and gotten these evil doings to stop, but other than some suspicions, based perhaps on my own prejudices, we really have no answer."

"What do you mean prejudices? Maybe it's intuition. You do have good intuition. Just believe in yourself."

"I wish I could. I realize that I put myself down. I guess I've always wanted someone else to validate me," Jan confessed. "I'm still looking for my mother's approval, and wondering what I did to bring on Sid's rejection. How pathetic is that?"

"What you did was to be yourself, and that just didn't click with what he apparently wanted. It sounds like he wanted a Stepford wife, and that isn't you."

"No, I guess not."

"And," Matt went on, "I like you just the way you are." He smiled and slid back into the water again, but caught his hand on a rough board on the way down. "Ouch! I think I got a sliver. Damn. Look at that." Matt showed his hand to Jan.

"Come on," she said. "Come back to the lodge, and I'll take it out for you." Jan jumped into the water to cool off again, and then they walked quietly back to the lodge together, now and then glancing at each other and turning away.

Sitting next to Matt on the big overstuffed sofa in the great room, with the bright floor lamp shining on his hand, Jan held the needle over the sliver, about to operate.

"Here goes. Are you ready?"

"I'm ready, Jan," he said, looking into her eyes, and enjoying the closeness. Jan gently took out the sliver, which was quite deep and took several minutes. Matt never flinched.

When she finished, she held on to his hand for a moment. This never would have happened with Sid, she realized. He'd have probably gone to the emergency room rather than trust me,

She let go of Matt's hand and turned away, feeling her cheeks flush hot. "Boy have I become needy and vulnerable," she thought. "Come on, Jan, get tough."

Chapter 17: Elan

Jan sat on the porch swing thinking about Sid and agonizing over whether she should call him. Not really wanting to hear his voice, she procrastinated as much as she could. Cliff and Stan ran out of the green room, slamming the screen door as they left to go out on a boat ride. The guys had all finished their work at the refuge for the day and were looking for adventure. Jeff had declined to join them, deciding instead to work on his summer writing project.

Jan called out, "Hi guys! I hear you're going out in the rowboat."

"Yes, Ma'am," Cliff answered. "We're going to row all around the lake."

"Well, it's a pretty big lake. You might get awfully tired," Jan commented, beginning to wonder if somehow she was behaving like a ma'am.

"Is it okay with you if we do this?" Stan asked. "Or do we have to be interrogated first and get your permission?"

"Oh, no. I'm just curious about things. Sorry to intrude," Jan responded, feeling the sting of Stan's curtness.

She watched them head to the dock and take out the boat, wondering again if she should call Sid. "Should I, or shouldn't I?" she said aloud to the summer sky. The next thing she heard was a kingfisher calling, his trill sounding to her ears just like a telephone ringing.

"Okay, okay, I get it," she said, looking upwards. Not wanting to use the lodge phone, in case Sid made her cry, she walked to the far end of the beach, sat on the grassy bank and hit number one on her cell phone. "I guess he won't be number one much longer," she thought.

He answered right away. "Jan, where the hell have you been? What were you thinking taking off like that and not telling me where you were going? If you think you are going to keep your job here by behaving like that, then you better have a good explanation. I'm very close to deciding to hire Serena Sanders to take your place."

"Sid," Jan interrupted. "Would it be possible for us to say 'hello, how are you' and chat a minute before we start dividing property?" She found her voice fighting to stay calm.

"Gee, I'm sorry," he said. "I didn't know I was required to be polite to someone who just disappeared off the face of the earth and left me hanging. Well, let me start over then. Just how are you, Jan? When are you coming back here? We need to negotiate this divorce."

"Well, it sounds like you haven't changed your mind then?" Jan asked, already knowing the answer.

"I thought that was clear. You want what you want and I want what I want and I guess the twain shall never meet."

"I gave in on everything, Sid. Everything but children. I do want to have a child someday, and I guess you never do."

"Correct. Now, I need to know if you want to keep the pickup truck along with your Mazda. I have no real use for that old truck, and I know you like it. Well, do you?"

"I guess. Do we have to decide that now?"

"I see no point in dragging it out. I really need a list from you of the furniture and stuff you want from the house, so I can sell it. I already have it on the market, in fact, so you need to come and pack up your stuff."

"Sid, we own that house together. We bought it together. How can you put it on the market without my signature?"

"A technicality. I don't really want it, and you can't afford it. I have no intentions of giving it to you, either. Maloney offered to handle everything for us for a reasonable fee, and I think we should take him up on it. He's been my family lawyer for twenty years and I trust him. You'll get a good settlement and we'll both be free. Of course, I want the Rolls and the vacation cottage at Winnie. I'm giving you a quarter of everything I have, and I think that's reasonable, since I came into this marriage with most of the wealth and made most of the income. I'm sure Maloney can show you on paper what is fair. He's already drawing up an agreement for us to sign. We can keep this simple."

Jan couldn't speak.

"Well?" Sid asked.

Jan was stunned, but then felt her blood beginning to boil, as this man to whom she'd been married for six years treated her like an old business deal that needed dissolving. Something snapped inside of her, and she felt a strength that she had not felt in more than six years.

"You may have put seventy-five percent of the assets into this marriage, Sid. But I put more than fifty percent of the love into it," Jan asserted. "I kept my vows and you didn't. I am not ready to discuss negotiations right now with you or your lawyer, and I will not sign any agreement made up by your lawyer. And if you sell that house without my consent, I'll sue you for fraud. From now on you will only be talking to my lawyer about these things. I will have her call you!" Jan hung up on him, with her hands shaking.

The phone rang and she looked at the ID. It was Sid again. She did not answer. She turned off the phone and put her head down into her hands. Her brain was swimming with hurt. "How dare he put our house on the market?" she thought. "How dare he decide to give my job to Serena, of all people? I can't believe I had any thoughts of saving this marriage. This is not the man I thought I loved. How dare he expect me to use his lawyer?"

Jan now felt more angry than hurt, and realized that being mad was a better feeling. It was clear that the marriage was over. She felt free in a way and stronger than she had been in a long while.

"Am I strong enough," she asked herself. "Am I strong enough to get through this divorce and to help Ida and Philippe get rid of the evil at the lodge. I hope so. Guess I'll have to find a lawyer."

Raising her head, Jan looked out at the clear waters of Seymour Lake with Elan Hill rising up out of the water in the distance, standing proud and alone in the middle of the deep glacial lake.

"How strong it looks," she thought. Jan stopped thinking and just let the mountain speak to her. A small cloud passed over the peak of the mountain, circled the cap for a brief moment, and drifted away. "Elan," she thought. "Elan means 'vigorous spirit'. Jan felt something inside like a surge of optimism. "Look at that mountain. It shouts 'enthusiasm'!. It is a message to me. I must find this in myself. Either I have it or I don't. Shall I admit to myself that I don't? No. I do. I do have the strength. I do." Jan fell back laughing, picked up the phone and jumped up off the grass and trotted along the edge of the crescent beach, with no memory of the pain in her legs she had felt earlier. She felt a new energy within herself, and knew that she was going to win, no matter what came her way.

Jan ran back toward the section of beach across from the lodge, and without taking time to change, but tossing her cell phone and flip flops onto the beach, she let out the vital force that had been dozing inside of her and plunged into the lake in her shorts and tank top. Diving down deep into the sparkling water, she swam for several yards underneath, startling perch and sunfish in her path. Rising up and feeling the cool lake water run off of her face and shoulders, soothing her still sore sunburned skin, she dove again and again, coming up each time to look at Elan Hill, and to feel a kinship with the hill, the lake, and old Israel Seymour himself. She leaped from the water like a breaching porpoise, reaching out her arms to feel the joyful splash on her body. Over and over she dove deep and leaped up again, splashing and turning, one with the water, one with the coldness and the mountain. Never had she felt so refreshed. Eventually, spent from her reverie, Jan pulled herself up onto the dock and collapsed in complete peace.

For almost half an hour, Jan lay on the warm dock, watching the white clouds drift by and feeling like a new person. Then she heard a cry of distress—and then another. Sitting up, she turned toward the cries and saw a rowboat several yards out from the beach. It was Stan and Cliff. Cliff was screaming, and Stan was yelling at him to be quiet and to swim to shore. Jan noticed that neither boy had on life vests, and that the rowboat was rapidly sinking. She watched as Stan swam towards the dock, and Cliff was sinking down with the boat. Quickly running to the beach for the kayak, Jan hopped in the craft and paddled as fast as she could out to where the boat was. Cliff was flailing around, and sank under water as she approached. Jan dove in, grabbed Cliff by the arm and pulled him towards the kayak. With all her strength she pushed the husky young man up onto the kayak and held onto him as he coughed up water.

"Hang on, Cliff," she told him, as she paddled toward shore, where a crowd had gathered. Someone yelled that an ambulance was on the way, and a doctor staying in one of the cabins came to check Cliff over.

"What on earth happened?" Philippe shouted to Stan.

"We were doing fine out there," Stan answered, "We were on our way back, when all of a sudden a piece of board in the bottom of the boat popped loose and water rushed in."

"And you guys went out with no life preservers?"

"Well, I know how to swim, and I assumed Cliff did."

"Well, he didn't. And he almost drowned."

"Well, that ain't my fault. I ain't his keeper."

"But you swam in without trying to help him," Jan shouted.

"He'd have pulled me down with him. I ain't dying with some idiot that doesn't know how to swim."

"Well, we're lucky he's okay. He is okay, isn't he, Doc?" Philippe asked the doctor who was leaning over Cliff.

"He'll probably be fine, but since he may have gotten some water in his lungs, he needs to go get checked out at the hospital. We'll send him over to the emergency room at the Newport North Country Medical Center. Someone needs to call his family."

"I'll do that," Philippe said. "I have the contact information for his folks down in Brattleboro."

"Philippe," Ida whispered, "We need to bring up the boat and have it inspected and call Sergeant Parker. This could be another attack on us."

"We'll do that—just as soon as this boy is taken care of," Philippe answered her. "Jan, thank God you were there and knew what to do. Thanks."

"Well, sometimes we're just in the right place at the right time," she said, and then looked up to see Matt standing nearby looking at her. He looked white.

"Are you all right?" Matt asked, coming over and putting his arms around her.

"I'm fine," she said, "I'm more than fine. I had a revelation today. I feel like I just made a leap of awareness."

"Really? I'd like to hear about that. Come on, let's go to the lodge. Cliff is in good hands."

The ambulance arrived and whisked Cliff off to Newport, while Philippe contacted his parents who were now on the way to the hospital. The crowd dispersed and Constable Fred stopped in at the lodge to ask some questions.

"Philippe and Ed Pease are dragging the boat out of the lake now," Ida told Fred. "We think from the way the boys described the floor popping a leak, it had to be sabotaged."

"I don't know if we could ever prove that, but with everything else going on here, it is in the realm of possibility," Fred said. "Then again, it could have just rotted out."

"Oh Fred, you know that Philippe keeps all of our boats and vehicles in tip-top shape. There's never a hole in a boat, much less a rotted board. We'd just never let that happen."

"Well, I know you wouldn't mean to let it happen, but sometimes things get away from people, you know, repairs just being hard to keep up with and all."

"Well, I'm not going to hear that, Fred. You just do your job checking this out. Someone is out to hurt someone around here, and I've had it. So don't try to tell me it was any oversight on our part." Ida was furious.

"Okay, okay, I get it," Fred assured her. "I just have to look at every angle, that's all. Not meaning to accuse anyone of negligence."

"Well, you better not use that word around me," Ida scolded him.

"What's going on, Fred?" Philippe asked, coming up from the beach. "We got the boat up onto the beach. Ed is staying with it till you get down there to look."

"I'm coming, I'm coming. I think it's safer down there than up here," Fred said, and Philippe gave Ida a quick glance of wonderment before heading back to the beach with the constable.

Later at the campfire, guests tried to relax and sing songs, but people were stressed out about the boat incident and discussing the other scary events.

Nate Loomis came out without his family. "Frances and I decided that the kids should stay in and watch TV tonight. We are even wondering if it's time for us to leave."

"No one could blame you if you did," Philippe sympathized. Then he told the guests that the constable believed the boat floor had been cut from underneath, maybe with an ax. "Just far enough through that when a body put their foot down hard enough it would give out and sink the boat. Definitely foul play."

"What kind of a cad would do that?" asked Ward Shapiro, putting a stick with a frayed end into the fire to make a small torch. "They must have known that it could have been anyone who would take the boat out. Even a kid who couldn't swim."

"They didn't care, obviously," Avis declared. "They didn't care who got hurt, on the boat, or the swing, or with the gas. This person is evil. Someone is going to get hurt."

"Well, Cliff is in the hospital. Is that 'hurt' enough yet?" Ward asked.

"Why are you asking me?" Avis asked, defensively. "And stop waving that torch around."

"I'm just asking," scowled Ward. "And I'll play with fire if I want to. Are you thinking you want to leave, yet?"

"No, not me. It's all kind of interesting. Like we're in some kind of a horror movie. You're the one who wants out," Avis said. Jan looked at her quizzically.

"Well, I think it's someone who is pretty sick," Matt said.

"Sick? He's damned evil," Annette retorted. "Only an evil person would do this stuff."

"I guess I don't think of people in terms of good and evil. I think that evil things are caused by sickness. Whoever is doing this needs to be in a mental hospital," Matt added.

"Well, you are much kinder than I am," Diana declared. "I'd like to hang this guy up by his toenails. My dad is so scared one minute that he doesn't want to leave the room. Just sits and looks at magazines. Then the next thing you know, he wants to find the guy and beat him up. We might as well leave, too."

"So, who was the last one to use the rowboat before the guys did?" Annette asked. "I think we need to find out when this happened."

"Good idea, Annette," Ed Pease nodded. "Who has used the boat?"

"Well, Avis and I used it on Thursday evening," Ward answered. "It was fine. No water came in. We went all around the lake. I have the sore arms to prove it."

"Yeah, and he has big clunky feet, so if it had been cut by then, it would have gone through for sure," Avis added.

"Thanks, dear," said Ward with a smirk.

"Anyone since then?" Ida asked. No one answered. "Okay. So, someone did it between Thursday night and when the boys took it out on Saturday. That doesn't give us much information."

Jan was sitting next to Ralph Ledger, away from the hot fire. She decided to throw some cards on the table.

"So where were you on Friday, Ralph?" she asked.

"Out in the woods, where else?" he answered with a laugh. "Looking for those moose of yours to shoot."

"And Saturday, when we went hiking?"

"Off in my truck. You saw me leave, Missy. I distinctly remember you giving me a big wave off. You suspecting me of messing up the boat? I would have done a more clever job than that."

"Well, that's good to know. What would you have done?"

He laughed. "I'm not sure, but I'd have made sure they were out farther."

"I don't think that's funny," Jan growled. "And, yes, I do have you on the list of possible suspects, if you want to know. We never know where you are."

"I don't have to report my comings and goings to anyone, now, do I? Course if you want to ride around with me and show me some moose hangouts...."

"No thanks. I think I'd rather not know where you've been," Jan declared, feeling frustrated. She got up and walked to the other side of the fire next to Matt.

"Heck, I'm turning in early," Ralph declared.

Ward and Avis continued bickering, Philippe asked everyone to relax and just enjoy the fire and listen for loons. When no loons were heard in five minutes, Ed began to blow softly on the harmonica—songs that made everyone a bit melancholy.

"You all right, Jan?" Matt asked, sitting next to her and briefly rubbing her back.

"I'm fine. I'm fine. Just irritated. I'm not sure I can agree with you, Matt, that there isn't evil here. I do hope the Good Shepherd is watching over us, if there is. I admire that you think well of humankind but I think this perpetrator is too clever to be a mental case."

"So, you think that a mental case can't be intelligent as well as sinister?"

"I don't know. I need some more spiritual input. Joseph Rainwater, where are you? I need you."

"I can't tell if you're becoming an Abenaki or if you're still a Christian, Jan," Matt teased her.

"I'm not so sure there is a big difference, Matt. Perhaps we use different words for the same forces in the world. I just know we need help with this situation. I plan to say my prayers before bed tonight."

"Do you need any help with that?" Matt teased.

"Ha. I think I can manage."

Suddenly a plaintive howl tore through the night air with the repeated "yeep, yeep, yeep" of an animal in pain. Then, Seymour came out of the shadows, running towards the campfire and almost into Philippe's lap.

"Porky got him," Philippe moaned. "Poor dog. Get the pliers, please, Ida." Ida got the needle-nosed pliers from the lodge and Philippe had Ed and Matt help him hold on to the wounded dog while he pulled out the quills. Seymour whined but seemed to know he was being helped, and didn't try to pull away.

"He's full of quills," Jan said sympathetically, while watching the procedure.

"Remember to pull them straight out," Ed said.

"Oh, yeah, I know," Philippe said, pulling on the quills. "This isn't the first time one of my dogs has played pincushion."

"Why straight out?" Jan asked, wincing as Seymour was whining and howling in pain.

Ed explained, "When the dog goes after a porcupine, soon as he touches him, the quills spring out into the victim and the quill absorbs moisture and swells up. It's like a sponge inside the quill. The hook pops out and gets stuck. It has to be pulled out right away, before it's hooked in. That's eight. Man, he's loaded with them."

Ida tried to soothe the dog, and Nate, Ward, and Avis decided to call it a night. They couldn't bear to watch any more. The poor dog squealed in misery.

"It's how the porcupine protects himself from enemies," Jan mused. "No animal could get past those quills, I bet."

"Except the fisher cat," said Ed. "The fisher cat knows how to get to the porky's belly and tear it right open."

"Wow. I'm learning things about the north woods I didn't even want to know," Jan said. "Nature is cruel."

"Yep," said Ed. "That's twenty-five quills. He must have a hundred or more. We need another plucker to get them all out faster."

Ida found another needle-nose and set to work, hoping they'd get all the quills out and that there would be no infection.

Chapter 18: Cloud Patterns and Candle Flames

Jan arrived early at the Morgan United Church on Meade Hill on Sunday morning, hoping to speak to the pastor and perhaps arrange to meet with him later to ask a few questions about the Baggett funeral. The white-haired, jovial Pastor Livingston welcomed the visitor to his church, agreeing to talk after the service. Jan had heard from Ida about his wonderful sense of humor and was impressed with his warm greeting and his friendly smile.

"I'm not sure that I remember very much about a funeral that took place six years ago, but I will give it a try, my dear," the pastor promised. "Just give me a half hour to chat with people during the coffee and refreshments and then we'll talk."

Jan was pleased that she had thought about checking in with him on Baggett, as well as being happy that she had made it to church and was not lost in a wildlife refuge as she was last Sunday. Taking her seat in a pew halfway back on the right side of the church, she looked over towards the left and, with a jolt, saw Joseph Rainwater sitting there. He smiled in her direction and nodded with an uncanny look of recognition, as if he had known that he would see her. Jan did not know how to react. "These shaman are interesting people," she thought.

The service began with the singing of "When Like the Woman at the Well".

Pastor Livingston put the congregation in a relaxed state of mind with a subtle joke.

"A parishioner asked his pastor, 'How can I get to be more compassionate?' 'You get to be more compassionate the same way you get to Carnegie Hall,' the pastor answered. 'Practice!'" A few chuckles drifted through the congregation.

"Well, I guess I'll never make Carnegie Hall," said Livingston.

After a couple of readings from the good book, the Pastor began his sermon on compassion. Jan gave Joseph a questioning look, which made him choke back a laugh.

"This church apparently is used to laughter," Jan thought.

Pastor Livingston spoke eloquently about forgiving those who have done wrong to us, understanding their handicaps and damaged hearts, and also helping them to heal. He advocated rehabilitation programs over filling our prisons to overflowing, allowing those who have done damage to property to make restitution instead of receiving punishment, and ardently preached against all kinds of cruel and unusual punishment, including the use of torture by governments. Jan was impressed, feeling a definite connection to the spirit of this church.

Afterwards, she had a cup of coffee and introduced herself to some of the congregation while she waited to catch both the pastor and the shaman. Because she didn't want him to escape from her again, she decided to corner Joseph Rainwater first. She stopped him just as he was slipping out the back door.

"Mr. Rainwater, I get the message about compassion, but I don't know how it applies to the situation at the lodge. And what are you doing in a Christian church? I thought you practiced the Abenaki beliefs."

"Jesus was a lover of the world, as you and I are," Joseph answered. "He is part of the Great Mystery, really. There is no separation between the Christian God and the Great Mystery, for surely God is in everything—every cloud, every tree, every spruce grouse." He continued walking as he spoke to her. "We are on a search for the truth, so we must be open-minded and understand that we are all one. That is why compassion is so important."

"I think I am compassionate. But who is it that you want me to be compassionate to?" Jan asked.

"Anyone you do not feel compassion for," the shaman answered. "But I want to warn you, Jan. Be careful. You are concerned about the Rambling River Company wanting to buy land around Seymour Lake, but that is not the source of the evil. Evil really does not exist in itself. Evil comes about through those who are hurt and unable to do good—unable to love. You must have your eyes open. The answer continues to escape you, like the flame of the will-o'-the-wisp. Look there." Joseph pointed up at the clouds gathering overhead.

"They look like flames," Jan said, looking up. "Like a row of candle flames." When she looked back, Joseph was disappearing into the woods, and although she thought of running after him, she remembered her appointment with Livingston and turned back to the church.

Pastor Livingston did remember the funeral of John Baggett after he had thought for a moment. "Of course. How could I forget? He was the poor fellow who was murdered at the lodge on Seymour Lake. That was a tough one. There were no family members to speak about him. He had a few relatives in Maryland somewhere, but none of them came. His lawyer had to do the eulogy, as I recall, and he didn't have much to say. Plenty of townspeople came, perhaps out of curiosity, and a few lodge guests, including one blonde woman who couldn't stop crying, but then, no one seemed to have anything bad to say about the guy."

"Was he a member of your church?" Jan asked.

"No. I didn't know him really. I had spoken to him at the lodge once or twice when visiting out of town relatives and clergy who stayed there. But, no, he never went to church—well, not here, at least."

"But you had his funeral here."

"Yes, that was arranged by his lawyer, Jake Hawkins, from over in Island Pond."

"What kind of a person is Jake Hawkins?" Jan inquired.

"Well, now, is this part of the official investigation?" Livingston asked, smiling.

"It's part of an investigation, yes," Jan answered. "Not directly about the murder, but perhaps related."

"Well, Jake's an okay guy from what I know. A straight shooter. No funny business. We've used him for some church legal papers now and then. I know of no problem with him. You don't think he murdered his client, do you?"

"Oh, no. I'm just looking at every angle I can find." Jan asked a few more insignificant questions and then bade goodbye to the pastor, complimenting him on his sermon and promising to come back soon.

"Well, you can thank your friend Rainwater for the idea for that one," Livingston said. "We've been pow-wowing all week about the benefits of compassion."

"I knew it," Jan said. "He seems to have influence on quite a few people around here."

The pastor nodded. "Yes, we're old friends, and he is full of spiritual ideas. We sit and talk about religion for hours, but I can't seem to convert him. I often borrow his ideas, though. I put a Christian slant on them, of course."

Jan smiled and headed back to the lodge.

The day was growing more cloudy and humid by the minute. The sun escaping through breaks in the clouds only seemed to increase the hot-tub feeling of the summer air. At the lodge, guests were trying to keep cool with fans and frequent trips to the lake for refreshing dips. People were on edge, snapping at each other. The Loomis kids were fighting over nothing. Nate Jr. chased Dora back and forth through the dining room, and around and around the great room. Dora chased Albert and Albert teased Celeste. All of them were screaming as if they were being attacked by demons.

Even the dogs and Lola were irritable. Rosebud kept lunging at Seymour and nipping at his feet as he tried to rest. When he got up to move to another spot on the lawn, the cocker spaniel would follow him and nip some more. Lola joined in the fun by leaping at Rosebud, hissing and scratching, as if she wanted to protect her buddy, Seymour.

Ward and Avis sat in the dining room, complaining about their deli sandwiches being stolen again from the refrigerator.

"And the last piece of blueberry pie I had in there, too," Avis whined.

"Wait a minute," Philippe requested. "Has anyone else discovered things missing? I thought our perp was done with the tame stuff."

"Right," Jan agreed, as she entered from the kitchen with a cup of herbal tea. "We have a lot more to worry about than missing food."

"Well, I had some Stewart's cream soda in the fridge, and that's gone," Frances answered. "I just didn't mention it, because it's almost not worth talking about, when you have more serious stuff going on, like murdered cats."

"We don't know what did that," Ida spoke up. "It could have been that Princess wandered off and met up with a fox. There are plenty of them around."

"My bones are killing me," Amos yelled from the great room. "There must be a storm coming. These old bones don't lie."

"Yes, Dad," Diana said to him. "There is a storm predicted. I'll go up and get you some of your arthritis pain meds."

"Let's go to lunch in Island Pond. Jennifer's will do," Avis said to Ward, more as a question than a statement.

"Sure, that would be better than just sitting around here waiting for the pictures to fall off the walls. Hey, look at that," Ward jumped up, pointing at the kitchen doorway. There was a bright blue spot where the cleaver had been hung on the now- faded wallpaper. "The cleaver's missing. Someone stole the meat cleaver."

Philippe and Ida looked up in shock.

Avis began to cry. "Oh no. Now someone has a weapon to kill us with." She put her hands over her face and shook with fear. "Now I am starting to get frightened."

"Now, Avis. Don't jump to any conclusions," Ida warned. "Nobody's going to be killed. Maybe someone just wanted to steal an antique. It happens now and then." But turning to Jan she said, "I actually could believe that, if it weren't for all of the other stuff going on. This scares me."

"If they wanted an antique, why not an old doll, or some depression glass? Why a meat cleaver?" Ward protested. "Come on, Avis, we'll go out to lunch and talk about this. Maybe it's time to leave."

Just as they were heading out the door, Annette came running out of her room screaming. "Blood! Blood! There's blood on my floor!"

"Blood? How can there be blood?" Jan asked. She and Matt, Philippe, and Ida ran into room nine. Frances and Nate grabbed their kids and went upstairs. Diana took Amos by the hand and said, "Come on, Dad, we're going for a ride!"

Philippe studied the small puddle of red liquid in the middle of the hardwood floor in the very spot where the body of Mr. Baggett had been found. "I'm not sure that's really blood. We'd better call Officer Parker." He went to the desk and dialed the state police.

"It sure smells like blood," Matt said, squatting close to the red spot. "This is another indication that there is some connection between Baggett's murder and what is happening now." Jan agreed. Ida nodded, and went to call the state police.

"Now let's not panic," Philippe pleaded. "And don't anyone touch that stuff until Parker gets here. He says he'll be right over, and for no one to leave." Diana rolled her eyes and led Amos outside to the porch.

"Oh, I can't take it. I need to get out of this room," said Annette, her voice hoarse.

"You can have room eight if you want it, now that Miranda's gone," said Ida. "And room ten is available upstairs. That is, if you want to stay at all."

"I do want to stay. I'm not letting this ghost scare me off. I'm going to stick it out until we find out what's going on. I'm staying in room nine. I may be terrified, but I'm also curious."

Ida and Jan went into the kitchen and put on a pot of coffee. "I think it's going to be a long day," said Ida. She blotted her forehead with a dish towel.

"Well, I'm going to take a nap, cause it was a long night," Ralph snapped. "What with that dog howling and babies crying."

When Parker arrived, all of the guests were anxiously waiting. Even Jeff and Stan, who were playing ping-pong in the great room, were now very curious about the blood spot, and happy to hang around for the investigation. Cliff had spent the night at the hospital and had just been dropped back at the lodge by his parents. He was now resting on the sofa in the great room watching the ping-pong game. The Loomis family was up in their room, reading stories to the children and eating peanut butter and jelly sandwiches. Ward and Avis were snacking on some leftover salads, Diana and Amos were relaxing in the porch rockers, and Ralph Ledger was still napping. The lodge was in a quiet state of expectancy.

Parker was accompanied by a forensics specialist who took pictures of the spot, gathered up the red liquid and then took more pictures. He and Parker talked secretively for a while, and then Parker said to the guests who had now gathered in the dining room, "It's not blood. It's fake. I have to tell you," he said, looking towards the three young men, "This is the kind of practical joke that can get someone thrown in jail. It's not funny."

"Hey, man," Stan objected. "It wasn't us. Everyone blames the teenagers. That ain't fair."

"I didn't do nothin'," Cliff said, looking fearful.

"Me, either," Jeff added. "I can understand why you'd think that, but none of us would do that. People are too scared. After that boat incident, we're all nervous."

"Well, someone did it," Parker snarled. "And, I can tell you true, I will find them out. And when I do, they will be damn sorry."

"So," Jan jumped in. "It sounds like you still think that all of the events here are just practical jokes or coincidences."

"Or some sicko's idea of fun. I don't think cat-killing is a joke, but that, of course, could have been a fox. I'm not even going to question you people any further. Whoever did this needs to fess up. One more mess like this, and I'm calling in the FBI. That will make it a federal offense and you'll go up the river." Parker motioned to his forensics guy and they were out the door.

"Is he serious?" Jeff asked. "A federal offense?"

"Oh, that's crap," Matt snorted. "A scare tactic. The FBI would laugh him right out of town. They wouldn't come here for a murder unless it crossed state lines or smelled of terrorism. He can't be bothered to put all the information together and just wants to believe it is one of us here at the lodge. I think we'll have to continue to investigate this ourselves."

"Can I talk to you for a minute?" Jan asked, beckoning Matt to the porch.

"Yes, you may, my lady," Matt answered, following her outside.

"Matt, let's quietly try to get a look at everyone's hands," Jan said.

"Let me guess. To try to see if anyone has traces of fake red blood on them?"

"Right," Jan answered.

"Okay, but it's been over an hour, don't you think they would have washed up?"

"Even if they think they washed it off, there might be some. Let's just try to get a quick look."

"Okay, I'll take the ladies, and you take the guys," Matt grinned. "I suppose it's worth a try."

Jan looked at Ralph's hands by bringing him a cup of coffee, Ward's by offering him a maple candy, Nate's by bringing him some more books for the children and handing them to him. The three teens she checked by handing them sodas. Then she stopped, deciding that it couldn't be Amos or Philippe.

Matt managed to look at Annette's hands by asking her to look at a poem he wrote quickly on a scrap of paper, Diana's by remarking on how her hands were definitely artist's hands and taking them one at a time to examine. Avis was more difficult, but he accomplished the task. He didn't pursue Frances.

"Well," Jan said. "Not a trace of red. I'm surer than ever that the perpetrator is not someone from the lodge. It has to be someone sneaking in."

"Oh, well," Matt said. "It was worth a shot. Kind of far-fetched, but I guess it's good to try anything. Sometime soon we will get a real clue. This guy will slip up and we'll figure it out."

"Matt, I'm exhausted. Would you excuse me? I want to take a nap and maybe sleep on this."

"Okay. But, how about I knock on your door in an hour or so and you let me take you to dinner over at that Cow Palace? I hear it's really good."

"Well, all right. Maybe we can go over some more details and get some insight after we take a breather."

Jan rested her head and soon was deep in a dream in which she found herself trapped in the middle of a giant campfire. Flames danced all around her, and Indian figures, all resembling Joseph Rainwater, danced around the flames. She could not get through the wall of fire to Joseph, and the flames came closer and closer, reaching out for her like fiery fingers, caressing her arms and legs. She woke up in a sweat. "Won't this heat wave ever break?" she asked out loud. After a quick shower, she rummaged through her suitcase for something nice to wear, and found a red rayon tank top that she had forgotten about. Her black skirt and some silver dangle earrings and matching necklace made the outfit suitable for a dinner date.

"Not bad," she said to herself, looking in the mirror. "Of course you are still married, and this is just a meeting to discuss our investigation. Oh, right, Jan, who are you kidding? Damn, I guess I really am confused."

No moose jumped out on the way to dinner, but the full moon gleaming through the gathering clouds cast El Greco shadows on the landscape, and Jan was fascinated with the effect. "Wow, Matt, do you get an eerie feeling from this—as if it were Halloween instead of early June?"

"I do feel it," he answered. "It reminds me of History of Art 101. It's like someone has been real busy changing the scenery all around us."

"Perhaps someone has," Jan agreed.

As Matt parked the Bronco in the restaurant parking lot, the moonlight seemed to flicker and dance on the herd of elk behind the fence at the adjoining elk farm.

"Wow, look at those beautiful animals," Matt exclaimed, hopping out and going over to the fence to take some pictures. "I've seen several elk in the wild, but this is really different. Look, they come right up to the wire."

Jan joined him and admired the beautiful red hides of the elk. "Look at the babies. They are so cute. I hope we aren't going to eat any of them."

"Not the babies, but you have to try some elk, for sure," Matt insisted, taking Jan by the arm and leading her through the antler archway into the restaurant.

"Wow, there must be a thousand antlers in this arch!" Jan commented. "I wonder if they keep track."

The pair was given a cozy table in the corner, with an oil lamp centerpiece. "You look beautiful in that red top," Matt ventured.

"Thanks, but we're here to discuss business, remember?" Jan asked, with a smidgeon of guilt.

"Was that the deal?" Matt teased. "Whatever you say, lady. I'm going to have an elk steak and the salad bar. How about you?"

"I guess the same. Everyone raves about the salad bar here, and the elk and buffalo meat. I've never had either."

"Oh, well you are in for a treat. Elk is very lean, and has a unique flavor." Matt gave the waitress their order, and also asked for a nice bottle of red wine to complement the elk.

"Here's to the beautiful and delicious elk," Matt toasted, holding up the wine glass, which sparkled in the lamp light. Jan noted the twinkle in his dark eyes, and felt like she was going to be dizzy.

"How about a little horseradish sauce on that steak?" Matt suggested.

"What? I don't know. I've never tried it," Jan responded.

"Are you kidding me? I figured you for the type who liked a little fire," Matt appeared surprised.

"Okay, I'll try just a dab," Jan said, smiling.

"You mean a dollop," Matt corrected.

"No, I mean a dab. A dollop is for sour cream."

"Oh." Matt laughed out loud. "Excuse me. A dab it is, then."

"I hate to think of those beautiful elk being killed."

"It's no different than killing a cow."

"I know. That's what Mr. Ledger says. I guess I have to start forgiving the moose hunters."

"Yes," said Matt. "Apparently the hunters are doing the herd a favor, keeping the numbers down. It also keeps the parasites down."

"Oh yes. Moose ticks and some kind of brain parasites."

"Yes. Ever seen that video of the moose with the tics?"

"No, and I don't think I want to," Jan said, putting her hand up. "Stop right there. Not while I'm eating."

Matt chuckled.

After dinner, Matt enticed Jan to drive out to the bog to look for moose. "Maybe we could find a will-o'-the-wisp. I want to see if they really exist," Matt said.

"Me, too," Jan added. "I have read about them in literature, but never seen one. Joseph says they exist here in the bog. And you know what else? The yellow flower he gave me, telling me it was my totem flower or something? That's called a swamp candle."

"No way."

"Yes way. The woman at the refuge identified it for me. "

"Maybe Joseph has a real sense of humor," Matt said.

"Well, he does, but this is not all a joke. It's spirituality. The Abenaki believe that all of nature speaks to us."

Matt parked near the bog, and they got out to walk in the moonlight. "Did you know that the full moon in June is called the strawberry moon?" Matt asked.

"That's pretty," Jan answered. "I wonder why? Maybe because the wild strawberries are out now? I guess that would make sense."

The pine boardwalk to the bog shone almost white in the moonlight, as Jan and Matt strolled out into the swamp. When they reached the bench at the viewing area, they sat quietly and looked out over the swamp.

A very slight breeze gently brushed their faces, but there was no sound. The bog remained quiet.

"I don't see any wisps," Jan said after a while.

"Well, you probably have to sit here for hours, and kind of make them think you're not here. I bet those wisps run off at the slightest sound. What are they supposed to look like?"

"Candle flames." Jan pulled a picture out of her pocket. "Here, this is a picture I found in the great room. Candle flames in the bog. This must be what they are."

"Wow. That's neat," Matt said. "What's the legend? Is it some kind of live creature?"

"It's like a spirit, I guess. Like a cross between a ghost and a fairy," Jan explained, sitting close to Matt on the bench and whispering. "At least that's what I have concluded from literature and from Joseph Rainwater. It's a flame that beckons you from the swamp, and makes you want to follow it. But if you follow it, you never catch it. You go deeper and deeper into the swamp, but the wisp retreats, eluding you, just escaping your grasp. In the legends, people get lost in the swamps and are never seen again. I suppose it's an allegory about something that keeps evading your understanding. Rainwater says I'm not seeing the whole picture yet. Something is missing, but what?"

"Maybe this," Matt said, as he leaned over and kissed her strongly on her mouth.

Jan returned the kiss, but something inside of her screamed, and she pulled back again. "No. Matt. We can't do this. It's too soon."

"I don't see why," Matt declared. "Your marriage has been over for some time. You only have to end it legally."

"That and I have to grieve it. And you have not finished grieving Julia. You know that's true, Matt. We're not ready." Jan rose and walked back to the car, with Matt following behind, rebuffed again. He glanced back only once, sensing a brief glow of light behind him.

Later, as Jan lay on her bed, listening to the lonely sound of rain falling on the tin roof, she felt grief, but she also felt hope, and allowed her dreams to come.

Chapter 19: Smoke and Rain

Monday morning it was raining like a monsoon with a mission. At six A.M. Jan lingered in bed after she was wide awake, thinking about the previous evening and her growing feelings for Matt. A tangy smell began to tickle her nose, and she wondered if Philippe had put a fire in the wood stove because of the cool rain, although the lodge was still very warm. The smell grew stronger and more pungent. When it began to burn her eyes, she leapt out of bed just as a smoke alarm sounded from downstairs, and the lodge came alive, with people running out of rooms, slamming doors and calling to each other.

Jan pulled on her blue jeans and a shirt and ran out into the hall, crashing into Avis. Black smoke began to billow up the stairway.

"Not that way!" Jan yelled. "Out through the deck!" Matt and the Shapiros ran into Jan's room and out onto the deck over the front porch. The rain pelted the guests as Jan pointed to the side of the deck where a fire escape ladder led down onto the grass. The Shapiros went down, but Matt ran back into the room.

"We have to check on the others," he shouted as he ran down the east wing hallway knocking on doors. The Loomis family, Diana and Amos, and Ralph Ledger followed him back to Jan's room and out onto the deck, as the black acrid smoke began to fill up the east wing. Frances Loomis, with baby Celeste in her arms, was crying as she hurried down the escape ladder and onto the lawn. Nate sent the other three children down before he followed after. Matt helped Amos and Diana, and then sent Ralph and Jan down the ladder, and then went last

People from the nearby cabins ran over with umbrellas to shelter the lodge guests from the heavy downpour. The owners of the Deli invited them all to come over to get dry, but they stood still, in disbelief, on the lawn looking at the lodge with the smoke billowing out of it.

Fire sirens filled the air, as fire trucks from Morgan and Island Pond came screaming up to the Lodge. An ambulance soon followed. A logger going by earlier had seen the smoke and called it in. Philippe and Ida came running over from the log cabin, and Matt pounded on the door of the green room in back of the shed, to awaken the three teenagers.

"Oh, my God, where's Annette?" Ida cried. "Has anyone seen her?" The firemen went crashing into the lodge through the front door, and Philippe ran around to the west side entrance of suite nine and banged on the window and door, to awaken Annette. When he didn't hear a response from her, he ran around to the front and alerted the firemen. They soon came out carrying a very limp Annette, and hustled her to the waiting ambulance. A few minutes later, the fire chief came out, and announced:

"The fire is out. It was contained to a wood stove and was mostly smoke, but with very toxic fumes. Someone put a bunch of wooden ducks in the stove in the living room and set it on fire. The paint and varnish made the black, acrid smoke, which is going to take a while to clear. Everyone should stay out for several hours. We have notified the Vermont State Police and they said they'd be over to question everyone."

"Oh no, not again," Diana moaned. "What will we do on a rainy day?"

The fire chief then said to Philippe, "The woman in room nine probably inhaled some nasty fumes, and we're sending her to the hospital in Newport."

"Dear God," Ida began sobbing. "Why is this happening? Is it my fault?"

"Your fault? Don't be silly, Ida," said Philippe. "If it's anyone's fault, it's mine. I said I was going to try to sleep here, but I couldn't."

"But, Philippe, I have been complaining a lot lately about all the work there is to do here. Maybe God wants us to leave."

"Do you really want to close down?"

"No, no, I don't, Philippe. I just get tired sometimes."

"Then God knows that." Philippe put his arms around her. "Hold it together, honey. We will get through this. Right now, I need you to take everyone to the log cabin and make them some breakfast." Ida was relieved to have a plan to focus on.

"You'll make sure Annette is all right?" she said, turning back to Philippe.

"Yes, Ida. The paramedics already said that she is breathing okay. They're just taking her as a precaution."

The firemen placed the big fans around the lodge to air out the place, as they had done with the gas fumes, only this time they needed more fans, and said it would take a lot longer to completely air out.

"You will also have a layer of smoke on everything. It would be best to call your insurance person and then a cleaning service," the chief said to Philippe.

"I'm on it," Philippe responded. "I'll call from the cabin."

When Philippe arrived at the cabin, Ida was serving waffles, and everyone was eating and chatting. Most of them were in their pajamas and robes but Philippe took note that Ralph and Matt were fully dressed.

"I'm so glad Seymour and Lola were here, and not at the lodge, last night," Ida remarked. "But of course, we are worried about Annette."

"I'm going to call the hospital, and then I'll call her emergency contact. I brought her file over from the lodge. She has a sister in New Hampshire who should be notified."

"I need to talk to you," Nate Loomis spoke up. "As soon as we can go back in the lodge to pack, I'm taking my family home to Kansas. We've had some fun, but it has been also scary, and this is more than we want to deal with anymore. I'm sorry, but Frances and I have talked. We have had it, and we are leaving."

"I really don't blame you at all," Philippe said, sadly. "And, I'm going to give you all of your money back. It's only fair."

"That's not necessary. I'll only accept it for the days we had left, because we really loved it here, and had a good time. And don't worry about us suing you or anything."

"Ouch. I hadn't thought of that, but I suppose someone could," Philippe said. "I'm sorry to see you go, Nate. But, I completely understand. I would too, under the circumstances. In fact, we have to consider closing down."

"Oh no, don't do that!" Avis cried. "Ward and I have been talking. We feel like we're a part of the family here, and we want to stick it out for the summer, no matter what! Right, Ward?"

"Right. We were nervous, but we've decided that we don't want to run away. We want to see this through. Whatever this is. Whatever is going on. We want to stay."

"Well, we'll see. For now, we'll have to see if the lodge is fit to stay in tonight. If not, we can put most of you up here, or pay for a hotel in Island Pond."

"I'm sure our room is okay," Jeff declared.

"That's true," said Philippe. "You didn't get the smoke over there. You guys will be okay then."

"Don't worry about me," Matt said. "I can always sleep in the Bronco."

"I won't hear of it. It's our job to make you all comfortable."

"Is it okay then if we go to work," Jeff asked, "or do we have to wait for the state police again?"

"Do you have to go to the refuge if it's pouring rain?" Philippe asked.

"Mathewson will put us to work in the center," Stan answered.

"Well, it's not like Parker's rushing over here, so I say go ahead and go to the refuge, and if he needs you, we'll send for you. All right?"

"Okay, Mr. Renault," Jeff answered. "Let's go, guys. Mathewson told us to get in early, and he'll be worried. Who wants to give us a ride?"

"That would be me," Ledger offered.

"Ralph, are you sure you're okay? Did you breathe in any black smoke?" Ida asked.

"I'm good, and I'm sure as heck not hanging around here all day." Ralph got up and headed out to his pickup. The boys hurried to the green room to get dressed, happy that they had not been in the main lodge.

"Good thing he's got a king cab," Cliff said, as they climbed in. "We'd get wet riding in the back again."

"Well, you're not supposed to be riding in the back of the pickup anyway," Ida called to him as they took off.

Jan reached Sergeant Parker on the phone in Ida's den at the cabin, and asked him why he wasn't on his way.

"I'll be there," he snapped. "Seymour is not my only problem."

"Well, this is serious, and it's been going on for weeks now. It's time you did your job and figured out who the perpetrator is here." Jan was angry and wanted Parker to take this investigation seriously.

"I'll be over. Don't worry your pretty little self, Missy. I figured you'd have it all sorted out by now. But since you don't, I'll have to come and help you. I pretty much know who it is anyway."

"You do? Who? Don't patronize me," Jan snapped. "If you know, and haven't put a stop to it, I'm going to have a thing or two to say about that."

"No one you suspect. While I'm getting ready, take a look at your boyfriend."

"What? What boyfriend?" Now Jan was furious.

"Oh, now, don't pretend. It's pretty obvious you have a thing for the photographer, and he is hiding a lot from you. I also got some inside track on him. He's not so innocent."

"You better explain what you mean," Jan demanded.

"Well, you just watch your back, and I'll be over soon. Don't let anyone leave town." He laughed a sinister laugh.

Jan could not believe her ears. "He is implying that Matt had something to do with all of this," she said to herself. "It doesn't make sense." Jan decided to run these accusations by Philippe.

By noon, the lodge was aired out, and the cleaning people had arrived to scrub down the smoke residue.

"Thank you for coming so quickly, Toby," Ida thanked Toby Barnes, the owner of the Barnes Clean It All service. "I'm afraid it's a nasty job."

"Not to worry, Mrs. Renault. We've had worse jobs. I promise you, you'll be happy." The crew of half a dozen men entered the lodge with several cleaning machines.

Meanwhile, the guests were still at the log cabin. Jan took Philippe aside and told him what Parker had said about Matt. "I just think Parker is a nasty character. He doesn't know Matt at all, and has no reason to suspect him."

"You said he told you he had some inside information?" Philippe asked.

"Yes, but what could that possibly be?"

"Who knows? But what do you think, Jan? You've been getting to know the man. Is Matt capable of something like this? I did notice that both he and Ralph were fully dressed this morning, when everyone else ran out in their night clothes."

"Oh, no. I'm sure he isn't. I've gotten to know him pretty well. Of course my track record for seeing through men isn't all that great."

"Yes, it is. You have learned a lot. I say, trust your gut. I'm going to call the hospital and check on Annette." Philippe stood up to go to the den, when he saw Kyle Dorsey dashing up the walkway in the pouring rain. "Looks like we've got company. Or you do."

Jan let Kyle in, and he reached out and hugged her as if they were old friends. "I was so worried about you. I heard a woman was taken to the hospital."

"That wasn't me. That was Annette DiPersio."

"Is she all right? Tell me everything." Kyle got out his note pad.

"Philippe is calling the hospital to find out. She may have inhaled some toxic fumes. She looked pretty listless. Someone made a fire in the woodstove, with painted wooden ducks and things, and there was varnish and paint burning... It was terrible."

Matt came in from checking on the cleaning company, and saw Jan sitting on the sofa with Dorsey. "Ah, now the big story, right, Kyle?"

"I mostly want to make sure Jan is okay, and everyone else."

"Of course," Matt snapped. "We're mostly fine. But someone could have died."

Philippe came back and announced that Annette was doing well and would be released in an hour or so. Ida sighed with relief. "Thank you, Jesus." Philippe and Ida sat down to talk with Diana, Amos and the Shapiros, while Jan, Kyle and Matt went out on the front porch of the log cabin. The rain was heavy, but coming straight down, so that the porch was reasonably dry.

"Wow, I haven't seen this kind of rain up here in a long time." Kyle declared. "The forecasters say it could last for days."

"I was getting ready to go out for an early morning moose hunt before I saw that it was raining," Matt said. "I wonder if they'd be out in the rain."

"No, they don't like the rain," Kyle proclaimed.

"I've seen them in the rain," Jan said.

"Matt, would you mind terribly if I talk to Jan alone for a few minutes?" Kyle boldly asked.

"No problem. I'll be around," Matt said as he got up and left.

"What's up, Kyle?" Jan asked.

"Well, I'm just wondering if you're thoroughly checking everyone out here at the lodge?"

"Meaning?"

"Meaning that since you are not really a trained detective, you might miss something, especially if you are a little prejudiced."

"Oh, now I get it," said Jan, irritated. "You're talking about Matt, aren't you? You said something to Parker to cast suspicion on Matt, didn't you?"

"Well, you don't really know much about him, Jan, do you?" Kyle continued.

"You're wrong. I know more about him than I do about you. He's a good person. He's not the one." Jan got up to walk away. "I can't believe that you would try to disparage him."

"Don't you even want to ask me why I would doubt him?" Kyle asked.

"No. I don't want to hear it," Jan jumped up and went inside, joining Philippe and Ida with the Shapiros and Peabodys. The deep grooves between her eyes and her tightly pressed lips gave away her annoyance. When she sat down in the dining room, she had a nagging thought that maybe she should take another look at Matt's possible involvement—just to be fair, but she quickly shook off that thought.

Kyle soon followed her in and approached Philippe. "I need to talk with you some more, Philippe, if you don't mind."

"Well, okay, but I think Parker is the one you should talk to for your story," Philippe answered him.

"I want to explore some other perspectives," Kyle insisted. Philippe shrugged his shoulders and motioned Kyle to follow him into the den of the log cabin. They chatted for a while and then Philippe came out, stomping his feet and heading for the back shed.

By late afternoon, people were going back into the lodge. Fortunately, the smoke did not get into the bedrooms, so they were spared having to wash the clothes and bedding although they would have a slight smoky smell for a while. The Loomis family packed up and everyone gathered in the dining room to say goodbye.

Ida hugged Frances, Philippe shook hands with Nate, and everyone wanted to hug and kiss the children, especially baby Celeste, who said bye-bye so sweetly.

"I'll miss you little darling," Amos told the baby girl. "I hope you don't forget old Amos."

Nate then announced, "We have a confession to make. Nate Junior has admitted to taking his sister's bathing suit and hiding it in the shed along with his boogie board. I have retrieved them both. He hid his board because some local kids made fun of him, saying that there were no waves here. He wanted to float on it and paddle around, like he does at home on the lake in Kansas, but not after they laughed. We are deeply sorry, and hope you'll all forgive us for adding to the confusion here, right, Nate?"

"Yes, sir," Nate Jr. said apologetically to the lodge guests and the Renaults. Chuckles rippled through the room.

Frances then added, "I'm going to make you a special Seymour Lodge Quilt and send it to you. I've gotten so many great ideas for nature crafts for my shop. We'll come back another year, and hopefully things will be much better."

"I assure you it won't be like this," Philippe promised.

Ida held her handkerchief over her face as the Loomis family ran through the rain to their caravan and drove away.

"I'm taking my dad upstairs for a nap," Diana announced, leading Amos by the hand to the back stairway.

Kyle Dorsey got up to go back to Newport. Jan walked him to his car, holding an umbrella over their heads, as Matt sat on the lodge porch with Ledger, watching.

"I'd love to take you to dinner again, Red. Just the two of us this time?" Kyle ventured.

"I don't think so, Kyle. I don't know where you're headed with your insinuations about Matt, or what's behind it, but you're way off base, and I'm angry about it."

"So, let's go to dinner and talk it over."

"There's just too much stress and my emotions are very erratic right now." Jan scowled, but he didn't seem deterred.

"Erratic emotions. Okay. Well, I will check back with you tomorrow on that, and maybe you'll feel better and change your mind."

Jan half smiled, but didn't answer. Kyle left, shrugging his shoulders in frustration.

After calling Officer Parker and leaving him a message insisting on being called back, Jan went to sit with Ledger in the great room.

"It's good of you to give those boys rides," she remarked.

"Hey, no problem. I was a kid once myself," Ledger growled.

"I have to confess to you that I feel bad that I have considered you a suspect in this case." Jan attempted to be conciliatory with the man.

"Oh, that's okay. I can be a bit scary. But are you saying that you now have another main suspect?"

"Yes, as a matter of fact. I think there is a lot more going on up here in the hills than we thought before."

"Can you tell me about it?"

"Not yet. But we'll all know soon. Right now I have a few more phone calls to make." Jan went into the back kitchen and sat at the desk under the Good Shepherd painting. Looking up, she said, "Give me strength."

Her first call was to Jake Hawkins, the lawyer and executor for Baggett's estate. She asked him the name of the woman included in Baggett's will. Hawkins said she could look the answer up in the town hall, as it was public information, but when she pressed him he agreed to tell her. "Let me get the file. Hang on."

Jan looked at the painting again, of the shepherd and his sheep. The face of Jesus appeared to be looking at her with compassion. "Compassion," she thought. "We all need compassion."

"Here it is. He left $20,000 to a friend, Annette DiPersio. The rest went to his niece Brianna."

"Wow, that's a surprise! Thanks, Mr. Hawkins. That information is very helpful."

"Don't tell me that after all these years, someone is going to find out who murdered the poor man?"

"Perhaps. It just might happen, Mr. Hawkins. I'll be in touch." Next, Jan dialed her friend on the *New Haven Courier*.

When Jan got through to her, Margaret had some interesting information for her. "I've been trying to call you at the lodge all morning, and I left messages on your cell earlier."

"I'm sorry about that. We've been just a bit preoccupied here."

"Well, I got some information from the *Baltimore Sun*. There was an obituary there for John Baggett of Morgan, Vermont, formerly of Baltimore. Nothing really new there, but in the same issue, there was an article about James Baggett being arrested and held in jail in Hagerstown, Maryland the same day as the funeral. Obviously that is why he could not attend."

"Hagerstown? Are you sure?"

"Positive. I have the articles in front of me. I'll email them to you."

"Okay, thanks a million, Margaret. This is significant. I'll call you in a couple of days. I did talk to Sid, and he will be hearing from my own lawyer. I'm not going to be railroaded."

"I'm glad to hear that, Jan. Now, how about calling your mother? She's frantic, and won't stop calling me. I've told her nothing except that you are alive and well."

"Okay, thanks. I'll take care of that soon." Jan hung up the phone and thought about her mother's judgmental hand waiting to come down upon her soon-to-be-divorced daughter." She dialed her sister, Eleanor, instead.

"Jan, where are you? Mother is going nuts."

"So I hear. Well, she will just have to wait. I'm okay. I'm working on an article up here in the Kingdom, and then I'm going back to Branford to deal with Sid and get a divorce lawyer. Would you please relay that information to our mother?"

"Chicken? Can't talk to her yourself? Not that I blame you. She can be difficult."

"I will deal with her at some point, but I know how she feels about divorce, and I just don't want to hear it right now. I'd appreciate it if you'd just let her know what's up and see if you can get her to chill out until I get a chance to call her."

Matt came into the room as Jan was hanging up the phone. He turned to leave, and Jan stopped him. "Matt, do you want to use this? I'm finished."

"Thanks. I thought I would call Ethan. Seeing the little Loomis boys drive off suddenly made me feel homesick for my son." Jan had noticed the lonesome look on his face.

"Could we talk later when you're finished?" Jan asked, smiling a sympathetic smile.

"Sure, any time."

Matt dialed the number for Ethan's cell phone.

Jan went out to a table in the dining room and sat down to write up some notes. She soon realized that she could hear Matt's conversation but was not motivated to get up and leave.

"Hi, buddy. How's it going?"

Matt listened, a smile flickering across his face. "I know, pal. I'm sorry. There's almost no service up here, and I've been working on an investigation. I should have called you. Are you having fun? What do you mean it's hard work? Oh, learning to tie knots and different swimming strokes can be hard, yes. Horseback riding? Wow, are you lucky. Rock climbing, too? That's fun. I climbed a big rock up here I bet you would like. You and I will have to go hiking some time. Sure, you're tired, but it's fun, right? I thought so. You're not really ready to come home then? Who's Alex? Sure, you could invite him to come and see you sometime."

Ethan went on and on, and Matt listened, mostly happy that his son was well, but the slight quaver in Matt's voice told Jan that he was feeling the distance.

Later, Matt sat on the porch swing by himself and Jan went out to talk to him. "Mind if I join you?" she asked. Matt blinked back a tear.

"Please do," Matt said, motioning to the space beside him.

"If you'd rather be alone, I can leave."

"I'd rather you join me, but only if you want to. I've felt you keeping a distance from me all day."

"I'm sorry. I guess that has been happening, but I've been busy," Jan said, sitting down next to him.

Matt looked at her quizzically. "I guess I should have expected it. I have been a little pushy with this relationship—more than you wanted, obviously. I have felt something very special here, but I understand that it is not returned."

"You're wrong about that, Matt. I have feelings for you, too, I'm just scared about acting on them. I think it's too soon."

"You said that. I get it, and you're right. It's soon. But it happens when it happens, Jan."

"And sometimes because we are vulnerable. Matt, I have something to tell you."

"Oh, boy. Do I want to hear this?"

"It's not about us. Sergeant Parker thinks you might be the perpetrator. He tried to tell me that he got some inside information on you, and that you are not what I think."

"What? That's a riot. He is about as useless as an umbrella in a tornado."

"I thought I ought to warn you, Matt. Of course I told him it was ridiculous, but he said that I might have overlooked something because I had feelings for you."

"What? Do you think for one minute that I could have done this? Killed a cat? Sunk a boat with kids in it?"

"No. Not at all." Jan looked in Matt's eyes. "Not at all. But do you have any idea what his so called 'inside information' could be?"

"No. I just think he's an idiot. What else?"

"I have to ask a question—as an investigator, and because someone else brought it up."

"So?"

"So, the other day, with the gas leak, you ran out half-dressed, but today you were fully dressed when I called you. Is there any particular reason for that?"

"Yes. I said that I was up early and planning to go out for a moose ride. I got dressed before I smelled the smoke." Matt excused himself. "I need a nap."

Jan sat a while on the porch, regretting that she had asked that question, but the rain began to slant towards the lodge, and she started to get wet and chilly. Back inside, Philippe was making a fire in the wood stove in the dining room.

Sergeant Parker pulled up in the cruiser, bringing Annette back from the hospital. Ida got her settled in her room, bringing her some tea and toast, and sitting with her for a while. Soon Annette was sleeping peacefully.

"I need to ask her some questions when she wakes up," Jan said to Sergeant Parker, and then told him about the inheritance.

"Well, that may or may not mean something," he said with a tone of dismissal.

"You're something else, Parker," Jan said angrily. "You discount a significant piece of information, yet you choose to believe some completely ridiculous allegations made by Kyle Dorsey against Matt."

"Oh, that," Parker responded. "Well, you're right. Dorsey admitted that it was only a feeling he had. Nothing substantial."

"I knew it," Jan fumed. "Why don't you do your job, Parker, and find some real answers, before someone gets seriously hurt or killed around here?"

"Oh come on, lady. I was right about the pranks. The kid admitted stealing his own boogie board."

"What? You think all of this is pranks? I can't believe you." Jan stormed up to her room, leaving Parker to talk with Philippe and Ida. She flung herself on her bed and tried to think logically through the events of the past few days. It seemed to her that she would have to rely on her own brain to sort things out, as Parker and Dorsey were not of much help, and neither was Constable Fred. The Abenaki shaman, who lived in the modern world as well as in the ancient realm of the forest, was friends with the local pastor, and was telling her to think with compassion. Her husband was divorcing her, she had growing feelings for someone else that she was not ready to have, and another man was lying to her out of jealousy.

"What is truth and reality?" Jan wondered. "What or who can I believe in?" At that moment, the picture of the Good Shepherd came into her mind. "Am I a lost sheep?" she wondered. "Is there a truth inside of me that comes from something beyond myself? From God? What else is there? Other people's opinions? I can only know what I see and hear—what I experience myself. What is in my gut. And what is it that I feel in my gut?" She let herself feel for a moment, without thinking. Then, she got up and went down the hall to knock on Matt's door.

"Door's open," his voice said. Jan went into the semi-dark room and sat down on the edge of Matt's bed. He lay there with his arms behind his head, a serious look on his face.

"I need you to know that I did not believe anything that Parker or Dorsey said," Jan began. "I've come to know you better than that. I was only informing you of what they were saying."

"Really?" Matt asked. "You had no doubts? Not even for a minute?"

"Not even for a minute. No doubts about your character at all. I mean it. My seeming suspiciousness was connected to them, not to you. I wondered right away where Parker had gotten that crazy idea, and I was right, it was from Dorsey. It was a low attempt on his part to discredit you in my eyes." Jan looked pleadingly at Matt. "He did not succeed. Please believe me. I'm sorry that I sounded as if he did."

"But you questioned me about why I was dressed."

"It was a question that would have been raised and I wanted you to have a heads up."

Matt smiled slightly and then reached out to Jan and pulled her down onto the bed with him. He rolled over on top of her and held her tightly, kissing her passionately. She slid her arms around his neck and returned the hugs and kisses. Then she pulled back.

"Wait. Stop," Jan said. Matt rolled over, exasperated.

"What's wrong, Jan? You know we have strong feelings for each other."

"Nothing is wrong, and yes, I know that. I know that surely, but I also know that it's not the right time. Forgive me. I want to be with you, but I want it to be right. I want us to wait. Can you understand?"

"Yes, Jan. I really do. I want it to be right, too. We have some other things to get out of the way, first, but I can't help wishing."

"Yes. Thank you, Matt." Jan leaned onto his chest and hugged him. "It will be hard to wait. But it will be better, believe me." They lay there, dozing together for an hour or more, until a loud crack of thunder woke them both up.

"I guess the storm is getting worse," Matt said. "And it's your fault."

"What?"

"Well, you had to mess with that little butterfly," Matt laughed. "You move a rock in California and you start a landslide in West Virginia."

"Very funny, Matt," Jan said. "Let's go check things out and find some supper."

Downstairs, guests were throwing together a meal from whatever they could find in the kitchen. No one wanted to venture out, even to the deli.

"It looks like we have some hot dogs in here, and rolls. There's probably enough for all of us," said Avis.

"And I think I saw some baked beans in the cupboard," Ward opened a row of cabinet doors and peered into each one. "Yeah, here they are. This will be great. I think I can make a fruit salad also. We have some apples here, and a pear, and a can of pineapple chunks."

Ida called over from the Log Cabin to see how they all were. "I don't want to stay on the line in a thunderstorm," she said, "but I wanted to see how you all were."

"There are just eight of us here," Jan said. "Matt and I, the Shapiros, the Peabodys, Mr. Ledger, and Annette. The boys are still at the refuge, and Matthewson called to say that he would bring them home later after he treats them to a pizza. We are going to feast on hot dogs and beans."

"All right, well, call if you need anything. Oh, and there's ice cream in the freezer that you can all have. Philippe brought it over this morning. Enjoy."

"Thanks. We will." Jan got out some plates and set two of the four-person dining-room tables. She invited Annette, Ledger and Matt to sit with her, hoping that Matt would understand her purpose.

"So how are you feeling, Annette?" Matt asked her. "I'm glad you're well enough to join us for dinner."

"Thanks. I haven't eaten all day. Even hot dogs and beans sounds like a gourmet meal. My, the storm is really persistent, isn't it?"

"Seems like room nine doesn't like you," Ralph Ledger ventured in a nasty tone. "Creepy sounds and blood and then smoke. Maybe the ghost of the lodge is after you. Maybe you did something bad to him."

Jan looked at Matt and held her breath.

"You're just a nasty person," Annette said. She took her plate to a table across the room. Jan followed, giving Matt a quick wink.

Matt apparently got the message and tried to start up a conversation with Ralph that might shed some light on his attack on Annette, while Jan offered her sympathies to the woman.

"I don't understand why he's so rude, do you?" Jan asked.

"No, and I don't want to talk about it," Annette said.

"Well, I know you've had a rough day, but I do want to ask you some questions, so we'll change the subject, okay?"

"Oh, okay," Annette answered, with a bit of anxiety. "What do you need to know now?"

"I have just one question, really," Jan said, hoping to calm her and catch her off guard.

"And what is that?"

Jan asked quietly. "I'm just wondering what your true relationship was with John Baggett, and why he left you $20,000."

Annette dropped her fork onto her plate. "I can't talk about that here," she said, raising her voice. Then she leaned towards Jan and whispered, "And how on earth did you find that out? Oh, yes, you're the investigator. You have no right to ask me my personal business."

"Annette, I'm not trying to hurt you. But it is public information, and the state police will eventually ask you, so I'm giving you a chance to think about it and talk about it with me first. You could be a suspect."

"A suspect? Are you kidding me? I was asleep when that fire started. I could have died, remember?"

"Sure. The police could think that was a diversion. They could also wonder why you didn't discuss your relationship with Mr. Baggett when he was killed."

"Why would I kill a sweet man who cared enough about me to leave me $20,000?"

"For the $20,000."

"Oh. But I didn't know about it."

"You didn't? Can you prove that?" Jan was pleased that Annette was talking. "Were you closer to him than you have let on?"

"Okay, okay. We were close. We were lovers. Are you happy now? Are you happy that you opened up my grief?" Now Annette realized that she had raised her voice again, and that the others were looking at her. She got up and went into her room, slamming the door. Matt saw that Ledger got a strange smirk on his face, though he said nothing.

The other guests finished eating without much conversation, and went off to their own rooms to sit out the storm.

That evening, the storm subsided to a light rain and Philippe and Ida joined the guests gathered around the dining-room stove for a small campfire. The stove in the great room still smelled of burning paint and varnish and needed to be thoroughly cleaned out.

"We're really all okay, aren't we, Philippe?" Diana asked him, holding on tight to her father's arm.

"I hope so, Diana, but I don't know anymore. That smoke could have killed people."

"I don't think it was meant to, though," Avis added. "It's still part of some sick person's attempt to get rid of us all. For some reason they want us out of the lodge."

"Well, that seems apparent," Jan said. "But why is the question. And just how far will they go to accomplish that?"

"What they've done so far is quite enough for me," Annette stated.

"I'm surprised you're still here," Ida said.

"Well, I'm interested in everything that happens here."

"Are you feeling better, Annette?" asked Jan.

"Yes, I'm fine. No ill effects, I guess. Now if the rain would only stop."

"Well, if you're up to it, I have a few more questions to ask you."

Jan's plan was interrupted as the three teenagers came slamming in the front door, exclaiming about the weather. "Did you hear that roads are washing out all over the area?" asked Jeff. "The roads are passable, but full of pot holes, and chopped up shoulders."

"Well, maybe it will dry up tomorrow. The road crews up here know how to patch things up pretty fast," Philippe said.

"I don't think so," Matt spoke. "The weather report this noon said that there could be two more days of rain."

"Yuk," said Ida. "Well, we were expecting some guests from Vancouver, but they called in to cancel. They must have heard about the weather."

"Or they heard about our evil spirits up here," Diana declared.

"Oh, now, don't go getting crazy on me, honey," Amos said to his daughter.

"What do you mean by that, Amos?" Jan asked.

"Well, she can get a little nuts at times, thinking about ghosts and evil spirits. You should see some of her crazy paintings."

"Dad, that's an awful thing to say," Diana whined. "Don't listen to him. He's just an old man with Alzheimer's."

"And that's a mean thing to say about me," Amos answered back.

"Well, don't go saying bad things about me like that, Dad."

"Ha, maybe she's the evil spirit around here, huh?" Ralph Ledger added his two cents, grinning at the distress.

"Would anyone like to watch a movie tonight? Kind of just relax?" Philippe asked.

"Ha, well I doubt that you have any movie we would want to see," Stan laughed. "Although I suppose you might have some horror stories, huh? Like *The Shining.* I bet you could write your own movie about the ghost of Seymour Lake Lodge!"

"Okay guys, that's not funny," Annette said. "We should just watch an old movie, like *Gone With the Wind.*"

"Oh, we have that one," Ida said. "I'll get it."

"Would anyone like to see some great pictures? I got a great one of the black bear, and some moose, and a beaver." Matt put his laptop on the table, and showed a slide show of his recent photos. Some of the guests came over to look. Stan seemed the most interested.

"Wow, these are great photos," he said. "Is that hard to do? To learn to take pictures like that?"

"Well, some people are naturally good at it. Others need time and practice, like with most things."

"Could you teach me?" Stan asked. "I mean, maybe sometime I could watch you. I don't have a camera anyway, though. Maybe some day I could try that."

"Tell you what," Matt said. "I have a couple of things to deal with here, and then we can talk about it."

"Sure, I'll hold my breath." said Stan.

"Time for the movie," called Ida, from the great room. She popped *Gone With the Wind* into the VCR and folks gathered around to watch.

"Let's get out of here, guys!" Stan said. Jeff and Cliff followed him back to the green room.

"Hey, Mr. Wildlife Reporter," Ralph addressed Matt. "I heard Dorsey say that he had some suspicions about you. How about it? Are you the perpetrator?"

"Dorsey was being an idiot," Jan interrupted. "There are no suspicions of Mr. Abbott."

"Really? Now isn't that a little bit of favoritism there? Aren't you supposed to suspect everyone until you know otherwise?" Ralph persisted.

"I really think the Shapiros have something to do with it," Diana charged. "They seem to be enjoying the whole thing. I've seen them taking notes and laughing a lot." She had a strange glassy look in her eyes as she accused Ward and Avis. "They are from New York, you know. You can't trust a New Yorker."

"Hey, that's not nice," Avis protested. "You really are a fruitcake, lady."

"Now, let's not all get touchy with each other here," Ida pleaded. "No one suspects any of the guests here, right, Jan? We think it's an outside job. Let's watch the movie."

Jan nodded, and looked out the front window toward the lake. The rain was coming down hard again, in sheets of water that waved like flags across the lake.

"Could it be any drearier?" she thought.

Chapter 20: Stalemate

Jan stayed in bed all morning on the second full day of rain. She dozed on and off, feeling waves of grief over the end of her marriage to Sid, interspersed with memories of a more tender time, when they had been in love, happy together, and hopeful for the future. When she woke, she sleepily looked around the room— dark although the drapes were open. The sky outside was gray-green and rain pelted the glass doors and ran down in torrents. The room was warm like sweat.

Jan glanced at her dream catcher on the wall beside her bed, with the loon eye beads staring back at her, hoping that it would catch a good dream and not a nightmare. Muffled voices drifted up from somewhere downstairs, but the pounding of the rain on the old tin roof lulled her back to sleep. Dreams of wild animals and strange people ran through her brain like a documentary of an alien planet. A loon kept swimming towards her in the water and then backing away. Soon a large flock of loons came after her, and she saw in their eyes, golden flames like will-o'-the-wisps. She reached for them, and swatted them away, awakening to find herself hitting the dream catcher on the wall. She lay in bed with her heart pounding rapidly in her chest, until she calmed and began to doze off again.

It was midday when she finally dragged herself out of bed, dressed, and went downstairs to a quiet lodge. There were no children running around, no dogs or cats, and no people arguing. Jan went into the kitchen to find some coffee, and found Avis taking lunch orders for the deli. Ward, Matt, and Philippe all wanted chicken wings and potato salad, Amos wanted a cold-cut grinder, and Ida and Annette wanted to share a calzone.

"I'll have some of Dad's grinder," Diana said.

"Maybe you will, and maybe you won't," Amos said, laughing.

"Let's get some extra chicken and salad, since maybe the boys will want some when they get back," Avis suggested.

"Mind if I tag along?" Jan asked. Huddling under a large rainbow-striped umbrella, the two women ran through the rain.

"At least it isn't thundering," Avis said.

The deli was packed full of customers, chatting about the rain, road damage, and the arson fire at Lake Willoughby.

"Yeah, that was a real fire, not a pretend one in the wood stove like the one over at the Seymour Lodge," one middle-aged gentleman in overalls remarked.

"Well, I heard that someone from there went to the hospital by ambulance," said Frita, the woman behind the counter. "Heard that the fumes were pretty nasty, too. They've been having quite a problem over there, I guess. Nothing to laugh about."

Avis looked at Jan, but Jan put her finger to her lips, urging Avis to keep her thoughts to herself. They gathered up the orders and some snacks for later, and headed back to the lodge. The teenagers were in the great room playing ping-pong.

"Mathewson called and told us to stay home today," said Jeff. "There are no visitors to the refuge and nothing to do outside or inside right now. So, I guess we get to goof off, unless of course we can help you with anything, Mr. Renault," he said, turning to Philippe.

"Not that I can think of right now, but Ida and I are going to run over to Island Pond to pick up a motor for the sump pump in case we need it in the basement. It's getting quite wet down there, and the old motor wore out last year after a storm like this."

"Be careful," Matt said. "I just heard on the television that some roads have washouts in the shoulders and there may be some high winds later."

"We'll be back as quick as we can," Philippe answered. "Jan, how about if you take charge of things while we're gone?"

"Sure, don't worry about a thing," Jan answered. "Not much can happen when we're all trapped inside in a rainstorm."

The innkeepers left and the guests lounged around, chatting, getting anxious with cabin fever. Cliff and Jeff kept playing ping-pong.

Stan had just finished the last of the lodge's pile of comic books when Matt came in and sat next to him. "Here Stan," he said. "This is an older camera of mine that I don't really use much any more. It was still in one of my bags. You can have it if you want. I'll show you some basics and you can practice taking pictures around the lodge. You'll have to use the flash inside, but if it ever stops raining, there are many wonderful things to photograph here in Vermont."

"You serious? I can have it?" Stan showed a hint of a smile, which no one at the lodge had seen on his face before.

"Yes, let's try it out." Matt took Stan into the kitchen and they began taking pictures of antiques.

Jeff headed back to the green room to work on his paper, and Cliff followed him, listening to the old boom box.

"It's so boring being cooped up," Annette said. "I even miss the Loomis kids running around and screaming."

Amos paced back and forth from the back stairway to the front stairway. There was quiet except for the sound of his shuffling feet. People read books, painted, and wrote poetry. Amos finally went up for another nap, and Stan joined the other guys in the green room.

In the late afternoon people began restlessly moving around the lodge, staring out the window and complaining about the rain. Ward spoke up. "Hey, who wants to play scrabble? A dollar apiece in the pot."

"Oh, you always beat everyone," said Avis. "I hate playing with you."

"I'll rise to the challenge," Matt asserted. "Come on, Jan, how about it? You in?"

"Oh, I'm afraid I'll embarrass you all," Jan laughed. "But, all right. Come on, Avis, watch Ward get beaten at his own game."

"I'll play, too," said Diana. "Words aren't my forte, but I don't feel like painting right now."

"Well, that's six of us. Just enough to make it interesting," Annette said. "Unless Amos wants to play. And where is Ralph?"

"I think he's upstairs. I heard him snoring earlier. I'm just going to watch, thanks," Amos responded.

Ward and Matt put two smaller tables together in the dining room and spread out the scrabble game. "There's more light in here than in the great room," Matt explained. "We'll be able to see what we're doing."

"Okay, then, everyone go ahead and draw seven letter tiles," Ward began.

"We all know how to play," said Avis, snottily.

"I don't know the rules, really," Matt said, apologetically. "but I know that we have to spell words with the letters on our tiles. Who goes first?"

Jan jumped in to answer that question. "Well, wait, before we draw seven tiles, we each have to draw one tile to see who goes first."

"So the letter furthest along in the alphabet goes first?" Matt asked.

"No," said Jan, "The letter nearest the front. A before B, etc. But, I'm afraid six people can't play, unless we have three teams. No more than four can play, since there aren't enough letters for that many."

"I'm on Ward's team!" shouted Annette. "Avis said he always wins."

"Yeah, against *her*!" said Diana. "I think we should draw straws."

"Oh come on," Matt insisted. "Just pick a teammate. Annette picked Ward. Who else wants to team up?" Matt looked at Jan, but she didn't speak.

"Well, then, I want Matt," said Avis.

"Then I guess that leaves Diana and me for the third team," said Jan, smiling teasingly at Matt. She put all of the letters into an old straw hat, and one person from each team drew a letter.

"You're first then," said Jan, looking at Matt and Avis.

After conferring, Matt put down the word "scary".

"With a double letter score on the Y, that's eight, plus six more, that's fourteen, and a double word score makes it twenty-eight," said Matt. "Read 'em and weep."

"Hey," said Ward. "I thought you didn't know how to play?"

"Well, maybe I have played a little here and there."

"I wonder why you picked the word 'scary', Matt," asked Annette. "Is it because we are all scared, by any chance?"

"Maybe," he answered.

"I'll tell you who's scary," said Diana. "That Ledger guy. He's a creepy hunter. He is mean to animals and not very nice to people. I certainly don't like him."

"Oh, now, he's not that bad," Jan spoke in defense of Ralph. "Although there is something about him that really bothers me, but I can't quite figure it out yet."

"I think he's nasty." Annette "He reminds me of an old woodsman I once knew. Kinda looks like him, too. Come on, let's play, Ward. Our turn."

They looked at their letters. Ward moved them around, and then played all seven to make the word "torments", attaching it to "scary" at the S.

"Now who's weeping?" Ward teased, looking at Matt. "That's thirteen points, times three for the triple word score, that's thirty-nine points, and of course the extra fifty points for using all seven letters at once. That's eighty-nine points, I believe."

"What? Fifty extra points? I never heard of that," Matt protested.

"It's true," Jan said. "Fifty points for using all seven letters at once. I guess Ward really is pretty good at this, after all, huh?"

"Pretty good?" Ward beamed. "You could all hand over the cash right now."

"We'll see about that," Jan said, giving Matt a sideways smile and wink. Matt looked back in surprise, wondering if Jan was as good at the game as she had implied.

"Okay, you two, take your turn," Matt said in challenge to Jan and Diana.

A loud crash was heard, coming from outside of the kitchen's back door.

"Oh, my God," Diana cried. "The madman is here." Ward and Avis jumped up and huddled together near the front door, in case they had to run out. Matt and Jan went toward the sound of the crashing, which was growing louder, and sounded like metal on metal.

As they peeked out the back kitchen window towards the shed's steps, they both began laughing.

"It's raccoons!" Jan laughed. "Two of them. They're raiding the trash cans. What are they doing out in the daytime?"

"They do sometimes scrounge for food in the daytime, especially if they have babies somewhere. Look at that big one," Matt said. "Where's my camera?" He went to grab it from the table and started snapping pictures through the window. The other guests came over to peek at the intruders.

"Hey, they're cute," said Diana.

"Obnoxious," said Ward. "Scared the heck out of me. And maybe they have rabies."

"Why are they running around in the rain?" Avis asked.

"Silly," Ward answered. "They're wild animals. They don't care about rain."

"Okay, you know everything, dear," Avis said.

Matt opened the door and yelled at the raccoons, and scared them off. "I don't think Philippe would appreciate us letting them scatter the trash all over the back yard. Let's get back to Scrabble."

"I believe it was our turn," said Jan.

Diana quickly put down the word "vice", attaching it to "torments" at the E. "Well, that's only eighteen points, but it's a start," she said.

"Why are we all using scary words? And why don't you like Ralph?" Ward asked Diana.

"I don't know. I just don't like him and that's all there is to it. He's a mean one."

"I think Jan has ruled him out as the perpetrator around here, though," Matt continued. She thinks this is something bigger than a one-man job. Go ahead, Avis, you take our turn this time. I know you're good at this."

"No kidding?" Ward asked Matt. "She really thinks that? How big? Like mobsters?"

"Well, I wouldn't go that far," Jan said, chuckling.

Avis played "dagger", connecting to "scary" at the R, and racked up eighteen points for team one.

"Dagger? Is that all you people can think of?" Ward asked. "Well, I don't think Ledger should be ruled out yet. He is one nasty character. I haven't gotten into a civil conversation with him yet."

"I'm too afraid of him to try," Avis added. "He's always staring at me and scowling."

Annette played "dread" down from the D in dagger and scored fourteen points. Ward laughed. "You guys are just no challenge for me," he bragged.

"Well, laugh at this, smarty pants," Jan chided, and played "sadistic" right across the bottom of "dread". "That's nine points for the word, with a double word score on the I, times three for triple word score, makes twenty-seven, times three for the other triple word score, makes eighty-one points, and, oh yes, the extra fifty for using all seven letters on my rack. That's one hundred and thirty-one points. Thank you very much."

"Argghh! I don't believe it," Avis whined. "I thought you would be good at this, Matt."

"Well, I guess that means one should never underestimate a woman reporter," Matt chuckled. "I suspected she was a ringer."

The game went on, with the players coming up with words like "gun", "murder", and "peril" before Jan and Diana won with three hundred and twenty-seven points to two hundred and five for Ward and Annette, and one hundred and thirty for Matt and Avis. The guests got up and stretched and went off to various spots in the lodge. Diana grabbed the six bucks winnings and gave three to Jan. Ward and Avis decided to nap, Diana went to paint in the kitchen where the light was brightest, taking Amos with her, and Jan and Matt went into the great room to see if they could get a weather report on the television. The room still had a strong odor of burning varnish.

Matt turned on the set and heard a grunt from the back corner of the room. He and Jan turned to see Ralph Ledger get up from an old over-stuffed chair in the dark and go up the back stairway. They were both too surprised to say anything.

"Yikes, I wonder if he was there the whole time," Jan said quietly to Matt. "Do you think he heard what people were saying about him?"

"I doubt it," Matt said. "Wouldn't he have come barging in, if he had?"

"I hope you're right," Jan responded. "I don't think I'd want to get that guy mad."

"He's already mad," Matt said. "And by that I mean 'loony', and not like the birds. Listen, here's the weather. More rain tonight and high winds."

"Great. We're under threats from every direction."

The phone rang. It was Ida, who explained to Jan that the winds and rain were so fierce between Morgan and Island Pond, with limbs coming down in the roads that she and Philippe were going to wait it out a while before trying to get home.

"Is everyone all right there?" Ida asked.

"Oh, yes, except for those who are bemoaning their loss in Scrabble," Jan told her, "and a visit from a couple of raccoons."

"Oh. Okay, well, it sounds like you are finding things to do, and no major problems. That's good. Don't worry about us. If we can't get home, we'll bunk at the Clyde River Hotel tonight, unless it washes out."

"Washes out?"

"Yeah," Ida said, half jokingly. "The river goes right underneath the hotel. No, really, don't worry. We'll be fine."

Jan hung up the phone, and it crossed her mind to call her mother, but she just wasn't ready to do it. Instead, she went over to the kitchen table to look at Diana's painting. It was a dark watercolor image of bloody knives arranged on a quilt-covered bed in colors of olive and sepia. It looked to Jan similar to the quilt in room nine.

Dinnertime came and the teenagers came in, dripping wet and looking for something to eat. They admitted that they had not been very frugal with their food allowances, and there wasn't much left in the green room suite. After some discussion, the guests were of one mind to make homemade pizza. Jan knew that there was bread dough in bags in the refrigerator that Ida had been thawing to possibly make some rolls. She thought that it wouldn't bother Ida any if they used it. Searching the cupboards again, they found canning jars of tomato sauce that Ida had put up the previous fall, a small can of mushrooms, a can of black olives, and a small tin of anchovies. With that, and some partial blocks of cheese from the refrigerator and some frozen sausages, they were ready to roll. The three young men volunteered to cook, so the others backed off into the dining room to wait. In about an hour, the pizzas were ceremoniously delivered by the enthusiastic cooks.

"We made one for the vegetarians with mushrooms and olives and two for the meat eaters with sausage and anchovies," announced Cliff. "There's something for everyone, so dig in."

Annette sat down next to Cliff. She wanted to talk to him about his ride to the hospital in Newport, and compare it to hers. Cliff said that he didn't remember a thing.

Jeff sat with the Shapiros and listened to Ward talk about New York City and stock-brokering. Avis snapped, "Ward, you're boring the kid to death. What makes you think he wants to be a stockbroker?"

Stan and Matt took a table in the corner and struck up a philosophical conversation about the pros and cons of a life of crime. "I really don't know what else I want to do," said Stan. "I never had much of an interest in anything."

"Well, you do now," said Matt.

"Photography?"

"Sure, and I bet if you let yourself, you'd find some other interests, like art or design. These pictures you took around the lodge are unique. You really have some potential here." Stan smiled and Matt offered to show him some more of his photos on the laptop.

Jan sat with Amos and Diana, and asked questions about the latest painting. Ralph Ledger remained in his room.

They were just finishing off the pizza when Ed Pease came in the front door with Joseph Rainwater. Ed had a tiny black and white kitten in his arms. Jan jumped up to greet them.

"Welcome, you two. Would you like some pizza? Or, I can probably make you something else if you'd rather."

"Oh, we're not here for dinner, Jan," responded Ed. "We're really just checking up on people. There's quite a bit of damage around town and more to come."

"The worst weather will be tomorrow," Joseph asserted. "Philippe must take precautions and batten down the hatches."

"Hatches?" asked Jan, reaching out to take the kitten from Ed. "Ah, how sweet."

"He's showing his age," Ed said. "He just means to protect the place. Close windows and doors up tight tonight. Tie things down outside. No loose trash barrels, like that."

"All right. Well, Philippe and Ida haven't gotten back from Island Pond, and may spend the night there. Are you sure you wouldn't like a bite to eat?"

"Well, maybe a little something, if you have it." The two men sat down and Jan went to the kitchen to fix them a meal. She found some chicken soup and some blueberry muffins to warm up.

Back in the dining room, Amos was chatting with Ed about Miranda, expressing his concern and how he missed her. Ed explained how he had found the little kitten in the woods. "It's most likely a feral cat. I bet Miranda can tame it. I'm going to take it to her."

Joseph was walking around the lodge, looking up at the ceiling and in all of the corners. Jan watched him in wonderment.

The rainy weather had begun to cool down the atmosphere considerably, so Matt made a small fire in the dining-room wood stove, and the gathering evolved into another indoor campfire.

"I find it interesting that your name is Rainwater," Jan began. "Especially since it has been raining here for days and doesn't look like it's going to stop soon. Do you have any special ability to predict rain by any chance?"

Joseph laughed. "Well, maybe a little. I watch the clouds gathering. But the spirits have their own agenda, and things can change. Perhaps the rain clouds bring a message. Perhaps they just remind us about the significance of water. The great mother earth needs good clean water, yet our New England rain has acid in it. It damages the trees. Damage will happen until we understand what we must do."

"Well, this is a bit too much rain, don't you think? Speaking of which, it's coming right in the front windows." Jan got up to close them. "We had them open because the nasty smoke smell from the burning wood ducks is still here."

"Leave that other one open, please," Joseph requested. "The wet air is very pleasant and cooling."

Ward seconded the request. "I am thankful for the cooling. It has been darn hot up here."

"Right now I'd rather be driving in our air-conditioned car out on the roads in sunny weather," Avis added.

"I'm glad to get a day off from the refuge," Cliff chimed in. "It gets really hot working out there sometimes. Especially when we're cutting hiking trails through the woods."

"Is that what you've been doing over there?" Diana asked.

"That's only a small part of it," Jeff responded. "We do a lot more. We work on preserving the whole Nulhegan basin, by providing a place for visitors to admire it, and perhaps understand about environmental issues. I actually helped to videotape a short movie for the visitor center."

"Really?" Avis asked. "That's great, Jeff. Do you see yourself staying involved in environmental issues after this summer?"

"Yes. I'm hoping for a scholarship to New York University for a degree in environmental studies. Ranger Mathewson may give me a recommendation, which will help."

"I'm sure he will. Is it possible for you to get a full scholarship?"

"I doubt it. I may have to take on some big loans. My family has no money to help."

"Well, perhaps you can find a patron," Avis smiled at him. "It certainly is a worthy cause, protecting our planet."

"Yeah, really," Amos spoke up. "If we don't have a planet, we don't have us for sure."

"Right, Amos," Ed agreed. "By the way, once this rain has stopped and the roads are safe, I'll bring you up to the farm to visit Miranda. Would you like that?"

"Oh, yes. I really would. Thanks so much. Please tell her I'm thinking of her."

"I will. Say, why don't we play some music? Any requests?" Ed got out his harmonica and began to play "Singing in the Rain".

Stan got up to leave. "I think I'll go hear some of my own music, if you don't mind." Cliff and Jeff soon followed, and Ed played "April Showers" and "Don't Let the Rain Come Down".

"My roof's got a hole in it and I might drown," Amos sang along. Avis and Ward laughed and went off in a corner to chat.

"Ward, I think I know of a good way to spend some of that inheritance from your dad," Avis said.

Meanwhile, Jan took Joseph aside to ask him questions about the messages from nature.

"Joseph, could you tell me more about what the animal totems are saying?" Jan asked, relating to him the story of the loons teasing her on the pond.

"Well, if you want a possible explanation, it could be that they were attracted to the agitation in yourself," the shaman answered.

"What? I don't understand."

"Your vibration."

"Now you sound like a new age prophet."

"I keep telling you, it's all the same, whatever name you give to it."

"All right, what about the moose? Why the mother and baby, the big male moose on the lawn, and the female with the collar?"

"Well, Matt gave you some obvious answers on two of those. The mother and baby connected to your inner desire to have a child. The female moose with the collar might be about your imprisonment in your own insecurities. I agree with him there."

"And the big bull on the lawn?"

"Well, what do you think, Jan?" Joseph challenged her to think.

"Well, I wanted to show it to Matt, but it ran off. It might mean that it's not time for a new man in my life, and that it's not the time to get involved with Matt."

"There. Do you see? You can understand what the world is telling you."

"Then I expect that the big moose I almost hit on my way here is also a warning."

"Perhaps," Joseph said. "You will see another, and you will see the whole picture."

Jan looked questioningly at the shaman, but the front door crashed open, and Philippe and Ida came in dripping wet, with their arms full of bags.

"The storm is causing some serious flooding," Philippe said. "The road is washed out along the edge of Willoughby. Trees are tipping over. The road between here and Island Pond is blocked by a fallen birch, and we had to drive down around through East Charleston on 105 to get back here."

"Well, I'm glad you made it," Ed said, slapping Philippe on the shoulder and grabbing some of the bags. "What's all this?"

"Well, candles, lamp oil, and parts for the sump pump. Ida has the groceries."

"Here, Ida, let me take some of those," Jan offered, as Ida came in with her arms weighted down with canvas grocery bags.

"We thought people might be trapped a while. Luckily we have firewood for cooking." Ida looked around the room. "How's everyone doing?" she asked.

"We're all okay. The boys just went back to the green room, and we haven't seen much of Ralph Ledger."

"I see Ed is here with Joseph. Maybe I should make some stew."

"We've fed everyone supper, Ida. Don't worry," Jan said.

Philippe came back from the kitchen shed with Ed. "We're going down the cellar and fix the sump pump."

Joseph then spoke up. "I feel an evil presence," he said, matter-of-factly. "It's here in the lodge." Just then, an owl flew in the open window and flew around the dining room, crashing into the walls and flying around and around, causing the guests to duck and run into other rooms. The owl then flew into the kitchen towards the back wall and crashed just above the Good Shepherd painting, but missed it. Three times the owl flew towards the painting, but did not crash into it.

Philippe grabbed a large towel and tried to catch the owl as it flew. Ida grabbed a broom and tried to shoo it towards the front door, but to no avail. The owl then headed into the great room, and the guests followed to see what it would do.

The owl crashed hard into the big mirror at the base of the back stairs, sending it smashing down in splinters. Jan thought suddenly of the hairy man that Miranda said she saw in the mirror, and she had a sudden revelation, but kept it to herself.

The big bird flew into a wooden swan hanging from the ceiling just before it found the open front window and flew out into the twilight.

"Wow, that was something!" Amos whistled.

"We're lucky the only damage is that old mirror," Ida said.

"It's a warning," Joseph stated. "The owl is wisdom."

"I think I get it," Jan said quietly to the shaman. "It's telling us something. It didn't damage the Good Shepherd, it only pointed to it, before it crashed the mirror."

"You're beginning to see," Joseph confirmed.

"I'll help you clean up this mess," Annette offered, taking the broom from Ida's hands and heading for the broken mirror.

After the sump pump was fixed and the mirror cleaned up, Ed and the shaman went off to the Pease farm in Ed's old pickup. As they were leaving, Joseph whispered to Jan, "You are about to be tested. Remain strong."

Jan decided to call her mother.

Chapter 21: Lightning Strikes

Jan went to bed very late, after watching the lightning storm over the lake send huge bolts down on Elan Hill as if trying to rip apart the mountain. The thunder pounded like rumbling timpani, and the raindrops tinkled like chimes on the glass doors. She snuggled down under her quilt, looking up at the dream catcher, listening to the music of nature, and thinking about her talk with her mother.

In the first place, she wasn't sure what had prompted her to call, when she had been avoiding talking to the woman for weeks. Perhaps it was Joseph's warning that she was going to be tested. Perhaps, if she was going to be threatened, deep inside she wanted her mother. Perhaps it was the feeling that if there was danger ahead, then things unsaid needed to be spoken. So she spoke to her mother. She told her about the impending divorce and received the anticipated reaction from her mother that she should try to stop it, and hang on to the marriage at all costs. There was also, of course, the issue of who was to blame, and the accusatory question of what she had done to wreck things.

Jan was proud of how she had handled the conversation, keeping her cool, yet telling her mother the truth—that although the divorce was Sid's idea, she had never been happy in the marriage and had gotten married at 28 under pressure from her to find a man and settle down before it was too late.

"I'm going to be my own person now, Mother," she had said. "Not controlled by you or by Sid. I'm going to take some time to find out who I am and what I want for my future. I am not Eleanor, and my life may be very different from hers, but I am still worthy."

At that, her mother had protested that she had always loved her, no matter what. Jan wasn't sure of that, but realized that she had a lot to think about and a lot to discuss with her mother at a later date. Right now, she felt a little alone, here in a lodge near the Canadian border, with no one to hold her. She had momentary thoughts of reaching out to Matt, but quickly overcame that needy feeling. Then a sense of peace about being alone and free allowed her to sleep soundly until morning in spite of the storm raging on and off all night.

In the early morning, Jan woke up to the soft sound of voices. She tried to turn on the lamp beside her bed, and realized that the power was out. Outside it was still flashing and booming, and it was hard to tell what time it was, although she sensed that it was a while after dawn.

"I wonder what this day will bring?" she thought. "I will handle it, whatever comes." She felt her new strength growing within her, and as the lightning still flashed over Elan Hill, she stretched, took deep breaths, dressed in her bright pink t-shirt and faded blue jean shorts and stepped out to seize the day.

Downstairs, Ida and Philippe were gathering up oil lamps from the antique shop and lighting candles and lamps in every room. A warm fire was glowing in the big wood stove in the dining room, and the smell of fresh muffins filled the air. Soon Philippe was cooking up eggs and sausage in big fry pans on top of the stove, and making coffee in an old percolator. Guests began straggling down to partake of the wonderful morning meal.

"It looks like this place has become a bed and breakfast of the first order," Jan said. "You never had more than the continental breakfast before."

"Well, we never had our guests subjected to such terrible weather and scary events before," Philippe explained. "I feel like we at least owe everyone some good food."

The phone rang twice. Before anyone could pick it up, it stopped. "Someone check and see if it's still working, or if it's just our prankster," Philippe requested.

Jan went over and picked up the phone. "We still have a dial tone," she said. "If anyone needs to make a call, they'd better do it soon."

Ida picked up Lola, who was rubbing around her ankles, and ran with her back to the log cabin next door. She left Seymour to hang out at the lodge for a sense of protection.

Annette stared out the front window at the green-black electrical storm, with the rain heavy again like a tropical downpour. Torrents ran in a river down the driveway and across to the beach. "It looks like the road is washing out right across from us," she said.

Amos and Diana ate a big breakfast and Amos decided to go back up to bed.

"Not much else to do," he said.

"Well, I'm going to read," Avis asserted. "I've never tried reading by lamp light, but I guess there's always a first time."

"I suppose I could try painting by lamp," Diana added. "Why not? Maybe I will. I'll get my paints and bring them down here."

Ida came crashing back in the front door in a bright yellow rain slicker.

"Wow, lady, you are one brave woman!" Annette exclaimed. "Either that or you're crazy.

"Oh, Philippe and I have been through many things and this is just another adventure," Ida declared, hanging up the raincoat and going to see if the fresh pot of coffee was ready.

"Good morning," Matt said, mostly to Jan, as he sat at one of the tables in the warm kitchen instead of the dining room. Ida greeted him and put a plate of breakfast in front of him.

"Coffee?" she asked.

"Yes ma'am," Matt answered. "High-test please." Matt began to eat, when suddenly water came dripping down from the ceiling right onto his plate. He jumped up and called to Philippe. "Yikes, it's coming inside now."

"Darn. I knew that old roof wouldn't hold forever," Philippe complained. "I should have built the second story over the kitchen last year as I intended."

"We didn't want to spend the money at that time, remember?" Ida reminded him.

"Well, I think we're going to have to spend some now." Philippe grabbed some sap buckets from the antique shop and placed them under the leaks that were now showing up in several spots in the kitchen and the attached back shed.

"There's a problem here, too!" Ida cried. "There's water coming down the chimney, right into the stove." The old wood stove popped and sizzled like a firecracker. Philippe checked out the stove in the great room, and saw that it had the same problem.

"Well, we're lucky we don't live at the bottom of a hill," Philippe said. "The radio told about some farmer over in East Montpelier whose whole barn slid down the hillside, cows and all."

"Heavens!" Diana said, returning with her paints. "Now that's a picture I wouldn't want to see. Wait, maybe I would." She sat down at the table nearest the front window and began to put color on paper.

The phone rang, and Jan ran to pick it up before the second ring. "Hello!" she bellowed into it. Sergeant Parker answered, although his voice was a bit hard to hear through the crackling on the line.

"Jan, I'm calling for two things. First, I want to apologize for the comments about Matt Abbott. I got sucked in by Dorsey, and I'm really sorry. Matt is no suspect. I also want to tell you..." Parker's voice faded out amid the crackling, and Jan shouted into the phone, "Hello! Hello! Parker, I can't hear you."

"I said, I have the name of the escapee from Drummondville. His name is Richard Bordman, but they know that to be an alias among many. He was in jail in Maryland once under the name of ..." more crackling.

"Parker?" Jan strained to hear. "What did you say?"

"Richard Leggett. Other aliases are Ralph Bagger and ..."

Silence.

"Oh, my God," Jan said to herself, hanging up the dead phone. "The Vermont State Police came through after all." She now had a good idea of what was really going on.

A loud clap of thunder and a huge crash were heard in the back yard. Ida looked out to see a tree down on top of Philippe's truck.

"Oh, no! This is awful," Ida cried. "We have so many trees around the lodge. We better all stay in the dining room, where we'll be safe. Philippe!"

"I saw it," he said, "There's nothing I can do right now. We have good insurance, so don't panic."

"Insurance won't keep us from getting killed," she cried.

"Ah, hon, that tree on my truck was old and rotted. I should have taken it down last year. The rest are good and solid."

Philippe spent most of the morning mopping up leaks and trying to patch the roof from the inside. The stove was cleaned out so it wouldn't keep smoking as water ran down the stovepipe.

"The guests will have to settle for cold sandwiches for lunch, I guess," Philippe said to Ida.

"What a mess. Philippe, I don't know how much more I can take of this. My nerves are getting frazzled. What is God's purpose?"

"Never mind, sweetheart. The sun will come out soon. It always does."

"And the lodge will be safe from evil in the sunlight?" Ida questioned, just before hearing a loud knock on the front door.

"Who on earth is visiting in this weather?" Ida wondered aloud, as she went to open the door. The porch was covered in water and rain was still driving in sideways towards the windows.

Ida saw that the two men wore the familiar uniforms of the US Border Patrol. She let them in and Philippe, Jan, and Matt gathered around to see what was up.

The officers introduced themselves as Jim Murphy and Herk Wilson. Trooper Murphy was a former Boston cop, over six feet tall, and Trooper Wilson was a small guy, stocky like a bull. Murphy told the group that the roads were washed out between Morgan and Island Pond and that, in fact, all the roads out of Morgan were closed due to either washouts or downed trees. They had been out all morning checking every back road for old camps or caves where a prison escapee might be hiding out, and happened to be here near the beach and the deli when they got the word that there was nowhere to go.

Ida invited the men in, took their coats and offered them sodas and sandwiches. "Your coats are soaked. Oh, and so are your clothes. We'll find you some dry things. Come on in and have some lunch. I'm so sorry that we have nothing hot. The power's been out, as you can see, and the stoves got wet from rain down the chimneys, so we can't use those either.

"Well, we're happy just to have a roof over our heads right now, thanks," Trooper Murphy said. "We're a bit tired of being out in the patrol vehicle, searching back areas that are going under water, and our four-by-four can't take much more, having jumped giant potholes and climbed over downed limbs."

"No sign of the guy, then?" Philippe asked. "I understand he got out weeks ago, and they thought he was headed down south somewhere."

"Right. Maryland," Herk Wilson explained. "He originally came from Maryland, and received letters from there, but we recently got a report of him possibly headed this way. When he was in jail, he apparently got mail from Island Pond, from a Mr. Orton of Rambling River Development."

Jan looked at Matt, and then at Philippe and Ida. They all looked frightened. Pieces of information were jumping around in their heads, but not making too much sense yet. Jan motioned for Matt to follow her into the great room.

"What's going on, Jan?" Matt asked. "What do you think Orton has to do with this escapee, and how does it affect us?" Jan quickly told Matt about Sergeant Parker's phone call and her building suspicions.

"It seems pretty clear then," Matt said, "And we need to talk to these border patrol right now! Ledger has left the lodge. His truck was gone when I got up this morning, and the door to room seven is open and he's not in there."

Jan approached Trooper Murphy.

"So, did you find this Mr. Orton over in Island Pond?" she asked, hoping to find out more details to support her suspicions.

"Nope," Murphy said. "The address he put down for the return address on his letters to Bordman was an empty warehouse. But we tracked down Rambling River Development over in Concord, New Hampshire, and Orton wasn't around. We were going to go back there today. We had a phone number for the company, and no one answered that, either."

"Well, I guess I have a few facts to share with you," Jan said, realizing her obligation and glad that there would be more brains working on this than just hers and Matt's. She hoped that these guys were sharper than Parker and Fred. She told them about Parker's call and all the aliases, the events at the lodge over the past two weeks, and her suspicions about Ralph Ledger. They all spent the afternoon trying to piece together the fragments of information.

When Jan thought about adding tidbits such as the owl flying into the mirror, the shaggy black bear tearing up the lodge, and will-o'-the-wisps, she bit her tongue. She decided to stay away from the spiritual aspect of the events to avoid not being taken seriously.

"It sounds like you really think the escapee is this Ledger guy, then?" Murphy asked. "And he's the one who has been terrorizing the lodge? The pieces do appear to add up in that direction. But, if so, he's left the lodge, and we have no way to go after him, or even to call for backup at the moment. You said that cell phones only come in down on the far end of the beach? Well, there is a huge washout between here and there. I guess we'll just have to wait out this storm and then see what happens."

"What about your truck radio?" Matt asked.

"That thing died the second time we floated down a wet dirt road onto a rock. We were lucky to get ourselves back up to the main road," Herk explained.

"Well, it looks like you two are going to have to stay the night," Ida said. "Since we had a cancellation, room ten is available upstairs and all made up with two beds, and you are welcome to use it."

"Thanks, Ma'am, we appreciate it. Please keep checking your phone service, if you will."

"Speaking of phones, Jan," said Matt, taking Jan aside, "I haven't had a chance to tell you. I spoke with Fitzgibbons last night late. He really loves your writing and even asked if you would consider applying for a job on the magazine."

"You're kidding," Jan said, in disbelief.

"For real. What do you think? Interested?"

"I'm flattered, that's for sure. I don't know, Matt. There is so much going on in my mind," she paused, "...and in my heart. I am going to need a lot of time to think. And what would you think, really, of me working in your territory?"

"No question about it. I'd love it," Matt said with assurance, looking at Jan with obvious affection.

"There's just so much... Please tell Mr. Fitzgibbons that I am flattered." Jan looked away and then went into the great room.

The afternoon was spent with guests gathered in the dining room and great room, Diana painting scenes of buildings getting washed away in mud slides and Annette writing dark poetry by the light of oil lamps. Avis and Ward were reading and talking, while Jan and Matt and the innkeepers talked with the border patrol. The dark, dreary day dragged on.

"I have to say I've never seen weather this bad in this area. It's possible there are tornadoes about," Wilson said. Philippe had managed to get the men some clothes from the log cabin, although they weren't really a good fit. Their wet clothes were hung over the kitchen stove, although there was no heat to dry them.

"Well, this happens about once in ten years up here in the Kingdom," said Philippe. "I remember a time like this when we lived down in St. J. The streets were like rivers. As soon as the sun came out, it all dried up in no time."

"Well, you know," said Wilson. "I am truly exhausted, and a nap right now would be a Godsend." Murphy agreed.

"I'll show them where to go," Jan said. "I want to get a jacket from my room."

She and the two men headed upstairs to room ten. They took a quick look around room seven, but soon realized that Ledger had cleared out completely.

"Do you think this was the guy? Right here at this lodge?" Wilson asked. "I wonder why the state police didn't figure it out."

Jan decided not to voice her opinion on that subject.

"Well, I don't know. All I know is I'm wiped out," answered Murphy, lying down on the bed nearer the hallway.

"Sure, give me the bed near the window, so I'll get killed when the branches crash in," Wilson laughed.

"Oh, hush up and sleep."

The Shapiros and the Peabodys also went up to take naps, since it was too dark and dreary to do anything else. Philippe kept trying to stop the leaks and picking up the phone to see if it was back on. Not yet.

Jan and Ida made a plan for dinner with the groceries Ida and Philippe had purchased in Island Pond, and cleaned up the dining room and kitchen as best they could with soap and cold water. Around seven, guests began to straggle back down, rested and hungry.

Cold fried chicken and ham and cheese slices were set out along with deli potato salad, macaroni salad, bean salad, gelatin with fruit, pickles and olives, rolls and butter.

"Hey, this is like a picnic," Amos cheered. "This place is fun."

Ida saw Philippe looking out the back kitchen window at his beloved pickup crushed beneath the fallen tree. "Not for all of us," she said.

The boys came in from the green room and ate their fill. Matt then took Stan aside to talk with him about coming down to Pennsylvania for a visit, and Jeff sat talking further with the Shapiros about his desire to help save the environment. Cliff volunteered to clean up the kitchen, and chatted with Ida about what it would mean to be a chef's assistant.

Jan talked some more with Murphy and Wilson, going over the details that they knew about the various aliases of the Drummondville escapee, who she now believed was Ralph Ledger, and his connection to Roger Orton and Rambling River.

"Bordman was a thief and knifed a couple of guys in some drug deals. I don't know what that has to do with real estate," Murphy said to Jan, a bit condescendingly. "However, we'll find out more about Rambling River and Bordman's connection once we can get back some power or phones. And as for your Mr. Ledger, the names could be a coincidence. As soon as we can, we'll get the goods on him from the FBI files, too. But, really, I think your theory is a bit far-fetched."

Jan sighed. "Do you? Well, you haven't heard all of it. I also think he is connected to the murder of the previous owner of this lodge." Jan saw their eyebrows go up.

"What? Oh, come on. You've been drinking too much of the local dandelion wine, I bet," Wilson teased.

Jan could not believe what she was hearing. "You have to be kidding me," she said. "Ralph, Richard, Leggett, Ledger, Bagger, Baggett. Orton and Rambling River? After everything I've told you, you still don't get it? Do you have to be an idiot to be a cop in Vermont?" Jan walked away, pounding her head with her hands and growling in frustration that even the US Border Patrol could not take this burden from her shoulders. However, she realized that if Joseph was truly predicting that she would be tested, it probably was going to be today.

That evening, several people stayed up to play cards in the great room, but Philippe and Ida went back next door, suggesting that everyone get a good rest for whatever tomorrow's adventures might bring.

"I'll turn in after I take all the money from these suckers," Stan bragged.

"Well, you just go on and try, young man," Herk Wilson said. "I'll have to show you young whippersnappers how it's done. Ante up a quarter, boys."

"Oh, high stakes, huh?" Ward laughed, sitting down at the poker table.

"I'm in," said Matt.

"Me too, I guess," Jeff said with hesitation.

"Not me, I'm broke," Cliff sighed.

Diana took her dad up to read for a while and turn in early, and Jan asked Annette to sit with her and talk a bit. She wanted to poke around for more details about Annette's relationship with John Baggett, and why he would leave her twenty grand.

"So really, Annette, was it serious between you two, or just a fling?" Jan pressed.

"I didn't really think it was serious, and I didn't realize that he did. Not until he left me the money. Then I realized how much I had meant to him. He was a very lonely man in many ways."

"Did you ever meet his niece or any other relatives?"

"No. He did talk glowingly about his niece, who was a missionary for several years. He rarely mentioned his son, and when he did, it was not in loving terms. I gathered that they had had a big falling out."

"So you never had contact at all with his son?"

"No, Jan. Why do you keep asking that?"

"You never even saw a picture of him?"

"No. Not even a picture," Annette asserted.

"Do you think he might look like his father?" Jan took out the picture she had of John Baggett and put it in front of Annette.

"I don't know. Maybe." Annette looked into Jan's eyes with sudden awareness.

Jan nodded, but Annette froze and then turned the conversation to poetry and weather.

The poker game dragged on for hours until Jeff cleaned everyone out of all their spare cash and Stan slammed his fist on the table and headed off to the green room suite. "You conned us, man," he said to Jeff. "You're a pro."

"Nope. I just learned to use strategy."

"Yeah, I'd like to know what that strategy was," Murphy said.

"Don't worry, it's completely legal," Jeff winked.

In spite of their earlier nap, the troopers were tired, and so was everyone else. It wasn't long before the lodge was dead quiet except for the ping of rain on the roof, and the rumbling of thunder beginning to fade into the distant hills.

Who knows what dreams wafted through the old lodge at Seymour Lake as border guards and guests slept calmly?

Blam! At one in the morning, a gunshot echoed through the lodge. Jan ran into the hallway of the east wing, where she met Diana and Amos breathless with fear and banging on the door of room ten.

"Hang on, I'm getting my pants on," Murphy called. The two border patrol came out into the hall, and Murphy had his pistol raised.

"Was that a gunshot?" Jan asked? "Or did something explode?"

"Well, we're going to find out," Murphy said in a strong voice that was reassuring to Diana. "Stay back now, folks, Herk and I will check this out. The two guards went quietly down the back stairs into the great room, where they were joined by Diana and Jan, who had followed them down, the Shapiros who came down the other stairway, and Annette from room nine. The lodge was quite dark, with only the light of a few oil lamps still glowing.

"Stay calm, folks," Herk Wilson warned. "There may be someone here, or it may have been just a log truck backfiring as it went by." A sound on the front porch made them jump, as the three teenagers from the green room came charging in. The others all crowded into the dining room to join them.

"We heard a gunshot!" yelled Stan. Philippe and Ida came in right behind them.

"Is everyone okay?" Philippe shouted. "Has anyone seen Seymour?"

"We don't think it was a gunshot," Murphy insisted. "Probably a truck backfiring."

"I'm sorry, but that was no truck," Philippe said adamantly. "Maybe something exploded. We should check the back rooms, and the furnace and hot water tank."

And from the dark corner of the kitchen, a figure came towards them. "Don't bother folks." His voice was deep and harsh. As he moved into the lamplight, they could see that Ralph Ledger was holding a shotgun on them. The meat cleaver hung from his belt loop. Diana and Avis screamed.

Ledger lunged towards them. He grabbed Annette by her long blonde hair and dragged her back towards the kitchen. Philippe started to reach for her.

"Don't!" ordered Ledger, pointing the shotgun at the innkeeper's face.

Chapter 22: Confrontation and Compassion

Philippe backed off, afraid that Ledger was serious.

Murphy pulled out his pistol and aimed it at Ledger, but Ledger fired at the ceiling and the patrolman dropped his gun. Diana screamed again and Ida ducked behind Philippe.

"Okay, okay!" Murphy hollered. "Don't hurt anyone. Don't hurt the lady."

"What do you want from us?" Philippe asked him.

"You'll see what I want. All of you get into the big room." Ledger pointed with his gun towards the great room and the others all did as he ordered, crowding into the game room.

"Over there!" Ralph shouted, indicating an area in the back near room eight.

They stood in a huddle, most of them afraid to move, but Stan kept fidgeting and looking around the room. Jan whispered to him, "Don't try anything. This man is dangerous." Cliff whimpered like he was going to cry.

Ralph kept peeking out the window to the street, and holding on tight to Annette.

"Ralph, why are you doing this?" Jan questioned. "This is not the way to solve your problem."

"What the fuck do you know about my problem, Missy?" Ralph shot back. "You and your damn investigating. I could have had everyone out of this lodge days ago. Now you went and made everything harder."

"I understand, Ralph. I really do. Only your name isn't Ralph, is it? It's James."

"You think you're so damn smart, huh? So you figured me out. How did you know?"

Diana tried to take her father back out to the dining room, but Ledger yelled, "Don't anyone move! I got nothing to lose and I'll shoot."

Diana froze. Avis sobbed and Ward put his arms around her. Ida looked angrily at Ledger and said, "You've been tormenting us for weeks. Why would you do that? What's your problem?"

"Shut up, lady. I'll do the talking." Ledger tightened his arm around Annette's neck and she whimpered.

"All of you shut up! I asked you how you knew," Ledger growled angrily at Jan. She tried to make her voice as calm as possible, but inside she was trembling.

"Well, the monogrammed 'B' on your jacket for one thing. It's not really for 'bear hunter' is it?"

"So? It could have been," Ledger snarled. Ida and Philippe and the others looked confused.

"You've never shot a bear, or a moose either. Have you?" Jan challenged.

"How would you know, Missy?"

"I learned from Ranger Matthewson that people don't use shotguns for big animals like that. You're not really a hunter, Ralph, so you're not here to check out the moose for the fall hunt. I know who you really are."

"What makes you so damn sure?"

"You also look like your father. I've seen pictures. And, you pronounced your name 'Leggett' once instead of 'Ledger'. It just made me suspicious. You did a pretty good job of covering things up for a while, though. You called the lodge phone from other places and hung up, and you snuck around turning lights on all over the lodge when others had left them off, didn't you?"

"You're all so stupid. It took you long enough to figure it out."

"Well, it's to your credit," Jan said to him, "that you were so clever. You stole things from people and pretended you had cigarettes stolen."

"Well, I didn't steal anything from any kid. No damn bathing suit or surf board. The brat admitted that, didn't he? And I want to know who took my damn beer!" Ledger looked around the room, squeezing Annette's neck tighter and waving his shotgun.

"I said don't move. You there, kid. You trying to get killed?" Ralph snapped at Stan who had been reaching for a lamp.

"Take it easy!" Philippe begged him.

"Fuck you. I'll do what I damn please. I got no use for the lot of you. I know what you all think of me, too, and I don't give a damn."

"Ralph, I think you have gotten a dirty deal in life," Jan said to him in a calm voice. "I think you're angry and some of it's justified."

"No one asked you to psych me out. It don't matter now."

"Okay. I won't try to psych you out. But what is it that you want from us, Ralph? Or should I call you James, now that we know who you are?"

"I wanted you all to leave this damn lodge, and I wanted them there to sell it." He pointed to Philippe and Ida. "But, no. They couldn't take a hint. I could have made a killing off of the deal, and settled an old score, besides. Now that you all know about me, I can't pull it off unless I kill you all."

"You wouldn't do that Ralph," Jan said to him, continuing in her calming tone, and trying to remember that Joseph urged her to think with compassion.

"Oh yeah. I'm quite capable of it."

"All right, I know you killed a bird and Miranda's cat. But I don't think you would really be able to kill a person," Ida begged.

"Those darn cats were a pain in the ass. The Siamese escaped me, but I made sure the other one didn't." He laughed. Ida put her hands over her face.

"You were pretty clever, to go off in your truck, then sneak back to stab the grouse and then drive away and just happen to come back with the kids. You did the same when you killed the cat."

"And you never had a clue."

"Right. And you sure got me with the snake in the bathtub," Jan smiled, trying to establish a rapport with this man who was obviously unstable and very dangerous. "But I really didn't think the dead car in the bog was very funny. Falling down with the swing wasn't real comical either."

"Well, I thought it was pretty damn funny, but I really wanted to give you a message about leaving. Tried to scare you off. You don't scare easy, Missy."

"Well, thanks, I guess. You also put the threatening messages in the guest book, didn't you?"

"So you're on to me. So what? This place needs to close down. It's evil."

"Ralph, I know that you've had a troubled life. You were in prison in Maryland, and you are the man who escaped from Drummondville, aren't you?" Jan fought off her fears and kept confronting him.

Ida gasped.

"So you know that, too? You think you've got me all figured out, don't you?"

"Sergeant Parker told me that you used the names Richard Bordman, Richard Leggett and Ralph Bagger," Jan informed him. "The 'B' on your jacket stand for 'Baggett', doesn't it?"

"You're James Baggett! You're John's son," Ida cried.

Murphy and Wilson started to move towards him, and again Ledger shouted, "I'll kill this damn woman. I swear to God. She's nothing but a tramp, anyway. Turned my father against me!"

Everyone looked bewildered, and Annette whispered, "James. You're James Baggett?"

"The one and only," Ledger answered angrily, "and you're the woman who stole my money." He dropped the shotgun and grabbed the cleaver, putting the blade to Annette's neck. "I should do you in right now." Annette squealed and grabbed at the cleaver with her hands, trying to move it away from her neck.

"Ralph, wait, please," Jan pleaded. "That's not the way. You'll just end up dead yourself. I know you feel you haven't been treated fairly. You told me about your father. He was mean and abusive to you, and then he left you out of his will. You wanted to own this lodge, but he didn't leave it to you. That must have really hurt. Ralph...James, let me help you. Let me help you to find the answers you need."

"Answers? Damn, I got answers." Ralph was getting more and more agitated. "This bitch got more from my father than I did."

"Ralph, I understand why you are angry. He disinherited you. But that was your father who did that. These people didn't do that."

"This one did!" Ralph yelled. He tightened his grip again, and blood oozed from a cut on Annette's neck. Jan knew she had to think fast and talk carefully. Ida, the Peabodys, and the Shapiros huddled into a group, and the two officers tried to look strong, but were obviously feeling helpless.

"James, I know that this wasn't all your doing," Jan disclosed. "Roger Orton put you up to this, didn't he?"

"How do you know about him? Yes. He offered me money to get the lodge to close down. It was a good deal. Now it's fucked up."

"He wrote to you in prison. Did he help you escape, too?"

"Now, that one I'm not answering, Missy."

"But he did lure you into escaping and coming here, didn't he?"

"You tell me, Miss Know-it-all." Ledger was getting more agitated.

"Please, James. There is a way out of this. You don't have to hurt anyone else." Jan was taking a big risk.

Murphy joined the discussion. "What do you mean 'anyone else'?"

Jan ignored his question. "Orton set up Rambling River Development and has been buying up land all over the area, and he really wanted this lodge on prime property on Seymour Lake. He wanted to set up a development scam, like he did at Lake Moosebegone in Maine, until he was found out, fined big bucks, lost his realtor's license, and was banished from the state. When the Renaults wouldn't sell him this lodge, he looked up the history of it and found out about your father, and contacted you. He thought you might want to get revenge and he was right, wasn't he? He used you, James. This is really his doing."

"Is this about revenge on your father?" Ida asked. "For disinheriting you?"

"Or for abusing you?" Jan asked. "But you already got back at him for that, didn't you, James."

"Shut up! That's enough," Ledger yelled. "Or I'll cut this bitch."

"That won't accomplish anything, James, but more trouble for you. This doesn't have to happen."

"It might make me feel better. Besides, it doesn't matter what happens to me."

"It matters to me, James," Jan said, calmly. "It matters to me, and it matters to God. Don't hurt Annette. She's not to blame."

Ledger looked shaky, and his arm began to move the cleaver. Jan was afraid for Annette. "Is that how you killed your father?" Philippe and Ida looked shocked at her words. Patrolman Murphy looked at his gun on the floor.

"With this very cleaver. I cleaned it and hung it back up on the wall so no one would ever know. And they didn't. Never looked at it. Stupid police. Yes, I killed him. The bastard deserved it. I spit on his grave."

"And you turned over his headstone? No one could blame you for being angry, James."

Ledger had a strange look and Jan wasn't sure if he was calming down or getting more anxious. Then through the shadows of the lamp-lit room, Jan noticed Matt coming slowly down the back stairway, and she knew she had to keep Ledger distracted.

"James, I know you're afraid, but I understand how you could have felt homicidal towards your father. He was abusive to you, and you knew he was going to disinherit you. People will understand that. They won't understand if you hurt anyone else. There is still hope for you to get out of all this trouble and with a good lawyer, you could be all right, you could have a future. If you hurt anyone else, you could end up dead, with no future at all."

"I've screwed up bad, Missy. Now there's no way to fix it."

"James, you can still end this now before it's too late. You don't want to wreck the rest of your life."

"It's too late, Missy," Ledger said. "I'll end up in prison again, and I'll never get out."

"James, listen to me." Jan kept his attention. "Even if you do go back to prison, you can find a meaningful existence there. Lots of people do. Have you ever felt God in your life? Have you ever wondered about what God wants of you? It's not too late to turn things to the good, to create a better future, both in this life and in the next. If you're in prison, I'll come to visit you."

Ledger briefly lowered the cleaver, as if entertaining a flash of hope. Seizing the moment, Matt pounced from behind and hit him over the head with a large antique wooden pestle.

Ledger slumped some and let go of Annette, who raced toward the door to the porch and ran out screaming into the rainy night. Then James recovered and turned towards Matt, raising the cleaver. Patrolman Murphy reached down and picked up his gun and fired at Ledger, hitting him in the leg. He dropped the cleaver, and the two officers jumped him. Matt and Murphy held him down while Wilson ran upstairs to get the handcuffs.

Within minutes, Ledger was cuffed to a heavy chair and the guests were hugging each other and crying with relief. Jan hugged Matt and asked him if he was all right.

"I'm fine. I should have hit him harder, but I've never struck a person before. I'm lucky that someone had a gun."

"I wondered where you were, and I thought you might have snuck out to get help."

"I was listening from the top of the stairway the whole time. You were magnificent, Jan. You kept things under control and probably saved lives."

Jan smiled.

Philippe spoke to the perpetrator. "You got duped, Mr. Baggett. If you hadn't tried to get my lodge away from me, you'd have never been found out for your father's murder. Now you will answer for that."

James Baggett glared at Jan. "You did me in, Missy. You pretended to care, but you never cared."

"You're wrong, James. I care," Jan insisted. "And I meant what I said. You can let God help you through this, and you can start a new life, whether in prison, or out of it."

James Baggett stared at her, with tears now forming in his eyes.

Chapter 23: Encore

Later that same morning, Jan sat with Matt on the porch swing, watching the big machines of the state road crews going back and forth with loads of fallen branches. State police cars followed them and television crews followed the police cars. The cleanup in the Northeast Kingdom would take several more hours, if not days, but the rain had finally stopped and the roads were now open in and out of the area. One report on the Channel Three News said that there may have been a tornado in Island Pond. Philippe heard that it was just a microburst, but there was probably a million dollars worth of damage.

At dawn, Philippe had heard Seymour howling and had found him locked in a closet in the back part of the shed, probably put there by Ledger to keep him from defending his owners. Now the dog was roaming around the lodge, wagging his tail and licking everyone's hands, apparently understanding that the crisis was over.

Diana and Amos had left early, promising to return next year. Amos said that it was the most exciting vacation he had ever had.

Ward and Avis offered to stay on a while and help Philippe clean up the mess around the lodge. Jeff, Stan, and Cliff volunteered to help also and Philippe put them all to work.

"After we clean up the storm damage, we are going to do some renovating around here," he said. "Who knows, Jan, we might even put in an air conditioner."

"What? Don't do that. It would spoil the charm," Jan laughed. "Besides, you'd only need it about four days out of the year."

"That's true, for sure, but maybe just a small one in the great room. We'll see. Anyway, Ida and I are going to touch up a few things and then maybe do a little traveling ourselves. We'll be hiring some people to help us with cleaning and laundry, and tending to the place when we're away."

"Good for you," Jan said. "Getting away from here for a while might be a good thing for you."

Philippe and Ida talked with Cliff about staying on at the end of the summer to work for them at the lodge, learning the skills needed to be an innkeeper and chef. Cliff was thrilled and was sure he could get his mother to agree.

Ward and Avis began to talk with Jeff about lending him the money for the environmental program in New York, as well as inviting him to live with them while he was in school.

Stan had a plan also, to visit Matt in Pennsylvania when he was finished with high school, and to learn some more about wildlife photography.

Matt's duffle bag was lying on the porch, and he was ready to head back to Pennsylvania. Jan's Mazda was all packed up to return to Branford.

"I think it's wonderful that Fitzgibbons wants to publish your article, Jan," said Matt. "Are you sure you won't consider coming to work on *American Wildlife?*" She smiled and started to respond, but stopped when she saw Kyle Dorsey's Porsche pull into the lodge driveway.

"Well, well, look who is here," she said just a bit sarcastically. "He must be looking for the big story."

"I'd sure like to give him one," Matt said, with a sideways smile. He got up and walked into the lodge.

"Hey, Red!" Dorsey said, bounding up the steps. "What's the word? I heard you talked down the crazy man and kept everyone safe."

"I am not taking any credit, and please don't call me Red," said Jan. "Matt is the hero. He subdued Mr. Ledger so the border patrolmen could arrest him."

"Don't you mean Mr. Baggett?" Dorsey continued, pulling out his note pad and pen, but ignoring the part about Matt being the hero. The buzz is that he's the son of the previous owner, and also the murderer? Is that true? Can you give me details?"

"Well, I don't know, Kyle. The police are still investigating. Parker is in charge and everything has to go through him," Jan fibbed, and wouldn't spill to Dorsey about all of the previous night's horrific events. "Or, you could just make up the story and distort everything like you did in your article about the gas."

"Okay. Then I'll get it from Parker. I can see you're agitated. It must have been really awful—from the stories beginning to come over the radio. Is there anything I can do for you?"

"I'm fine, Kyle, and at least its over. The perpetrator was caught and arrested and the lodge is once again safe for guests."

"Well, that sounds good. Somehow I thought the story would be much bigger than that, though. Baggett's son killed him out of anger, and then wanted to destroy the lodge. Is that it?"

"I guess so," Jan answered.

A Channel Three News truck that had been parked behind the lodge, then pulled away, and Sergeant Parker followed behind, honking and waving as he left.

"Why didn't you tell me they were here?" Dorsey asked Jan, as he tried to run after Parker and flag him down. Failing to get Parker's attention, he looked back at Jan, got in his Porsche and drove off.

Jan went into the lodge to take one more look at her favorite painting.

"Well, Jesus, my good shepherd," she prayed. "I guess you were with me all the time, keeping me safe. I know you don't just fix everything like magic. I know we have to do the work ourselves, but I really do appreciate the guidance when I was lost. Stay with me please, while I find my way back to myself."

Jan took one last look around the lodge, and promising to be back soon, she went out the front door to the porch swing.

Matt came back out and sat again with Jan, the two of them just sitting quietly with each other and taking in the scene of the beautiful lake, people returning to the beach, a pontoon boat floating by, blue herons flying over, and Elan Hill standing sentinel.

"As for the job in Pennsylvania, I really don't think that is where I want to be," Jan said.

"I understand. I didn't really expect that you would. But, it ought to tell you something about your talents, that an editor like Fitzgibbons likes your work."

"It does. Really, it does, Matt, and it means a lot to me that you liked it, too. I do think that my life's purpose has something to do with writing and environmentalism. I need to explore more just what that is. I'm going back to Connecticut to get divorced, and to wrap things up there, and then I think I'm going to come back to Vermont, maybe to open a detective agency or something, and to write on the side. I think I can do whatever I want to do, once I know what that is."

Matt smiled. "I'm positive that you're right about that." He reached out and gently touched her arm.

"I know I'll have to go through a grieving process before I'm ready to move on, Matt. And, I'm not so sure that you have finished grieving Julia."

"Well, you are probably right about that, too. I'm going to work on that back in Pennsylvania, and spend a lot of time with my son, and my mother, letting them both know how much I love them. One day soon, I'd like to bring them up here to the North Woods and see if they would be interested in moving here. I'd really like to see you again though, Jan, and I kind of hope it will be soon."

"I'd like that, too, Matt." Jan smiled at him. "You are very special to me, and I do think this relationship invites investigating. Let's just see what happens."

Philippe came out of the lodge and Jan and Matt stood up to talk with him. "Sergeant Parker is headed over to Concord to pick up Roger Orton. He has also spoken to the Vermont State Attorney General's office, and they are already investigating Rambling River, and Orton's connection to the fire at the Sheldrake. It turns out that he tried to buy that place and they refused to sell. I'm sure he will be shut down, and some of the land deals around here will be eradicated due to illegalities. Orton's check to Mr. Addison bounced and he won't be retiring to Florida on that land deal, but I think Mr. Orton is going to be going on a long vacation, and I don't mean anyplace comfy."

"That's good to know, Philippe," Jan sighed. "I hope you're right that Orton goes to prison this time, so he can't start over again in another state."

"Philippe, what's the word on Annette?" Matt asked.

"She lost some blood, and needed a few stitches, but she's okay. I just talked to her on the phone and while she's getting a transfusion she's writing 'The Ballad of Seymour Lake'."

"Ha. I can't wait to read that one."

"She's one very lucky lady. It's a damn good thing you came down those stairs when you did. Matt, I'm so very grateful for that, and for your helping Jan with the investigation."

"I won't say it's all been a pleasure, but"—he looked at Jan and winked—"some of it was."

"You come back any time, Matt. You're always welcome." Philippe shook Matt's hand.

"I second that," said Ida, appearing in the doorway. "Have a safe trip to Pennsylvania," and gave Matt a big hug.

Jan and Ida shared a long embrace and a teary goodbye.

"Now, if you two will excuse me," said Philippe, "I'm going to go look at the newspaper ads and see if I can find a new pickup truck. We have some guests arriving tonight and others tomorrow, and I need a truck to get some work done around here."

Ida took the hint and went back inside the lodge. "I guess I have beds to make," she said.

"I'm helping you!" Cliff offered.

Jan and Matt walked down the porch steps. The sun shone brightly on the wet grass and the flower beds, which had perked up nicely, with lupine and columbine waving gently in shades of pink and blue. Jan noticed with a smile that in between the other plants, were glowing yellow swamp candles.

"Look, Matt. Joseph said these were my flower."

Matt bent down and picked one and gently placed it in her red hair. "So who leaves first, Red, you or I?"

"I do," Jan answered, and lifted her face towards his.

Matt kissed her gently. "You have promised to call soon, and email too."

"I will," Jan said, squeezing his hand. She slid into her little red Mazda and, with a wave, headed west on

Route 111, feeling a little sad, but strong and determined. Rounding the bend just before Derby Line, there she stood in the middle of the road—a female moose! Jan stopped. The lady moose stood tall and strong, looking Jan in the eye.

"Okay, girl," Jan said. "I get it." Then, when she was good and ready, the moose strolled off into the woods. Jan sighed deeply and headed for the interstate.

About the Author

Susan Winters Smith was born in Norwood, Massachusetts and grew up in Central Vermont in the little village of Shady Rill. She has lived in Connecticut for most of her adult life, with her husband, Stephen. She graduated from Montpelier High School in 1965 and the University of Vermont in 1969, later earning a Master's degree from St. Joseph College in West Hartford. She has written stories and poems all of her life, while going to school, raising three children, caring for a handicapped uncle, and working in the fields of special education, free-lance journalism and social work. Susan is a member of CAPA, NWU, LVW, and IPNE. Her many interests include genealogy, arts and crafts, sewing, music, gardening, nature, environmentalism, religion, spirituality, and photography. Susan has had articles and a poem published in newspapers and genealogical journals. Her works in progress include poems, several children's books, and novels.

The Mystery of Hunger Mountain

In the upcoming sequel, Jan Whitlock returns to Vermont after her divorce to open a Creativity Center for writers, artists and musicians. She buys and renovates the old farmhouse in Shady Rill that she had always admired as a child, building hiking trails and meditation areas to inspire her guests. Some friends from the Seymour Lake Lodge, including Matt Abbott, become program participants.

Vandalism, perhaps connected to the wisp of smoke she sometimes sees in the distance, makes her wonder if not everyone in the area is happy with her presence. Questions arise around the endangered flora and fauna of the Middlesex Town Forest, and the integrity of its protectors. The dead body of a beaver and rattlesnake poacher found under the bridge on one of the hiking trails raises even more questions and Jan is once again, involuntarily engaged in detective work.

CPSIA information can be obtained at www.ICGtesting.com
Printed in the USA
BVOW03s1129070214

344261BV00014B/382/P